NEVER TOO LATE

THE EXTRAORDINARY JOURNEY OF MELVIN KLAPPER

DAVID J. MEISELMAN

ISBN 978-1-63784-464-9 (paperback)
ISBN 978-1-63784-466-3 (hardcover)
ISBN 978-1-63784-465-6 (digital)

Hawes & Jenkins Publishing
16427 N Scottsdale Road Suite 410
Scottsdale, AZ 85254
www.hawesjenkins.com

Printed in the United States of America

For Eve Claire for sharing with PopPop
her world of wonder and innocence.

Also by David J. Meiselman

Attorney Malpractice: Law and Procedure
Collection of Poetry
Ten Rules for Business Success
Welcome to the Hollow

ACKNOWLEDGMENTS

First and foremost, to my love of fifty years, Myra Packman, who has made everything possible. And fun. Admittedly it's not easy to have one's words microscopically scrutinized by a former editor-in-chief of her law review, but it undoubtedly made the story better.

Oorah to my wise and generous friend Don Keelan, a fellow Marine Corps veteran, a CPA, a successful businessman, a community leader, and an all-around great guy. Semper Fi, Don.

A sincere and heartfelt thank-you to all my friends (you know who you are) who offered their encouragement and support along the way. It got me back to the desk.

PROLOGUE

What I'm about to share with you may seem unbelievable, but it's pretty much a matter of documented record. Well, maybe not all of it.

Before I get started, there's some stuff you need to know about Melvin Klapper.

Approaching his seventy-fifth birthday and recently retired, Melvin lived in a small, simple, moderately well-maintained white house in need of paint on Maple Street in Springfield, New Jersey, the town where he grew up.

As a better than average student who loved sports, though not much of an athlete himself, Melvin had graduated from Springfield High School in 1965.

That September, still a virgin and barely needing to shave, he kissed his childhood sweetheart, Martha McPherson, goodbye and joined the United States Marine Corps. After two grueling thirteen-month tours in Vietnam, suffering through a week-long bout of malaria with a near-fatal 105-degree fever and sustaining shrapnel wounds in his left hip, lower back, and buttocks that left him with a barely discernible but permanent limp, Melvin was honorably discharged in September 1968 and eagerly returned home to Springfield.

Back home, Melvin went to work for Barney Wilson, who owned the local grocery store on the corner of Main and Elm. While in high school, Melvin had worked summers and holidays for him, and even the cantankerous Mr. Wilson was more than happy to welcome Melvin as his fourth full-time employee.

During his third year at Wilson's, Melvin married Martha—remember her? Martha's father, Doc McPherson, had wanted Martha to go to college and marry a successful lawyer or banker, but Martha loved Melvin with all her soul, and that was that.

Over the years, Martha provided a warm-hearted, nurturing home where she and Melvin proudly raised their daughter, Grace. After graduation from Springfield High, where Grace was an honor student and editor of the school newspaper, she went on to the local community college and then got her four-year degree in education from the nearby state university.

Following college, Grace went to work as a sixth-grade teacher at Springfield Elementary, where she met and fell in love with Chris Walker, an eighth-grade math and science teacher. Melvin and Martha treated Chris like the son they never had, though Chris never quite returned the warmth and affection. A few years later, Grace and Chris had a beautiful baby boy named William, named after Melvin's father, then deceased.

For fifty years, until 2019, Melvin unpacked deliveries, stocked shelves, took inventory, worked the cash register, carried customer's bags to their cars, and kept the store neat and clean as a pin. In all those years, Melvin rarely missed a day of work. And when he did, just about every customer asked with sincere concern where he was.

When Melvin retired at age seventy-two, Wilson's had grown to become the premier supermarket in Springfield with more than fifty-five employees. A big farewell party was held for Melvin, although most of his fellow employees had only been there a few years.

And that is where we pick up our remarkable but true story. Come. It's time to meet Melvin Klapper.

CHAPTER 1

Friday, July 8
Springfield

Although he liked and respected Dr. Mendelsohn, Melvin was not looking forward to this day. Only two years had passed since Martha had succumbed to breast cancer. Of course, Melvin realized that hadn't been the doctor's fault, but all the same, it was painful to walk back into that same office.

Just seeing the lettering on the thick glass door, "Stanley Mendelsohn, MD," with "Oncology" below the name, sent shivers through Melvin. Bad memories flooded his mind. All the conversations, the tears, the unanswerable questions. He recognized that Mendelsohn had a deservedly fine reputation and knew his stuff, but Melvin, never a big fan of doctors to begin with, was filled with trepidation as he approached the office. Melvin knew full well that death could now be at *his* doorstep.

Having recently experienced sporadic abdominal pain as well as pain in his lower back, which was sometimes relieved by aspirin or Advil, Melvin had gone to his family physician of many years, Dr. Roland Benedict, who had ordered an MRI. The scan had reported what appeared to be a four-to-five centimeter tumor near the head and neck area of the pancreas. Knowing that Melvin's situation was extremely serious and in need of urgent medical attention, including a biopsy, Dr. Benedict had referred Melvin to Dr. Mendelsohn.

Mendelsohn had wasted no time scheduling Melvin for a PET scan and endoscopy, and so today, Melvin would learn the results.

*****

Opening the door, which seemed unusually heavy, Melvin was hit in the face by a burst of cold air. The air-conditioning was on full blast, requiring the receptionist to wear a sweater even on this hot summer day. Maybe the air-conditioning was to keep people awake, Melvin speculated. Maybe it was to minimize the smell of whatever was sprayed in doctors' offices to make them seem clean and sterile, giving patients a false sense of confidence that all would be well.

The receptionist, an innocent-looking young lady (they all seemed young and innocent to Melvin these days), greeted Melvin with a pleasant face and upbeat voice.

"May I help you?" she asked.

"Yes, thank you. I'm here to see Dr. Mendelsohn. I have a two p.m. appointment."

"Are you Mr. Klapper?"

"I am. That's Klapper with a *K*."

The receptionist smiled. "Could you please fill out a few forms for us?"

"Yes, of course," replied Melvin.

Taking the three printed pages on a clipboard with a Springfield Savings and Loan pen attached by a white string, Melvin wondered why he had to fill out the same forms every time he walked into a doctor's office. But he accepted it as a part of the routine doctors had to adhere to, while doubting the doctor actually had the time or inclination to read all this information before seeing each patient.

After filling out the forms and bringing them back to the receptionist, Melvin selected a coffee-stained, outdated *Sports Illustrated* from the magazine rack with Tiger Woods on the cover and returned to the uncomfortable metal chair, so typical of waiting rooms. He couldn't help but notice how patients in the waiting area sat far apart from each other as if cancer were contagious, spreading through the air like a cold. Maybe it was just for privacy and solitude, not having to talk about themselves or their condition with others. Certainly, that was how Melvin felt.

It had taken Melvin a year to get at least somewhat past Martha's death. "Widow fog," he had heard it called. He understood that term better now. Yes, fog was an apt description of how it felt to lose a dearly loved spouse. At first, he'd felt ashamed that he continued to live on, but Melvin, being Melvin, had gradually bounced back by doing volunteer work at the library, reading to those whose sight was impaired.

Thinking about anything that might distract him from the coming examination and conversation, Melvin did not at first hear Helen, Dr. Mendelsohn's nurse of many years, call his name. Then he heard her say, "Melvin, the doctor will see you now." Getting up from his chair, approaching the inner door, Melvin tried to read Helen's face as to what was coming. She knew, he thought. They always did. He wasn't sure why, but he felt like a schoolboy being sent to the principal's office.

Helen was thin without being gaunt. Handsome in a mature, well-mannered sort of way. The shape of her face, adorned with small gold earrings and just the right amount of makeup, along with her starched whites and perfectly coiffed hair, made her seem both sympathetic and capable, which she certainly had been during Martha's ordeal.

Holding the door open, she said, "Hi, Melvin, how have you been?"

"Hi, Helen. I think I'm okay, but I guess I'm here to find out for sure." This was Melvin's way of trying to get a raised eyebrow or curled lip or other subtle reaction out of Helen so as to glean a hint of what was to come. But there was nothing, not even a twitch.

Helen escorted Melvin into one of Dr. Mendelsohn's examination rooms. Melvin had been there before. He remembered it all too well but looked around to see if anything was new or different. No, it looked the same. It was a room of about ten by twelve with white walls, a beige-speckled linoleum floor, an examining table with a thin paper sheet covering, an X-ray box on the wall next to anatomy charts doctors must get for free, a blood-pressure device that looked like it probably had a hundred years ago, latex gloves in a plastic dispenser, various instruments, a small sink with an even smaller mirror above, and a tiny desk with a backless stool where Dr. Mendelsohn would sit and make notes.

Function over form, thought Melvin. Rooms like these remind us, intentionally or otherwise, that we are mere patients. Powerless, with little or no control over our circumstances. We come and we go. *Wouldn't it help*, Melvin wondered, *to paint the walls a warm and soothing color or to install carpet, to play soft, calming music, anything to make patients feel cared about or at least comfortable?*

Melvin sat on the edge of the examination table and waited, trying to be a patient patient. He always thought that was funny. He could hear Dr. Mendelsohn talking slowly and gently in the hall outside the door. A moment passed. Dr. Mendelsohn knocked twice and entered the room, wearing a three-quarter-length white smock with his stethoscope dangling out of one side pocket and several pens affixed to his breast pocket. He was carrying papers, but not the papers Melvin had filled out earlier. No, these looked like lab reports. All in all, Mendelsohn might have stepped straight out of central casting. But honestly, Melvin preferred it that way.

Dr. Mendelsohn always looked the same. Thin-boned, mostly bald, shoulders beginning to stoop, with small but sincere brown eyes, he wore a lightly starched white shirt with a neatly knotted bow tie, laced, thick-soled brown shoes, and round rimless glasses. Although he rarely offered a smile, he emitted a warm and benevolent voice that came from his heart. Like many doctors, he wore a watch that had all kinds of indecipherable dials and buttons. It looked more like a Swiss army knife. If he was trying to look smart, it was working, thought Melvin.

Melvin stood when Dr. Mendelsohn entered the room. They shook hands. Melvin looked to make eye contact with Dr. Mendelsohn, but the doctor was not to be caught out so easily. Still, Melvin was not getting a good feeling.

"So, Melvin," said Dr. Mendelsohn, "how are things?"

"Pretty good, Doc," Melvin said. "Still some aches and pains in my lower back and on my left side, but for almost seventy-five, I feel pretty good."

"Are you sleeping well?"

"I was never a big sleeper, so I guess I'm about the same as always."

"How's your appetite?"

"I'm not hungry that often. I'm probably eating too much ice-cream, but I figure at this age, what the heck?"

"Okay, let's take your blood pressure."

Melvin returned to his perch on the examining table, and Mendelsohn took the measurements with his usual gentle but crisp efficiency, again avoiding Melvin's probing gaze.

"Not bad, 142/88. Your pulse is eighty-six. Both are probably a bit elevated from being in a doctor's office but within normal limits for your age. Are you getting any exercise?"

"Not much anymore. I putter around the house, mow the lawn, but my back acts up, so I don't really do that much."

"Are you still taking your blood-pressure meds?"

"Yes," Melvin said, even though he sometimes forgot to adhere to the carefully timed regimen. A beta blocker and an ACE inhibitor had been prescribed for Melvin by Dr. Benedict during Martha's illness. After she passed, she headed a prescription of Xanax to help take the edge off while Melvin was mourning. An almost full plastic bottle of 0.5mg Xanax sat quietly collecting dust in his medicine cabinet. While they had helped to relax Melvin in his moments of sorrow, he did not like the drowsiness that seemed to set in and linger for a while afterward.

Mendelsohn cleared his throat. "So, Melvin, I have the results of your scan, endoscopy, and biopsy and wanted to discuss them with you."

"To be honest, Doc, it's a bit scary when your doctor, especially an oncologist, calls you to come in."

"Well, Melvin, to return the honesty, I wish I had better news."

"What do you mean, Doc? I feel pretty good."

"You may feel okay today, but I'm afraid it's not going to last. I have to level with you. You have cancer of the pancreas, and it has spread to nearby organs, specifically your liver. The cancer has spread very rapidly, unusually so, and it has metastasized to at least three lymph nodes, which will further accelerate the spread. The reports are not good, not good at all, I'm sorry to say."

"How could it get so bad so fast without us knowing about it?"

"I'm surprised your symptoms haven't been worse, but it explains your lower back, side, and occasional abdominal pain. Most of the time, the patient calls with complaints of pain, and that's when we pick it up. Maybe you have a high tolerance for pain. But it is the nature and character of pancreatic cancer not to make itself known until it is already well advanced."

Melvin was stunned. It was like a punch to the solar plexus. He felt the air leaving his lungs as if never to return. He was glad he was sitting on the table because otherwise he was pretty sure his legs would not have supported him. After a moment or two of silence, Melvin asked, "Is there anything we can do, like surgery?"

"I'm afraid not," Mendelsohn answered. "The cancer has spread far and wide. Once it's in the lymph nodes, there's really very little we can do."

"Doc, are you saying I'm going to die from this?"

Dr. Mendelsohn did not respond right away. Finally, he looked directly at Melvin. "In all likelihood, yes."

"Is there anything you can do?"

"If you want to try some combination of chemo and radiation, it may buy you some time on the order of weeks or months, but it won't be pleasant and may even make things worse. Sometimes it accelerates the spread of the bad cells. And it's no walk in the park."

In typical Melvin fashion, his first reaction to this sad and upsetting news was to feel badly for Dr. Mendelsohn. He could see the years of sorrow taking their toll on a good man who had chosen a profession that required discussions like this.

"Doc, how much time are we talking about here?"

Again slow to respond, Dr. Mendelsohn nearly whispered, "It's hard to say for sure, but probably around six months. Twelve at the most but quite possibly less."

"Wow," said Melvin. And then more softly, "Wow."

It was all Melvin could say as he stared without actually seeing anything.

"Unfortunately," Dr. Mendelsohn continued, "your pain will get worse both in frequency and intensity. There's no question about it. You have to be prepared for it, Melvin. I can give you pain meds that work fairly well, but eventually, you'll need hospitalization. I'll see you every week if you want. From here on out, it's really your call. I'm here to help, and you know I'll do everything I can. You can call me anytime."

"Doc, the good news is that I'll get to be with Martha again, and that's just fine with me."

"Would you like to sit here a while and think about things? I can see a patient in the meantime, and then we can get back together and chat again, if you'd like."

"No thanks. I have my grandson, Billy, coming over this afternoon, and I want to be at home for him when he gets there."

"Okay, I understand. Do you want Helen to walk you out to your car?"

"No, I took the bus here today. The fare is less than the cost of gas, and I'm having to watch my budget. So I'll just catch the bus on your corner. Listen, Doc, I know you're just doing your job. I appreciate you being straight with me. I've had a pretty good life. I consider myself a lucky guy."

Placing his hand on Melvin's shoulder, Mendelsohn said, "Melvin, you've always been a good man. It's my privilege to know you. Helen will be in touch to set up your next appointment. I'd like to repeat some blood work, and we'll talk again after I get those results back, okay?"

"Sure, I understand. Thank you."

Dr. Mendelsohn left the room, quietly closing the door behind him.

Melvin took a few deep breaths and considered the possibility that the lab results were actually those of another patient or that Mendelsohn had misinterpreted them. He contemplated a second opinion. But only a few seconds passed before he recognized wishful thinking for what it was. Hope was not a strategy. There was no genie to grant his wishes. He had been down that road with Martha and knew better now. No, the test results were his. Dr. Mendelsohn had read them correctly. Melvin knew he had some serious thinking to do about how he was going to spend his last few months.

CHAPTER 2

Friday, July 8
Springfield

Melvin found himself on the street with no memory of how he had gotten there, walking to the bus stop like a robot on automatic pilot. All he could think about was the inevitability of what Dr. Mendelsohn had told him in clear, simple, and frightening terms. No chance of clemency or pardon.

The next thing he knew, he was on the bus. When had it come? How had time become so fractured? He was glad he had decided to take the bus that morning. He would never have been able to drive home. The bus was packed, filled with people on their iPads and phones. A group of kids was laughing and throwing wads of paper at each other. Not an empty seat. It was wonderful to see. A young woman cradled a tiny sleeping infant in a pink blanket. So many lives with so much to look forward to. Melvin was happy for them. He wanted to tell them how lucky they were but knew better than that. Being told your life would soon come to an end did not justify creating a scene that would only scare people.

He took a deep breath and smiled a small smile of acceptance. It was time to calm down and begin coming to terms with his situation. His Marine Corps training kicked in—so many years ago but still a part of him. His mind cleared. His heart steadied. Now was not a time for panic. All the same, Melvin sensed that the Marine adage of "adapt, improvise, overcome," which had served him so well in Vietnam and afterward, might not be enough this time.

He would be seeing Billy in a few hours and did not want to bring his troubles to his sweet, good-natured grandson. It was Billy's tenth birthday, and Melvin was not going to let anything spoil the day, especially now that he knew his days with Billy were numbered. Well, to be fair, he had always known that. He had just thought the number was going to be a lot bigger.

Melvin knew he had to perk up. He would deal with his problems after Billy went home. He wondered if he should tell Grace the news when she was dropping Billy off. Maybe afterward, when she returned to pick him up.

As he pondered the appropriate time to tell Grace, an poorly attired elderly woman boarded the bus and stood in the aisle shuffling her feet, desperately looking for a seat. She could barely walk even with the assistance of a cane. She kept glancing from side to side with the hope that someone might give up a seat for her. Melvin watched this frail woman—well, into her eighties if not nineties—struggle to keep her balance as the bus lurched into motion. No one budged. Not an inch. She was invisible to the other riders.

So Melvin did as he always did. He stood and asked the woman to take his seat. She thanked him with a well-articulated and surprisingly strong "God bless you" while staring straight at him with knowing and piercingly iridescent eyes that made Melvin feel an internal glow of earnestness and promise, a feeling he had never quite experienced before. But then she had moved past him and settled herself into his seat.

Melvin's stop was next. As he exited the rear of the bus, he glanced back at the elderly lady, but she was gone. Someone else was in her seat, a young kid whose eyes were glued to his phone. Melvin shook his head—another one of those fractured moments in time. Was this how it would be from now on? It was peculiar to say the least. He felt like a stone skipping across the surface of a pond. He wondered if Martha had experienced disconnected moments like this.

As Melvin began the one-block walk to his house, he noticed a tow truck backed into his driveway. Even though his left hip was bothering him more than usual, he picked up his pace and arrived at the driveway in time to see a stout, bull-necked, partially bearded man of about twenty-five, wearing a sweaty, faded Rolling Stones T-shirt and oil-soaked shorts that reached his knees, attaching a tow line to Melvin's 2018 Honda.

"Hey, what are you doing?" asked Melvin. "That's my car."

"Are you Mr. Klipper?" growled the guy.

"It's Klapper. Mind telling me what's going on?"

"Sorry, pal. I got a work order. Just doing my job. I left a copy by your door. Read it and weep."

Watching and listening to this exchange from the sidewalk was Henry, the local mailman. Henry was a short, clean-shaven, balding man of about forty-five who couldn't have weighed more than one hundred and thirty pounds. On his thin left wrist was an inexpensive big-faced Timex watch with a blue fabric band that had faded from sweat and sun.

Perched on his Penn State Nittany Lions cap were sunglasses with black frames and gray lenses. He had no wedding band or other jewelry. In a too-large USPS shirt, brown shorts that covered his knees, held up by a well-worn leather belt, he looked like a teenage nerd in need of some protein. With a subdued but affable demeanor, he had previously told Melvin that although he was a college graduate, he took the job delivering mail because he liked being outside even in the winter, that the walking was great exercise, and most importantly, that he had no office or boss to deal with.

Although Henry had worked Melvin's route for years, Melvin did not know Henry's last name, where he lived, or whether he had family. Melvin was not the kind of person to pry. If information came out naturally in conversation, then fine. If not, that was fine too. But Henry and Melvin always chatted when they saw each other, especially in good weather, when Melvin would be sitting on his porch. Now like a quarterback making a handoff, almost without looking, Henry nonchalantly handed Melvin his mail as they watched the tow truck pull away with the front of Melvin's car dangling sadly and helplessly in the air.

Turning to Henry, Melvin said, "I missed one or maybe two payments, and after all these years and they swoop right in with no warning? Is that legal?"

"Used cars are worth a lot these days," said Henry. "They can make more money selling that car than they can on your payments. And the contracts are all in their favor."

Could this day get any worse? Melvin wondered. Losing his car, which he wasn't using much anymore, was of course a very minor problem compared to the news he had received from Dr. Mendelsohn. But the car had sentimental value to Melvin; Martha had picked it out on their anniversary a few years ago. It had been meant to cheer her up after a particularly difficult time with her cancer treatments.

Melvin had taken too many body blows in a few short hours. Walking up the three brick steps to his porch, he stopped for a moment to catch his breath. He was comforted by the sight of his favorite white rocker. Next to it was Martha's matching rocker. Melvin liked the two chairs sitting side by side just like old times. Four brass plant hooks jutted out from the overhang of the roof, but without their plants, there was a noticeable absence of color and life. Porch hooks without plants appeared sad and lonely. They needed nature's vitality to be useful. Without Martha, Melvin had no clue about what plants to hang or how to care for them. The abandoned hooks reminded Melvin of how much he missed Martha. He didn't mind the feeling at all, especially on this day.

The worn brown wooden front door with the brass numerals 2420, sided by two glass panels, was unlocked. For some reason, Melvin only locked the door at night, and even that he often forgot to do. On the glass panel to the right of the door was a faded VFW decal that had seen better days. Melvin didn't belong to that organization, but they had given him the decal because of his military service. Out of respect for other veterans, Melvin had put it up.

On the left-sided glass panel was an even older decal from the Girl Scouts of America. This odd-shaped three-leaf-clover emblem had been affixed proudly to the glass when Grace had sold the most cookies in her pack. Protected from inclement weather, these reminders of the past endured.

This was the first day in a long time that Melvin had noticed these decals and what they symbolized. The meaning of time, both past and future, was now very different than it had been just a few hours earlier.

Melvin's house was the typical post-Depression 1,900-square-foot layout on a lot of approximately 4,400 square feet, or about one-tenth of an acre. On the east side of the property was a narrow driveway that led to a one-car garage built out of the same wood siding as the house, painted white. The garage, now used solely for storage, had not housed a car for many years even in snowstorms. It was easier for Melvin to brush snow off the car than to shovel the driveway. Between the house and the driveway were two dented metal garbage pails with covers nowhere to be seen, and a faded-green garden hose with a rusted grommet that sprawled out in loose coils like a stunned boa constrictor. A terra-cotta flower pot that Martha had used for red geraniums lay on its side, forlorn and abandoned.

Built with federal assistance by the city of Springfield in 1938, the house included three bedrooms and two bathrooms upstairs. Downstairs was a kitchen that had been "remodeled" by Martha in the late seventies after Grace was born, a connected living and dining room, fashionable at the time, and a half bath next to the stairs leading to the basement. The living room had a bay window looking out onto the street and a wood-burning fireplace that hadn't been used since Martha took ill. There was a small lawn between the four-foot-high cyclone metal fencing that enclosed the property on three sides (not the driveway side) and the porch. The Klappers were the second family in the house, having bought it from the DiPietros in 1974, with some assistance from Martha's father, for $33,500.

Melvin spent most of his time sitting in the living room about ten feet away from the one TV in the house, a beloved thirty-six-inch Sony that Grace had bought for her parents several years earlier. This was Melvin's comfort zone. His bookshelf, just a long arm's length away, was crowded with biographies, his favorite genre, which he would read over and over until the bindings became frayed. Churchill, Lincoln, Jackie Robinson, and Einstein helped Melvin escape from the boredom and sometimes disappointing life he knew was his. He was especially tickled by their clever and witty quotes. He tried to memorize them for no particular occasion but was never quite able to do so. The courage and accomplishments of these individuals inspired him—but only momentarily. The more lasting lesson was that some men achieved greatness while others only read about it.

He would plop down into his big, cushy chair covered with a tartan plaid fabric that had endured thirty years of Melvin and still looked pretty good. It wore like iron, which Melvin marveled at each time he sat in it. Melvin fondly remembered buying the furniture with Martha from Jack's on Main Street, a third-generation Springfield institution. A hand-carved red oak breakfront with shelves above and three drawers below sat behind and to the side of the TV. It was filled with memories. Pictures of Martha, Melvin, Grace, Billy, and a few other relatives as well as some long-lost friends sat there trying desperately to make Melvin feel surrounded by love.

Martha had made and kept friends easily, but most of those relationships had not survived her passing. Other than the customary Christmas cards, very few people still reached out to Melvin. He was a man with many acquaintances but few, if any, true friends. Certainly no one to confide in.

One of Melvin's regrets was not having gone to college upon his return from Vietnam. The GI bill was available, but he did not have confidence that he could handle college courses. Plus, he'd needed the money a job would provide. As the years went on, Melvin had come to realize that his decision about college was another one of those moments where his lack of self-confidence had held him back from achieving something meaningful. He had shared this disappointment in himself with Martha, who had assured him that although he would have done well in college, he had been very successful without it. But Melvin had never been never sure that Martha truly felt that way. Whenever the subject came up, she'd reminded him that he could always go back to Springfield Community College.

Two six-foot-tall cherry trees chosen by Martha stood guard on the lawn. They bloomed in the spring and occasionally a second time if the fall was mild. They were hardy flowering trees that required little or no maintenance. There had once been a modest lawn in the back of the house, but that had been changed to a brick patio many years earlier when Melvin had mistakenly thought that laying brick would be an easy and fun project. That was when Melvin had learned that his lower back was still an issue for him from his wartime wounds and that he would have to be forever mindful of overdoing strenuous physical labor.

From just about anywhere in his house, Melvin could hear the TV from next door. It seemed to be on all day, serving as a companion to Mrs. Brewer, an elderly lady living alone. Mrs. Brewer was hard of hearing and kept the volume high to compensate. Melvin had never complained. Maybe he also played his television too loud and just didn't realize it.

In his small kitchen lit by a dim seventy-five-watt fixture that hung from the ceiling, Melvin stood next to his dinette set, almost leaning on it for support, and sorted through the mail that Henry had handed him. He didn't open the envelopes. He didn't have to. He knew what they were—bills, bills, and more bills. Melvin laid them down gently on the table and then placed his bent head in his hands as if praying. He stood there for a minute, unmoving. He didn't cry, didn't say anything, and didn't feel sorry for himself. He just wondered what he was going to do from this moment on. Picking his head up, he focused on Martha's sweet and tender eight-by-ten picture on the kitchen wall. It always made him smile. He went over to it, looked at Martha, and kissed her.

"Martha, what should I do?" asked Melvin. "It's not easy without you. I miss you, my love. I may be seeing you sooner than planned."

CHAPTER 3

Friday, July 8
Springfield

Melvin suddenly realized he had lost track of time. Grace and Billy were due any minute. He had to collect himself, act as if everything were fine. No, better than fine. Great. Just perfect. Nothing would ruin Billy's tenth birthday. Nothing.

Melvin splashed his face with cool water. It felt refreshing. Wanting to be free of the clothing he had been wearing at Dr. Mendelsohn's office, he put on his favorite beige chinos, a clean polo shirt, and his sneakers. His bedroom closet was small compared to the adjoining closet Martha had used and which Melvin, contrary to advice, had left untouched. He still needed the occasional fragrance that her closet, filled with her clothes, provided. Having recently lost a few pounds, Melvin's belt was now on the never-before-used next-to-last loop.

Melvin was a man of simple tastes. His wardrobe consisted of just a few items. But he still took pride in being neat and maintaining his gig line. He had passed on to Billy the Marine Corps lesson of aligning the seam of your shirt, belt buckle, and trouser-fly seam.

Melvin quickly combed his still-attractive mane of white hair. Back down in the kitchen, he grabbed a glass of water from the tap and his portable radio and went to the porch to wait for his grandson.

Melvin and Billy had an exceptionally close relationship. While they shared a love for the New York Yankees, it went far deeper than that. There was a certain understanding and a special feeling they had for each other. Billy would rather be with Melvin than just about anyone else, and Melvin felt the same about Billy. When they weren't together, they would speak by phone almost every day. Billy would call Melvin to talk about the game or school or Amos, his much-loved golden retriever. Not a word about girls—yet. For Melvin, talking to Billy kept him young, engaged, and on his toes.

On occasion, Billy would call his grandfather "Melvin," which made them both laugh and feel like the friends they were. Because of their close and comfortable relationship, Grace and Chris could get away for mini vacations or a "date night." Billy loved sleeping over at his grandfather's house, where he could eat junk food and stay up late and talk with Melvin. They would talk about everything and nothing.

While Grace enjoyed and respected her son's feelings for her father, Chris wasn't all that pleased about it. Too often, Chris felt left out. There were times when Billy would go to Melvin with questions that Chris felt should have been directed toward him. Chris felt that Billy seemed to prefer spending time with Melvin more than being with his father. Chris, a college graduate and successful educator of children, could not grasp what Billy's connection was with Melvin, who had spent his life stocking shelves at Wilson's supermarket. What was it that Billy saw in Melvin that he didn't find in his own father?

These thoughts troubled Chris and created an awkward barrier between him and Melvin and even to some degree with Grace, who would try to allay these concerns, but she too noticed that Billy often favored Melvin over Chris. She suggested to Chris that he lighten up on Billy, treat him more as a son rather than as a student, play catch with him, take him bowling, watch television together, and go to the movies or the zoo or for walks in the park. In other words, just hang out together and have fun. Most importantly, he should hug Billy a lot like Melvin did.

Melvin hadn't been on the porch for more than two minutes before Mrs. Brewer, the hard-of-hearing next-door neighbor, walked by. Martha had always thought Estelle fancied Melvin and, having lost her own husband many years before, was a bit too friendly with him, especially when Martha wasn't around. Melvin had assured Martha that she had nothing to worry about.

Actually, Melvin remembered that Estelle had been a looker at one time and was still to this day jokingly referred to as "Miss Gingersnaps." This was because when she was about eighteen, she had been selected to be in the print ads for the local cookie company that sold gingersnaps all over the country. Of course, that had been about fifty years ago, and there wasn't much ginger or snap left in Estelle.

But she and Melvin went back a long way, and Estelle was always nice to Melvin and he to her. Estelle stopped in front of Melvin's gate.

"Hi, Melvin. How are you doing today?"

"Not too bad," Melvin fibbed, not about to share his sorrows with Estelle.

"I see they took your car." Without waiting for a response from Melvin, Estelle went on, "You're better off without it. I haven't had a car since Carl passed away twenty years ago, and I haven't missed it a day."

"And how have you been, Estelle?" asked Melvin, trying to get past the car incident.

"A bit lonely to tell you the truth. Eating and watching the telly alone is not fun. You ought to come over sometimes. Better to have companionship."

"My favorite companion is about to visit with me."

"Oh, your grandson? What a terrific little boy. A real whippersnapper, as they used to say. My grandkids live in California, and I don't get to see them much. You're a very lucky man, Melvin."

After a slight moment of hesitation, Melvin replied, "Yes, I am…a very lucky man. Big day tomorrow. I'm taking Billy to his first major league baseball game. He's going to be ten, and I thought it would be a great birthday present. He's excited, but I'm even more excited. I just know it's going to be a special day that neither of us will ever forget. I can feel it in my bones."

Estelle raised an eyebrow. "Better take it easy," she warned. "We're not as young as we used to be. You know what they say: It's better to be on this side of the grass."

She laughed out loud before continuing on her way, failing to notice that Melvin had not acknowledged or responded to something she thought was a real knee-slapper. But her lighthearted remark seemed to Melvin to carry a weight of meaning and portent he would never have noticed before today. How quickly things had changed.

CHAPTER 4

Friday, July 8
Springfield

Waiting for Billy, Melvin couldn't help but review the events of the day. How could he be so sick yet not feel sick? Should he get a second opinion? Should he do chemo and radiation as Dr. Mendelsohn had mentioned? Although he had heard from others how difficult a course that was. The nausea, the loss of hair, the fatigue. Whom should he tell and when? What about the house and personal items? Did he need a lawyer? A new will? Did he have to make his own funeral arrangements? *Ugh!*

Thankfully, the trance was broken by Bart Slaughter, the fourteen-year-old bully of the block, probably cursed from the outset by his last name. Practically living on his black thick-wheeled BMX Jet bike tricked out with high-rise handlebars, Bart would often stop at Melvin's house, and although he never actually got off his bike or approached Melvin, he would lean on the fence and start a conversation by calling out, "Hey, Mr. Klapper, wassup?"

Melvin treated Bart with respect despite the fact that most of the kids in the neighborhood avoided him as did many of the adults on the block. Bart's old man had skipped town a few years back with another woman, leaving his mother, a nice gal, with an alcohol problem. Bart's older brother, Wayne, had been in and out of the courts for minor but increasingly serious violations of people and property. He didn't seem to be around much. Bart was trapped.

Melvin was able to connect with Bart by treating him with courtesy and goodwill, welcoming his stops. After a while, it became obvious that Bart went out of his way to stop and talk with Melvin. On this particular day, in need of conversation, Melvin got out of his rocker and walked slowly off the porch to get closer to Bart, who remained on his bike on the other side of the four-foot-high chain-link fence.

As Melvin approached, Bart lifted himself off the fence and stood over his bike. Bart was taller and broader than he appeared from a distance. Melvin could see why the other kids were scared of Bart. Melvin could see that Bart was a bit surprised by Melvin walking toward him but not as much as when Melvin put his right hand out to greet Bart, who appeared as if he had never previously engaged in a handshake, wiped his hand on his pants, and awkwardly stuck his hand out to meet Melvin's. Bart had a damp, flabby, loose handshake that Melvin wanted to correct but did not.

Melvin started a conversation by admiring Bart's bike, and then most unexpectedly, Bart asked Melvin about what it was like working at Wilson's supermarket.

"Why do you ask?"

"When I was riding past the store yesterday, I saw a Help Wanted sign and figured I could sure use the money. My pop stopped sending us money a few months back, and my mom had her hours cut back at the diner, so it's about time I pitched in."

"That's great, Bart. Good for you."

"Mr. Klapper, could you put a good word in for me?"

Melvin hesitated. "To tell you the truth, son, I need to know that you'll be nice and polite to people. I'm sure you know your reputation isn't all that great. Now you've always been nice to me, so if you give me your word that you'll be the same with everyone else and be easy to work with, I'll call over to Wilson's for you. What do you say?"

"Mr. Klapper, it's easy to be nice to you because you're nice to me. I'd like to be like you because everybody likes you. For an old guy, you're cool. I know people don't like me, but they don't give me a chance. So yes, I promise."

"Bart, try being nice to others first. You'll be surprised how nice they act in return. Let me see what I can do."

"Thanks, Mr. Klapper." Off rode Bart.

Melvin watched him pedal down the block, hoping he had given Bart a ray of sunshine in an otherwise cloudy future, then checked his watch, the only jewelry he wore other than his wedding ring, which he hadn't taken off since 1972. It was now nearly five o'clock. Where were they? Billy was usually home from school by 3:30 p.m., and they only lived fifteen minutes away.

Before Melvin could get back to his porch, he heard Billy yelling, "Grandpa, Grandpa," from the rear window of the car as Chris pulled up in front of Melvin's house. With his baseball glove on his left hand and a blue Yankee cap on his head, Billy immediately jumped out of the car and ran to Melvin. Billy's dog, Amos, named after Billy's favorite chocolate-chip cookie, had his tongue wagging out the rear window. Billy and Amos were pretty much inseparable.

"Hey, Grandpa," said Billy.

"Billy, Billy, Billy," said Melvin as he hugged Billy and kissed the top of his head. Billy was all of sixty-two pounds soaking wet on his 4'4" frame. His arms and legs were just starting to develop muscle. He was well coordinated and popular at school with both boys and girls as well as teachers. It didn't hurt that he was both smart and cute with big brown eyes protected by long and full eyelashes. Most importantly, he was a sweet and sensitive kid, blessed with a big and giving heart.

Grace, who had meanwhile emerged from the front passenger seat, greeted Melvin with her customary big smile, kissing him on his cheek and hugging him like she meant it. She was carrying an overnight bag with all that Billy would need for tonight and then tomorrow at the game. Probably enough stuff for a week.

From behind the wheel, Chris gave Melvin a half-grin and wave. Melvin had long ago accepted the fact that Chris was not enamored with him and didn't have a great deal of respect for Melvin. That was all okay with Melvin as long as Chris was a good husband and father. Melvin remembered what he had told Chris when he informed Melvin that he wanted to marry Grace. Melvin had said, "I have two requirements that you must promise to always honor. One is that you never cheat on my daughter, and two is that you must never raise a hand to your wife or your children. If you can honestly make and keep these promises, then you have my blessing."

As far as Melvin knew, Chris had honored Melvin's two requirements, and so regardless of how Chris treated Melvin, he was more than accepting of Chris even if it wasn't the intimate, loving son-in-law relationship Melvin had hoped for. So long as Grace and Billy were happy, it was good enough for Melvin.

Melvin wasn't in the advice business, but when it came to the safety and well-being of his daughter and grandson, he would not hesitate to say what he felt was appropriate. At Billy's birth, Melvin had told Chris that the best way to be a good father was to be a good husband. Chris had not verbally acknowledged that counsel, but as far as Melvin knew, Chris was a good husband. Grace wouldn't accept anything less, having grown up in the loving and respectful home Martha and Melvin provided.

Standing in front of the house by the steps leading up to the porch, Grace began to give a long list of instructions to Billy and Melvin, including what to eat, when to go to sleep, to brush his teeth, stay close to each other in the train, take an umbrella if it was raining, don't overeat at the game, don't talk to strangers, to call if anything was needed, and so on and so forth. Both Billy and Melvin were listening with one ear, maybe half of one ear, because they knew from past sleepovers that they were going to do what they wanted and that Grace would never really know. Grace knew this too but felt better saying what a responsible mother should say.

"Okay, it's time for you guys to go," said Melvin once Grace had come to the end of her list. "We're good. Don't worry about us."

"We'll be back to pick Billy up tomorrow afternoon around five," Grace reminded him.

Before the car was even out of sight, Melvin and Billy simultaneously turned and raced to the front door to see who would be first in the house. Melvin always let Billy win, but this time, Billy beat him fair and square. Melvin wondered if carrying Billy's overnight bag had slowed him down or if the cancer was to blame. He sensed that this was a question he would be asking about many things in the weeks and months ahead.

"So, my wonderful, fabulous, handsome grandson, what should we do first?" he asked.

"Can we have pizza and ice cream?"

"You bet. Let's walk to Randazzo's for pizza and then hit the ice cream store on the way back. What do you say?"

And off they went. Melvin noticed that when they walked together, they didn't hold hands as much as they used to, which he missed but recognized as a sign of Billy growing up. Both Billy and Melvin proudly wore their Yankees caps and talked about their favorite players, batting averages, and whether the Yanks could make up the thirteen games they currently trailed the first-place Red Sox. At Billy's request, Melvin brought his joke and riddle book, which would allow each of them to take turns at dinner reading jokes and asking riddles. While Billy loved to laugh, he enjoyed even more making Melvin laugh. Melvin knew this, so he laughed as much as he possibly could.

Melvin loved posing riddles to Billy, enjoying the momentary lapse in conversation while Billy tried to figure out the brain teaser. "Billy," Melvin started, "here's one for you. A man leaves home, turns left three times, and upon returning home finds two men with masks. Who are they?"

"Say it again, Grandpa."

Melvin repeated it.

"Hmm, that's a good one. What's the answer?"

"A catcher and an umpire," Melvin said.

Billy laughed out loud. "I should have gotten that one, Grandpa."

And on they strolled.

After overeating pizza and meatballs at Randazzo's, followed by giant ice cream cones (with sprinkles for Billy) from the Springfield Sweet Shoppe, a meal that Grace would hopefully never know about, both Melvin and Billy were stuffed to the gills. When they got back to the house, they put on the TV to watch the Friday night Yankees–Red Sox game, the first of a three-game series at Yankee Stadium. The game had a 7:05 p.m. starting time, so the first pitch was about to be thrown. Billy watched while pounding his leather glove like he was waiting for a ball to come right to him through the television screen. Melvin sat back and watched Billy. What a joy. This was what he would miss.

Melvin had been teaching Billy how to play chess but, not wanting to push it on him, waited to see if Billy was in the mood. Sure enough, around the third inning, Billy suggested they play a board game.

"Sure, pick out whatever game you'd like."

"How about chess, Grandpa?" said Billy as he went through the games piled on top of each other on the two bottom shelves of the living-room breakfront.

"You bet," said Melvin. "Remember how to set up the board?"

They sat on the floor for nearly two hours in front of the television talking chess while knowing instinctively when to look up to see a home run or great catch.

"Grandpa, I really like chess. It's hard but fun."

"Billy, chess is a lot like life. Always remember that at the end of the game, all the pieces go back into that little wooden box."

"What does that mean?"

"It means that no matter who you are or how successful you are, you should always respect other people. There's no room for arrogance. At the end of the day, we're all the same. Whether you're a king or a pawn, we all end up in the same place."

Melvin enjoyed seeing Billy's mind at work. The kid had a good mind, could grasp concepts, and had his father's head for math. Hopefully, he had his mother's warmth and personality. He was quickly picking up the game. He liked the different ways in which the pieces could be moved.

How much more could Melvin teach his grandson in six months?

CHAPTER 5

Friday, July 8
Springfield

It was 11:30 a.m. when Melvin realized that he and Billy had fallen asleep on the floor. Pillows from the couch were under Billy's head. The chessboard was still there with its pieces in place. The postgame show was just finishing up, bemoaning the fact that the Yankees had lost to the Red Sox 6–5 and were now fourteen games behind.

Knowing he could no longer lift Billy, Melvin nudged him and said, "Okay, Billy, it's time to go upstairs."

"I think I fell asleep, Grandpa."

"Me too. C'mon. It's late. I'll tuck you in. Remember, Mom said you had to brush your teeth. And then I have a bedtime story to tell you. You want to hear a bedtime story?"

"You bet. Is it a good one?"

"It's better than good—it's great. C'mon, let's go upstairs."

In anticipation of the story, Billy quickly got into his PJs, brushed his teeth, and jumped into bed.

"Okay, Grandpa," shouted Billy, "I'm ready to be tucked in and hear a great story."

Billy snuggled into the cool sheets. He loved the soft, fluffy pillow and wondered why his pillow at home was so much heavier and harder to mush into position.

Melvin sat comfortably on the left side of Billy's bed and put his right hand gently on Billy's chest. He couldn't help thinking that this had been Grace's bedroom, Grace's bed. How many times over the years over the years had he sat here, first with his daughter, and now, when Billy stayed over, with his grandson? Melvin was trying to slow the moment down so he could savor it. He knew there wouldn't be many more times like this. He wanted Billy to remember this moment long after Melvin was gone.

"So, Billy," Melvin began, "I'm going to tell you a story, a story about you and me. It's not so much a story as it is an idea, a belief, a feeling that I can't really explain or fully understand myself. This is not an exact science, so it's somewhat uncertain and unpredictable. Maybe it's about trust and faith. I don't know. I have to say all this to you so you are prepared later to think about what I'm about to tell you."

Billy was silent, not knowing what his grandpa was saying or what was about to happen next.

"Tonight is the perfect night for me to be telling you this, Billy. Why? Because you're about to have your tenth birthday." Billy stared at Melvin with rapt attention, clutching the bed covers under his chin, preparing himself in anticipation of a scary ghost story.

"The night before my tenth birthday," Melvin began, "my father told me what I'm about to tell you. I don't know if this happens in other families. But as my father told me, we get a chance in our family to make a secret wish on the night before our tenth birthday." Melvin paused to emphasize the "secret wish" part. "Tonight, my boy, is a special night for you. It's a night you will remember forever, and someday, you'll share this tradition with your son or daughter or grandchild on the night before his or her tenth birthday."

Billy was silent. Melvin got his thoughts together and continued, "Like many things in life, there are some very important rules that you must play by if the secret wish is to have any chance of actually coming true. Do you understand everything so far? Do you want to hear more?"

"Yes, but I'm scared."

"No need to be scared, Billy. Nothing bad will happen, I promise. Either your wish will come true or it won't. I believe it depends on what you wish for. The better the wish, the better the chances that it will come true."

"Okay, I'm ready. Tell me more."

"You have to pay very close attention to what I'm about to tell you. There are three rules, and you must remember and respect each and every one of these rules. Do I have your word of honor?"

"Yes, Grandpa," said Billy as he crossed his heart with his right hand and pointed his left hand skyward. "I promise and hope to die."

Melvin winced inwardly at this inadvertent reminder of his diagnosis but went on to outline the rules in a serious but affectionate voice.

"Rule number one. You get to make only one wish on this night, the night before your tenth birthday. It may come true, and it may not come true. It may happen right away, or it may not ever happen. There's no guarantee. I don't know why, but that's just the way it works. So it's impossible to know if your birthday wish will come true. The important thing to remember is that you have to make your wish truly special to improve your chances. So while there's no way of knowing if your wish will be granted, I think a really good wish has a better chance for success. So be very thoughtful and make it something really, really special."

Pushing the covers toward Billy and repositioning himself on the bed, Melvin could see Billy was hanging on every word, clutching his blanket and anxiously awaiting what Melvin was going to say next.

"Rule number two. The wish can never be about something for yourself or for things like money or diamonds or a mansion or a fancy sports car. It's much more important than that. It's really about wishing for something that money *can't* buy. Remember,

Billy, things or objects that may give you temporary joy will not make you happy in the long run. Only people can do that."

Melvin realized this was a concept that Billy, though smart for a ten-year-old, would need to ponder. So he again rearranged himself on the side of the bed, giving Billy time to process the words and the meaning behind them.

"So far, so good?" he asked.

Billy nodded.

"The last rule," said Melvin, "is very important if you want your wish to come true. You can never tell anybody what you wished for. Only you can know what the wish was for. Even if the wish comes true, you can't tell anyone. That's just part of the deal."

Billy was transfixed. He gazed at Melvin, but it was not an empty gaze. Melvin liked that. It was what he had hoped for, and it was nothing less than what he expected from Billy. Nothing was said. Nothing needed to be said. Billy just kept looking at Melvin, his eyes filled with curiosity and wonderment. Melvin looked back at Billy with adoration and devotion. Both knew they were sharing an extraordinary moment.

"Billy, what do you think of all this?" Melvin asked at last.

Billy paused before answering. "Did you make a wish the night before your tenth birthday?"

Melvin liked this question. It meant that Billy was processing what had been said. "Yes, I did."

"What did you wish for?"

"Remember rule number three?"

Billy nodded.

"We're not allowed to tell anyone what we wished for, so I can only tell you that although I didn't wish for it, I've had a wonderful life. I've never been rich or famous, but I try to be kind and generous and respectful and to be there for others in their time of need. I've gotten a lot in return just being nice and helpful to friends and neighbors and some people I didn't even know. Even though I didn't wish for it, I met and fell in love with your grandmother, had a wonderful daughter, your mother, and now I have a terrific grandson. Life has been very good to me. Yes, I can tell you that I think my most important wishes in life must have come true."

"What did you mean about a 'good' wish having a better chance of being granted? Like what?"

"I suppose a good wish is one that comes from the heart." Melvin tapped Billy's chest lightly. "That's the best way I can describe it. To help someone else, to do something good for other people. That to me would be a good wish and would improve your chances that your wish would be granted. Does that make sense to you?"

Billy moved right along. "How do you know if your wish is granted?"

"Oh, you'll know. Believe me, you'll know."

"Who grants the wish?"

"I would tell you if I knew, but I don't. I don't think we're supposed to know the answer to that question."

"Can you tell me what your wish was if it didn't come true?"

"Hmm, let me think about that." Melvin wanted to answer all of Billy's questions in a way that would demonstrate his respect for the rules. "I didn't wish for it, but if I could have, I would have wished that I could play for the New York Yankees. But you can't wish for things like that for yourself. So obviously that wish would not have come true. But I'm still a big Yankees fan."

"Did Mom get a wish when she was my age?"

"I told her the same things I'm telling you tonight, but she never said a word about it to me after that night, so I don't really know if she believed me enough to make a wish or whether she's just following rule number three of not telling anyone what she wished for. Since she knew you were going to be here tonight, I was waiting to hear if she was going to discuss the wish with me, but when she didn't, I felt she was either leaving it to me or simply forgot the whole thing. But having a son like you is all your mother ever wanted. She couldn't wish for anything more important or better than you. And hopefully, someday you'll pass this all along to your children or grandchildren."

"Does Dad know about this?"

"Not from me. He would only know if your mother told him, and I have no idea if she even remembers any of this."

"Can I talk about it with her?"

"Yes, so long as you follow the three rules."

Billy, now thinking out loud, said, "Can I wish to be the strongest or fastest person in the world like Superman or the Flash? That way I could save the world."

"I can't tell you what to wish for—that's up to you. But if you want to improve your chances of your wish coming true, my advice would be to try and save the world in a way that doesn't require you to become Superman."

Billy was again silent but thoughtful. Melvin knew his words had not been wasted. The rest was up to Billy.

"Big day tomorrow," said Melvin as he got up from the bed, pulling the covers up to Billy's chin. "Time, young man, for you to get some shut-eye. Your first big-league baseball game."

"Can I eat all the hotdogs I want?"

"You bet, kid. It's your tenth birthday only once, and I guarantee it's going to be a special day, like no other day you've ever had before. I can feel it in my bones. I hope it turns out to be a day you remember for the rest of your life. I know it will be for me. Love you, Billy."

Melvin leaned over, kissed Billy's forehead, and started to leave the room.

Billy asked, "Grandpa, can you leave the door open?"

"Sure," said Melvin.

"Love you, Grandpa," Billy said.

Outside Billy's door, Melvin stood silently in the hallway, wondering whether he had properly presented the wish and whether he had answered Billy's questions. In the fall of light through the door, he could see Billy, though he did not think Billy could see him.

Billy reached to the nightstand and grabbed his glove, which he and Melvin had oiled to make a good pocket, and put it on his left hand. He then flipped his Yankees cap off the bedpost and made sure it was firmly on his head. After a moment of staring straight ahead and up at the ceiling, Billy squeezed and held his eyes tightly shut. Then he fell asleep with his glove on his hand, the Yankees cap on his head and a smile on his face.

Later, as he lay in bed, Melvin reflected on the day. He had gone from the depths of despair with Dr. Mendelsohn to the pure joy of being with Billy. He felt exhausted, but also, for some reason, he felt renewed. In his heart, without knowing why, he felt sure that tomorrow was going to be a great day. Then with a smile on his face, he fell asleep.

CHAPTER 6

Saturday, July 9
Springfield

Melvin was already dressed and in the kitchen nursing his second cup of coffee when Billy came down for breakfast.

Melvin had put Billy's favorite cereal on to the table—Wheaties, breakfast of champions—along with a banana and milk. As they ate, the radio played in the background, tuned to the local sports station, with the radio pundits debating whether the Yankees could make up their fourteen-game deficit. The consensus was that the Yankees' season was effectively over and that they should start playing their rookies to give them experience for next season. None of this negative talk diminished Melvin's excitement about the day ahead or lessened Billy's enthusiasm.

Melvin had been curious to see if Billy would mention anything about what he had told him the night before. But Billy said nothing. Whether that was in keeping with the rules Melvin had outlined or because, like his mother, he had already forgotten the whole business, Melvin didn't know. But he had his suspicions.

"Billy, let's leave around eleven," Melvin suggested. "It will take time to catch the train to 125th Street. Then we have to switch to another train going uptown into the Bronx, where we get off at 161st Street. Then we can walk a few blocks to the stadium. Sound good?"

"But that's three hours away, Grandpa. I'm ready to go now. What can we do between now and then?"

"We can finish our chess game or play Monopoly or anything else you like."

"Let's play Monopoly. I like that game."

Billy went to get the Monopoly box from the breakfront, while Melvin washed the breakfast dishes and placed them in the rack to dry. They then sat down at the dinette table and for two hours threw dice, bought and sold properties, and tried to make the time go faster. Billy was starting to get as good at Monopoly as he was at chess, which thrilled Melvin. He knew Billy had a good future ahead of him. That was the important thing, after all, not whether Melvin would be around to see it.

It was finally time to go. It was a warm July day but not oppressively hot or humid. Billy wore white shorts with a blue Yankees shirt and his red high-top Converse All-Star sneakers that Melvin had given him last Christmas. Melvin had shown Billy how to wear his cap with its bill slightly curved just the way it should be to look like a pro. With his glove already on his left hand, Billy was more than ready. Melvin wore his chinos and his "lucky" green short-sleeved shirt that Martha had gotten for him many years before. He only wore it on special occasions, and taking Billy to his first big-league game was about as special as occasions got.

When they got to the station, a crowd had already begun to assemble, waiting for the train to 125th Street. Billy had never been on a city train before, so Melvin found it interesting when Billy felt for Melvin's hand. Just standing on the platform, they could feel themselves surrounded, almost engulfed, by the hum of anticipation, although the game was still a good hour away.

Both train rides went smoothly and were on time, always an accomplishment in New York City. The crowd was in a good mood despite the Yankees being so far out of first place. It was now 12:30 p.m. Getting off the station at 161st Street, Melvin could feel the exhilaration building in Billy, who had been unusually quiet during the trip. As if carried along by the human wave of fans, Melvin and Billy made their way to Gate D of the stadium. It had been several years since Melvin had attended a game. He too was swept up in the thrill of being with fifty thousand people watching a Saturday game between the Yankees and the Red Sox. What could be more magical than a game between these two storied rivals on a clear July day?

Upon entering the circular concrete corridors of the stadium, Billy was enthralled by all that was going on. It was as if his head were on a swivel. Melvin purposely walked slowly, giving Billy time to take it all in—the smell of the food, the barking of the vendors, the crush of the crowd, the store selling jerseys and all things baseball, and the voice of the public announcer echoing from the field introducing important guests and former Yankee stars. It was everything Melvin had hoped it would be. And for Billy, it was way beyond what he'd imagined it would be. It was bigger. It was better. It was louder. It was an experience he had never had before and could never have again. Your first major league game happens only once.

"Grandpa, this is great."

"I'm glad you like it. I think so too."

Their seats, when they finally made their way to them, were way back in the center field bleachers. Although he didn't comment, Melvin was disappointed, but tickets had gotten so expensive over the years that these were the best available seats Melvin could afford. Five minutes to one and there wasn't an empty seat in the house. The roar of anticipation from fifty thousand people was building. It was standing room only.

Melvin and Billy's seats were in the middle of the row, so people already seated had to stand up to let them pass by. Baseball fans like seeing kids at a game and are almost always respectful of seeing a parent, let alone a grandparent, getting a kid to become one of them. The smell of the beer was both pungent and enticing. Never a big drinker, Melvin remembered it as mostly water, but it sure was a part of being at a ball game. He wondered how they made something so bad smell so good. Billy wanted peanuts, so Melvin passed a $10 bill across the row to the vendor in the aisle, who passed an $8 bag of peanuts right back across the row to Billy. Teamwork in action. To avoid annoying his new neighbors, Melvin told the vendor to keep the change.

Everyone rose en masse for the singing of the national anthem by an eight-year-old girl who had a voice that had been gifted to her by God. She silenced the crowd until everyone joined in at the end and then applauded her and themselves. The umps were already on the field. The infield looked flawlessly groomed. The bases were gleaming white. The outfield grass looked like it had just been painted loden green.

For a few minutes, Melvin lost himself. To his amazement, he was taken aback by the majesty of the moment, the beauty of it all—the sights, the smells, the sounds. Watching all these years on television, he had forgotten how wonderful it was to be an actual part of this experience. It was stimulus overload, an all-out assault on one's senses. He loved being there. Billy broke the spell, poking Melvin to ask questions about the scoreboard.

There was thunder emanating from the crowd that seemed to circle around the packed stadium as the Yankees took the field. The players looked small from where Melvin and Billy were sitting.

"Grandpa, we're so far away," Billy bemoaned. Melvin felt disappointment, his and Billy's.

Before Melvin could respond, a very big African-American man with a bald head and a thick mustache leaned in past Melvin toward Billy and said in a rich baritone voice, "Hey, kid, this is where the real people sit."

Billy did not know what to say or where to look, but Melvin did. Extending his right hand, he said, "Thank you."

"You're welcome," said the man so softly as almost not to be heard while shaking Melvin's hand. Melvin realized that his neighbor's hand had just swallowed his own and that being so large he must have learned over the years to shake hands in a gentle, barely touching manner, the way prizefighters do. Melvin instantly liked this guy.

After a minute or so of thinking about what to say next, Melvin started a conversation with this neighbor on his right, who was obviously much too large for his seat. He was wearing a short-sleeved shirt that barely contained his upper arms and shoulders. He was alone but seemed to know some of the people sitting in the area. It was obvious that he knew the game and was a dedicated Yankee fan.

"This is my grandson's first major league game," began Melvin. "It's his tenth birthday, and I thought this is about the best gift a kid could get."

"Yeah," responded the man in the seat next to him, "my uncle got me into the game when I was about the same age as your grandson, and it's been a big part of my life. Being in the crowd on a beautiful day like this. What could be better?"

"Did you ever play?" asked Melvin.

"Not much baseball. Mostly football. I played the line, both offense and defense, in high school and then some semi-pro until I got too old and slow. That's a young man's sport. Know what I mean?"

"I'm Melvin Klapper. That's Klapper with a *K*."

"Nice to meet you, Melvin Klapper with a *K*. I'm Aaron Winfield. My friends call me Winnie." Melvin saw the man smile, and it was a smile that was big and broad and sincere. It wasn't a facial smile. It was a whole-body smile. There was something about this guy that made Melvin feel like he had known him for a long time—or sorry that he hadn't.

"Hey Melvin, want a beer on me?" asked Winnie as got up to leave his seat.

"I'm good," said Melvin, now realizing how tall and wide Winnie actually was.

"Hey kid, you want a soda?"

Billy looked at Melvin to see if it was okay. Melvin nodded.

"Thank you," said Billy.

While Winnie was gone, Billy asked Melvin why he was talking with a stranger, something his parents had told him not to do.

"Billy, he seems like a nice man who's alone and probably wants some conversation."

Winnie returned with a beer for himself and a soda and a box of crackerjacks for Billy, who had already devoured a hotdog and a bag of peanuts. Billy was starting to like Winnie too.

With very little hitting and few walks, the game was moving along at a brisk pace. Billy had already enjoyed two Yankee fan "waves," which Billy had only done in his house while watching it happening at the game. Billy quickly got into the spirit of things when everyone around him, including Melvin and Winnie, stood to join the fun.

Bleacher fans, unlike some box-seaters, willingly take the time and make the effort to not just watch the game but to actively participate or at least vocalize. Very few pitches go by without some comment from bleacher fans. Winnie, sharing baseball lore with Billy, told him that the wave had happened for the first time in 1981 in Oakland, when the Athletics were playing the Yankees in a playoff game. It took off from there. Billy loved to know these tidbits of information. They would become committed to memory.

Billy was asking Melvin all the right questions. If the foul pole was in fair territory, why wasn't it called the fair pole? Where did the announcers sit? Who cleaned the stands after the game was over? Who mowed the lawn? Melvin enjoyed Billy's inquisitive mind. At one point, Winnie overheard a conversation between Billy and Melvin and joined in by softly saying, "That's some smart kid you got there, Melvin."

CHAPTER 7

Saturday, July 9
Yankee Stadium

This Saturday afternoon game between the New York Yankees and Boston Red Sox was being carried live by ESPN despite the fact the Red Sox had a fourteen-game lead on the Bronx Bombers. The traditional rivalry between the Yankees and the Red Sox made their games worth watching regardless of the standings. It was being announced on television by the best baseball duo in the business, former Dodger great Scott Whaler and thirty-year booth veteran Dan Earling. The pair had worked together for several seasons, were beyond knowledgeable about baseball, and were easy on the ears. According to some viewers, they were also easy on the eyes.

In his fourteen seasons with the Dodgers, the only team for which he had ever played, Whaler was a five-time all-star catcher and six-time Golden Glove winner. He had 275 career home runs and had been a key part of three World Series championships. At thirty-eight, he was only three years into retirement and was a sure bet to be nominated to the Hall of Fame when he became eligible in two more years. The fans liked him as did the players. Whaler could get information from and interviews with players no one else could. He had been offered numerous managerial jobs, even a front-office position as a general manager. But he enjoyed his less physically demanding schedule, the learning of a new skill, and the handsome remuneration far too much to go back into uniform or sit behind a desk.

Earling was a legend in his profession, with a smooth, melodic voice ideal for radio or television. He had broadcast major events not only for baseball but also for football, golf, and basketball. Earling was in constant demand by the networks for any sport he was willing to do. But his first love was baseball, having played at Pepperdine as a center fielder while also a starting guard on the basketball team. Although his dream of making the big leagues had fallen short, Earling truly loved broadcasting.

"The game is now in the top of the sixth inning here in New York," Earling drawled, "with Boston leading the Yankees two to nothing behind some great pitching by Olivio Otero, and the home crowd is getting restless. There hasn't been much for Yankee fans to cheer about lately, Scott, especially coming off a heartbreaking defeat last night. The Red Sox now have a fourteen-game cushion against the fourth-place Yankees, who just can't seem to get it going this season."

"Yankee Manager Russ Higgins has tried just about everything, Dan," Whaler chimed in. "He's rotated his pitching staff, changed the batting order, even brought players up from the minors, but so far, nothing has worked to turn the season around. Looks like they could be running out of time this year. They certainly aren't swinging the lumber today."

"Okay, here we go," Earling said with the genuine enthusiasm for the game that had endeared him to fans, "with Red Sox cleanup slugger Brock Dennison coming to the plate. Dennison is a big man at 6'4" and 225. He led the league in home runs last year with forty-eight and is having another good season this year, tied for second-most homers in the American League with twenty-six. He's already knocked in fifty-five runs, and his last time up, in the third inning, he drilled a laser line-drive double to drive in the two

Red Sox runs. Brock has been hot lately, going twelve for his last thirty-five at bats, including five home runs. Dennison has been the only offense in the game so far."

"Lefty Manny Rojas is on the mound for the Yankees," Whaler said. "Other than giving up that two-run double, he's pitched a very good ball game, striking out six so far and walking only one. Rojas is a crafty nine-year veteran who's going to pitch carefully to Dennison and try not to give him anything too fat to hit. The key to pitching to Dennison is either to jam him so he can't extend his arms or keep it away from him so he can't pull it. It's easy to say but hard to do with a guy who manages to hit home runs regardless of how pitchers throw to him."

"And the first pitch...is low and outside for ball one," said Earling. "Beautiful Saturday here in the ballpark. Sold-out crowd of about fifty thousand. Not a seat to be had in this stadium when the Red Sox come to town even when the Yankees seem out of the race. Rojas checks with his catcher, gives a nod, goes into his windup, and Dennison swings and misses a rising fastball. That was some high cheese."

"I think Brock was looking for a breaking ball and was way behind that fastball," added Whaler. "Rojas got away with that one."

"One–one count. This is a good battle between two experienced players at the top of their games."

Dennison stepped out of the batter's box, glaring at the pitcher as most big hitters do, took a deep breath, tightened the batting glove on his left hand, knocked some dirt out of his cleats, adjusted his cap, and stepped back in, looking ready to clobber one.

"Rojas takes the signal from his catcher Glenn Worthington, winds, and throws a bullet right down the pipe."

Dennison swung, and the sound coming from the collision of bat and ball said it all about where that ball was going. With the ball soaring high and far, higher and further than most home runs, Dennison flipped his bat, pointed to his cheering dugout, admired the flight of the ball, and began his home-run trot. The crowd was watching in awe.

"No question about this one, folks," Earling said. "That's way, way outta here. Wow."

Yankee center fielder Jay Jones never even moved, just stared at the ball as it flew overhead, knowing it was far beyond his reach.

As the bat-propelled missile, a white blur traveling at a speed well in excess of one hundred miles per hour, began to descend, with the entire stadium—including players, umpires, and announcers—glued to its trajectory, Melvin suddenly realized that it was on course to hit Billy squarely in the face.

Without thought, Melvin thrust his bare left hand inches away from Billy's face and caught the ball squarely in his palm. The thud of the impact reverberated through the stadium. Even people watching at home heard the ball thwacking into Melvin's hand.

A stunned silence fell. Then as if catching its collective breath, the crowd burst into spontaneous applause. Melvin and Billy only dimly heard the applause and cheers. They did not see their faces up on the Jumbotron. They did not realize that people all over the country were witnessing this moment. All that existed for them was that white baseball in Melvin's hand, inches from Billy's face.

"What the hell?" said Winnie. "Are you kidding me? That may be the greatest catch I've ever seen, and I've been watching baseball games my whole life."

A chant began to spread through the stadium.

"Throw it back! Throw it back!"

This, of course, was a tradition in many ballparks. When the opposing team hit a home run on your turf, any fan who recovered the ball was expected to throw it back onto the field. Anyone who did not could expect to be roundly booed by the crowd and generally treated as a traitor to the team.

Winnie told Melvin, "You gotta throw it back, Melvin."

Billy grabbed Melvin's arm. "Grandpa, I want the ball for my room. Please don't throw it back."

Melvin didn't know what to do. He didn't want to upset Billy and ruin the day, but they'd be in for some pretty rough verbal abuse and maybe worse if they defied the crowd, which could also ruin the day.

Winnie, seeing Melvin's dilemma and with Billy now tearing up, laid his big hand gently on the boy's shoulders. "It's just the way baseball is played, Billy."

Melvin nodded. "Winnie is right, Billy. We have to throw it back. But I promise I'll get you a ball before we leave, okay?"

"Okay, Grandpa," Billy said, and Melvin could see how much it cost him to say it, "I understand."

"Good boy," Melvin said. "I'm proud of you." At that, he stood up and without any apparent effort threw the ball directly into the glove of the Yankee catcher at home plate, approximately 460 feet away.

You could hear a pin drop. It was beyond eerie. Something unnatural had just occurred. Time seemingly stopped. The catch of a minute ago, which the crowd and announcers were still buzzing about, had now if possible been surpassed by Melvin's throw. No crowd of fifty thousand men, women, and children should be totally devoid of sound unless witnessing a moment of historical proportion. They were sharing a unique and exceptional experience. No one spoke. A stillness and serenity had fallen upon this gathering of people. Players on both teams started to slowly come out of their dugouts looking into center field. Umpires removed their face masks and did the same. The catcher holding the ball kept looking at it.

"Did I just see what I just saw?" Winnie asked as though in shock.

Melvin gave a baffled smile.

"Grandpa, I didn't know you could play baseball," Billy said.

"Neither did I, Billy," Melvin said. "Neither did I."

Billy looked up at Winnie. "Was that good, Mr. Winfield?"

"Good? Was that good?" Winnie kept shaking his head and looking at Melvin as if he were an alien from outer space. "After just seeing possibly the greatest catch of all time, I just saw the greatest throw of all time."

An ardent fan of about forty, sitting with his friends behind Winnie, tapped Melvin on the shoulder. "Hey, Pops, who the hell are you? Are you a former player?"

Melvin, not knowing what to say, just smiled and shrugged.

Still staring at Melvin, Winnie said, "Seriously, how did you do that?"

"I don't know," Melvin replied. "I honestly don't know. It just happened."

Back in the ESPN booth, Dan Earling offered the following observation: "You know, Scott, anyone can get lucky on a catch, but you can't call it luck when a guy, no youngster—actually an elderly gentleman, I might add with all due respect—throws a ball in the air on the fly perfectly to a target 460 feet away. That was the longest throw I've ever seen by far."

"Dan, I've had the good fortune of playing with some of the greatest players in the game," Whaler replied, "and I have never seen a ball thrown that far. I have no idea how what I just saw could possibly happen."

"And bear in mind, Scott," said Earling, "he had no running start, no momentum whatsoever. He just stood and threw. Is that even physically possible? And the catcher didn't even have to move to catch it. It fell right in his glove. I have to watch the tape again in slow motion to believe what I just saw."

Back home, standing and gawking at his television, Melvin's son-in-law, Chris, was screaming for Grace to join him in the den. Grace, who was in the kitchen, had no idea why Chris was shouting her name but ran to the den to make sure he was okay. There she watched in amazement the replay of her father's miraculous catch and ever more miraculous throw.

"Why didn't you ever tell me Melvin played pro ball?" Chris demanded.

"He didn't," replied Grace.

"Did you see the distance on that throw?" he marveled. "The accuracy? That doesn't just happen, Grace. That's world-class athletic ability and a lifetime of training. Hell, I don't think most pros would be able to make that throw!"

Back in the stadium, Winnie said, "I need a beer, maybe two or three. Can I get you guys anything?"

"Can I have a beer, Grandpa?" asked Billy.

"No, I don't think your parents would want me to do that, but you can have ice cream." Melvin reached into his pocket to give Winnie money, but the big man waved him off.

"Not today, pal," he said. "This one's on me. You've earned it, Melvin Klapper with a *K*."

"Thanks, Winnie. You're a good man."

CHAPTER 8

Saturday, July 9
Yankee Stadium

Just as things seemed to be settling down, two stadium attendants came down the aisle to the row Melvin was sitting in and asked him to come with them.

"Are you throwing me out?"

"Sir, just come with us."

"Did I do something wrong?"

"Sir, we're not here to argue with you. We need you to come with us…now."

Fans in the area who could hear what was going on started yelling at the attendants.

"Hey, leave the old guy alone."

"Piss off, you jerks," offered another baseball aficionado.

Billy was starting to get frightened at which point Winnie stood up. And when Winnie stood up, people took notice.

"The guy just threw the ball back," said Winnie to the attendants in a very deep and serious voice. Starting to feel the heat of the crowd defending Melvin, the attendants didn't respond when Winnie bellowed, "Just like it's always done. What's the big deal?"

While the attendants were being jeered and booed and being given the New York one-finger salute, some easily angered fans, probably having had a few beers too many, started throwing peanuts at them. Words were said that Billy shouldn't have heard, but that was the way it went sometimes. Melvin tried to assure Billy that they had done nothing wrong and need not worry.

But Billy, like Melvin, felt uncomfortable with all that was going on around them. Having never been to a game before or sitting in a crowd this big or this noisy, it was easy to understand Billy getting scared. As the situation was becoming one of disorder and potential bedlam, two burly New York City police officers rushed down the aisle to the row where the attendants were standing.

The older of the two cops approached the attendants and said, "What's going on here?"

"We're trying to get that guy over there"—they pointed at Melvin—"to come with us."

"Why? What did he do? Are you trying to eject him? Isn't he the old guy who made that incredible catch and throw?"

Fans all over the stadium were starting to boo, assuming that Melvin was being ejected. More cops were double-timing over to the scene. The game had resumed, but no one was watching it. Even the players were trying to catch a glimpse of what was going on.

After not initially acknowledging the altercation, announcer Dan Earling finally said, "We seem to have a commotion of some sort going on over by where the catch and throw were made. We can't see what it's about because it's so far away, but we do see quite a few of New York's finest and can certainly hear the boos. What do you think, Scott?"

"It looks like they're trying to eject the fan who made the catch and throw, but I can't understand why. As far as I can tell, he didn't do anything wrong. I hope the Yankees know what they're doing. This old guy is going to be famous by tomorrow, and if I were the Yankees, I wouldn't start up with him."

One of the cops who had just joined the huddle was clearly a senior officer. He was older, had gold bars on his uniform, and the other cops were gingerly moving out of his way, making room for him. After being momentarily prepped by two other cops, he walked over to the attendants and said, "Listen, boys, I'm not letting you throw that old man out unless you have a damn good reason. It's as simple as that."

"We're not here to throw him out, Captain. We got a message from the owner's suite that they want to meet the old man and give the kid a ball. You know, good public relations."

"Why didn't you say that before you started all this trouble?"

At that point, the officer, brushing the attendants aside, entered the row where Melvin, Billy, and Winnie were seated. As he made his way to Melvin, the fans in the row watching all this occur right in front of them stood as straight as soldiers to make as much room as possible.

Seeing the officer on his way to them, Melvin grabbed Billy's arm around the elbow. "Don't worry, Billy. Everything will be fine. It's just a misunderstanding."

Could this day get any crazier? he wondered. *Grace may never let Billy stay with me again.*

Winnie leaned into Melvin and whispered, "Just be cool."

As the officer approached, Melvin got to his feet. In a show of apparent support, Winnie stood too. Billy remained seated, clutching his glove.

"Are you the guy who caught that ball?" asked the cop.

"Yes, sir," replied Melvin.

"Were you the guy who threw that ball to home plate?"

"Yes, sir. Am I in trouble?"

"Oh no, just the opposite. These attendants aren't here to throw you out. The owner of the Yankees wants to meet you and give the kid here, I assume your grandson, a ball."

"Really? Do I have to go now?"

"Totally up to you, but it could be a thrill for the kid here. I suggest you go get a ball, maybe get a picture or two. The owner's not a bad guy, just a little stuffy if you know what I mean." He glanced over to Winnie. "You with them?"

Winnie hesitated, but Melvin said, "Yes, Officer, he's our friend."

"That was one hell of a throw, mister. Glad I was here today to see it. So what do you want to do?"

Winnie was nudging Melvin in the back to say yes. Melvin looked to Billy for an opinion. "Billy?"

"Grandpa, I think we should go get a ball."

"Winnie?"

"Are you kidding, man? This is a no-brainer."

Melvin asked, "Can our friend come with us?"

After a moment of hesitation, the cop said, "Sure, why not? I'll personally walk you over there, okay?"

Melvin respectfully responded, "Thank you, Officer."

Melvin, holding Billy's hand, followed the officer out of the row and up the aisle. Winnie, looking more like a bodyguard than a fan, stuck close to Melvin. Spectators they passed went out of their way to applaud, give Melvin a pat on the back, or shake his hand. Even Winnie was getting pats on the back. Cell phone cameras were clicking away.

After about ten minutes, they reached a private elevator. The officer who had been escorting them handed them over to the elevator operator, who said, "Welcome to Yankee Stadium, gentlemen."

And so up they went in a plushily carpeted, rosewood-paneled, cloudlike lift that silently and swiftly brought them to a part of the stadium that 99.99 percent of fans wondered about but never got a chance to actually see.

"Here we are, gentlemen," the elevator operator said as the doors slid open. "I'm sure you'll enjoy your visit."

"Holy shit," Winnie burst out. Then he added, "I'm sorry. Didn't mean to say that out loud."

For Melvin, who was usually pretty calm and centered, this was like an out-of-body experience. Everything he looked at was handsomely crafted and decorated, the woodwork, the furniture, the art. Even the lighting fixtures, those hanging from the ceiling and the gold wall sconces, were things Melvin had never before seen in person. To his left was a sitting area with two very large dark-green suede couches and four club chairs covered in a material of mostly yellow and some red. A thick black-marble cocktail table that had to be at least four feet by six feet sat centered between the chairs and couches.

Beyond the sitting area were two wide doors with several wide-shouldered security guards standing in front of them. The guards didn't appear to have guns, but they didn't look like they needed them.

Directly in front of Melvin, about forty feet away, were two spotlessly gleaming glass cabinets, each about ten feet wide and six feet high, filled with neatly and thoughtfully placed Yankee memorabilia. Melvin, with his arm on Billy's shoulder, could see that the cabinets contained trophies, baseballs, gloves, bats, and what looked like old programs and lineup cards. The professional lighting of these items reminded Melvin of being in a museum.

Quietly taking it all in, Billy was mesmerized by the sheer size as well as elegance and glamor all around him as well as the deference everyone was showing them. Winnie grabbed a hold of Billy's arm and guided him over to the display cases. A second or two later, Melvin joined them.

"Look, there's Yogi Berra's glove from when he caught Don Larsen's perfect game in the 1956 World Series! And that's the bat Roger Maris hit his 61st home run in with in 1961," Winnie enthused.

To Billy, these were just names. But to Melvin and Winnie, they were living, breathing reminders of baseball's glorious past and their love for the game.

While hypnotized by the items on display, which Winnie identified for Billy, a friendly faced, well-dressed man of about fifty, wearing perfectly pressed gray slacks, a blue sport coat, and a starched white shirt with a striped tie, approached.

"Hello, I'm Warren Hecht. I'm the manager of the executive level. I understand you're guests of Mr. Carter, the owner of the Yankees. Before I bring you into Mr. Carter's suite, may I please see some identification? Routine procedure. I'm sure you can appreciate the need for security." Hecht was polite and pleasant, but he meant business.

"No problem, here's my driver's license," Melvin was quick to volunteer.

Mr. Hecht looked at it and wrote down Melvin's name on a little blue notepad. Winnie then handed his license to Mr. Hecht, and once again, Mr. Hecht noted the name.

Billy spoke up and said, "I have no driver's license, but my name is William Walker."

"That's perfectly okay, young man," said Mr. Hecht. "Welcome to the executive level of Yankee Stadium, Mr. Walker." Billy beamed. He had never before been called Mr. Walker. He couldn't wait to tell his father.

"Right this way, gentlemen," said Mr. Hecht and led Melvin, Billy, and Winnie down a lengthy private hallway ending in two very large oak doors with antique brass handles. On the door were brass letters that read "Owner's Suite." Guards stood to either side like sentinels.

Mr. Hecht knocked on the door and waited until a voice invited them to enter Then he held the door open, motioning for Melvin, Billy, and Winnie to enter.

"Yes, please do come in," echoed the voice of Langdon Carter, whose family had owned the team, solely or by significant majority, for more than seventy years. Carter looked every bit as rich as he actually was. A member of the lucky sperm club, he wore it well with perfectly coiffed hair, cuffed linen slacks, an Armani shirt opened at the collar, polished Lobb shoes, and what had to be a perpetual tan. He reminded Melvin of the actor George Hamilton.

The team had been purchased for $10M by Carter's billionaire father, Nelson Addison Carter, before he was born. Now forty-seven, Carter had inherited his father's money and dapper good looks but, according to newspaper accounts, not his easy charm.

Beside Carter stood a tall, thin man, also nattily dressed. "Gentlemen, I'm Gus Christianson, general manager of the team, and I'm sure you recognize Mr. Lang Carter, my boss and the owner of the New York Yankees."

Mr. Hecht, who had entered behind Melvin, Winnie, and Billy, now introduced them by name, never once referring to his notepad. He then left the room as unassumingly as he had entered.

Melvin, meanwhile, was taking in the room. There was no getting around it: It was drop-dead gorgeous. So this was what it was like to be rich, he thought. A blue-colored Yankee carpet with thin white pinstripes covered the floor. Four tufted leather couches with brass nails, a full bar with six padded and backed stools, a conference room table that could easily sit ten, partially covered by a bank of phones, a credenza with platters of the biggest shrimp ever resting on ice, cold cuts meticulously folded amid cheese with fruit and pastry nearby, most of it uneaten. *What a waste*, thought Melvin. In a bucket atop the bar was a large silver tureen with several bottles resting in ice, one of which looked like champagne. Melvin hadn't had champagne since he and Martha had celebrated their fortieth anniversary.

Four televisions provided a view from anywhere in the room. One very large television was on the wall near the bar. Three other televisions, smaller but still sizable, hung from the ceiling or were affixed high up on a wall. A closed door to the side opposite the bar probably led to the bathroom, Melvin surmised. But hands down the best part of the room was the view it offered of the field, slightly down and across so everything was in view. You could sit inside in air-conditioned comfort, looking out through the flawless glass or walk through a door to the outside seating area that had enough room for twenty people.

Carter didn't mince words. "Melvin, did you catch that home run?"

"Yes, sir, I did."

"In your bare hand?"

"I guess so."

"Don't you know for sure?"

Winnie jumped into the conversation. "I was right there. Saw the whole thing. He caught the damn ball right in his palm. I saw it and heard it."

Turning back to Melvin, Carter said, "And was that you who threw the ball back onto the field?"

"Well, sir," said Melvin almost apologetically, "I didn't want to, but the crowd told me I had to because the Red Sox hit it."

"No, no, you did the right thing, Melvin. Can I call you Melvin? We just want to be sure it was you who actually threw that ball."

"It was me all right. I just stood up and threw it."

"It's right there on your TV," added Winnie.

A momentary silence fell as everyone watched the replay. The miraculous catch. The prodigious throw. Even Melvin could scarcely believe it. He cleared his throat. "Would it be possible to get a ball for my grandson?"

"Of course," Gus said and grabbed a ball from a nearby basket filled with them. "Here you are, son, an official major league baseball." He handed the ball to Billy then gave Melvin a smile. "Nice boy you've got there."

"Melvin, please don't be offended," Carter broke in, "but can I ask you a personal question?"

"Sure, those are usually the best ones," responded Melvin.

"How old are you?"

"I'm not offended at all. I'm pleased to say that I'm going to be seventy-five this October."

"Ever play ball?"

"No, not really. But I've always been a big Yankees fan."

"Are you retired?"

"Yes, sir."

"What did you do?"

"I worked in Barney Wilson's grocery in Springfield, New Jersey, for fifty years."

"Hmm," said Carter, "if I may ask, what do you do these days to keep busy?"

"To be honest, not a whole lot. I mow the lawn, chat with my neighbors, hang out with Billy, read biographies, and watch or listen to Yankees games."

Speaking now with more certainty, Carter said, "Melvin, how would you like to try out for the New York Yankees?"

Gus just about fell on the floor.

"What? Are you kidding?" inquired Melvin.

"Would you be willing to come back to the stadium tomorrow morning to meet me, Gus, and our manager, Russ Higgins, on the field, say around ten o'clock?"

"Can my grandson come with me?"

"You bet."

"And my friend Winnie?"

"Absolutely." Winnie and Billy were beaming. Melvin was not quite sure what had just happened, but whatever it was felt awfully good.

As the trio turned and started to make their way out of the suite, Carter said, "Would you gentlemen like to sit here and watch the rest of the game with us?"

"That's very nice of you to offer, Mr. Carter," said Melvin, "but we'll go back to our seats if that's okay with you."

"Sure, Melvin, whatever you like."

"So tomorrow at ten?" Gus reminded the trio.

"Tomorrow at ten. Where do we go? How do we get in?"

"Just go to the Diamond Club entrance. There'll be someone there waiting for you. Don't forget to bring your glove."

"Oh, I don't have one anymore. That was a long time ago," said Melvin.

"Okay, we'll have one for you. Do you have cleats?"

"No, but I have sneakers that I take walks in."

"Sounds swell," said Gus, already past the point of disbelief. "Bring whatever you have."

"Grandpa, are you really going to try out for the Yankees?" asked Billy.

"Looks like it," said Melvin. "I'm sure it's just a PR stunt, but where's the harm? We'll have an experience we'll never forget."

"Melvin, you saw the reaction of the crowd," Carter said. "This team is fourteen games out. Our fans need something to make them feel good about Yankees baseball. Something to make them smile and give them hope. The players too. You'll be giving this organization and its fans a big shot in the arm."

Gus looked like a light bulb had switched on in his head. "Boss, you are one of a kind," he said admiringly.

"It's Melvin here who's one of a kind," Carter replied.

CHAPTER 9

Saturday, July 9
Yankee Stadium

As Melvin, Billy, and Winnie were making their way back to the elevator, Mr. Hecht appeared and handed Billy an 8" × 10" glossy picture from the Jumbotron of Billy and Melvin hugging after Melvin's throw. Spectators around them were all standing, smiling, cheering, and clapping.

"Billy, the Yankee organization wanted you to have this remembrance of today."

Billy took the photo, gazing at it as if it were already his most prized possession. "Thank you, Mr. Hecht. This is awesome."

"And Melvin, I just want to shake your hand," he added. "It's been quite a day. Nice to meet you, sir. I hope we meet again."

"Thank you, Mr. Hecht. It's been a pleasure meeting you."

Nodding goodbye to Winnie, Mr. Hecht said, "Enjoy the rest of the game, gentlemen."

The rest of the game passed in a blur with the Yankees rallying to a 5–3 victory. As the unlikely trio exited the stadium, Melvin was congratulated again and again by fans as if he had personally batted in the winning runs.

Once outside, Winnie stopped. "Melvin, be honest with me. Are you coming back tomorrow?"

"Sure, why not?"

"I'll admit that I don't understand what happened here today. And now it's all hazy. I don't want this day to end. If we never meet again, Melvin Klapper with a *K*, I'll never forget today. Thanks for including me."

With his arm around Billy's shoulder, Melvin matter-of-factly said, "See ya tomorrow, Winnie. Don't be late."

"Oh, I'll be here. You guys better show. Ten o'clock."

Walking toward the train with Billy's hand in his and feeling proud, Melvin said, "Billy, didn't I tell you this would be a special day?"

Billy just smiled, holding Melvin's hand tightly.

A long line had formed to go through the turnstile to get to the train. Although everyone in line was incredibly friendly to Melvin, both he and Billy were exhausted by the events of the day. So it was a godsend when a cop came up to Melvin and offered him a ride home. Billy was ecstatic, never having been in a police car before.

While Melvin was wondering what the neighbors would think of seeing Melvin in a police car, Billy asked if they could put the siren on.

"Sure," said the cop, "we can manage that."

And off they sped, the siren wailing, Billy's smile wider than ever.

Grace and Chris were waiting on the porch when they pulled up to Melvin's house.

"Looks like you've got a welcoming committee," said the cop as Melvin and Billy exited.

"That's my daughter and son-in-law," Melvin explained. "Thanks for the ride, Officer."

"Anytime," the cop said and drove off, giving the siren one final whoop.

"I can explain everything." said Melvin, turning to Grace and Chris.

But before he or Billy could say anything more, Chris said, "We saw what happened at the ballpark today. It's all over the news and social media. It's all over everything!"

"Did this really happen, Dad?" asked Grace.

Before Melvin could answer, Billy jumped up and down. "It really happened! Grandpa made this incredible catch and then threw the ball a mile, then we met the Yankees' owner, then I got a ball, then I got this picture!" He held up the 8" × 10" glossy Mr. Hecht had given him. "And then we got invited back for tomorrow."

"What?" replied Chris. "Why would they invite you to come back?"

Melvin responded matter-of-factly, "They want me to try out for the team."

Chris seemed at a loss for words after this statement.

"Dad," said Grace, "I don't recall you ever playing baseball."

"I played a bit when I was younger. But nothing to speak of."

"So what are you going to do?" Chris asked.

"I gave the man my word that I'd be back tomorrow. So if it's okay with you, I'd like to go back with Billy if he wants. I think he's my lucky charm."

"I want to go. I have to go. Please, Dad. Please. Please."

Chris looked to Grace, who nodded approval.

"It's a Sunday, no school, so okay," said Chris almost grudgingly. "How about I drive you to the stadium and wait for you outside?"

"You can come in with us, Chris," said Melvin. "These guys are great. They won't mind."

"What guys are you talking about?"

"Well, the owner of the Yankees, Lang Carter, and Gus Christianson, the general manager."

"I don't believe this," Chris said to Grace. "Are we all nuts? Melvin, you're on a first-name basis with the owner of the Yankees?" Without waiting for a response from Grace or Melvin, Chris added, "And what time are you supposed to be there?'

"Ten a.m. sharp."

"Okay, this whole thing is crazy. But Billy and I will pick you up at nine."

"Dad, get a good night's sleep," said Grace with a big reassuring smile and holding Melvin's arm by the elbow. "I have a feeling you're going to need it."

Melvin, whose back was beginning to act up after all the excitement, said, "Okay, kids. Go home. See you boys in the morning. Love you, Billy," he added with a wink.

After Melvin and Billy hugged goodbye, Billy said, "Thanks, Grandpa. What a day. Winnie was right. We'll never forget today."

"Winnie? Who's Winnie?" asked Chris.

CHAPTER 10

Sunday, July 10
Yankee Stadium

Already at the stadium, having carefully read the voluminous report about Melvin, Gus tried to figure out his position Carter should ask. Gus was still in a state of confusion and bewilderment. He read and reread the report several times to make sure he had his facts right.

At 7:55 a.m., Gus went to Carter's office. He was neither surprised nor comforted seeing Langdon striding out of the owner's private elevator and toward his office.

"Sorry to get you here so early on a Sunday, Lang, but I thought you'd want to hear this as soon as possible," said Gus, carrying the report like it was a tray of vivid yellow diamonds.

"It's okay, Gus. I'm all ears. Tell me what we came up with."

Taking a deep breath, looking directly at Langdon Carter and without looking down at or flipping through the pages of the report, Gus began, "Well, for starters, Melvin's a freakin' war hero. Won two purple hearts and a bronze star with the Marines in Vietnam."

"What, that old guy?"

"He wasn't always an old guy. That was fifty-five years ago."

"How does he live?" Langdon asked

"Like a pauper, mostly off of social security, Medicare, and a military disability."

Now it was Langdon's turn to sound astounded as if hit by a thunderbolt. "What disability?"

"Supposedly he has a limp from taking a bullet in the hip and shrapnel in his behind, although I didn't notice any limp yesterday." Gus continued, "He pretty much has no money, the house has no mortgage, his car has just been repossessed, he has no insurance, no charge cards, no jewelry to speak of, he has a landline but no cell phone and one television to watch the ball games. He has about $6,300 in the bank plus whatever he might have under the mattress. He spends his money mostly buying things for his grandson, and—get this—he donates $25 a year to each of four local charities. He buys nothing for himself, eats pizza at least twice a week at a pizza joint called Randazzo's and a lot of ice cream, which seems to be his favorite meal. No alcohol, no cigarettes, no girlfriend, no poker games.

"As if that isn't enough, he visits his wife's grave on holidays, birthdays (his and hers), and their anniversary. He'll sit there for hours and just talk to her like they're sitting in the kitchen having dinner. He has a daughter, Grace, a schoolteacher in Springfield, who is, you guessed it, the mother of Billy, that cute little kid."

"No way. This guy is too good to be true. Are there really people like this?" Langdon Carter managed to say. He was visibly dazed and unsure of what to say next.

"There's more, Lang," Gus went on. "He reads the newspapers, including the comics, to blind people at the library every Monday. And he collects toys for kids at Christmas. You know, the Marines run that Toys for Tots program. Everyone, and I mean everyone, spoke well of him. The guy is loved. *I* love him.

"So, Lang, I was wrong about him. Dead wrong. He's legit. We got something here. Something special. I still don't know how he could throw a ball like that or whether he'll even show up today, but something truly incredible, maybe inexplicable, is happening here."

The room went silent. Gus sat down, wiped his forehead with a hankie, and just stared at Lang Carter, awaiting his response. Gus could see Lang thinking while tapping his fountain pen on his oversized walnut desk, laser focused at the wall portrait of his father as if asking for divine guidance.

Finally, Langdon Carter turned toward Gus and said, "If this isn't a stunt, we can make a fortune off of this guy. But the question remains, How did he catch that ball, and how did he casually throw a baseball 460 feet? Answer that one for me."

It took no time for Gus to respond, "I can't explain any of it, Lang, but we all saw it. I've watched the video a hundred times. He did it. I don't know how, but he did it."

"What about the big guy?"

"Name's Aaron Winfield. Not much time to dig into him other than to find out he's former NYPD. Twenty-one years. Clean record. Honest guy. Well regarded by the few colleagues we could contact on such short notice. We can find out more if you want. Now head of security at a Springfield bank. Lives alone with his wife, no kids. Neighbors like them. They keep to themselves. Apparently, he comes to about ten games a year and sits pretty much in the same section. No record of Klapper ever being at the stadium. Not sure if they knew each other before yesterday, but they seem like awfully close friends to have just met."

"Odd couple, odd trio," Lang said thoughtfully. "The whole damn thing is odd." Gus just listened without commenting.

The quiet in the room was broken by a knock at the door.

Manager Russ Higgins was in Langdon Carter's office only when he was either being called on the carpet or being told how to handle an overly critical press. So it was with some surprise that the manager of the Yankees for the past three seasons was voluntarily walking into the owner's office—in full uniform no less. Higgins knew that neither Gus nor Carter were particularly thrilled with the team's performance this year. Although memories in sports only seemed to last a season, Higgins did have three consecutive winning seasons under his belt, and his teams had gone deep into the playoffs before being eliminated. That he had not yet produced a world championship would surely be a topic of conversation when his contract renewal came up for negotiation at the end of this season.

Higgins was short, stout, stubborn, and took no crap from anyone, including the Yankee general manager or even its owner. Both Gus and Langdon knew this about Russ and were careful to pick their battles with him. Russ Higgins was an earnest man, fearless, motivated, hardworking, and sincere. His gravelly voice was in sync with his leathery and experienced face, which made him appear older than his fifty-eight years. With a strong chin and a prominent, unhealed broken nose from his boxing days in the Army, he was proud of his four-and-four ring record but more so of his never having been knocked down.

Russ was more of a baseball man than Gus and Langdon put together. He had forgotten more than they would ever know. He treated his players with respect. In turn, the players respected him, personally and professionally. Russ always had their backs with the press and with management.

He would never knock a player in public and rarely even in private. He knew how hard it was to have to go out and perform every day in front of thousands of screaming fans, especially in New York with its aggressive baseball press and the incessant talking heads on radio.

After just about every game, Russ would have a beer or two with any players or coaches who wanted to sit around and talk baseball. Similarly, the press liked and respected Russ. He never shied away from them, no matter how badly that day's game went or how unpleasant the questions thrown at him were. Best of all, Russ really didn't care if he was fired, because he knew there was a job always waiting for him somewhere else. And there was always fishing.

This season had been especially tough for Russ. He wasn't sure why. He had good players, but they hadn't jelled yet. Sure, his players had injuries, but so did those of other ball clubs. He tried switching lineups, bringing players up from triple A, changing pitching rotations. So far nothing had clicked. Lagging behind the league-leading Red Sox by fourteen games in July, Russ knew that time was running out on this season.

Gus had spoken to him more than once. Russ understood that was the job of the general manager when things weren't going well. Russ appreciated the difficult and demanding role of general manager but told Gus that he had to be more aggressive in acquiring players who were available, such as closer Javiar Lopez from the Giants or hard-hitting center fielder Elvin Lewis Jr. from Kansas City, both of whom were rumored to be available for the right price. Russ was looking for something, anything that could ignite the spark that the Yankees needed so badly this year. The team was loaded with talent and had the potential to win it all but seemed to lack that intangible factor that could turn a losing team into a winning team.

"Hey, Russ," called Gus as soon as he saw the manager coming into Carter's office.

"Morning, boys," responded Russ, removing his cap. Langdon groaned and cursed but only to himself whenever Higgins wore spikes into his office. He thought it would ruin his carpet. Gus always assured him that the spikes Russ wore were like the soft spikes worn by golfers and that no harm would come to Lang's luxurious blue carpet.

"Are you gents waiting for a little old man with a kid and a guy who looks like a professional wrestler?"

"I don't believe it," said Gus, looking at Lang. "Klapper with a *K* actually showed up." He turned to the manager. "Russ, we—and that includes you—are going to give this old man a tryout this morning."

"You gotta be kidding me," said Russ as he scratched his crewcut in an arguably disrespectful rejection of the idea. "Well, before I embarrass myself with this stunt, are you gentlemen sure you know what you're doing, and if so, would you mind cluing me in?"

Up until now, Langdon Cater had been merely observing the back and forth between Gus and Russ, hoping not to get caught up in it by having to take a position.

"Russ," interjected Lang, "you saw the catch and throw this guy made yesterday the same as we did, right?"

"Yeah, I saw something. But what I saw was impossible. In this case seeing may not be believing."

"I suppose you can say that, but I know what I saw, and unless you have an explanation as to what we all saw we're going to give Mr. Melvin Klapper with a *K* a tryout today. I'll leave it to you to run it as you see fit, but let's find out, once and for all, what this old man is all about. Okay? Fair enough?"

"I've been in this game a long time, Lang. Damned if I know what's going on. Craziest thing I ever did see. But you're the boss, so let's go and get it over with."

"No press around?" questioned Gus.

"Nah, just my coaching staff and a few players working out."

"Okay, so no one knows he's here, right?"

"Not as far as I know," replied Russ.

Rising with determination from his high-back dark-blue leather chair, Lang pretty well summed it up. "Boys, let's see if we have ourselves a seventy-five-year-old baseball star."

CHAPTER 11

Sunday, July 10
Yankee Stadium

When Melvin, Billy, and Chris arrived outside the Diamond Club gate at 9:55 a.m., Melvin was disappointed not to see Winnie. He wondered if the big man was having second thoughts. The drive from home had been eerily quiet, almost uncomfortably so. Chris barely uttered a word. Even Billy, apparently taking cues from his father, was not his usual talkative and animated self. So Melvin, sitting in the back seat behind Billy, kept quiet, just wanting the drive to be shorter and faster than it was. To his surprise, he did not feel nervous about what lay ahead. Instead, he was excited to see how the day would turn out. Above all, he was glad Billy was with him.

Winnie appeared at the stroke of ten, striding toward them in black jeans and a red short-sleeved shirt that did nothing to hide his intimidating presence. On his head was a NY Yankees cap. On his face was a grin that exuded positivity and pure cool.

The mere sight of Winnie made Melvin feel elated. *What good fortune*, he thought, *to have a guy like Winnie in your corner*.

Melvin put his hand out in greeting, but Winnie ignored it, leaning down to give Melvin a hug. "You ready, Melvin?"

Before Melvin could answer, Chris jumped in and said in not the most friendly tone, "Who are you?"

"That's Winnie, Dad. He's our friend."

"Hey, Billy," said Winnie, tousling his hair, "you as excited as I am?"

Finally Chris put out his right hand and said, "I'm Melvin's son-in-law, Chris. So you're the famous Winnie I keep hearing about?"

"I'm not the famous one here. Your father-in-law was all over the television last night and this morning. I'm just glad to be along for the ride. Hey, it's ten o'clock. Shouldn't we head in?"

Two NYC police officers were chatting amiably in front of the entrance to the Diamond Club. One was an older white man who looked to be nearing retirement age. The other was a younger Asian woman. They broke off as the group approached.

"And where do you guys think you're going?" asked the senior cop.

"My friend here," said Winnie, pointing to Melvin, "has a tryout with the Yankees this morning. We're here to support him."

After the cops stopped chuckling, the older guy said, "I've heard a lot of stories by gate-crashers, but this is the best one yet. Thanks for the laugh. Now move along."

"Hey, Sarge," said the younger cop, "isn't he the guy from TV?"

The older cop did a double-take right out of the movies so that Melvin had a hard time keeping a straight face. "Well, whattaya know?" the cop said. "That was some catch and throw, pops."

Just then, a Yankees employee came to the gate from inside the stadium and informed the officers that Melvin and his friends were the invited guests of Mr. Carter.

That was all that needed to be said. The gates swung open, and in went Melvin, Billy, Winnie, and Chris. The younger cop wished Melvin good luck.

"Yeah," chimed in the sergeant, show 'em what us old geezers are capable of."

"I'll do my best," Melvin said, one arm around Billy's shoulder.

The staff member guided them through the labyrinth of corridors to the Yankees' locker room. This was no high school gym locker. Melvin was mesmerized. The uniforms that would be worn that day were neatly pressed and hanging at each player's locker. Their spikes were polished and sitting in wait next to a stool at each player's locker. The room smelled like leather, wood, talcum powder, and mentholated liniment—an aroma found only in the locker rooms of athletes. In preparation for the game, attendants were setting out fresh fruit, protein drinks, and power bars.

The staff member told Melvin that he would give them the grand tour later, but now he was going to take them straight out to the field. Melvin nodded, finding himself unable to speak. He knew he was wide awake and not dreaming, yet everything seemed too incredible to be real.

That sense only increased as he entered the dugout and saw the field, the soon-to-be-filled stands, the enormous scoreboard, and the aptly named Jumbotron, where he and Billy had been displayed up close and personal for thousands of screaming fans less than twenty-four hours ago.

Melvin found his voice at last. "Can we?" He gestured to the field.

"Of course," their guide replied.

Melvin ushered Billy up the steps of the dugout and onto the field. Winnie followed with Chris bringing up the rear. They advanced about fifteen feet and then stopped as if at some invisible boundary.

"I never thought I'd be standing on this field," said Winnie, shaking his head in obvious disbelief. "If there is any more hallowed ground in baseball, I don't know it."

"It's something all right," Melvin said, his arm still around Billy's shoulders. "What do you think, Billy?"

"It's better than Disney World," Billy pronounced.

His parents had taken Billy there a year ago for his birthday, and Melvin could not help noticing how Chris's expression tightened as, thanks to Melvin, Billy seemingly dropped what had been one of his most prized experiences down a notch.

A few players wearing shorts and T-shirts were doing wind sprints in the outfield. The batting cage by home plate had a player taking his swings, while those waiting to hit were congregating and chatting outside the cage. A coach, standing behind a partial pitching screen for protection, was lobbing balls for the batter to hit, while a few others were shagging flies in the outfield.

The crack of the bat hitting the ball was an unmistakable and captivating sound. There was nothing else like it. It was so much louder in person than on television, thought Melvin. He could not remember ever having seen grass so green or a sky so blue.

Melvin was so engrossed in his surroundings that he was oblivious to everything else. But Winnie noticed a short, stout man in a Yankees uniform emerge from the dugout and walk toward them like a man about to endure some onerous task he had not willingly undertaken but was determined to see through. He gave Melvin a nudge. "Don't look now, but that's Russ coming our way."

That got Melvin's attention.

The manager of the Yankees was walking toward them methodically, unhurried, just as Melvin had watched him walk to the mound many times prior to pulling a pitcher. Higgins was short, stout, stubborn, and took no crap from anyone. His gravelly voice and leathery face, with a crooked nose from his boxing days in the Army, made him seem older than his fifty-eight years. After three consecutive winning seasons, to call the current season a disappointment would have been an understatement. The team had good players, but they hadn't jelled yet. Sure, some of the players had injuries, but so did those of other ball clubs. Higgins had tried switching lineups, bringing players up from triple A, changing pitching rotations, but so far nothing had clicked. Lagging behind the league-leading Red Sox by fourteen games in July, Russ knew that time was running out.

Upon reaching them, Higgins doffed his cap, put out his hand to Melvin, and said, "I'm Russ Higgins. Are you Melvin?"

Melvin took the proffered hand. "Yes, sir. I'm Melvin Klapper, and this is my grandson, Billy. It's an honor to meet you, sir."

"Okay, so no one calls me *sir*. You can call me Russ. Hello, Billy, how do you like being on the field at Yankee stadium?"

"It's awesome."

"Melvin, I'm told by my bosses that you're here for a tryout. This is highly unusual, but what you did yesterday was also highly unusual. No offense, but did you really throw that ball?"

"Yes, sir—I mean, Russ—I did."

"Ever play any organized ball?"

"No, not really."

"You think you could make that throw again today?"

"To be honest, I have no idea, but I hope so."

"I hope so too. If that was you yesterday, maybe you're a better player than you think. Okay, Melvin, you ready? Did you bring a glove?"

"No, I don't have one."

"Not a problem." Higgins turned and yelled toward the dugout. "Hey, Earl,"—referring to Earl Endicott, a venerable Yankee coach—"could you get a left-handed glove out here for our friend Melvin?" Turning back, he eyed Melvin's footwear critically. "Melvin, I see you're wearing—what are those—sneakers? You got cleats?"

"No, I've never worn cleats. I thought it would be best to wear something comfortable, and these are my best walking shoes. Is it okay with you if I play in these?"

"I guess it'll have to do. Just don't want you getting hurt out there."

Earl brought Melvin a glove. Melvin put it on his left hand and hit the pocket a few times. It was a Rawlings, big and well-oiled with a deep, dark pocket that left no excuse for an error. It smelled so good that Melvin brought it closer to his nose just to get a deeper whiff. This did not go unnoticed by Higgins, who had started to get a sense for Melvin and liked the old guy. He hoped what was about to happen wouldn't be too humiliating for him and his grandson. Lang and Gus were standing by the first-base coaching box, looking on with their arms folded and faces like brick walls.

"Okay," Higgins said. "Now all you need to look like a big leaguer is a uniform. How tall are you?"

"I was five-eleven, then five-ten, and now probably closer to five-nine."

"So you're shrinking?" asked Higgins with a smile.

"That's what happens as you get older, but I don't mind."

"What do you weigh, Melvin?"

"Well, I used to be 180 and pretty strong, but now I'm only about 165 and pretty mushy," said Melvin as he pushed his stomach with his right hand.

Russ called out to Yankee locker room manager Walter Dombrowski,. "Walt, got a uniform for Melvin here?"

While Melvin went into the locker room to change, Russ went over to Lang and Gus.

"Fellas, I just don't get this. Something very strange is going on here. And yet I like the old guy."

"I still can't believe he showed up," said Gus. "I admit this whole thing is bizarre, but it will only take another five or ten minutes of our time. Here he comes now. Uh-oh. Looks like something happened."

"Where's your uniform, Melvin?" Russ asked.

"They didn't have one that fit me right, but that's okay. I'm good to go."

Melvin, with the glove still on his left hand, wearing chinos and the lucky green polo shirt Martha had bought him years ago, in his comfy walking shoes, looked about as ready for a major league baseball tryout as a penguin would look walking into an emergency room.

"How about fielding some grounders at third base?" said Russ. "Hey, Bert, can you cover first to take Melvin's throws?"

Elbert "Bert" Lansing, a utility infielder for several years with a few different ball clubs and now a Yankee coach, looked over. "Sure thing, Russ." He trotted out to first base.

"So what should I do?" asked Melvin.

"Go to third base, Melvin," Russ managed to say both sarcastically and respectfully, using his arm to guide Melvin in the right direction. Melvin started to jog toward third base, trying to imitate the players he'd been watching all these years on television. But his left hip gave him a ping and then a second ping, so he decided to walk instead. Russ, now standing with Lang and Gus, mumbled, "Not exactly Babe Ruth."

"No, more like Pee Wee Herman," said Lang, not known for his sense of humor. Caught off guard by a joke from Mr. Langdon Carter, Gus and Russ looked at each other and laughed out loud, making Lang feel like one of the boys.

At home plate, Coach Endicott started to fungo a few balls to the third-base area, easy and slow at first, all of which Melvin handled flawlessly. This was now a different Melvin than the Melvin of a few minutes ago.

"Hit 'em harder," snapped Russ. The balls came faster, and still Melvin glided smoothly to his left and to his right, scooping up each grounder and throwing perfectly to Coach Lansing at first base. Billy and Winnie were smiling and fist pumping. Chris just sat there stunned and expressionless.

"Pinch me," said Russ as he held his arm out to Gus.

"Get him out into center," responded Gus.

"Okay, Melvin, get out in center field," said Russ.

After waiting a few minutes for Melvin to settle in center field, batting coach Lou Hudson, a .280 lifetime major league hitter, started by hitting soft fly balls and then some more difficult to judge and handle line drives into the outfield—to Melvin's left, to Melvin's right. Gracefully, Melvin floated around, getting under each ball, catching them with confidence and composure. Melvin threw them all back to the infield with accuracy and strength.

"Melvin, come on in and take a break," said Russ. Melvin returned to the bench, where Winnie and Billy greeted him with high fives, fist pumps, and wagging heads. Other players and coaches had noticed what had just occurred. No question about it. They were watching Melvin, this old guy, and trying to make sense of it all.

"I ain't believing this. What we're seeing just ain't possible," said Russ. "What the hell is going on here, gentlemen?"

Without waiting for a response, Russ continued with a little more respect in his voice than before, "Okay, Melvin. Take a breather."

Lang had been quiet so far. Whenever Lang got quiet, Gus got nervous. Lang Carter was staring hard at Melvin, now sitting on the bench between Winnie and Billy, having a drink of water with his glove still on his left hand.

"Hmm, do you think he can hit?" asked Lang.

"Why the hell not? He seems to be able to do everything else," Gus replied.

Melvin was exhilarated but tired and sweating. He was glad to be back on the bench.

A moment or two later, Russ walked over to the bench. "Hey, Melvin, want to take a few swings?"

"Okay," said Melvin. He left his glove with Billy and stepped up out of the dugout.

"There's a bunch of bats leaning against the batting cage. Find one you like and step right in," instructed Russ. The few players still at the cage heard Russ and knew they should let this old guy hit a few if he could.

"Hello, boys," said Melvin as he approached the cage. Their only response was a slight nod. Melvin lifted a few of the bats. They all seemed so long and so heavy, but he knew everyone was waiting on him, so he grabbed the lightest bat he could find and walked into the cage. On the mound pitching from a mostly protected screen was pitching coach Wally Young.

Wally nodded at Melvin and asked, "How do you like 'em?"

"I don't know. Can you just make them easy for me to hit?"

That got a snicker or two, but Wally, being a good guy, said, "Sure thing."

Melvin took a few practice swings. He couldn't remember the last time he had even held a bat, but here he was on the field at Yankee Stadium with a Louisville Slugger in his grip. After letting a few pitches go by him, Melvin swung and hit a few weak grounders then a few fly balls and then some line drives deep into the outfield. Everyone was paying attention now, especially Lang, Gus, and Russ. Winnie and Billy were out of the dugout. Billy was jumping up and down. Winnie was clapping on every good hit. And then Melvin Klapper proceeded to hit three balls in a row out of the ballpark into the stands—all solid, well-hit balls.

No one knew what to say, so no one said anything. The players behind the cage just stared at each other in awe of what they had just seen. Melvin was exhausted, so he just returned the bat to where he had taken it from, said "Thank you" to Wally, and walked back toward Billy and Winnie. Billy ran onto the field to hug Melvin, while Winnie stood and applauded. Not knowing what to do but not wanting to be left out of the moment, Chris joined in the clapping.

Finally, Gus said, "This just gets crazier and crazier."

"I need an eye doctor or a psychiatrist or both," added Russ.

CHAPTER 12

Sunday, July 10
Yankee Stadium

Lang Carter knew a business opportunity when he saw one. Turning to Gus, Lang said in his most serious and direct way, "Sign this guy…and I mean right now, today, this moment. Before the Red Sox get wind of this. Give him whatever he wants. No haggling. Just get it done before he leaves today. Even if it is a PR stunt, we'll make a fortune off of this guy."

Lang turned and walked toward Melvin sitting in the dugout. "Melvin, you did great out there today. You and the New York Yankees make a great team." And then he was gone.

Gus had been given his orders. He knew what he had to do, but he had no idea what it would take to get Melvin to be a New York Yankee. Russ was now in a small group of coaches and players over by home plate, reviewing what they had just seen. Chris sat quietly on the bench, while Winnie, like a radio announcer, recapped all the plays Melvin had made. Billy just listened and loved it.

"Hey, Melvin, got a minute?" said Gus from the first baseline. "C'mon out."

Melvin made his way out to where Gus was straddling the first baseline between home and first base.

Gus didn't beat around the bush. "Melvin, how would you like to play for the New York Yankees?"

"Are you kidding?" said a stunned Melvin.

"No, siree. We really like you, Melvin. We think you'd be a great addition to our ball club."

Melvin couldn't believe what he was hearing. His legs got wobbly. He tried to keep his composure. "I don't know what to say. This whole weekend has been a shock to me."

"It's been quite a shock to us too," Gus admitted. "How much would you want to play for us, Melvin?"

"Want?"

"Yeah, in terms of salary."

"When I left Wilson's, I was making $41.75 an hour plus Christmas bonus and health benefits, so I'd appreciate it if you could match that."

"Very funny. Let's get serious. We have about seventy-five regular season games left this season. How much do you want?"

"I have no idea, Gus. Whatever you think is fair."

"You're a tough negotiator, Melvin, so how about $7.5 million? That's about $100,000 a game. Waddaya say?"

Melvin tried to look calm. "I've got to ask my agents."

"What," groused a surprised Gus, "you have agents?"

"Yeah, Winnie and Billy. Would you excuse us for a minute?"

Leaving Gus somewhat stunned with his mouth open, Melvin walked to the dugout and whispered, "Guys, they've offered me $100,000 a game for the rest of the season. Can you believe it? What should I do?"

Without hesitation, Winnie said, "Are you kidding? They offered what? Melvin, don't screw this up."

"It's not about the money, Winnie."

"There may be more important things in life than money, but you need money to accomplish them."

Missing the importance of the financial discussion going on between Melvin and Winnie, Billy asked, "Can I come to the games when there's no school?"

Winnie jumped right back in, "Hold on a minute here, guys. Let's stay focused. Grab the money, Melvin, plus two box seats right behind the Yankee dugout for every home game plus parking in the players lot, and you want it all in writing in twenty-four hours. Nothing less." A silent Melvin nodded in agreement and turned to walk back to Gus.

"And free hotdogs," added Billy.

Wanting to be inclusive, Melvin said, "Chris, what do you think?"

"To tell you the truth, I have no idea what's going on or what to say. You're doing fine without any advice from me."

"Okay, boys, I get the idea. Let me see what I can work out with Gus."

Winnie, Billy, and Chris could see Melvin and Gus standing face to face. It seemed amicable. This time, Melvin was doing the talking, and Gus was doing the listening. Then they were seen shaking hands and smiling.

"Melvin, can you start tomorrow?" asked Gus. "We have a one o'clock game against Baltimore."

"What's tomorrow? Monday? I'm really sorry, but I have a prior commitment for tomorrow that I have to honor. I can't let those people down. But I'm good as of Tuesday."

"Okay, Melvin. We have a deal. I'll send the paperwork to your lawyers."

"Gus, I don't have any lawyers. Just send it to my son-in-law, Chris. I'll get you his address."

Winnie saw Gus and Melvin shake hands again, and Gus patted Melvin on the shoulder, which he took as a good sign that a deal had been reached.

"You boys are okay," said Gus as he entered the dugout. "We'll see you all soon. Melvin, see you Tuesday."

"Okay, Gus, and thank you."

While Gus was heading back into the locker room, Russ made his way over to the dugout.

"That was really something today, Melvin. How do you feel?"

"To be honest, I'm a little tired. Wouldn't mind some ice cream though."

"All of you, c'mon back with me. I think we can find some ice cream for everyone. Billy, I heard you want a tour of the Yankee locker room, right? I'll arrange that for you."

Russ was now in full enjoyment mode of the most unusual day of his career. If Saturday's events were not enough to challenge his sense of baseball reality, then Sunday would surely take the cake. Russ got ice cream for the boys and gave Billy a cook's tour of the clubhouse.

"Melvin, did you and Gus work things out?" asked Russ.

"Yes, I think so."

"Good. When do you start?"

"Tuesday."

"Okay, that's the last day of our home stand against Baltimore. Starting Wednesday, we're on the road for six games, three against Cleveland and three against the White Sox. We'll have a uniform and everything ready for you by Tuesday's game. Even shoes and a glove. Just so you know, you'll be sitting on the bench for the foreseeable future, learning things you need to know. Keep your eyes and ears open. In time, I'll see where I can find a spot for you."

"Okay, Russ, you're the boss. See ya Tuesday. C'mon, guys. Time to go home."

Russ couldn't help but look at this motley crew as they walked away, scratching his head in disbelief and wondering what the next crazy day would bring his way.

Once outside the stadium, Winnie said, "Melvin, what a day. I mean, man oh man, what a day. Two incredible days in a row. I can't wait to tell the guys at the bank about this weekend."

"Let's stay in touch, Winnie. I want you to be part of this, whatever it is and however long it lasts." Winnie shook hands with Melvin and Chris and patted Billy on the head.

“Don’t forget me, boys,” said Winnie as he turned and walked away. Melvin wondered if Winnie had a car or was going to the train station. It bothered Melvin the way he and Winnie had parted ways without saying anything more. It felt awkward. Winnie deserved more, but Melvin didn’t know what to say.

CHAPTER 13

Sunday, July 10
Springfield

Riding in the front of Chris's car, Melvin felt exhausted but elated about the prospect of being a New York Yankee. He didn't know or understand how something so incredible could happen or how he'd become able to catch, throw, and hit a ball like he did today. He knew how proud Billy was of him, which made Melvin feel ten feet tall.

As the car turned down his street, Melvin saw a crowd of people gathered in front of his house. There were NBC and CBS news trucks with satellites on their rooftops, three police cars, and a squadron of cops standing between the crowd and Melvin's front gate. *Oh boy*, Melvin thought to himself. He realized that the Yankees must have already made an announcement. He'd been hoping for a little quiet, but as Winnie had told him earlier, those days were over. Winnie had said he was now a "public figure" and that he had better get used to the publicity, the paparazzi, and people wanting a piece of him—a fair price, it seemed, for the chance, the thrill of a lifetime, to play for the New York Yankees.

"There he is," yelled a teenage boy as Melvin was spotted walking toward the crowd. Then the cameramen and the reporters rushed to Melvin, barking questions at him, not even allowing for an answer.

"What's it like to be a New York Yankee, Melvin?"

"Melvin, how old are you really?"

"Why did you wait until now to play baseball?"

"Is this all a stunt?"

"How much money are you making?"

Melvin heard every word. And some of the words bothered him. They were like daggers. Why weren't they happy for him? Why so cynical? This was just the kind of confrontation Melvin had sought to avoid his entire life. He was hardwired to keep a low profile, stay off the radar, and avoid personal exposure. He was not a person to ask questions of others or expect to be put on the spot by others posing personal questions of him. He had not yet learned how to ignore the press or just smile and keep moving. But as usual, despite his discomfort, Melvin was friendly to all and thanked everyone for their good wishes.

Melvin was relieved to see a few faces he knew. There was Estelle shaking her cane at the media, and there was Bart guarding the house like a bouncer. Bart had apparently appointed himself Melvin's unofficial home security service. It was difficult for Melvin to make his way through the crowd until two officers, acting like Moses, parted the sea of people.

Finally, Melvin made it to his front gate. He invited Bart and a few neighbors he knew to come in. No reporters were allowed in. The police started to disperse the crowd, and the media were packing up their gear. As Melvin started to go into his home, he saw that Chris and Grace were parking their car down the block and were waving to him to get his attention. Melvin was happy to see them and was hoping that Billy was there, but Melvin didn't see him. Melvin opened his front door halfway but waited as he watched Chris and Grace walk toward him. Yes, Billy and Amos were with them.

Melvin signaled to the police to let Chris, Grace, and Billy in. The crowd was thinning. The show for today was hopefully over. Billy came running and hugged Melvin.

"Hi, Grandpa. Mom thought we should all be together tonight, so we jumped in the car."

Grace hugged Melvin and said, "You okay, Dad?"

"I'm doing just fine," replied Melvin. Melvin went to shake Chris's hand, and for the first time in many years, Chris clumsily hugged Melvin, maybe out of newfound respect, not heartfelt affection, the way Melvin would have liked. The moment was awkward and took Melvin by surprise, but Melvin recovered enough to say, "Well, that's nice."

Melvin, Chris, Grace, and Billy, along with Bart and Estelle and a few other neighbors, feeling part of a select crowd, went into the house. Amos sat between Billy and Melvin.

"I'm sorry I have nothing to offer you folks. I wasn't expecting company."

"That's okay. We just came to see you," said Grace.

"I can go and bring in pizza," offered Bart. Melvin was pleased to see Bart's enthusiasm.

"Why don't we all just sit and relax?" Melvin proposed. And everyone looked for a place to sit in a room that only had seating for two. So Grace and Chris brought in four chairs from the dinette set in the kitchen and two folding beach chairs that had been in the hall closet for twenty years.

"Melvin," Chris began, "when exactly did you become such a great baseball player? And how come we never knew about it? Is there something you want to tell us? Because we have no explanation, and it's making us look and feel very left out."

"I don't feel left out, Grandpa," Billy said, apparently feeling a need to defend the grandfather he loved so much.

Melvin, smiling at Billy, was glad when Grace jumped in.

"Dad, what Chris is saying is that we had no idea that you could play baseball at such a high level—and at your age, no less. It's just kind of…well, miraculous."

"Mom, Grandpa was so good that the Yankees signed him to a contract."

Chris jumped right in again, sounding a bit envious, "And paying him an outrageous amount of money."

"Does that really matter? I'd do it for free. Who wouldn't?"

Chris kept up his questioning. "What are you going to do with the money?"

"Oh, Chris," moaned Grace, "please, this isn't the time for money talk."

But Chris was not to be stopped. "Did you hire a lawyer or an agent to negotiate for you?"

"No," said Melvin, "I had Billy and Winnie."

"Billy and Winnie?"

"Yep, that's all I needed. And I asked the Yankees to send the contract to you so you could review it. Is that okay with you, Chris?"

"Oh sure, Melvin," said Chris, suddenly surprised but proud. Grace just smiled a knowing smile.

Once again, Billy joined in the conversation to support Melvin. "Winnie's a great guy. We met him at the game. He was sitting next to Grandpa."

"Wait a second, a guy you just met is now your financial advisor?" chirped Chris.

"Yep," replied Melvin, "Winnie knows his stuff, and we three all get along great, right, Billy?"

"You bet, Grandpa."

"Dad, maybe you should have spoken with Chris before doing anything rash."

"The Yankees are being more than generous. I'm happy. What else matters?"

"I think," said Chris, "that maybe you're being used as some part of a publicity stunt. And that you're going to end up embarrassed."

"It's hard for a seventy-five-year-old guy to be embarrassed. I know you folks want what's best for me, but I think it's all going to work out."

Responding to loud knocking at the door, Melvin said, "Maybe we should let others in."

But Chris, in his earnest but somewhat agitated state, jumped up and moved toward the front door. "I'll get rid of them."

When Chris opened the door, Melvin saw that it was three neighborhood kids whom he had seen before, all about Billy's age. "Come on in, kids," invited Melvin with a wave.

Chris had to move aside so they could come in.

"Can we have your autograph, Mr. Klapper? Please?"

"I just want to shake the hand that threw that ball," another youngster said.

"Hey, how many kids get the chance to be in the home of a major league baseball player?" asked Grace.

Seeing Billy feeling overshadowed by these kids who all knew each other, Melvin said, "Hey, guys, I want you to meet my grandson, Billy, who was at the game with me. He met the owner of the Yankees and got a ball and photograph you would love to see."

"Wow," said the kid with hair as red as a fire truck, "you're so lucky. What was it like?"

"It was awesome," responded Billy.

"Next time you're in this neighborhood, you can play ball with us."

"Okay, thanks." That was exactly what Melvin had been trying to accomplish.

Chris couldn't help jumping back in. "So, Melvin, when do you start playing?"

"I report to the stadium Tuesday," said Melvin. "They already told me I'd be riding the bench, but I'm okay with that. They know what they're doing. By the way, as part of the deal, I got two box seats right behind the Yankee dugout—One for Billy and one for Winnie or whoever else wants to come."

"For how many games?"

"For the rest of the season."

"Can I sit there once in a while?" asked Chris rather meekly.

"Of course, Chris. You and Grace can sit there whenever Billy has school or homework or when Winnie can't make it because he has to work."

"Oh great," Chris said almost sarcastically, "and what does your new best friend, Winnie, do?"

"You met him. Didn't you guys talk?"

"No, he was too busy cheering for you."

"He was a NYC police officer for almost twenty-one years and now heads up security at Springfield Savings."

"You'll love Winnie, Dad, once you get to know him."

"We have to get Billy home and ready for school tomorrow," said Grace.

"Yes, and I need to shower and sleep," said Melvin.

Everyone started to leave. Grace and Melvin hugged. Billy and Melvin gave each other a high five, then Melvin kissed the top of Billy's head as he often did. Amos was up and at the door, knowing it was time to leave.

"I don't believe what's going on. This whole thing is just crazy," were Chris's parting words.

*****

Finally alone, Melvin was understandably weary from the events of the past forty-eight hours. He felt guilty that he had still not shared the news of his cancer with Grace, but Melvin didn't want to spoil this incredible moment of joy. Sitting at the kitchen table with a spoon and pint-sized container of pistachio ice cream, he tried to recap for Martha all that occurred, from Dr. Mendelsohn's terribly depressing news to the mysterious and the vanishing lady on the bus to telling Billy about the wish to the catch and throw to meeting Winnie to being in the suite of Yankee-owner Lang Carter to the tryout and then agreeing to play for the Yankees for $7.5 million. Melvin thought he saw Martha smile.

It may all be a dream, Melvin realized, but what a dream it was. "Please don't wake me," was all that Melvin could say to himself over and over. To help calm down, Melvin turned on the television. Despite the constant stories about Melvin that seemed to dominate whatever channel he clicked onto, Melvin fell asleep in his tartan chair as peacefully as always.

CHAPTER 14

Monday, July 11
Springfield

The clock said 6:15 a.m. The birds were busy singing their morning song, and the early summer sun was trying to break through the clouds. Melvin was fully awake but still felt as though he were dreaming. Was he really going to be a NY Yankee?

But that was not until tomorrow. Today was Monday, which meant Melvin had to be at the Springfield Public Library by 10:00 a.m. to read to the usual ten to fifteen sight-impaired people who would listen so attentively and then applaud so gratefully. He admitted to himself that he loved doing this and truly appreciated the appreciation these people shared so generously.

Sometimes Melvin would choose a short story. Other times, he would read from the newspapers. There were times when people in the group made a request or brought a book of poetry or short story with them for Melvin to read. Melvin tried to accommodate the group because he knew it was about them and their enjoyment. If anyone was offended by something, Melvin would simply switch to material acceptable to all. The intimate gathering was composed mostly of those in the fifty-five to seventy-five age group, of modest means, fairly well-educated, who enjoyed a good laugh and were polite beyond expectation.

After the last few days of emotion and excitement, Melvin was looking forward to the simplicity that Monday morning at the neighborhood library would bring.

But this Monday was not going to be like past Mondays. Upon entering the library, Melvin saw a crowd of at least one hundred people welcoming him with smiles and enthusiastic clapping. Melvin was taken aback. He had been hoping for a nice, quiet, peaceful morning, but now he realized those days were probably over as Winnie had predicted.

Melvin had brought with him a few popular magazines that he thought the group would like, but on this Monday, it wasn't going to happen. The crowd just wanted to ask questions and tell Melvin how proud they were of him. So Melvin decided to take it all in stride. He understood that these were good, well-intentioned people who were thrilled and honored to know someone who had suddenly and unexpectedly become somewhat of a celebrity. So Melvin answered their questions as best he could and graciously accepted their compliments and good wishes.

By 11:30 a.m., everyone seemed tired, including Melvin. He never got to read the magazines he was still carrying. So when Melvin started to wrap things up in a pleasant and respectful way, the already reduced crowd was only too happy to leave the library and return home or grab a quick lunch. As Melvin began to walk slowly toward the door, he was approached by Jean, the demure and reserved librarian who had two years earlier organized the reading group and asked Melvin, whom she knew to be an avid reader and local retiree, if he was willing to be their reader and moderator.

"Melvin, may I have a word please?" asked Jean in her usual soft but nevertheless assured way.

"Of course," replied Melvin. "I'm sorry, Jean, for all the commotion here today, but I was caught totally off guard."

"That's okay. I understand. Listen, I want you to know how happy I and the rest of the staff are for you. We really are. You're a very nice man. But does this mean you won't be reading to the group anymore?"

"Jean, I don't know what to say. I love my Monday mornings here at the library. I look forward to it every Sunday night, and it's a great way to start my week. But as you may know, as odd as it may sound, I've been offered a job with the New York Yankees, so I guess my time will be spent playing baseball."

"Yes, Melvin, of course. I understand that. Excuse me for saying this, but we're a bit puzzled. How can you do all these things that men in their twenties and thirties do? They are bigger, stronger, and younger than you. Is there a secret you can share with me?"

"No, Jean. I can't really explain it. I'm just enjoying it for as long as it lasts."

"I think I can speak for everyone when I say we'll miss you, Melvin. Please come back and see us from time to time."

"Of course I will. I'll miss my time here at the library, but I'll be thinking about you folks."

CHAPTER 15

Monday, July 11
Springfield

Leaving the library, Melvin decided to treat himself to a large pistachio cone at the Springfield Sweet Shoppe. When he got there, the owner, Arturo, reached out, shook Melvin's hand, and said, "That was some piece of garbage in today's paper. What a bunch of crap. But you better get used to it, Melvin."

Melvin found a bench under the tree out front to enjoy his cold and refreshing treat and find out what Arturo was talking about. It didn't take him long to get to the front page of the sports section, where the lead article was by syndicated *Boston Globe* columnist Vic "the Vulture" Coleman.

As a rabid sports fan, Melvin was of course familiar with Coleman, who was big and boisterous and never even tried to give the impression that he was kind or courteous. Having the power and reach of a nationally syndicated column, Vic Coleman didn't really care what anyone thought of him.

Vic "the Vulture" was a longtime die-hard and unabashed Red Sox fan and Yankee hater. As a feared and fearless sports journalist, his columns could make or break someone. Knowing he was connected to Red Sox brass, Boston players were careful to stay on his good side. Vic was sharp-tongued and, being big and beefy, wanted to be thought of as a brawler but had never been known to be in an actual fight. Loud, gruff, sloppily dressed, and reeking of cologne to conceal the stink of his cigars, Vic loved his position of power and enjoyed every minute of it, holding court at the bar at Grill 23 on Berkeley Street.

Vic's column, originating in the *Globe*, was carried in numerous newspapers across the country, including New York, where it was reluctantly read by Yankee fans. Vic took a special delight in attacking and criticizing anything that had to do with sports in New York, especially the Yankees, their players, and their fans. How had he found out about the Yankees signing Melvin?

When Melvin reluctantly turned to the front page of the Sports section, he found a big, bold headline that read,

The Latest Yankee Stunt
Victor Coleman

Our least favorite team, the New York Yankees, are up to it again. Having a miserable season, trailing our Red Sox by 14 games, Yankee management has decided to divert attention from their losing ways by coming up with a gimmick. But the gimmick is so insulting and embarrassing that we almost feel sorry for our hapless friends in the Bronx.

Believe it or not, and I for one must admit that it is truly hard to believe, the Yankees have apparently decided to add a nearly 75-year-old man to their active player roster. Not only is he almost 75, but he has no history or experience playing baseball or any sport for that matter.

So we ask most incredulously, what the heck is going on here? You'll recall that this is the old man who supposedly caught a home

> run ball off the bat of Red Sox slugger Brock Dennison last Saturday and then threw the ball back to the catcher approximately 460 feet away. Now we all know that didn't really happen because it couldn't have happened. But the Yankees would still have you believe it did just so they get some publicity while their team loses game after game.
>
> I'm not an expert in trick photography or how video can be manipulated, but when your common sense tells you something is impossible, then it is. We all know that children and cars can't fly, but on television and in the movies, they can. And just because you see it on television or in the movies doesn't make it true. Okay, so I admit that I do not know how the Yankees pulled this off, but regardless, we all know it's one big fraudulent scam being pulled on the public.
>
> More importantly, it hurts the game of baseball, which is about true events and accurate reporting. So I'm taking this moment to call upon Major League Baseball Commissioner Wendell Steinhouser to immediately investigate the situation, question the parties involved, and issue a report to the public without delay. All legitimate baseball fans feel this way, so it is incumbent on the commissioner and Major League Baseball to clear this up before it leaves a permanent scar on the sport we all love so dearly.

Melvin could not believe what he had just read. But it made him stop and think. Was this all a hoax? Was he being deceived? Was Chris right that Melvin was just an innocent dupe and would end up embarrassed?

Melvin needed to speak with Winnie but did not know where Winnie lived. Nor did he have Winnie's phone number. Melvin was so upset he did not know what to do other than go home and hide behind closed doors and pulled blinds.

Around 6:00 p.m., Melvin turned on the news to hear the weather for the next day's game at the stadium only to hear Vic's column being discussed. The anchor read a statement issued by the commissioner's office, in response to the Coleman article, which said in part, "Any action on the part of Major League Baseball regarding the allegations of a *Boston Globe* article would be premature at this time, although we reserve the right to do so at a later date if deemed warranted."

Melvin took that as a good sign, hoping the attempt to create a scandal would blow over.

After falling asleep in his favorite chair, Melvin heard his name being called. At first he thought he was dreaming, but then he saw a figure at the window pane next to the door. *My God*, thought Melvin. It was Winnie. Melvin couldn't wait to let Winnie in.

"Winnie, what are you doing here? How did you know where I lived?"

"Melvin, where you live is not much of a secret anymore. It's all over the Internet. And I'm here because I wanted you to be aware of a hit piece on you before you went to the stadium tomorrow."

Holding Winnie's elbow as a sign of appreciation, Melvin said, "Winnie, you're a sight for sore eyes. Yes, I read the article and wanted to talk about it with you but didn't know how to get in touch with you."

"Okay, here's my home number and cell phone number. Better to call the cell. Alva, my wife, gets a little cranky when the home phone rings. Melvin, you have to get a cell phone. It'll let you and Billy stay in touch when you're on the road with the team. Tell the Yankees to set you up."

"Winnie, tell me honestly, what did you think of the article?"

"Pure BS from a jerk. That's what I think. Is that honest enough? He's just a troublemaker. He hates everything about New York, especially the Yankees. Probably instigated by the Red Sox being jealous of the Yankees signing you. Let it go. Pay it no mind. Just focus on tomorrow. Melvin. Enjoy the experience. Don't let anyone rain on your parade. I've got to run. On my way to the bank for tonight's shift. Just wanted to make sure you were okay. Be cool, buddy."

Reaching out to hug this soft-spoken giant, Melvin said, "Winnie, you're the best. You have no idea how much better you've made me feel. Thank you."

CHAPTER 16

Tuesday, July 12
Yankee Stadium

If Melvin didn't actually wake up with a big smile, he sure thought he did. It was like the first day of school, a little scary but a lot more exciting. Melvin had been told to come to the Stadium at 10:00 a.m. for a 1:05 p.m. game time, but he couldn't wait. By 7:00 a.m., he was out the door and on his way to the Bronx. Passing a newsstand on the way to the train station, Melvin noticed that his house was pictured on the front page of one of the papers. He laughed. He was becoming accustomed to being famous in America. It didn't take long nowadays.

To avoid the eyes of other people, Melvin donned an "I Love New York" hat and kept his head down, reading a book about baseball facts and figures. Although he was a big fan, he knew that there was a lot he didn't know but should if he was to be a real major leaguer. Maybe it was because it was a workday with people rushing about to get to their offices, but nobody seemed to recognize or even notice him. He was thankful for the anonymity.

Arriving at the stadium, Melvin wasn't sure where to go, so he returned to Gate D, where he had entered on Sunday. But the cops on duty there advised Melvin to go to the players' entrance instead and directed him to it.

Melvin got a little bit lost at first but ultimately found his way. He approached the gate and the officers stationed there. "Good morning. I'm supposed to report to the Yankees this morning, but I don't know where to go."

"What's your name?" one of the officers asked.

"Melvin Klapper, sir."

"Is that Klapper with a *K*?" joked a wise-guy policeman as his fellow officers sniggered.

"Yes, sir, that's me," said Melvin proudly, "Klapper with a *K*."

"You're way too early, pops. There's not much going on yet. Most players come in after ten for a day game. But I guess you're welcome to go in now if you'd like. Know where to go?"

"No, sorry, I don't."

"Okay, c'mon, old-timer. I'll show you."

After walking down a few corridors and turning a couple of corners, the cop said, "Okay, you're here. Through those doors straight ahead is the Yankee locker room. Good luck to ya, pops."

Melvin was dazzled. Although he had quickly passed through the locker room on Sunday, he had not had enough time to savor the moment or actually look at what was there to be seen. Being so early, he could take his time without his gawking being too obvious or embarrassing. Now Melvin could see that the space actually consisted of several rooms. The carpet with the Yankee logo, the spacious wood lockers, the team bulletin board, the generous buffet table starting to be prepared, the trainers' room that included massage tables, a workout room with weights, bikes, and all kinds of torturous-looking equipment, steam showers, and hydrotherapy spa-like baths.

Neatly pressed uniforms hung on hangers in each player's locker, embroidered with the player's number on the back, players whom Melvin watched and rooted for on television. How strange to now be in the presence of those he had idolized for so many years. The sensation was more moving than even he had anticipated.

One of the proud traditions of the Yankees, distinct from most other major league teams, was not to have players' names on their uniforms. This was consistent with the Yankee philosophy that it was a team sport and that individuals should not be bigger than the team. Melvin liked the spirit behind the policy. Spit-shined cleats were neatly placed by the chair in front of each locker. The aroma of it all was intoxicating. Melvin had become a kid in a candy store.

Fortunately for Melvin, Walter Dombrowski, who was in charge of the locker room, came over to greet the newest member of the team. "Morning, Mr. Klapper. Remember me? We met briefly on Sunday. I tried to get you a uniform that fit. You're kinda early, but that's okay."

"Hi, Walter. Please call me Melvin. Yeah, I couldn't wait to get here, but I have no idea where to go or what to do."

"Mr. Klapper, I mean Melvin, this is the first time I've been younger than a player on the team, so thank you for that. I always feel so old around these young boys. But they're a great bunch. It's a really good locker room. They get along and work hard. I know their record is not so good this season, but it ain't for want of trying."

Melvin couldn't help but wonder how these young athletes would treat him or whether they would even talk to him. Did they too think it was a stunt like Coleman and Chris had said?

"Okay, Melvin, your locker is right over here. You're next to Willie Niles, our second baseman, a three-time all-star, and on the other side of you is Pete Warner, a Yankee veteran at third base and a co-captain. Pete asked for you to be next to him. You couldn't ask for a better next-door neighbor. Willie is a bit on the quiet side, but Pete is super friendly. You'll love being next to him. Your uniform is hanging in the locker, and there are your cleats by your chair."

"The team provides you with two uniforms," continued Dombrowski, "which we clean and press until a new uniform is needed, but you're on your own for cleats because a lot of players customize their shoes. Not knowing what you're used to, I left a few different gloves in your locker. Tell me which one you like, and I'll order a backup for you. Best to rotate two or three at a time just in case. So check it all out. I'm here if you need me. Welcome to the New York Yankees, Melvin."

It was hard to comprehend having a locker between two great players that Melvin had been watching on television just a few days before. Melvin walked slowly around the room, trying to absorb it all—one step at a time, eyes bulging, neck swiveling from side to side. Seeing the names on the front of each locker of some of the greatest players in all of baseball, touching the uniforms, smelling the leather, amazed at how the locker room staff prepared for every home game, there was so much to take in, but Melvin was up to the task.

Melvin's pinstripe uniform was a bit loose. He certainly did not fill it out like the other players—more stomach than chest. He had been given the number seventy-five. It made him smile. Someone on the Yankees had a sense of humor. Now dressed, Melvin stood in front of the full-length mirror for what seemed like hours and muttered to himself, "Martha, I wish you were here to see this because I'm in the New York Yankees locker room wearing a pinstripe uniform with my soon-to-be age on the back."

Players started filing in while Melvin sat by his locker, fully dressed, wearing his glove on his left hand. Some players noticed him but said nothing. Others nodded. Most just went about their business, apparently not seeing the newest addition to the team. Then Pete Warner strode in, stopping to say hello to everyone and getting warm greetings and fist pumps in return.

Like most of the players, he looked bigger and stronger in person than on television. With his buzz cut and square jaw, he reminded Melvin of a Marine drill instructor. Warner was a good 6'2" and weighed about 210 with thick wrists and Popeye-like forearms. He walked right over to Melvin. Pete's sheer size made Melvin feel small and yet at the same time protected. It was a feeling Melvin could not recall having experienced before other than meeting Winnie on Saturday.

"Hi, I'm Pete Warner. I guess you're Klapper, right?"

"Yes, sir. I'm Melvin. Honor to meet you."

Warner laughed and said, "There are no *sirs* around here—except maybe you. My name is Pete, and if it's okay with you, I'll just call you Melvin. Waddaya say to that?"

"That would be just fine. Thanks, Pete."

"Now turn around and let me see how you look."

Melvin turned his back to Warner, who said, "You look good, Melvin."

As the room started to fill in, Warner shouted out loud enough to fill the room, "Hey, fellas, come on over and say hello to Melvin."

And to Melvin's amazement, the players he'd been admiring from his living room were now right in front of him, shaking his hand and patting him on the back. Melvin sat down out of fear he would faint if he continued standing. He thought of asking for their autographs but knew it was not the right moment.

"Pete, I don't know what to do."

"No problem, Melvin. Just tag along with me."

The players went out onto the field for batting practice. Melvin watched in awe as baseball after baseball flew out of the field into the stands. Melvin was reluctant to take a few swings, afraid he would miss the ball entirely. So he just stood there, feeling and wanting to be invisible. Just being on Yankee Stadium dirt was enough to give Melvin a sense of achievement he had always wanted but had never had.

After about thirty minutes, the team returned to the locker room to resume final preparations for the game. Just before game time, Higgins walked in, dressed and ready for the game. He called the players to gather up so he could speak to them as he did before many of the games. Melvin stood by his locker, not sure of where to stand.

"Okay, boys," Higgins began, "we have seventy-four games to go. If we play .650 ball the rest of the way, we can make up the fourteen games. We're a damn good ball club, much better than our record so far, and I have tremendous confidence in us. We just need to win a few games, so everyone hustle and play like you mean it. We're the New York Yankees. Let's act like it."

While the players dispersed back to their lockers for last minute preparation, Higgins walked over to Melvin.

"You okay?"

"I'm a little overwhelmed, but the fellas have been great to me, especially Pete."

"Good. Keep your eyes and ears open. Always be ready to play. I have no plans to call your number, but if and when I do, you have to be ready. So keep your head in the game. Got it?"

"I'll be ready, I promise."

Melvin loved the sound of the cleats on the concrete walkway from the locker room to the dugout. It sounded so right. Melvin, having never before worn cleats, found them to be slippery and was afraid he'd fall, so he walked very deliberately. Apparently, it took a little practice to learn how to walk in cleats on hard surfaces. Last in line to leave the locker room, Melvin found a corner seat on the bench.

"Klapper, get on the field and warm up," barked Higgins. "Find a player to have a catch with."

A couple of players included Melvin in their warm-up routine and were impressed with how easily and gracefully this old man could throw a ball.

After about fifteen minutes, the players retreated to the dugout to get ready for the game—last-minute drinks, tightening their taped wrists, retying shoelaces, opening new packages of gum, making sure their sunglasses were properly affixed to their caps, looking at the lineup card, discussing the opposing pitcher and what he threw for his out pitch. High fives to psyche themselves up. It wasn't unlike being in the military. It was about teamwork. Melvin quietly reclaimed his seat on the bench as the Yankees took the field. It was now game time at Yankee Stadium. "Here Come the Yankees" was playing as it had been since 1967.

Melvin peeked up behind the dugout and saw that his two box seats were empty. Winnie, Grace, and Chris were at work, and Billy was in school.

Yankee catcher Glenn Worthington, not wearing pads, sat down next to Melvin. He had been sidelined from a foul ball that caught his shoulder just under the protective pad intended to prevent such injuries.

"How you doing, Melvin? Feeling a little nervous?" asked Glenn in a friendly manner.

"You could say that. Actually, I'm more than a little nervous. I think frightened would be more like it."

"That's to be expected. It's a lot to take in. You'll get past it. I've been in the bigs for six years, and I still can't believe I'm here. My name is Glenn." He put out his hand to shake.

"Nice to meet you, Glenn." His hand felt rough and calloused.

"Melvin, just so you know, I'm the guy who caught your throw last Saturday. That was quite a toss. Had some real pepper on it after all that distance."

"I had no idea I could do that. I was as shocked as everyone else."

"If you did it once, you can do it again. So no worries. And if you have any questions, just ask. I don't know everything, but I know a lot."

"Can you tell me a little about the field?"

"Sure, the mound is sixty feet, six inches from home plate. The mound is elevated to give the pitchers momentum. Pitchers and hitters debate this all the time. Pitchers like an elevated mound so they can push off, while hitters think it gives the pitchers an unfair advantage. The key to pitching is really very basic. It's about changing speeds and changing the level of what the batter's eyes see."

"What about the dirt? It doesn't look like ordinary dirt."

"It's not. It's a combination of sand, clay, and silt. It has to provide for drainage and softness but be firm all at the same time. It's a real science. It has to allow for traction and resilience and yet allow for a true bounce. Believe me, as a catcher I live in the dirt, so I know it well."

"Boy, have I got a lot to learn. I thought I knew a lot watching on TV all these years, but being here in person is very different. So please keep educating me. I really appreciate it."

"Sure thing, Melvin. Let's have a catch later."

"That would be great, Glenn, thanks."

Like most home teams, the Yankee dugout was on the first base side of the field. The wooden bench was lower than Melvin expected. Being lower than the field, most of the players stood close to the field on the top step of the dugout to better see what was happening on the field.

Melvin was trying to feel and act like he was one of the guys, but he knew he wasn't. He knew he wasn't really part of the team. No one was rude or disrespectful to him, but he felt like an oddity, someone who didn't really belong in the dugout of the Yankees or, for that matter, any major league team. The players were ignoring or at best tolerating his presence. It was obvious that some of the players probably agreed with Vic "the Vulture" that the Yankees were pulling some type of publicity stunt.

During the game, most players chatted among themselves, while others either sat or stood quietly, cheering when appropriate. The conversation was usually about the opposing players, most often the pitcher and what to expect when up at the plate. Close calls, especially balls and strikes, were complained about as was the glare of the sun when catching pop-ups and fly balls.

No one spoke to Melvin or even acknowledged his presence. Melvin understood it was his first day in the busy and pressure packed "office" of athletes going about their business.

Melvin was struck by the efficiency of it all. Even the groundskeepers were seriously attentive and meticulous, almost obsessive, about their work.

As Melvin quickly learned, the umpires were their own breed. Some were friendlier than others, but all were watchful and acted as if responsible for the game going well. They did not like to be challenged. Umpires worked hard and got through their own "minor leagues" before being skilled enough to make it up to the majors. To Melvin's surprise, the players talked about the umps before and during the game, usually about the home plate umpire. Did he call high or low strikes? Did he have a big or small strike zone? Would he allow a player to disagree with a call or was he quick to toss a player who argued with him? Umpires had reputations just like the players.

While Melvin sat quietly on the bench, his thoughts wandered. Would he be too nervous to swing a bat or throw a ball? Would Higgins take the chance of playing Melvin, or was he just placating Carter? Could he visit the centerfield monuments of Ruth and Mantle and other Yankee greats? Would Vic "the Vulture" continue to come after him? Would the commissioner take some type of action against the Yankees or even against Melvin? Would his cancer get worse?

One of the Yankees on the bench not far from Melvin was Luke St. Germain, a tall, lanky pitcher currently sidelined with a rib injury. He caught Melvin's attention because he was able to flip a baseball over his shoulder and catch it behind his back. It was hypnotizing to watch. About the third inning, Luke strolled by Melvin and introduced himself.

"Hey, Klapper. I'm Luke. Born and raised in N'awlins, great food, beautiful women, mosquitoes the size of small birds, half underwater, half under indictment." If it was meant to relax Melvin, it did. Glenn laughed as Luke continued his stroll from one end of the dugout to the other, tossing a ball from one hand to the other.

"Luke is a great guy to have on your team," Glenn said quietly to Melvin. "Always has a funny saying, but make no mistake: He's all business on the mound. You'll get to know him."

Melvin returned to his thoughts. Would he get to sign the Yankee autograph wall? The inner sanctum was not known to most fans. It was Yankee tradition that players who had worn the pinstripes and played in a major league game for the Yankees got to sign the wall in permanent ink. The part of the wall inside the Yankee logo was specifically reserved for those who made the Hall of Fame. Would Melvin play that one game needed to sign the wall?

Having lost 6–3, it was time for the Yankees, still fourteen games behind the first-place Red Sox, who also lost, to begin a six-game, seven-day road trip to Cleveland and Chicago.

CHAPTER 17

Wednesday, July 20
Yankee Stadium

After a mediocre three-and-three road trip, the Yankees were back on their own turf with two games against St. Louis and four games against Cleveland. The week had gone without incident or fanfare. Melvin just sat quietly on the bench, not really involved on the field, in the locker room, or in the dugout. So far he was a nonentity, but as Russ had told him, it was Melvin's job to observe, to learn, and to be ready at all times. As usual, Melvin did his job. He hadn't been away from home for a week since he and Martha took a trip to Florida with Grace back when she was in high school. Melvin spoke to Grace and Billy twice during the week but had nothing new to report. There was still no mention to Grace or anyone else about his conversation with Dr. Mendelsohn.

While talking to Grace, who had her phone on speaker, Melvin could hear Chris in the background telling Billy that the whole thing was some kind of weird stunt and that Melvin would never actually get to play. When Billy got to talk, he wasted no time in asking, "Grandpa, are you ever going to play?"

Melvin responded truthfully, "Billy, I have no idea. My job right now is to keep my head in the game and be ready if and when the team calls upon me."

Nothing much had changed that week. He was pretty much treated like the other players, included in everything but still barely noticeable. Most of the players had their cliques to go out for dinner with or go see other sports events as most of the players had friends in other sports in New York. Melvin was getting used to it. Thankfully, a few players like Pete and Glenn tried to make him feel comfortable. Russ and several of the coaches, as well as Walt Dombrowski, went out of their way to make Melvin feel part of the team. But how could he? He knew that without contributing, he would never be truly accepted.

The Yankees had just lost a key game at home to the Cardinals when Terry Miller, one of the best bats in the lineup, hit into a game-ending double play with the bases loaded and the tying run on third base. This was one of those games that might have turned the season around if it had been won. Melvin had watched Miller on television for the last few years and knew him to be a reliable bat at the plate. Miller was a proven hitter but was unfortunately mired in a deep slump that was obviously impacting his confidence and in turn contributing to the team's decline. Melvin could see that Miller's swings were tentative and lacked the commitment and confidence it took to hit major league pitchers.

After the game, the players routinely showered, dressed, and left the ballpark. Almost all were gone when Melvin saw Miller still in uniform, sitting on the chair by his locker with his head down. He was obviously feeling dejected and disappointed. Some of the players tried to console Terry as they made their way out, but Terry knew he had let the team down at a crucial moment in a big game. Terry was popular with his teammates, the staff, and the fans. Melvin thought he was a stand-up guy.

After considering how he could help, Melvin approached Terry.

"Hey, Terry, tough game, huh?"

"Yeah, pops," he said, as some of the players were now calling Melvin. "How you doing so far?"

"I'm just trying to be patient and to be ready as Russ told me to be."

"Don't worry. The way things are going, you'll get your turn soon enough."

After a pause in conversation, Melvin said, "Son, I hope you don't mind my saying this, but don't get down on yourself." Melvin pulled over a stool from the adjacent locker.

"I know," replied Terry, "but I feel like I'm letting the whole team down."

Melvin replied, "I've been looking at your stats. You're a lifetime .295 hitter. You hit .320 two years ago and .310 last year. So the question is why then and not now?"

"What do you mean?" asked Terry.

"Well, I've been watching you swing. I'm no batting coach, but do you know that you've lowered your bat in your stance? It's too close to your body, so you can't fully extend your arms. When you swing, you're uppercutting rather than hitting down on the ball. You're not driving the ball as you usually do because I think your swing path is not on its usual plane as a result of your bat position. And then subconsciously, because it doesn't feel right to you, you raise the bat too high and hit lazy ground balls as you did today."

Terry's eyes widened. "When did you look at my swing?"

"Well, on TV and now in person. I hope you're not upset with me for saying all this."

"Hell, no. At this point I'd welcome advice from the guy selling hotdogs."

"I would suggest looking at footage from the past two years and just trying to get back that bat position. Maybe try it tomorrow."

"Tomorrow?" said Terry. "Heck no, how about right now? And, pops, can you stay a bit longer?"

"Sure, Terry. If you want me to."

Terry and Melvin, still in uniform, went looking for Walter, who ran the locker room with an iron fist and a big heart.

"Sorry to bother you, Walter," said Terry, "but can one of the guys set up the batting cage? I need to take a few swings."

"For you, Terry, no problem. Who's going to pitch to you? And catch?"

"Would you pitch, Melvin?"

"Sure, I'd love to."

"I just saw Bert," said Walter, referring to pitching coach Elbert Lansing. "Maybe I can ask him to stay and catch for you boys."

"That would be great. Thanks, Walter," said Terry.

About ten minutes later, the cage was set up, and Melvin was on the mound with a bag of balls, while Coach Elbert Lansing was behind the plate putting on his protective gear.

It took Melvin a while to get his pitches over the plate and to know how fast to throw them. But Terry was patient. At first, Terry kept popping up and then hitting weak ground balls. So Melvin got off the mound and walked over to Terry at home plate.

Repositioning the bat while Terry was holding it, Melvin said, "Lower is here, and away from your body is here. Now just swing from that position and tell me how it feels." Melvin stepped away while looking at Terry.

After a few practice swings, Terry said, "Heck, it feels like my old swing."

Melvin returned to the mound.

His next pitch was hit solidly to center field. Then Terry drove a home run to left. Then another home run to left, even deeper. Terry started to smile. Coach Lansing muttered, "I don't believe it. Who is this old man? When did he become an expert in hitting?"

"I don't know and don't care," said Terry.

After getting quickly showered and dressed, Terry said, "Pops, can I buy you dinner?"

"No, son, that's okay. Time for me to go home and rest up for tomorrow. Who knows, maybe I'll get to play this week."

"You will. Sooner or later, you'll be out there. Just hang in there. And, Melvin, I owe you big time. I can't wait to play tomorrow. Thanks."

CHAPTER 18

Thursday, July 21
Yankee Stadium

As usual, Melvin showed up at the ballpark earlier than the other players. He did this because he loved being there and didn't know how long this dream would last. And by being there first and leaving last, he avoided the uncomfortable face-to-face contact with the players, coaches, staff, and ever-prowling media.

It was a beautiful day at the stadium. Terry came right over to Melvin to shake his hand. A few players who saw the exchange wondered what that was about, but no one said anything. Terry got right out for batting practice and continued to swing the bat as he had in years past—one line drive after another. The guys around the cage were surprised and happy to see such a dramatic and sudden turnaround in Terry's hitting, especially after what had happened the day before. Melvin, pleased to see Terry feeling good again, just sat quietly, still excited just to be riding the team's bench.

The game against the St. Louis Cardinals, leading the central division in the National League, was in the second inning when

Terry came to the plate. Melvin could barely wait for Terry to swing a bat during the game.

Veteran Yankee announcers Paul Winters and Jake Moore, along with former all-star outfielder Deion Jackson, were doing the day's game on the Yankee network.

"I'm glad to see that Higgins stayed with Miller despite his slump and the game-ending double play yesterday," said Jackson, who knew what it was like to be in a slump. "As a proven veteran, he deserves that vote of confidence, and I hope he comes through today."

Doing the play-by-play, Paul Winters filled the audience in. "On the mound for St Louis is Nestor Giles, who has a fall-off-the-table curveball and a sneaky, fast slider. Giles wheels and pitches…low and outside, ball one."

"Miller, batting fifth in the order today for manager Russ Higgins, has been struggling of late, so he's due," Moore added.

Winters picked right up. "Giles nods to his catcher, throws, and it's a line drive to left center, one hop to the wall. Left fielder Simmons picks it up and throws it in, holding Miller to a stand-up double. Miller is clapping as are his teammates."

Terry gave a thumbs-up sign to the bench, which Melvin, sitting quietly, knew was meant for him.

"They need Miller's bat to get hot if they want to get back into the pennant race," said Jake Moore.

A bloop single to right brought in Miller, and the Yankees got on the board with a one-to-nothing lead. His teammates all high-fived Terry when he got to the dugout, but only Melvin got a hug of gratitude. A few players saw this, but no one really understood why.

With the Yankees losing 3–1, Terry tied the score in the sixth inning with a two-run blast, his first homer in twenty-one games. The only person who felt better than Terry was Melvin. But again, the Yankees lost the lead.

In the ninth inning, with the Yankees down 5–3, Terry was at the plate with another opportunity, unsuccessful the day before, to be a hero. Every little leaguer grew up dreaming of winning the game for their team in the bottom of the ninth. But it didn't happen often.

His walk to the plate from the on-batters circle signaled that Terry had his confidence back. He wanted to be at the plate at this very moment. He knew his swing was back in the groove. Melvin was filled with subdued anticipation. Melvin could no longer remain seated on the bench. He soundlessly lined up behind the other players hanging onto the railing of the dugout.

The pitcher, catcher, and infielders gathered on the mound as Pitching Coach Cliff Dodd made a visit to give instructions on how to pitch to Miller. The home plate umpire broke up the huddle, and Terry was ready to step into the batter's box. With men on first and second and two out, both dugouts were on the top step. Everyone in both bullpens was anxiously watching because as everyone in the ballpark knew, the game was on the line.

On the very first pitch, Terry belted a soaring home run to dead center. Terry raised his right arm in victory as he rounded first base. Now winning 6–5, the Yankee bench went wild, running onto the field to greet Terry at home plate. They knew exactly what this meant. Terry Miller was back. A game-winning second homer of the day with five ribbies made it a Terry Miller day.

It was a fun and raucous Yankee locker room. Winning did wonders for a team's psyche. Would this turn the season around? While everyone was congratulating Terry, he went to the center of the room and announced for all to hear, "Hey, guys, I want you all to know that the credit for today's win goes to Melvin. He stayed late with me here last night, helping to get my bat in the right position to fix my swing path. I don't know how he knew, but he did. So, Melvin," said Terry, holding up a bottle of orange Gatorade, "you're today's hero."

Melvin was awestruck. Embarrassed, he did not know what to say or where to look. So he just sat as humbly as possible, with his head half bowed, smiled softly, and semi-waved for a moment or two as the Yankee locker room gave him a curious but respectful round of applause.

After the game, some of the players, including Terry and Pete, invited Melvin out for a celebratory beer. Melvin, feeling honored just to be invited, respectfully declined, saying he had to go home to talk with Billy, his grandson.

"Hey, Melvin," said Pete, "you have to get a cell phone like the rest of us. That way, you can talk with your grandson from anywhere."

"Okay, how do I do that?"

"Just ask your kids. They'll help you. Great day. Thank you," said Terry.

"See you tomorrow," added Pete.

"Good night, boys," replied Melvin, very happy and satisfied.

CHAPTER 19

Thursday, July 21
Springfield

When Melvin opened the door to his house, the phone was ringing. Melvin grabbed the receiver and caught Billy just as he was about to hang up.

"Where have you been, Grandpa? I've been calling for an hour."

"Just walked in the door, Billy. The game ran long, and we sat around and talked for a while. One of the Yankee coaches was kind enough to give me a ride home, but there was a ton of traffic. Did you see the game?"

"I saw Terry Miller hit a home run to win the game. Looks like he's out of his slump. When are you going to play, Grandpa?"

It wasn't like Melvin to talk about why he was late getting home, how he helped Terry, or about whatever role he may have played in today's win or that the Yankee players gave Melvin a standing ovation in the locker room. Melvin would savor that moment for as long as he was allowed to do so, privately and quietly.

"Soon, Billy, one day soon. I'm just trying to stay ready. Will you be coming to the stadium Saturday? I'm hoping you and Winnie can be there."

"I have to ask Mom and Dad, but if Winnie can make it, I'd like to come too."

"Okay, I'll call Winnie and get back to you right away. But plan on being at the game Saturday."

Melvin hesitated before calling Winnie, but since Winnie had given Melvin his phone number, he figured it must be okay. After five long rings and just as Melvin was about to hang up, he heard a very somber and sedate "Hello."

"Oh, hello, this is Melvin Klapper calling for Mr. Winfield."

"Hi, Melvin, it's me, Winnie."

"Winnie, you sound awful. You okay?"

"This is not a good time to talk, Melvin. Can I call you back later or maybe stop by your house?"

"Sure, Winnie. Anything you want. Can I help in any way?"

"No, Melvin. We'll talk later." Winnie hung up.

When Winnie got off the phone, he looked at his wife, Alva, and said, "You satisfied now?"

"No, I'm not satisfied. I still don't understand why you're hanging with a seventy-five-year-old white man and his ten-year-old grandson. What's going on here, Winnie? I'm entitled to an explanation."

"Nothing is 'going on.' These are friends I met at the stadium. Just nice people. What's wrong with that?"

"What's wrong is that it's not normal for a forty-five-year-old black man, a former police officer, now bank security, to be palling around with people like this. What is it about them that attracts you?"

"They're just nice people. It makes me feel good to be with them. Isn't that enough?"

"No, Winnie, it's not enough. It makes me wonder about you. And why would these white people want to be friends with you? Are they running a scam?"

Laughing, Winnie said, "These people couldn't run a scam if their lives depended on it."

"Well, you better watch yourself, Aaron Winfield. I say stay away. White folks always cause us trouble. Remember your place.

Remember who and what you are. Don't trust what you think you see. Remember, even salt looks like sugar."

Winnie sat pondering what Alva had said to him. He knew she had his best interests at heart. He knew she was trying to protect him. But Winnie did not feel that he needed protection from Melvin and Billy. Alva's words played over and over in Winnie's head until he stood up and said, "Alva, I need a walk."

After walking about with no particular destination in mind, Winnie decided to go see Melvin. Although it was now about 8:30 p.m. and starting to get dark, Winnie figured he owed Melvin an explanation as to why there had been so much mystery on the phone.

Knocking on Melvin's door and looking through the side glass panel, Winnie could see Melvin getting out of his chair. When Melvin saw that it was Winnie, he smiled, but Winnie didn't smile back. Melvin was concerned and upset before he reached the door.

"Come on in, Winnie. I was worried about you. You sounded so terrible on the phone I didn't know what to say. But I'm glad you're here. You okay?"

"Not so good, Melvin."

"Why? What's the matter? Can you come to the game on Saturday?"

"I don't know, Melvin. Alva thinks I shouldn't be doing this."

"Doing what?"

"Well, being friends with you."

"Why not?"

"To be perfectly honest Melvin, you're a seventy-five-year-old white dude, and I'm a forty-five-year-old black dude."

"So? Why does that matter?"

"It's hard to explain, Melvin. Alva and I have been together since high school. We've been through a lot. Alva hasn't had a good experience with white people, and to be totally truthful, neither have I."

"I don't understand."

"No, you wouldn't. And I'm not saying anything bad about you or Billy. Please know that. But I was definitely passed over for promotions, and with my outstanding record of performance and conduct, there was no other explanation. It's just a fact that Alva and I and other black folks live with every day."

After a period of silence, Melvin said, "I don't know what to say. I feel terrible. Are you saying we can't be friends?"

"I don't know, but you have to admit, it's pretty odd."

"I don't see it that way. We're friends if we want to be, if we like each other, if we trust each other. You're a great guy, Winnie, and I don't think it was an accident that you were sitting next to me last Saturday."

"What do you mean?"

"I don't know what I mean, but you're a big part of this, whatever this is, and I want you to continue to be a part of this with me for as long as it lasts."

"We'll have to see how things go, but I'm sorry. I won't be at the game Saturday." Winnie stood up and walked out the door. There was no hug, no handshake, not even a goodbye.

Melvin began to tear up. He felt Winnie's pain but knew there was nothing more he could say or do.

After gathering himself, Melvin called Grace.

"Hi sweetheart, I hope I didn't wake you. How are you?"

"Hi, Dad. Busy, but we're doing great. How about you?"

"I'm okay. I just wanted you to know that Winnie will not be coming to the game Saturday, so if you or Chris want to bring Billy, there are two box seats waiting for you."

"I can't, Dad. I have a school function, but maybe Chris can. I'll run it by him."

"How's Billy? Can I say hello?"

"He just went to bed, so how about talking tomorrow?"

"Sure thing. Tomorrow works. Good night, sweetheart. Let me know about Saturday."

"Will do. Good night, Dad."

Melvin felt abandoned. Here was this wonderful day, one of the most wonderful days in his life after marrying Martha and the birth of Grace. And yet he was all alone.

CHAPTER 20

Friday, July 22
Yankee Stadium

It was a typically hot and humid midsummer night in the Bronx with a 7:05 p.m. starting time. The crowd was filling in, and soon, every seat in the house would be occupied. The Yanks were still only playing .500 ball and had been unable to cut into the fourteen-game Red Sox lead. This was going to be a big four-game series against a Cleveland ball club that always played hard against the Yankees, even in New York.

The game was slogging along with pitching dominating the hitting. As a result of the heat, the managers were mindful to keep their pitchers and position players from exhaustion by substituting players more than usual, especially with a day game coming on Saturday and a rare doubleheader (due to a rain out in April) on Sunday. By the eighth inning, each side had used four pitchers even though it was only a 2–2 game. The eighth and ninth innings went without much action. Both teams looked lethargic. In the top of the tenth, Sandro Alvarez, Cleveland's all-star catcher, launched an opposite field fly ball that seemed to just float into the second row of the right field stands. In the bottom of the inning, the Yankees responded by loading the bases with no outs but only managed to score one run. At the end of ten exhausting innings, the score was knotted at three—six up, six down.

By the twelfth inning, with almost all the players on both rosters having gotten into the game, Melvin was still sitting on the bench. Higgins had even used a good hitting pitcher to pinch hit in the eleventh, making Melvin feel embarrassed. But he kept his head high and in the game, always ready if and when called upon.

It was now the bottom of the inning with the Yankees at bat. First baseman Jesse Wolcott led off with a single over the leaping shortstop's head and was sacrificed over by a perfect bunt laid down by the speed merchant Caesar De Conto. It was the relief pitcher's turn to bat. Joe Lusiak had pitched well and had another inning in him if Higgins needed it. There were three Yankee pitchers left, but Higgins needed them for the weekend games. Higgins looked around before he turned to the bench.

"We need a single!" He scoured the dugout. There was no one left but Melvin. Russ had no choice.

After nine games of sitting and watching, Melvin heard Higgins say, "Melvin, grab a bat."

But Melvin already had a bat in his hands as he had for the last three innings. Higgins put his arm on Melvin's shoulder. "Melvin, need any advice?"

"I don't think so, but I'll take any you have."

"Okay, here it is. Swing hard, run fast, turn left."

Melvin smiled, which was exactly what Higgins was hoping would happen.

Melvin exited the dugout, mindful not to slip on the concrete steps. The Yankee bench was pretty much silent except for Terry Miller and Pete Warner.

"You got this, Melvin," yelled Terry.

"Nice and easy, Melvin," said Pete. "Just relax up there."

Although the crowd had thinned out, there were still at least twenty thousand loyal fans in the stands. Walking toward home plate, Melvin could barely feel his feet on the ground. Then he heard, "And now batting for the NY Yankees, number seventy-five, Melvin Klapper." Initially, the crowd did not react. And then there was mild and uncertain applause.

"Well, Yankee fans," bellowed Yankee announcer Paul Winters, "we're finally going to see Mr. Klapper. His first major league at bat."

"To be honest, Paul, there's just about no one else left," said Jake Moore.

"I'm actually pulling for the old man," added Deion Jackson, who himself had experienced many game winning hits. "What a great baseball moment."

Melvin tried to calm himself. A couple of deep breaths. This one at bat, he knew, would get the name Melvin Klapper on the wall at Yankee Stadium. Who would have imagined this just a few weeks earlier? He looked at the box seats. They were empty. No Billy, no Winnie to root him on. How he wished they were there. But he knew it was time now to focus on the job at hand. He knew how big the moment was but also knew he had to be under control to make the most of this opportunity. "Just relax, make good contact," he murmured to himself wondering if everyone in the stadium had heard him.

When he got to the plate, which took longer than he thought it would, he put his hand out to shake with the home plate umpire and said "Hi, I'm Melvin Klapper. Nice to meet you." Notoriously grouchy ump veteran Vernon Dietz was so stunned he reacted instinctively by shaking Melvin's hand and then wondered what had just happened. Never in his twenty-two years as a major league umpire had a player sought to shake his hand during the course of a game. Melvin then tipped his hat to acknowledge the pitcher and the catcher. The Yankee dugout was laughing and clapping. Melvin realized he probably shouldn't have done any of this, so he attempted to make amends by saying to the catcher and ump, "Sorry, boys, I'm just so nervous."

*****

Cleveland catcher Alvarez jogged out to the mound while the ump brushed off home plate. Melvin just started looking around. Seeing the stadium from the batter's box was an incredible view. It looked so huge. He saw the fans standing, many smiling, some laughing. The entire Yankee bench, only a few feet away, was up on the top step urging Melvin on. He could barely hear them. He could barely see them. It was all a blur.

"The guy is seventy-four freakin' years old," said Alvarez to his battery mate. "Just throw it over the damn plate so we can go out for a beer."

Stern-faced pitcher Travis Henderson nodded in agreement as Melvin looked around, taking it all in. He couldn't believe it, but it was true. He was coming to bat for the New York Yankees in Yankee Stadium. *If I'm dreaming*, Melvin said to himself, *please don't wake me*. This was a mantra he seemed to repeat every day.

The infielders were playing him straight away, and the outfielders were shallow, not a lot of room out there. He saw Wolcott taking his lead on second. Wolcott was at best an average-speed runner, but there was no one left to pinch-run. All of the players on both teams were now on the top step of their respective dugouts leaning on the guard atop the protective screen, keenly aware and maybe somewhat bemused by the unusual circumstances of the moment. Were they taking part in baseball history? Were they part of something so unexpected, so unusual that it would be a story they tell their grandchildren someday? Or would this turn out to be an embarrassing moment for Melvin, the Yankee organization, and possibly all of baseball? Not a good swing thought, Melvin realized.

"Play ball," yelled Dietz as he pulled his face mask on and pointed to Henderson on the mound. Melvin stepped into the batter's box. He took a few practice swings. He was ready, or at least thought he was. All eyes were on Melvin. He could feel it. The pressure was enormous.

Announcer Jake Moore was enjoying the moment as much as everyone else. "This has turned out to be quite the game. The oldest person ever to play major league baseball. Used to be the great

Satchel Paige, who played at, I think, sixty. So Melvin Klapper has ole Satchel beat by about fifteen years."

Henderson went into his windup and threw a bullet right down the middle at ninety-five miles an hour. Strike one. To Melvin it was just a shadow. He heard it hit the catcher's mitt, but he never actually saw the ball after it left the pitcher's hand. He stepped out, knowing he had better focus in a hurry before he would be back on the bench.

"That was some high cheese," said Johnson.

After a few practice swings to keep loose, Melvin stepped back in. Once again, it was the same pitch. This time at ninety-seven miles per hour. Strike two. Melvin could barely see the ball, let alone get a bat on it. It came upon him so quickly. Hitting in the batting cage before the game was one thing. Hitting ninety-seven-mile-an-hour fastballs in the pressure of a game was very different. Melvin wondered whether he was frozen at the plate. That happened in tense moments, especially with rookies or players who didn't get much playing time. Melvin was in both those categories, knowing that with two strikes, he now had to protect the plate. It was never good for a hitter to be 0–2. Melvin thought he had better be ready to swing even though he expected a waste pitch to get him to swing at a ball outside the strike zone.

"And the pitch…low, ball one. One and two," said Moore. Melvin stepped out and tried to get some much-needed air into his lungs.

Wasting no time and brimming with confidence, Henderson wound up and threw again. Melvin expected a fastball, and that was what he got. The ball came whizzing by about waist-high. Melvin tried to check his swing. The home plate ump called it a ball outside, but the catcher, thinking Melvin had swung, pointed to the first base umpire, who confirmed that Melvin had not swung. So the count was now 2 and 2.

Melvin was starting to get a little more comfortable. His first major league at bat. He had now seen his first four major league pitches. He was ready. He stepped out of the batter's box and took a few deep breaths.

Henderson shook off two signs, probably just to make Melvin wonder what pitch was coming, and then he nodded slightly to his battery mate. He wheeled and delivered.

Melvin swung and hit a soft blooper over the shortstop's head between left and center field. Wolcott lumbered around third and scored. The Yanks had won a long and tiring game 4–3.

Fans were jumping up and down like pogo sticks, amazed at what they had just seen. Equally amazed were the announcers and the players. No one cheered louder for Melvin than Brian Baker.

Melvin was mobbed at first base by his ecstatic teammates. They poured water on him, slapped him on the back, and hugged him. Someone lifted him off the ground, but Melvin was so filled with joy that he didn't even notice who it was nor did he care. He now had a major league base hit. No one could ever take that away from him. Nor could anyone have been happier at that moment. If only Billy and Winnie had been there to enjoy it with him.

The celebration continued in the locker room. It was as if the Yankees had won the pennant.

The announcer Paul Winters said, "The Yankees win a big one tonight on the bat of a seventy-four-year-old named Melvin Klapper, and that's Klapper with a *K*."

Russ awarded Melvin the game ball. All the players were reveling in what had just occurred but not as much as Melvin, who maintained his customary humility and modesty by quietly enjoying the moment, a moment he never thought could or would happen in his life. It was now a little after eleven, which was late for an elderly gent who usually was asleep by ten. Melvin thought to himself that he would have to adjust his bedtime hours.

Mobbed by media and fans as he left the players exit of the stadium, Melvin was offered a free ride by a middle-aged Uber driver who was a big Yankee fan. Melvin jumped into the SUV and talked all the way home with the driver, who knew a lot about the Yankees. As the SUV was turning onto his block, he saw hundreds of people outside his house. He asked the driver to stop so he could figure out what to do. Fortunately, the police were right behind him with lights and sirens blaring. The SUV moved out of the way.

After just sitting and watching for a few minutes, the police got control of the situation, and the crowd thinned. The street was now open for cars to go through, and so Melvin asked the Uber driver to drop him off in front. Before the driver would move, he asked Melvin for five autographs. Melvin asked why five. "Because I have two daughters and two nephews, all big Yankee fans. And one is for me," he said laughingly. Melvin smiled and signed his name five times.

With assistance from the police, Melvin was able to get into his house but not before he heard the now-smaller crowd chant, "Melvin, Melvin, Melvin." He waved to the crowd, tipped his cap, and was glad to be inside his house. He was concerned that all this commotion would disturb his neighbors. Every once in a while, Melvin would sneak a peek outside to see what was going on. The crowd had dispersed. One police car remained.

After a midnight snack of toast and orange marmalade, which he had learned to like because it was Martha's favorite, Melvin decided it was finally time to turn in. But as he was climbing the stairs, he heard several loud knocks at the door. Because it was so late, Melvin decided to ignore it, but he wondered whether the police were still out there. So he came back down the stairs and went to the front window, where he first saw the police car and then five of his teammates on the porch.

Melvin opened the door. "Hi, boys, what's up?"

"Melvin, we decided to pay you a visit," drawled Luke St. Germain as they brushed by him into the house. Pete was there as were Jesse Wolcott and Glenn Worthington.

"Come on in," said Melvin jokingly after they were all well into the house. "Boys, I've got to get my sleep."

"It's okay, Melvin," said Terry. "You won a game for us tonight. Let's celebrate. What have you got to drink?"

"Nothing, sorry. I don't drink."

"That's okay," said Wolcott. "The only purpose of alcohol is so white people can dance."

"That's not true," responded Worthington.

"I was just kidding," said Wolcott.

"So was I," replied Worthington, and everyone laughed.

Looking around, Pete said out loud, "Melvin, aren't the Yankees paying you?"

"Oh yeah. They've been very generous."

"Then why are you living here?"

"I like this house. It's my home."

Pete realized he had hurt Melvin's feelings. "I'm sorry, Melvin. I shouldn't have said that."

"It's okay, Pete. I know you meant well."

Looking at Martha's picture, Glenn asked, "Who is this?"

"That's Martha, my wife. She passed a few years ago." A tear came to Melvin's eyes.

"Very pretty lady, Melvin," said Terry.

"And here's a picture of my daughter, Grace, her husband, Chris, and their son, Billy."

"Oh yeah, he was with you when you made the catch and throw. Right?"

"Y'know you can bring him into the locker on certain days," said Terry. "The kid would love it."

"Wow, that would be great. What a thrill."

"So, Melvin," asked Luke, "you have no car, no cell phone, and no booze?"

"Sorry, Luke. How about a steak dinner on me tomorrow after our day game? You boys pick the place. Whoever wants to come. How's that?"

Only Pete responded. "Melvin, we just wanted to make sure that you're feeling part of the team and enjoying it."

"Oh, believe you me, I'm enjoying it. You boys are welcome to stay, but I'm going to sleep. Good night."

As Melvin made his way up the stairs, he heard the front door close.

Melvin was asleep ten minutes later.

CHAPTER 21

Saturday, July 23
Yankee Stadium

Despite his game-winning hit the day before and in defiance of Yankee fans chanting "We want Melvin" throughout the game, Melvin did not play, and the Yankees lost 5–2. No one said anything about going out for dinner.

Sunday, July 24
Yankee Stadium

Melvin was not in the lineup for either game. Newspaper columnists and sports radio fans were asking why. What happened to Melvin? Manager Russ Higgins decided to be interviewed and was ready for the questions about Melvin. Russ, being as diplomatic as he could be, said, "Melvin is a valuable member of our team and will play when called upon like the rest of the players."

"Russ, you know he's not getting any younger," said the interviewer, thinking how clever he was. Russ just walked away. The Yankees split a doubleheader and remained fourteen games out of first.

Monday, July 25–Wednesday, July 27
Yankee Stadium

The Yankees hosted the Seattle Mariners for three games. Melvin didn't play. The Yankees lost two out of three and remained fourteen games behind the Red Sox. The season continued to slip away.

Thursday, July 28
Springfield

This was a much-needed day off. Melvin visited Grace, Chris, and Billy, bringing in two large pizzas and four quarts of ice cream so that everyone had the flavor they liked. Billy asked a lot of sensible and thoughtful questions about Melvin's teammates, which Melvin answered as best he could. Chris asked questions about how Melvin was going to handle the money. Grace was asking who wanted which pizza. Melvin was happy to be with them.

Friday, July 29
Atlanta, Georgia

The Yankees hit the road for a trip that would last through early August. They played three in Atlanta, three in Texas, and finally three in Boston. It would be a long, hot, and grueling ten days. The Yankee season looked over as they were running out of time to catch up. Melvin was not in the lineup. The Yankees looked lifeless as they lost their first game against the Braves 4–1.

Saturday, July 30 and Sunday, July 31
Atlanta, Georgia

The Yanks won on Saturday and lost on Sunday. The road trip was off to a 1–2 start. Melvin hadn't played since July 22. New York papers were all over Gus and Russ for having a losing season. Why did they bother signing Klapper if they weren't going to play him? That was the question so often heard. So was it all a publicity stunt like Coleman said, just to distract from their awful season? Calls to change managers were beginning to take on traction.

Sitting on the bench was very tough for most players but not for Melvin, who wasn't like most players. He remained exhilarated just being in the locker room, hanging out with the players, seeing the various stadiums. Sure, he wanted to play, but he would bide his time. His chance would come.

Monday, August 1
Arlington, Texas

The Yankees started a three-game series against the Texas Rangers at Choctaw Stadium in Arlington, Texas, located between Dallas and Fort Worth. Outside the stadium, it was 101 degrees with 88 percent humidity, reminding Melvin of his days in Vietnam, but thankfully, inside was air-conditioned. A capacity crowd of 48,000 baseball fans had come hoping to see Melvin Klapper. But once again, Melvin was not in the lineup. The Yankees lost the first game 8–1, garnering only three singles.

Tuesday, August 2
Arlington, Texas

Having won only one out of four games so far on this road trip, the Yankee locker room and dugout were solemn. The New York media along with the Yankee front office were asking questions, but unfortunately, there seemed to be no answers. Lang was all over Gus, and Gus was all over Russ. But Russ was at a loss to understand why the season was going so badly and what, if anything, he could do to turn things around. This was his worst managerial season in a long career, and it was keeping him up at night.

In the bottom of the seventh inning of a rather boring game in which the Rangers were leading 3–1, the young Yankee right fielder Brian Baker, running after a fly ball at full speed, crashed into the outfield wall, fell to the ground, and did not move. Time was called as Russ and trainer Eddie Montero ran out to him. After a few minutes, Baker slowly walked off the field with the aid of several pitchers from the Yankee bullpen. He was done for the day and maybe longer. Subsequent X-rays determined that he sustained a concussion and two fractured ribs. Baker was going to be sidelined for several weeks.

At a loss to know what to do, Higgins decided to put Melvin in to play right field. In the bottom of the eighth, Melvin caught a long fly ball and made a great peg to third, just missing the Ranger tagging up from second. When it was Melvin's turn to bat in the ninth, Higgins thought about a pinch hitter, but the players clearly wanted Melvin to get up.

"He's earned it, Russ," said Pete. "Let him hit." Higgins reluctantly agreed.

Melvin hadn't played since his pinch hit ten days earlier. When Melvin stepped into the batter's box, it was as if everyone started paying attention. The crowd came to life as did the announcers. The Yankee dugout was excited to see Melvin at the plate. They were all pulling for him. Up to this point, there had been no spirit in the Yankee bats or spring in their step. They were just going through the motions.

On a 2–1 count, going with an outside fastball, Melvin lined a sharp single to right field to lead off the inning. The bench seemed to wake up. The gloominess had somehow been lifted. With just a simple base hit, smiles and hope had replaced frowns and despair. The Yankees went on to score four runs that inning and won the game 5–3. The players loved it as did Melvin. Higgins was scratching his head in wonderment.

In the postgame coaches' meeting, Higgins said, "What do you guys think of Melvin starting a game?"

"The way things have been going, what have we got to lose?" said Coach Homer Burgess.

Russ went on, "I'm getting a lot of pressure from above. I don't really care about that, but maybe they're right. Maybe Klapper should be playing. But I'm not going to play him unless you're all on board. So speak up."

Earl Endicott, usually the first coach to use his voice, didn't hesitate to offer his opinion. "I think we should take it one game at a time, but I say play 'im."

Lansing jumped right in. "I say the old man plays. He did make that catch and throw, and we know he can hit. So why hold it against him that he's seventy-five? Maybe seventy-five is the new twenty-five."

"Russ, I agree with the boys," said Burgess. "You have to admit that the guy is getting the job done, so I say we roll the dice."

After a moment or two of thought, Russ agreed. "My old man used to say, 'Don't dismiss the obvious just because it's obvious.' All right then," declared Russ, "we have a unanimous vote to play Melvin. Let's start him tomorrow."

As soon as the meeting was over, Russ sent a text to Gus. "Klapper starts tomorrow. All staff on board."

Gus responded with a big thumbs-up.

Wednesday, August 3
Arlington, Texas

After being with the Yankees since July 12, Melvin finally started his first game. Playing right field for the injured Brian Baker and batting ninth in the order, Melvin in his first at bat struck out on a 3–2 slider. In his second at bat, Melvin grounded back weakly to the pitcher for an easy out.

"You see?" barked a grumpy Higgins to nearby Coach Burgess, doubting his decision to play Melvin. But the players had confidence in Melvin, and the coaching staff, including Russ, could see and feel that it meant a lot.

Even more significant was that Melvin felt himself getting comfortable at the plate. The rust of sitting on the bench was wearing off. His timing was improving. He was feeling good and couldn't wait to get another at bat. Hopefully Russ wouldn't pull him because of his two poor bats earlier. Pete and the other players were very supportive and encouraging. More of his teammates were talking to him now than before.

In his third at bat, Melvin singled to center, and in the eighth inning, he smacked a double off the left field wall that missed being a home run by inches. Winnie, watching the game on TV, noticed Melvin hobbling a bit into second base. So in his first major league start, Melvin had gone 2–4 with two ribbies. More importantly, the Yankees had won. It was the first time in a while that the Yankees had won two in a row. Russ and the coaches could sense something happening.

Sunday, August 7
Boston

After the winning day game in Texas, the team flew to Boston for a weekend series beginning Friday night. The Yankees could put a dent in the Red Sox lead by winning at least two if not all three of these games, not easy to do at Fenway. Enjoying the Thursday day off but with increasing lower back pain, Melvin took two Aleve and decided to visit some historical sites. He loved the different Boston neighborhoods. He was hoping he'd be in the lineup Friday night, although Russ hadn't said a word. Melvin was excited to see Fenway, a ballpark he had admired from afar for many years, a ballpark with great history, where the scoreboard was still updated by hand, the team Babe Ruth played for before they famously traded him to the Yankees.

Fenway Park, the oldest ballpark in the major leagues, opened in 1912 and was now a baseball shrine. The first pitch was thrown out by Boston's then mayor, John F. Fitzgerald, JFK's grandfather. It was overshadowed at the time by the sinking of the *Titanic*, which had occurred a few days earlier.

To Melvin's surprise, he was in the lineup, now batting seventh. The Yankee hot streak, if winning two games in a row could be called that, continued their progress with a three-game sweep of the Red Sox. Melvin, now hitting a lofty .667 with four hits in six at bats, wrapped up the road trip on Sunday with a single and his first home run.

The Yankees were now eleven games out. It was still a huge deficit, but they seemed to have come alive. They were a different ball club. The players adored Melvin. He was great to be around and always easy to be with. Players went out of their way to just sit and talk with him, not only about baseball but about life in general, the military, kids, etc. They were learning from him as he was learning from them.

But the really big story of far greater magnitude and with longer-lasting effect was how Melvin was impacting and actually changing the outlook and attitude of the nation's elderly. All over the country, people over sixty-five were turning to sports, exercise, and other physical endeavors that they previously thought were not doable at their age.

Workout classes were being formed in community and recreation centers. Television segments and even half-hour shows devoted solely to the elderly were suddenly on every channel. Physicians specializing in geriatrics could not explain Melvin's phenomenal achievements but readily acknowledged that it was giving inspiration and confidence to the elderly that they could do much more than they thought they could. Less illness and fewer office visits among our older population became a trend.

Melvin was on the cover or front page of every newspaper and magazine. His name was recognized everywhere, in all parts of the country and with all age groups. Solicitations for endorsements were flooding into the Yankees. By popular demand, Yankee games were now being carried nationally by ESPN as the incredible surge in the popularity of baseball was sweeping the country in all age groups but especially with seniors. Fans, media, and the team loved it. Everyone was in for the ride.

When a weary and achy Melvin arrived home at 8:00 p.m. on Sunday night, he found a room-temperature pizza on the kitchen table with a note from Grace, Chris, and Bill, which said, "Sorry, we had to leave to get ready for school tomorrow. You played great this weekend. We watched every game. We love you. Talk tomorrow. Love, us."

Melvin, so glad to be home, missed them dearly as he did Winnie.

CHAPTER 22

Monday, August 8
Yankee Stadium

The Yankees returned home feeling good about how the road trip had turned out. Sweeping three from the Red Sox in Boston renewed their hope that just maybe, if they played really well, they could make up the eleven games. But it was August, and they knew that time was running out. The media in New York were talking relentlessly and writing nonstop about Melvin and how he may have turned the Yankee season around but that the Yankees had to have him in the lineup to win. Melvin was exhausted and in more pain than usual from playing every day. He could certainly use a day off but didn't want the manager to be blamed by the media for not playing him. Although his back and hip were bothering him more than they had, Melvin said nothing and played when called upon.

Getting ready for a seven-game home stand against Detroit and then Boston, the players were happy to be back in their own locker room. Pete saw Melvin walking around as if he were looking for someone or something.

"What's up, Melvin?"

“No big deal, Pete, but I can’t find my bat. It’s the only one I’ve been using, and I like it.”

“Has anyone seen Melvin’s bat?” Pete called out. No one responded that they had.

“Walter says it was in the bag when we left Boston,” Melvin said to Pete. “He remembers putting it in there. It’s gotta be here somewhere.”

Walter went to Higgins. “Russ, something ain’t kosher here. I know I put Melvin’s bat in the bat bag like I always do with all the bats. That bag has been sitting in the locker room for about three hours. Some players took their bats out. Maybe someone took Melvin’s by mistake. Can I snoop around a little tonight when everyone’s gone?”

“You bet, Walter. Snoop away. In the meantime, let’s help Melvin find a bat he likes.”

“I’ll just use another bat,” said Melvin, “no big deal.” Melvin walked around the bat rack, hoping to find another bat that felt right in his hands. It was fascinating how major league batters got accustomed to their bats and rarely changed bats during the course of a season as if it would somehow bring bad luck. Unless they were in a slump, in which case they’d try any and all bats. Although not quite as comfortable in his hands as the bat that was missing, the new one Melvin picked up seemed good enough. After all, it was just a bat.

Over the next four games, Melvin got up fifteen times without a hit. For whatever reason, the new bat or otherwise, Melvin seemed to have lost his touch at the plate. He could barely make contact. Melvin’s batting average plummeted to an anemic .240. Walter searched everywhere but could not find Melvin’s bat. The Yankees lost three out of the four games and fell back to fourteen games out of first place.

Because of Melvin’s slump, Billy was getting ridiculed at school about his grandfather being old and decrepit. The other kids blamed Melvin for the Yankees doing so poorly. Grace told Billy not to let the other kids bother him. “How many of their grandfathers are playing for the New York Yankees?”

Melvin was down. Could a bat make that big a difference, or was it just him not being able to handle major league pitching? Maybe teams had figured out his weakness at the plate. Melvin needed Friday off to collect his thoughts and catch up with Winnie, Grace, and Billy.

Friday, August 12
Yankee Stadium

Preparing for a big three-game series hosting the Red Sox, the Yankees knew that a proud Boston team, having recently lost three straight to the Yankees in Boston, would be out for blood. At the same time, the Yankees knew that they had to win at least two of the games to chip away at the thirteen-game deficit.

But the weather gods were apparently not aware or didn't care that these two teams wanted to play baseball that night. Steady drenching rains started around 3:00 p.m. and didn't let up. Melvin and his teammates just sat in their locker with an occasional visit to the dugout to check out the condition of the field. It was bad, and the forecast was for thunderstorms all evening up until midnight. It was Melvin's first rain delay game, and it was interesting for him to see how each player had his own way of dealing with whiling away the time. Some played chess or backgammon; others played cards. Video games were big with some, while others sat quietly meditating or listening to their favorite music with earbuds. Still others broke in a new glove or signed baseballs. There was sporadic chatter, mostly about the weather and how it could affect the game.

Overall, it was a learning experience for Melvin, who used his time to read a biography of John F. Kennedy. He was often interrupted by players who just wanted to chat with Melvin about baseball, books, television shows, movies, or food. He liked it when players sought conversation with or advice from him. It made him feel like he belonged, a feeling of camaraderie he had not felt since the Marines. Even though he was in a slump, Melvin's teammates treated him with admiration and affection. For the first time in his life, Melvin was actually looked up to by talented, skilled, successful people. What a feeling.

At about 9:15 p.m., the umps advised both teams that the game was officially rained out and that it would be made up as part of a day-night doubleheader on Sunday. The players were glad to get back into their street clothes and go home or on dates or wherever most young men went on a Friday night in the Big Apple. Melvin went home.

Saturday, August 13
Yankee Stadium

It had been a terrible week for Melvin and a step backward for the team. Melvin felt responsible, but both Higgins and the coaches told him that baseball was a team sport and no one player won or lost a game. Melvin knew that was true, but it didn't make him feel any better. Because without Melvin hitting, the Yankees weren't winning.

About an hour before the game was scheduled to start at 1:05 p.m., with the players getting ready for the big series with the Red Sox, a must-win situation, the injured right fielder Brian Baker sheepishly walked over to Melvin holding the missing bat.

"Hi, Brian, what's this?"

"It's your bat, Melvin."

"Wow, Brian, that's great. Where did you find it?"

"I didn't find it. I stole it."

"What are you talking about?"

"I was jealous of your success and was afraid you'd take my place in right field. So I did something stupid. I apologize."

It was one of those rare moments when Melvin felt anger. His opportunity to play for the New York Yankees had been jeopardized by an act of treachery, by a teammate no less. Disloyalty was not part of Melvin's makeup, and he had no tolerance for it in others. He reminded himself that this wasn't the Marine Corps and that what Baker had done was boneheaded but not a matter of life and death. Realizing this, Melvin tried to calm himself before saying anything. He took a deep breath.

Meanwhile, other players drew closer to learn more.

"I'm really sorry, Melvin," Baker said. "My bad. I don't know how I could do something like that. But I'm here now to own up to it."

Melvin weighed his words. His initial anger was subsiding. Now he was feeling badly for Brian. This guy's career was on the line.

"I understand why you did what you did," Melvin said at last, "but I'm only playing while you recuperate from your injury. Honestly, if the only reason I can hit is because of that one silly bat, then I don't really belong here, do I?"

"Oh no, Melvin, you belong here," responded Brian, "and I'm as happy as everyone else that you're here."

Pete, overhearing the conversation and getting beet red in his face and neck, told Brian in no uncertain terms that his stunt was selfish, that it had hurt the entire ball club, and that his teammates deserved to know what he'd done.

"I know, Pete. It could end my time here and maybe my career, but I screwed up big-time and am ready to admit it to everyone right now."

"Hold on a minute, guys," said Melvin calmly. "As I learned many years ago, it's better to respond than to react."

"What's the difference?" asked Pete.

"It may not sound like a big difference, but responding is thoughtful and deliberate while reacting is too often immediate and rash. You get better results by responding, not reacting. It's harder but better."

"Melvin, you never fail to amaze me," said Pete.

Melvin stood up and looked at everyone. "Let's not throw the baby out with the bathwater. Yes, Brian made a mistake, but he owned up to it. I say we let it go. Let's focus on winning. We need to win these games and can't afford to be distracted. It won't help the team to embarrass Brian. How about it, Pete?"

"It's your call, Melvin."

Melvin said, "C'mon, boys. We have a game to win." The small group listening to what had occurred dispersed.

With a gesture that meant all was forgiven, Melvin went to shake Brian's hand, but instead, Brian grabbed Melvin and gave him a bear hug, knocking Melvin's cap off. Not knowing what to say, Melvin said nothing.

"Thanks, Melvin. I'll never forget you."

Patting Brian on the back, Melvin said, "It's okay, Brian. We all learn along the way."

Melvin put his old bat into the locker.

Seeing this, Pete said, "Melvin, what are you doing?"

"I meant what I said to Brian. I should be able to hit with more than one bat. What happens if it breaks?"

"Melvin, you old codger, you really are something," said Pete calmly, shaking his head and smiling.

"Pete," said Melvin a few minutes later, "I couldn't help but notice that you have several sayings or quotes taped to the inside of your locker door, and I see you look at them before heading out onto the field. If it's not too personal, would you mind very much telling me what they say?"

Warner, who had starred as a running back at Clemson for two years and probably would have been a top NFL draft pick before getting a big bonus to sign with the Yankees, said, "No problem. You're the only person who's ever asked me. You see the top one? It says, 'The player who complains about the way the ball bounces is probably the one who dropped it.'

"The one below it says, 'When you win, nothing hurts.' That was Joe Namath.

"And the bottom one is from Benjamin Franklin, who said, 'By failing to prepare, you are preparing to fail.' I've been carrying advice like this around with me since high school football."

Melvin read them to himself and liked all three, having never heard them before. They told him a lot about the kind of man and athlete Pete Warner was.

"That really great, Pete. Thanks for sharing."

Melvin went on to get three hits that afternoon as the Yankees won by a convincing 9–3 score. Brian Baker was now Melvin's biggest cheerleader.

After the game, Walter approached Melvin and asked, "Melvin, you got your bat back?"

"Yep."

"How?"

"Brian found it."

"Is that right?" asked Walter, sounding incredulous and rubbing his chin. "And where was it?"

"I don't know. Didn't ask."

Walter hesitated and said thoughtfully, "I understand."

"Thanks, Walter. You're a good man." Melvin winked.

Walter was no slouch in the ways of the world and with silent recognition of Melvin knew that a smart person may know what to say but a wise person knew whether to say it or not.

With Saturday's win, the Yankees were again within twelve games of the Red Sox with a doubleheader coming up the next day. The pressure was on, but it was a good pressure because Melvin and the Yankees felt it was now their time for a run at the Sox.

Melvin invited the team out after the game, but it seemed everyone had plans, so Melvin was once again alone. He was debating whether to call Winnie when his new cell phone rang.

"I saw the game today," said Winnie. "Three hits. Not too shabby for an old man."

"Winnie, I was just about to call you. How'd you get my number?"

"I called Grace to see how Billy was doing, and she told me how they helped you get a cell phone. Grace said it was quite the experience going to an Apple store with you. She gave me your number."

"You around to get together for dinner tonight?"

"Well, actually, yes. Alva is away at her sister's house in New Jersey, so I'm available. How about Vinny's at seven?"

"Great. This is turning out to be a really good day. See ya later."

*****

When Melvin arrived at Vinny's at 6:50 p.m., Winnie was already seated at a table. He waved to Melvin. People recognized Melvin and said hello, but in New York, people see celebs all the time, and it's just not cool to bother them in their personal time. Vinny's was one of those classic Italian restaurants that has been around forever, never showy but elegant in a quiet, confident way, the kind of place where they called the red sauce gravy, where the tomatoes were DOP San Marzano, and where the aromatic basil, plump burrata in flavorful virgin olive oil from Tuscany vineyards, and soft baby veal were the real deal.

Vinny was the name of the founder and presently the name of the owner-chef grandson of the original Vinny. They took no reservations. People they knew and liked got seated. Good-looking couples got seated. Loud, stupid people, not so fast. Waiting at the bar was the usual protocol, with the hope that after a few drinks Rudy the bartender would help get them a table. From 5:00–11:00 p.m., the place was always packed. As Yogi Berra once said, "Nobody goes to that restaurant anymore because it's too crowded."

Melvin, who could not afford Vinny's just a few weeks ago, was surprised that Winnie suggested it but had decided it would be an honor to treat Winnie tonight. He was so glad to see him. Their last conversation had not ended well, and Melvin was upset that he might never see Winnie again.

As Melvin approached, Winnie stood up to greet his friend. Melvin had almost forgotten how big Winnie was. Melvin's hand seemed to just fold into Winnie's.

They sat down, both obviously glad to be together once again.

Before Melvin could say how happy he was that Winnie called, Winnie said, "I owe you an apology, Melvin."

"You do? For what?"

"For laying my personal situation on you, especially at a time like this, with all you've got going on."

"Winnie, are we friends or what?"

"We're friends, Melvin. How's Billy? I miss that kid."

"He hasn't been to a game. Without you, he can't come because for whatever reason, Chris won't take him. I think for some reason, he doesn't want Billy to see me play. By the way, Billy is wondering where you've been. He keeps asking, but I didn't feel it was right to share our discussion with anyone."

"Look, Alva and I had a long conversation, actually more than one. I understand her point of view, and she understands mine. She's not wrong, but I need to see things in a brighter, more promising light."

"Does this mean you can come to the games?"

"That's exactly what it means," he said with a bright smile.

"How about tomorrow? It's a Sunday, so Billy can probably come. Look, I've learned how to text. I'll text Grace and see what she says. Will you pick Billy up if she says okay?"

"Of course."

Melvin jumped on his cell phone much to Winnie's amusement. "Grace, can Billy come to the game tomorrow? Winnie can pick him up at 11:30. Okay, kid?"

The lack of an immediate response probably meant that Grace was talking it over with Chris. Chris may say no, but hopefully, Grace would prevail.

Melvin and Winnie had a fabulous dinner at the end of which a sizable bill was delivered to the table. When Melvin went for his wallet, Winnie grabbed the check and said, "It's on me tonight, Melvin. I owe you a lot, and I always pay my debts."

"Thanks, Winnie, but you don't owe me a thing. Wow, this has been a great day." At that moment, Melvin received a text that read, "Yes, Billy will be ready at 11:30 a.m. Can Winnie or you bring him home afterward?"

"*Yes, yes, yes*," responded Melvin.

CHAPTER 23

Sunday, August 14
Springfield

Melvin awoke beyond eager to get the day going. The Yankees were winning, Melvin was hitting again, and his dinner conversation with Winnie had hopefully repaired and restored a relationship that meant a great deal to Melvin. Things were looking up.

It was going to be a cool, sunny day at the ballpark, perfect weather for Melvin, a welcome relief from mid-August humidity in New York. The heat took a toll on him. His hip was starting to hurt more often, but over-the-counter pills seemed to bring some temporary relief. More than before, it seemed like the pain had radiated from the back to the side and once in a while to the left side of his abdomen. But as long as it could be tempered by anti-inflammatories, Melvin felt it was under control enough not to see Dr. Mendelsohn. Melvin had not yet disclosed to anyone the situation regarding his cancer.

He couldn't bear telling Grace or, even worse, Billy. If pills he could buy in the drugstore seemed to work, maybe Dr. Mendelsohn was wrong. Melvin was due to go back for repeat blood tests in August but put off calling to set up an appointment since he naively felt that he had it under control. He also knew he would be getting a call any day now from Helen at Dr. Mendelsohn's office, so Melvin decided to wait until she called and then act like he had forgotten.

Most of the media had been extremely kind to Melvin. He knew full well that it was his age that made the story so interesting to so many. His was a feel-good story that the press glommed onto, at least for today. He was thrilled that his story was inspiring an entire generation of people over sixty-five to go back to physical activity.

The surge in popularity of pickleball, tennis, jogging, dance lessons, yoga, Pilates, and even weight lifting was noted all over the country. Gyms were full of older people. New videos were online specifically for the elderly. Sales of vitamins were increasing profits for supplement manufacturers. New clubs and clinics were sprouting up at country clubs, YMCA's and senior living facilities. The impact of Melvin's success was evident throughout the country. Active older people were now being referred to as "Melvin's." It even lifted the spirit of younger people who now viewed getting older in a new and more optimistic light. Everyone was pulling for Melvin because pulling for Melvin was pulling for themselves.

Similarly, the story about the Yankees was really a story about a nearly seventy-five-year-old man who was tearing up the league and turning a losing, insecure team into a winning and confident team. Melvin had brought the fun back to New York, baseball, and the New York Yankees. And he was having the time of his life. Melvin couldn't wait to get to the locker room, to greet his teammates, and to see what the day would bring. His enthusiasm, smile, and positive way of thinking had infected the entire ball club, and they were just floating along, riding the Melvin wave.

Knowing that Billy and Winnie would be in the stands on this bright August Sunday filled Melvin with anticipation. He was hoping he wouldn't let them down. This was the last game of a six-game homestand against the archrival Red Sox, but unfortunately, Vic "the Vulture" Coleman was not going to waste the opportunity.

For his Sunday column, Vic was on the front page of the *Globe* with his headline and story.

MLB Part of Klapper Coverup
Victor Coleman

Ever since the New York Yankees supposedly signed a 75-year-old codger who had no prior baseball or athletic experience to a contract, this reporter has been requesting and is now demanding that Major League Baseball uphold the integrity of the game by investigating the legitimacy of this unbelievable narrative.

We are being told to believe that all is on the up and up when we are intelligent enough to know that it can't possibly be true. Yet the commissioner sits on his hands, dithering away, while the sport is placed in jeopardy by some stunt the Yankees have managed to conjure up.

All sports fans, no matter who they root for, want the game to be fair and square. Without honesty, there is no true sport. The league owes it to millions of fans as well as to the future of baseball to answer a few questions.

Who is Melvin Klapper? Where did he come from and when? Has anyone actually seen proof of his age?

How did Klapper and the Yankees come together? Why did no other team even know about him?

How is he able to hit major league pitching having never even played organized baseball before?

> Are we to believe that anyone on earth can throw a baseball 460 feet from a standing position with no windup?
>
> Has Klapper been chemically tested by the league to make sure that he's not on performance-enhancing drugs?
>
> These are just a few of the relevant questions sports fans are asking. It's time for the Yankees to 'fess up about Klapper. If they don't do so immediately, this reporter, who has been writing about sports for thirty-five years, demands that the league step up and do their job, restoring sanity and respect for our national pastime.

Melvin was stunned to hear this column read aloud in its entirety on television at 6:30 a.m. on a summer Sunday, followed by a panel discussion of whether performance-enhancing drugs could explain Melvin Klapper's remarkable hitting and throwing. Why did this have to come along when everything was starting to look so promising? What was he to do? How should he react? What would Billy think?

Melvin knew that Yankee management would not be happy about this column. The Yankee organization, a winner of forty American League pennants and twenty-seven World Series titles, a bastion of sports history in America, would not enjoy being attacked. How would his manager and teammates react?

It didn't take long to find out. As soon as Melvin got to the stadium at about 9:00 a.m., he was told by Walter that General Manager Gus Christainson wanted to see him in his office right away. Was Melvin about to be fired?

Melvin had only seen Gus in passing since they agreed to compensation, but other than occasional nodding, there had been no actual conversation. Gus customarily made his intentions known to Higgins, and that word would pass down to the players, including Melvin, by Higgins himself or through the coaches.

So Melvin was upset to hear that Christainson wanted to speak directly to him at this time. It couldn't be good.

Melvin, still in street clothes, made his way up to the GM's office. Sandra, Gus's secretary, was not at her desk. Maybe because it was a Sunday. Melvin didn't know. So he knocked on Gus's door before hearing, "Come in."

"Good morning, Melvin," said a somber and displeased Gus Christiansen.

"Good morning, Gus. Am I in trouble?"

"That's what we're here to find out. Let me tell you at the outset that this meeting is at the suggestion, the strong suggestion I may add, of Mr. Carter."

"I understand."

"You heard of course about the *Globe* article this morning?"

"Yes, I haven't read it, but I heard it on TV."

"Melvin, as much as we dislike Coleman, that column of his is very upsetting to Mr. Carter and to me. Can you understand that?"

"Of course, I'm upset too."

"Melvin," said Gus, taking a deep breath, "we appreciate what you've done for us since coming aboard, and we're willing to make a statement in support of you and the organization, but I need to ask you something, and please think carefully before you answer." Again Gus paused. "Is there anything we should know? If the league tests you for performance-enhancing drugs, will anything be revealed that would embarrass us? This is obviously very important to you and to us, so please take a moment to consider your answer."

Melvin thought about his hip and wounds from Vietnam but felt there was nothing there to reveal. Then Melvin thought about his cancer. Well, Melvin thought, that was no one's business, and it certainly had nothing to do with Coleman's column.

Knowing that he was not taking performance-enhancing drugs or doing nothing illegal, Melvin said, "Gus, I'm not afraid to be tested. I would never do anything that would embarrass myself or the Yankees. You gave me an opportunity to live a dream. I can't really explain what's going on, but I don't think you or Mr. Carter have anything to worry about. Let them test."

"Okay, Melvin, we just wanted to give you a chance to clear the air. Because if you want, you can resign today, right now, and the Yankees will take no action against you. But if this turns out to be some kind of fraud and you persist in perpetuating it, I can't guarantee your legal future."

"Gus, I suppose I should be scared by what you're saying, but I'm not. Let Coleman say what he wants. We have games to win, and I don't think the team should be distracted. Gus, don't worry. I won't let you down."

"Thanks, Melvin. For whatever reason, I believe you. Getting a few hits today will be the best response to that jerk's column. By the way, do you know what they say about Coleman?"

"No, what?"

"His enemies hate him, but his friends really hate him."

Melvin laughed and said, "Thanks, Gus. See ya later." Gus just stared at Melvin as he got up and walked out of the office. Gus knew that if Melvin was lying, Gus's career could be over. He would become a joke around baseball. Lang had nothing to worry about. His team would still be worth $5 billion, and Gus would be the fall guy. Yet despite the obvious risk, Gus believed Melvin and was willing to put it all on the line for him.

About two hours later, the Yankees issued a public statement.

"Contrary to the irresponsible words written in today's *Globe* regarding NY Yankee Melvin Klapper as well as the entire Yankee organization, the NY Yankees denounce and totally refute their front-page story. We stand firmly by Melvin Klapper. While we do not believe that the league has the authority to examine or test any one particular player on the basis of mere speculation, especially in the heat of a pennant race, neither Mr. Klapper nor the Yankees object to the league doing what it considers necessary and appropriate to bring this contrived and absurd complaint to a swift conclusion. We also expect and request that when this columnist's alleged concerns are resolved in support of Mr. Klapper and the Yankees, the *Globe* issue a front-page apology and take the warranted disciplinary action against Mr. Coleman."

The Yankees had spoken. Their message was loud and clear. Melvin was grateful for their support but asked himself what would Coleman do next.

*****

By 11am, the Yankee statement was posted on the bulletin board in the Yankee locker room. Lang and Gus wanted every player to see that Melvin had their support. This was necessary for team unity at a time when the players were starting to play winning ball, and neither Lang nor Gus wanted this column to throw the players off, which was what they believed was the purpose and timing of the column.

As Melvin's teammates filled the locker room, all the talk was about how "the Vulture" had struck again. Some of the players laughed at the column, while others were angered. Melvin was just upset and prayed that it wouldn't affect the team. He hoped that Chris wouldn't use it to keep Billy from coming to the games. As if that weren't enough, would Alva use it against Winnie?

Melvin retreated to his locker, trying to stay as inconspicuous as possible. Pete and a few other team leaders had apparently been in a meeting with Russ and the coaches as they all entered the locker room together.

Higgins went to the middle of the room and put one leg up on a chair. "Let's huddle up, boys."

He waited for the players to shuffle closer into a circle around him. He never looked at Melvin. Pete and Terry moved over toward Melvin as a sign of support as did other players who had nearby lockers.

"That piece of crap Coleman is a stooge for the Red Sox. The only purpose of that column was to distract us from beating his team. Why else was it timed for today when we just happen to have a doubleheader against the Sox and everyone knows we're closing the gap? Let's not be angry or lose our focus. We stand by Melvin. If the Yankee brass is satisfied about Melvin, so am I. So go out there and play Yankee baseball. Melvin, you're batting third today. That's our response to that column."

Higgins and the coaches walked out of the locker room. The tone had been set. The players liked it. Some applauded. Melvin felt better knowing he had the backing of his teammates.

It was almost game time for the opener of the doubleheader. Melvin kept peeking from the dugout to see if Winnie and Billy were there. Not having heard from Winnie or Grace, Melvin assumed everything was okay. Maybe Chris had not heard about the article. He rarely followed sports, although now he was trying to at least look interested in baseball, hoping that by doing so Billy would talk with him more.

The networks knew the importance of these two games even before the *Globe* article. The entire country was now following Melvin, who had created millions of new baseball fans. Melvin had captured the imagination of the American public. The networks put their best announcers in the booth, Scott Whaler and Dan Earling, who had broadcasted the July 9 catch and throw that rocketed Melvin into the spotlight. They certainly had not forgotten their good fortune to see and describe what had happened that afternoon at Yankee stadium. Now that ESPN had committed to carrying all the Yankee games due to the national interest in Melvin, Scott, and Dan once again had the good fortune of being there for the big games, possibly a Yankee run at the Sox, and of course to watch Melvin.

The *Globe* article had now added even further interest and excitement to the already hectic scene. Moreover, the Yankees had definitely shrunk the Red Sox lead, and so NY fans who had pretty much given up this Yankee season were back to their usual rabid devotion to the team.

When Melvin was in the dugout, he could see the stands filling up. All these people spending a beautiful summer day watching grown men, some older than others, play a game of baseball. How lucky Melvin felt knowing he was part of that human experience. It would be a crowd of nearly fifty thousand, about what the Yankees were drawing whether at home or on the road. Melvin knew the importance of this game but was emotionally drained from the hubbub caused by the article and his overriding concern about whether Winnie and Billy would be there for at least the day game.

The Yankees took the field. Melvin slowly loped to right field. When the lineups were announced over the loudspeaker, Melvin's name got the loudest and most sustained round of applause. Melvin took this as a sign of support by the fans, and his teammates didn't mind. They knew that Melvin had become the main attraction. The Red Sox players were, of course, booed by the Yankee crowd. When Melvin got out to right field, he waved to the fans with his hat. They stood and applauded. Melvin had never before seen the stadium at capacity from his position on the field. He looked around and was awestruck. And then he saw all he needed to see: Winnie and Billy taking their seats. "Thank you, Grace," Melvin said to himself.

The Red Sox got off to a quick start by scoring two runs in the first inning. They had come to play. But then the Yankee hurler Luis Caramone settled down until the sixth inning, when Red Sox outfielder Sammy Leon whacked a line drive home run to left, making it 3–0 Sox going into the bottom of the sixth.

Melvin was batting third for the first time. Being in such an important position in the lineup, Melvin felt a little extra pressure, but he appreciated the message being sent to the public, the League, and the Red Sox. In his first at bat, Melvin grounded to short. In his second at bat in the third inning, with two out and runners on first and third, Melvin turned on an inside pitch and drove it down the left-field line. It was a fair ball by inches, rolling into the corner with the left fielder in hot pursuit.

A faster runner might have made it to third, but Melvin struggled to make it to second. His hip was definitely bothering him despite the pills he'd taken an hour prior to the game. Most observers just thought it was because of age that Melvin couldn't run any faster, so no one said anything about it. Neither did Winnie, who had previously seen Melvin limping ever so slightly.

Melvin also was mindful of the unofficial baseball rule to prevent killing a potential rally that a runner should never make the first or last out of an inning at third base.

The two base runners scored easily. The Red Sox lead was now 3–2. Despite both teams having scoring opportunities in the seventh and eighth innings, the game remained 3–2 going into the home ninth. The Red Sox brought in their fastball-firing closer Dean Smith, who at 6'5" and 240 pounds often reached 100-plus mph. With Smith, known as "high heat" on the mound, the game was usually over.

As he was fourth to bat in the inning, Melvin would only get to bat if a Yankee made it on base. The first Yankee to bat was a pinch hitter for the pitcher. He struck out on four pitches. The next batter was shortstop Caesar De Conto, who had a good eye at the plate. Smith, as usual, was just rearing back and throwing as hard as he could—nothing fancy, just an old-fashioned hardball. But Caesar was a savvy batter and managed to foul off some pitches until working a 3–2 walk. The speed merchant trotted to first.

It had been a close pitch, and the Red Sox bench erupted when it was called ball four.

Although MLB rules forbid players and coaches from leaving their position to argue balls and strikes, they certainly did so quite vociferously from the dugout. Usually the home plate umpire ignored what was said, but this time, umpire Lamar Ryder had heard enough. Lamar was known for having a short fuse. He took off his face mask and walked toward the Red Sox bench. He issued some type of warning and then turned back toward home plate. But apparently, someone on the Red Sox bench couldn't resist and said something more that Ryder didn't like, so he turned back to the bench once again, pointed at someone, and gave the "You're outta here" sign. Order was restored.

Melvin came out onto the on-deck circle but would only come to bat if Willie Niles, batting second, didn't hit into a double play. The fans were on their feet. Melvin saw the third-base coach flash the sacrifice bunt sign, but apparently Willie missed it. He swung at the first pitch and popped it up to the second baseman.

Now Melvin, still using his new bat, was walking toward home plate.

The crowd of more than fifty thousand was screaming, "Melvin, Melvin, Melvin." He saw Winnie and Billy out of the corner of his eye. They were standing, clapping, and screaming.

The announcers seized the moment. They had been talking about the article on and off the whole game, including reading the Yankee statement twice. Both agreed that Melvin should submit to testing if he had nothing to hide, just to get past all the accusations.

Dan began to set the stage. "As if we didn't have enough drama in this game, here's the moment we were all hoping for. The tying run is on first, the winning run at bat, and who's at the plate? Melvin Klapper. That's Klapper with a *K*, the nearly seventy-five-year-old Yankee who has been hitting the daylights out of the ball at a very respectable .300 pace. And he's up against one of the toughest pitchers in all of baseball, Dean Smith, who takes no prisoners. So the Red Sox have who they want on the mound, and the Yankees have who they want at the plate. Quite the moment, huh, Scott?"

"As a former player, I can only imagine what must be going through Melvin's head at this moment. The pressure is absolutely enormous."

"Smith looks ferocious out there," said Dan, "but Klapper seems to have his usual calm and composed demeanor. The entire stadium is rocking. This is one of those baseball moments that every fan prays to watch. Melvin steps in. He's expecting nothing but hundred-mile-an-hour fastballs. Melvin knows he'll have to begin his swing while Smith is finishing his windup."

Smith reared back and threw a pitch that looked good but was called a ball.

Melvin stayed in the batter's box, took a few easy swings, and waited for Smith's next bullet. This one was high, but Ryder called it a strike.

"Was that a makeup call by the ump, Scott?" asked Dan in the booth. The count was one and one.

With a man on first, Smith took his half windup and threw a pitch in the dirt, trying to get Melvin to swing at a waste pitch.

"Two–one count," said Dan. "This will be a big pitch. Smith asks for a new ball, walks off the back of the mound, rubs it up, and returns his right foot to the rubber. He winds and throws. High, ball three. Now three and one."

Melvin didn't want to walk. He loved this moment, but he knew it was his job to get on base, keep the rally alive, and let the next batter, Pete Warner, get to bat. *Don't be overanxious*, Melvin reminded himself. *Only swing if it's a good pitch.* And it was a good pitch. Looking for a strike, Smith threw a pitch right down the middle into Melvin's sweet spot. Melvin's eyes got big. He saw the ball, which wasn't moving that fast. He could drive it. Melvin swung, and the ball jumped off his bat into right center field. Did it have enough to get over the ten-foot wall? That was the deepest part of the field at 410 feet, and it took quite a hit to clear the wall. Everyone was looking at the ball and the outfielders. The Yankee players were out of their dugout, watching and waiting.

Dan described the action. "De Conto has already rounded second and will easily score the tying run if the ball is in play. It could be off the wall, Scott. The outfielders are going back, back…it's out of here. Oh, my goodness gracious, Melvin Klapper has done it again, folks. The Yankees win 4–3 on a home run by Klapper."

His teammates were all there at home plate, jumping up and down, waiting for Melvin, who seemed to be almost walking from third to home. This important game was in the Yankee win column. Some Red Sox players were watching, maybe out of disbelief. Smith had already left the field, head down, looking like he was about to throw his glove at someone or something.

Melvin was so proud that Winnie and Billy were here to share in this extraordinary moment. On his way to the dugout, he went over and hugged them both. "I have about an hour before I have to be back to get ready for the second game. Let's have something to eat."

Winnie was still clapping and smiling that big smile of his.

"Grandpa, Dad said I couldn't stay for the second game. Can you ask Mom?"

Winnie jumped in, "Melvin, I had to promise Grace that I'd bring Billy home after the first game. Otherwise, no dice."

"Okay, so let's have a quick snack together. Winnie, can you come back for the second game?"

"I have to check with Alva. Let's grab some food."

"Okay, let me shower and change. I'll meet you guys by the players parking lot in about fifteen minutes. We'll find a spot to sit and eat. I'm starving."

*****

Melvin was as glad to hug Billy as Billy was to hug the grandpa he was so proud of.

Melvin could see how well Billy and Winnie got along. Winnie was becoming like an uncle to Billy, and Melvin couldn't have been more happy to see the two of them together.

Melvin had brought out sandwiches, chips, and sodas from the locker room buffet table set up for the players in between games for Billy and Winnie as they sat at a picnic table outside the Yankee player entrance. Most of the players, exuberant with their win of the first game, just hung around taking it easy, getting mentally prepared for the second game of the day. It was exhausting but exhilarating for Melvin to have to play two games in one day. His hip and back were gradually but surely getting more painful, but Melvin would gladly do whatever Russ and the team asked of him. And as Pete quoted Joe Namath, "It doesn't hurt when you win."

CHAPTER 24

Sunday, August 14
Yankee Stadium

It was the second game of the day-night doubleheader. Pete Peterson was pitching for the Yankees, and Russ Tarnower, a savvy Red Sox veteran, was hurling for the visiting team. This game was worth two games in the standings. A win by the Yankees would get them to within ten games, while a loss would set them back to twelve games. So everyone knew the importance of this Sunday night game, covered nationally by ESPN.

Melvin was tired. Playing two games in one day was pushing him about as hard as he could possibly manage. The continuous play was taking its toll. His hip was bothering him as was an increasing pain in his lower back and side. Melvin took another two Aleve capsules, hoping they would get him through the game. He'd give Dr. Mendelsohn a call in the morning.

He looked for Winnie but didn't see him.

The game began right on time. Once again, the Red Sox jumped on the Yankee starter, scoring a run in the top of the first. It sent the message that the Sox were not about to roll over for the Yankees. Melvin hit a single to center in the bottom of the first but was stranded at second. He got another single in the fourth. Again, the Yankees could not capitalize on it. The game went into the bottom of the seventh with the Sox still ahead 1–0. Would the seventh inning stretch wake up the Yankee bats? The home crowd was pleading for a rally. There were so few hits that the game was moving along quickly. The Yanks had only four hits, all singles, two of which were by Melvin.

The Sox were not doing much better, but they had that one big run that could be enough to pull the game out.

In the home seventh, the first Yankee up singled sharply to left. Maybe Tarnower was tired after throwing eighty-two pitches. The second batter, attempting to sacrifice to get the tying run to second, laid down a perfect bunt between the pitcher and third base. The throw to first by Tarnower was late, and now the Yankees had two on with no outs.

Higgins decided to pinch hit with lefty Tony Tucker, a rookie who was showing promise. He seemed to like hitting when the pressure was on. On the first pitch, Tony hit a rocket right at the Boston first baseman, who speared it and tried to double up the runner at first, but he couldn't beat the runner to the bag. Still, only one out, and the crowd could sense that the Yankees were threatening. The next batter, Jay Jones, hit a lazy fly ball to center field, not deep enough for the Yankee runners to tag up.

Now it was Melvin's turn at bat. Only seven outs were left in the game for the Yankees. Down by a run. Tying run on second, go ahead, run on first. Two outs. The crowd rose to its feet. It was as if everyone in the stands felt that they were at bat. The Yankee players all moved to the top step of the dugout. Melvin had begun to relish these moments.

Announcer Dan Earling seemed as eager and as impassioned as everyone else. "It seems that every time the Yankees need a big hit, Melvin Klapper walks to home plate. After just thirty-six major league at bats, Klapper is currently hitting .361 with two home runs and seven runs batted in. Melvin already has two hits in this game, both singles. Klapper is taking his time, walking slowly and calmly up to the plate as he usually does. Pretty big moment here, Scott."

"Dan, is this another Melvin Klapper story about to unfold? Tarnower is just glaring at Melvin, but being glared at doesn't seem to matter much to Melvin. Maybe he's too old to be intimidated," said Scott, half-jokingly, half-seriously.

"I think the guy lives for these moments," said Dan. "I wouldn't want to be Tarnower right now. He knows Melvin can hit and that Melvin almost always comes through in these moments. This is a huge game for the Sox. Bigger for them than the Yankees. Being swept three games in two days could send the Sox into a slide. The Yankees, on the other hand, even if they drop this game, leave here knowing they're on a roll."

"Here we go," Dan continues. "Melvin steps in. Tarnower taking his time, being very deliberate, taking his right foot off the rubber, making Melvin wait."

Melvin knew it was a pitcher's tactic to throw off the batter's timing, but Melvin had already learned how to do the same to the pitcher. So Melvin stepped out of the batter's box. Home plate umpire Larry Fine clapped his hands and bellowed, "Today, gentlemen, while we're still young."

In response, Melvin turned to Fine and said, "Thank you, Larry."

Tarnower, still taking his time, nodded in agreement with his catcher, throwing a high inside fastball. Melvin couldn't get out of its way. The ball hit Melvin flush in the head, and he went down on his back. Melvin didn't move. His protective helmet, which blunted the force of the ball, was lying next to him. The Yankee bench went berserk and started charging the field. Then the Red Sox came out of their dugout. Both bullpens run all the way in from the outfield to the infield, where the umpires and coaches were doing their best to prevent the pushing and shoving into becoming an all-out brawl.

While this was going on, the Yankee manager and team doctor were examining Melvin, who was now on one knee, shaking his head and signaling that was all right.

Melvin stood up, still somewhat shaky on his feet like a prizefighter after landing on the canvas, gathered himself, and glared at Tarnower. After a moment or two, regaining his stability, Melvin started walking slowly but assuredly toward the pitcher. Tarnower was still on the mound, encircled by teammates protecting him from any Yankee looking to throw a punch.

Melvin was unafraid as he said "Excuse me" to just about every player he passed from both teams. There was no doubt that Melvin was headed to the mound, where Tarnower looked uncertain and concerned as to what was about to unfold. The players, having never before seen anything quite like this, didn't know what to make of it. Was Melvin looking to fight?

Finally, Melvin made his way through the mass of Yankee and Red Sox players and coaches. He approached Tarnower, who towered over Melvin but who was clearly confused as to why this old man was now coming at him.

About three feet away from Tarnower, with both teams now surrounding the two players, Melvin looked up at Tarnower and said, "Listen, son, I understand that you're just trying to brush me back—it's all part of the game—but please don't hit me with your fastball. It really hurts. Just think of me as your grandfather, okay?" And then Melvin shook hands with a stunned and speechless Tarnower, patted him on the arm, and walked away.

Umpire Larry Fine gave the players a moment to break up the scrum and then said, "Okay, everyone, just settle down. Klapper, you go to first. Bases loaded. Two outs. Play ball."

Everyone on the field, in the stands, and at home watching the game knew what Klapper had done. No player, coach, or umpire had ever seen anything quite like it before. His gesture had resolved the entire situation quickly and peacefully. People in the stands didn't hear what was said but saw Melvin and Tarnower shake hands.

The Red Sox manager, realizing that Tarnower, now embarrassed and dumbfounded, was no longer in a mental state to pitch, took his tall right-hander out of the game to a cacophony of boos. His day was definitely over. Melvin had given him a lot to think about.

A Red Sox relief pitcher, not entirely warned up or ready to pitch, came in and gave up a bases-loaded home run to Yankee catcher Glenn Worthington on a 3–2 count. Melvin was happy because he could now circle the bases slowly. Glenn almost caught up to Melvin, and when Melvin turned around, he saw Glenn, no speedster himself, smiling right back at him. The Red Sox were clearly shaken by what had occurred, while the Yankees were once again amazed and proud of Melvin Klapper.

Even Yankee owner Lang Carter, sitting in his suite, was wearing a smile of contentment. He leaned over to Gus and said, "That old guy is worth every penny."

The Yankees went on to score four more runs in the eighth, winning the game 8–1.

It had been quite the weekend.

The Yankee locker room was all over Melvin. Every player and coach went to hug him. They knew he had done something extraordinary. It was something no one had ever seen before. In all of baseball's nearly two-hundred-year history, this was probably the only time a hit batsman had gone to the mound and shook the hand of the pitcher who threw the ball.

Melvin couldn't understand what all of the hullabaloo was about. He had done what he thought was the right thing to do under the circumstances. Because Melvin didn't think the pitch was thrown at him intentionally to hurt him, he wasn't mad at Tarnower, although it was no picnic to be hit by a ball traveling ninety-five miles an hour. What mattered was that he Yankees had reduced the Red Sox lead to ten games.

Melvin's phone didn't stop ringing. There were already thirty-three text messages, and he hadn't showered yet. How had these people gotten his cell phone number? He had only given it to Grace, Chris, Billy, Winnie, Gus, Russ, and Pete.

He saw that Grace had called to see if he was okay. Billy had been allowed to stay up to see the game. Along with Chris and Grace, Billy was glued to the television. He started crying when his grandpa got hit with the ball. Seeing his grandfather on the ground upset and frightened Billy. But moments later, seeing Melvin shaking hands with the Boston pitcher with the crowd cheering reminded Billy how special his grandfather really was.

Winnie had seen the game at home from the fifth inning on after he and Alva returned from dinner out with friends. Winnie jumped out of his chair when Melvin got hit. His instinctive reaction was either to punch or arrest someone, but Winnie knew there was nothing he could do. When he saw Melvin get up, he breathed for what seemed like the first time in an hour. Initially, Winnie was puzzled by Melvin walking out to the pitcher, but then he knew something special was about to happen. He said to Alva, sitting there and knitting with no attention being paid to the TV, "Watch this, Alva."

"What am I looking at?"

"Something amazing is about to happen."

She looked up in time to see Melvin shake hands with Tarnower.

"And that's why I'm friends with Melvin Klapper," said Winnie.

Alva just sat and watched in silence, not quite appreciating the significance of the moment.

Although the "hot streak" of the Yankees did not go unnoticed, the lead story in every newspaper, on every channel, on every sports and talk show on radio, was the handshake. Melvin had unintentionally started a national discussion about sportsmanship. The picture of the handshake was everywhere. It was being discussed in schools at all levels. All teams in all sports of all ages were aware of what had happened on the field of a major league baseball game. A simple gesture by a simple man had changed the conversation of a country.

Melvin was now enormously popular and had become an incredibly important national figure, having transcended the world of baseball. Even players on opposing teams liked and admired him. In just a few short weeks, Melvin had become an idol to kids, their parents, and their grandparents. The Melvin phenomenon was everywhere. The Victor Coleman article was long forgotten. Or was it?

CHAPTER 25

Monday, August 15
Springfield

Finally, a day off. Melvin needed the rest badly. His left hip pain was getting more intense and occurring more often. He accepted this as simply a consequence of his playing and running more. The new pain he was feeling seemed to be in his lower back and side and was starting to bother him after dinner and then much of the night. Although he had lost five pounds since joining the Yankees, he was developing a bloated belly, something he had never before had.

Melvin called Dr. Mendelsohn's office at 8:30 a.m. and spoke with Helen.

"Helen, can I come in to see Dr. Mendelsohn? I'm not feeling too good. The team leaves first thing tomorrow for a long road trip, so I would appreciate it if you could see me today."

"Sure, Melvin," said Helen. "I'm confident that Dr. Mendelsohn will find time to see you. I'll speak with him and call you right back."

"Thanks, Helen."

Melvin sat in his easy chair, reading about Winston Churchill while waiting to hear back from Helen. After about an hour, he decided to watch television to keep occupied while waiting for a phone call. He turned to ESPN, a channel he hadn't even had on his TV a few weeks earlier, but Grace had purchased for him all of the sports channels that his cable provider carried. Melvin actually liked watching ESPN, except for some of the gratuitous shouting that seemed to be in style nowadays.

The usual morning show was showing the highlights from Sunday, and there was almost nonstop coverage of Melvin going out to shake hands with the pitcher who had hit him with a fastball.

The ESPN broadcaster, someone Melvin had never seen before, was discussing the Yankee surge, crediting Melvin for it but spending most of his time talking about the handshake. Melvin couldn't believe all the time and attention being devoted to something that didn't seem like that big a deal to him. It made him smile that such a small, momentary gesture could mean that much to so many people.

"It's really another unbelievable part of the Melvin Klapper story," said Otis Taylor. "The catch, the throw, the game-winning hits, turning around the Yankee season, the national interest in baseball that he has single-handedly created, the inspiration for millions of Americans, especially our elderly population, and now this truly incredible display of sportsmanship. This demonstration by Klapper could change the way sports are played in America and maybe the world. It could catch on with other teams, players, and coaches. On all levels, in all schools. It could be his legacy not only to baseball, not only to sports, but how we respond to adversity in our everyday lives."

His broadcasting partner was a woman named Connie Ferris, who had been a star basketball player at UConn a few years earlier. "Sorry to rain on this parade, Wally," said Connie, "but we just got this announcement coming across our feed issued moments ago by the baseball commissioner's office. I will read it out loud, as I'm seeing it myself for the first time."

"'Major League Baseball hereby advises Mr. Melvin Klapper and the New York Yankees that a physical examination, including all necessary and appropriate tests, will be required of Mr. Klapper. This process will be conducted by two highly qualified physicians chosen by the league, subject to approval by the Yankees and Mr. Klapper. These examinations will be conducted in New York City within the next two weeks. Whether the results will be disclosed publicly depends upon the findings and recommendations of the commissioner, following the report of the doctors. No further statements will be issued at this time.'

"Wow, what a blockbuster," concluded Connie.

"You're right," said Taylor. "That's a bombshell, maybe a game changer. I guess Victor Coleman's column demanding an investigation into Melvin Klapper resonated with the commissioner. This should be fascinating. Apparently, both the Yankee organization and Klapper already said they would cooperate, so it looks like they have no choice now. Do we have any information as to who the doctors will be?"

"No, no word on that yet," Ferris continued, "but they'll have to be the best in the profession. Hope they're not Red Sox fans," she chuckled. "So I suppose this will happen after the Yankees return on August 26, eleven days from now."

Picking right up on this breaking news, Otis said, "It will also be interesting to see how this announcement affects the team and most importantly how it affects Klapper. A very unique and dramatic moment in sports."

"Yes," added Ferris, "and maybe even the entire country. Let's stay tuned to find out who the doctors are, when exactly this will happen, how the team and Klapper respond, and whether we will ever get to know the results. We live in interesting times, my friend."

*****

Hearing this, Melvin turned ashen. He could barely move, although his mind was racing. He hadn't expected it so quickly or so publicly. He knew immediately what it meant. A physical exam had never been mentioned before. They had only been talking about testing for performance-enhancing drugs. This was now a very different situation and potentially a huge problem for him. There was no way that these doctors would miss finding his cancer, and then the whole world, including Billy and Grace, would hear the bad news before Melvin was prepared to tell them.

The phone rang. "Melvin, this is Helen. Dr. Mendelsohn said he can see you at noon. Does that work for you?"

"Yes, Helen, that's great. Thank you. See you at twelve." Melvin's mind was on fire. He wasn't expecting this very troubling turn of events and had no idea how best to handle it.

Instead of taking the bus this time to Dr. Mendelsohn's office, Melvin called an Uber driver as he had become accustomed to doing. With his new cell phone, texting, and Uber transportation, Melvin couldn't help but wonder if people being courteous to each other would keep up with the speed of technology. A police car and two officers were outside Melvin's house as they seemed to be all the time to make sure everything stayed calm and peaceful. Thankfully, their presence had kept the gawkers and sightseers to a minimum, restoring the quiet enjoyment Melvin and his neighbors had before Melvin became a Yankee.

Within a minute or two of Melvin arriving at Dr. Mendelsohn's office and without being asked to fill out any forms, Helen came out to greet Melvin with a polite smile and escort him into an examining room.

"Hi, Melvin, Dr. Mendelsohn will be right with you." Melvin liked that Helen's demeanor toward him never changed. Whether he was a star for the Yankees or simply a husband present in support of his wife, Helen treated him with the same respect. She knew he was dying but acted like she didn't because sympathy was not a cure. As Melvin reminded himself, *sympathy* was just a word in the dictionary between shit and syphilis. Getting him an immediate appointment was how Helen could best help Melvin.

"Thank you, Helen."

Looking around the room, Melvin wondered how many more times in his life he would be seeing Helen or Dr. Mendelsohn.

There came a knock at the door, and in stepped Dr. Mendelsohn, looking as somber and serious as always.

Extending his hand, Dr. Mendelsohn said, "I don't know how you're doing it, Melvin. Louise and I are watching Yankee games just to follow you. Frankly, I'm amazed that you are able to play at all, let alone at the extraordinary level of performance we're seeing."

"No one is more amazed than me, Doc."

"So Helen mentioned that you are in pain."

"I don't like whining, but my hip bothers me now that I'm running so much, and I'm pretty sure that's from where I was shot. But what's really bothering me is the lower back and side pain," Melvin added, rubbing his left side, "which is worse when I lie down. I also seem to be getting a big belly, although according to the scale I've lost five pounds in the last five weeks.

"Melvin, everything you're noticing is consistent with pancreatic cancer. You're starting to see signs that it's advancing. Signs such as fatigue, weight loss, swollen abdomen, back pain, and nausea. And yes, the backache is often worse lying down, at night, or after eating. What probably happened is that the cancer has spread to your liver or abdomen or both."

"So what do we do?"

"There's nothing much we can do. At this point, it's untreatable. The trouble with pancreatic cancer is that it's difficult to diagnose until it's too late because there are no early signs or symptoms. We can try chemo or radiation, which may prolong your life, but they do not provide a cure and can cause other problems, including increased weakness and discomfort. We can do a CT scan to check your organs, but there's very little that can be done to change the course of this miserable disease."

"So that's it? I just wait to die?"

"As I mentioned, we can try chemo to relieve your symptoms or a combination of chemo and radiation. It could buy you some time. But the answer at this point, I'm afraid, is palliative. The only surgical option is a long and difficult Whipple procedure, but it's often not successful. I'm not recommending it at this late juncture of your cancer."

"What's *palliative* mean?"

"It's a specialized form of medical care that focuses on providing relief from pain and other symptoms of a serious illness. It's a quality-of-life approach. We can do that here, or I can refer you to Dr. Arthur Andrews, a specialist in such care. Totally your call. It may make you feel better. It's something you should consider."

"Are there any meds you can prescribe to ease the pain?"

"Sure, I can prescribe an opioid, but it could interfere with your ability to play. If you want, we can start with a low dose of Tramadol once a day and see if it's effective. It should dull at least some of the pain and hopefully relieve anxiety. You can take Advil or Motrin with it if it helps. I'd like to do the least dosage possible so it doesn't interfere with your mental state or the quality of your performance. We can step it up if need be. We have stronger painkillers like Percocet or Dilaudid if necessary, but let's try to avoid them if we can—at least for now."

"Okay, Doc, whatever you say."

"Sorry you're going through this, Melvin. I want you to know I care and, if it means anything to you, so do millions of people across the country. I'm always here for you. Here's my home phone number and my cell. Call me anytime, and if Louise answers, she will probably gush all over you, so be ready. Here's the script. The pharmacy is just a few doors away, so go and fill it when you leave."

"Thank you, Doc."

"Call me if you need anything, Melvin."

Melvin didn't see Helen on his way out. He wanted to thank her, but she must have been with another patient, and Melvin wanted to get to the pharmacy, a place he had previously visited when Martha was sick. On his way there, he passed by an optometry office next to the pharmacy that still had a sign in the window that read, "If you don't see what you're looking for, you've come to the right place." That always tickled Melvin and made him smile, something he needed badly on this day of worsening news.

While waiting for his prescription to be filled, his cell phone buzzed. It was Gus.

"Hey, Melvin, you heard the news, right?"

"Yes, Gus, I did."

"The commissioner's office called us with the names of three docs they suggested. We can agree to any two. Do you want to know who they are?"

"Not really. Doesn't make a difference to me. What do you suggest?"

"We checked them all out. All eminent, all seem honorable with no ax to grind. So okay with you if we go ahead picking two of them?"

"Sure, that's fine. Do I have to do anything?"

"No, just show up. I'll get back to you with the date. Probably the twenty-sixth or twenty-seventh, when you get back from the road trip. Sounds like it will be conducted at New York-Presbyterian Hospital. I'll go with you if you want."

"Thanks, Gus, let me think about it." Melvin had learned to both like and admire Gus, who had a tough job to do as general manager but seemed to have a soft spot for Melvin. Gus always seemed to go out of his way to help Melvin.

After getting his prescription filled and giving thought to his conversation with Gus, Melvin called Winnie.

"Winnie, I need some advice. You around?"

"Sure, Melvin. I'm at the bank now, but my shift ends at six. Where do you want to meet?"

"Can you come over?"

"I'll be to you around seven. Should I bring in some pizza?"

"Yes, and some ice cream if possible. Pistachio or mint chocolate chip."

"Done and done."

Melvin now had his new pills as prescribed by Dr. Mendelsohn but decided not to take any unless and until really necessary. Melvin thought he should be careful about not getting addicted, and then he smiled to himself, knowing that was not the real problem he was confronting.

Melvin had not sat on his porch in a long time, but today, he did. He grabbed a glass of cold water from the tap and just sat in a rocking chair next to Martha's rocking chair, thinking about the day and how best to go forward. He could barely wait to talk it over with Winnie and get his input.

Seeing Melvin sitting on the porch, one of the uniformed police officers walked to the front gate and said, "Hey, Melvin, how you doing?"

"Pretty good, Officer, how about you?"

"You boys gonna pull this out?"

"We're sure gonna try. You a Yankee fan?"

"Only my whole life and my whole family for as far back as we know. We're BICs."

"You're what?"

"Bronx Irish Catholic. BICs. BICs are always Yankee fans."

"Good to know. What's your name?"

"Tim Finnerty."

"Tim, I feel better knowing you're here. Thanks."

"Melvin, just keep playing hard. Don't let the bullshit throw you off course. They're just trying to upset and distract you."

"Thanks, Tim."

"I better get back to my station before the commander comes by. Good luck, Melvin. We're pulling for you."

While waiting for Winnie, Melvin saw Bart on his way coming toward Melvin's house. Melvin and Bart hadn't seen each other in weeks. Bart pulled up to the gate and jumped off his bike. Officer Finnerty was on top of Bart in a heartbeat.

Bart said, "Hey, man, we're friends. I just stopped to say hello."

"It's okay, Tim. He's a local boy."

"Can I come up to the porch?" asked Bart.

"Of course," said Melvin, waving Bart in.

Bart shook hands with Melvin, more firmly than the last time. "How's it going, Mr. Klapper?"

"Bart, I'm really more interested in how it's going with you."

"Great. I love my job at Wilson's. They treat me real nice, and they said I can work as many hours a day as I want plus weekends. I'm getting along with everyone. Just so you know, it seems all we talk about is you. I told them we're friends and that I've been in your house. Mom got a full-time job at the frame store on Main, so between the two of us, we're doing okay."

"Great. That's what I was hoping to hear. Keep up the good work, son."

Melvin saw Winnie pulling up in his Toyota SUV. There was now a "local traffic only" sign at the top of Melvin's block. Whether it actually discouraged anyone was unknown, but it made the residents living there feel better. Being a former police officer, Winnie knew the proper procedure: Slow down, roll into a stop, hands visible, lower the window, and check in with the cops first. After a minute or so, the cop looked up at Melvin, who gave a thumbs-up sign. Winnie was then told to park right by the house.

When Winnie came toward the porch, Bart had no idea who this big black man was or what was going on. He kept glancing between Winnie and Melvin to try to get a fix if this guy was friend or foe. Melvin stood up to greet Winnie, who was carrying a big pizza box and a bag presumably filled with ice cream. They hugged, but it was more like a chest bump because Winnie's arms were occupied. Melvin introduced Winnie to Bart, who was awkwardly unsure how to act in this situation. Melvin thanked Bart for stopping by.

"Bart, keep me posted on your progress. Remember, I only want to hear good things about you. The nicer you are to everyone, the nicer they'll be to you."

"Thanks, Mr. Klapper. Nice to meet you, Mr. Winfield."

"Take care, Bart," said Winnie.

"C'mon, Winnie. Let's go inside," said Melvin. "I have a lot to tell you."

CHAPTER 26

Monday, August 15
Springfield

Melvin set the table, while Winnie put the ice cream in the freezer.

It didn't take long before Winnie asked Melvin, "So what's with this medical exam the league ordered?"

"That's what I want to talk to you about. I have some very personal stuff to tell you. I need to do this so you can give me advice as to how best to handle what's going on."

"Wow, sounds serious. Is it serious?"

"Yes, I'm afraid so."

"Okay, lay it on me."

"I was expecting a test for performance-enhancing drugs, which I was not worried about, but now it seems the commissioner has ordered a full physical exam, which is very different."

"Waddaya mean?"

"I'm concerned with what the doctors will find."

"What will they find?"

"First of all, I got wounded back in Vietnam, and it causes me some pain and a slight limp."

"That's not a big deal. I noticed your limp the first day I met you. If anything, it makes what you've been doing all the more amazing. That's what you're worried about?"

"No. There's more."

"What more?"

"I have cancer."

"What kind of cancer?"

"The terminal kind."

"Hold on. What?" said Winnie as he stopped eating.

"Pancreatic cancer, stage 4."

"What exactly does that mean?"

"According to my oncologist, a few months at most."

The conversation hit a long pause. Winnie was digesting what he had just heard, while Melvin stared at him, waiting for a response.

Finally, Winnie spoke. "Wait a damn second. How could that be possible? How can you be playing major league baseball if you're dying?"

"Beats me, but here's my problem. I haven't told anyone. You're the first to know."

"What about Grace?"

"Nope. No one. I learned a long time ago not to talk about my problems. Eighty percent of the people who hear them don't care, and the other twenty percent are glad it's not them. So I keep my mouth shut."

"Does the team know?"

"No, and my contract has a clause requiring that I tell them of any significant changes in my mental or physical condition."

"Holy shit, Melvin. This is crazy. Way more serious than I was expecting. I thought you were going to tell me you had a twenty-year-old girlfriend or were caught shoplifting a quart of pistachio ice cream."

"I only wish. Winnie, I'm in a big mess and feel like I've been dishonest with everyone. So what do I do?"

"I need to think on this for a few minutes. Let's take a break." Winnie got up from the table and went outside, where it was starting to turn a dusky red. Melvin remained at the table, still waiting to take his first bite of dinner.

Winnie had been trained in the police academy that in tough situations a good officer had to scrutinize, analyze, prioritize. After about twenty minutes, Winnie came back into the house and in his booming voice said, "Okay, here's my advice. Ready?"

"Ready."

Winnie, now pacing around the kitchen, hand stroking the top of his shaved head, said, "Okay, first things first. You have to assume that everything will come out. There are no secrets anymore, and nothing is confidential. Either the commissioner will disclose it, or it will be leaked by someone somehow. So based on that premise, the first person you have to tell is Grace. No question about it. That will lead to a discussion as to whether Chris and Billy need to know. But since they're going to probably find out anyway, you might as well tell them up front. It would be far worse if they hear it from someone else or on the TV or at school. You, not Grace or Chris, have to tell Billy. Straight up, man to man. He's a smart kid. Treat him that way. It's going to be emotional and difficult for all of you. But absolutely, you gotta do it. The sooner the better so they have time to digest the news and get to the other side of it.

Looking at Winnie, Melvin sat attentively without moving a muscle. He knew there was more. Winnie continued to pace back and forth, rubbing his head and neck. Winnie was clearly upset but doing his best to work through the dilemma confronting Melvin. Melvin waited.

"Second, you should ask to meet with Carter and that guy Gus."

"The owner and general manager?"

"Right. You gotta prepare them for the doctor's report. Hopefully get them on board supporting you. If it doesn't affect the quality of your play, they should back you up. You'll probably find out right away if they have the backbone to do the right thing here, but be prepared for anything from firing you on the spot to suing you to publicly attacking you in an attempt to distance themselves from you. Now if that goes okay, you have to tell Higgins and ask permission to address your teammates. This is tough stuff, Melvin, but it is what it is. Get it all out before the report comes out. And let the docs know right away so they see how straight you are with them."

Melvin was trying his best to absorb and assimilate it all. He knew what Winnie was saying made perfect sense. It was the right way, maybe the only way, to deal with this terrible situation. Play it straight. It was not Melvin's way to lie or mislead. As he was taught growing up, tell the truth, take responsibility, live with the consequences. Thank goodness for Winnie to remind him of what he already knew.

"Do we go public with it before the exam?" asked Melvin.

"Hmm, I wouldn't. Let the doctors' report and then the commissioner's report tell your story. People will only love you that much more than before. Coleman and the Red Sox will rue the day they demanded an investigation of Melvin Klapper."

"Winnie, a couple more questions."

"Shoot."

"Would you come with me to the doc's?"

"Me? You sure you want me to come?"

"Yes. I'll feel better if you're with me."

"I'd be honored, Melvin. Let me see if I need to trade shifts with some of the guys at the bank. Should be able to. I need to know the date and the time."

"Okay, as soon as I know it. Probably the twenty-sixth or twenty-seventh, when we return from our road trip, which begins tomorrow. So my next question, more of a request really, is would you mind being my spokesperson?"

"Huh? What does that mean?"

"Issuing statements on my behalf as needed. For example, I need a statement in response to all the letters and phone calls I'm getting that want me to do ads, sponsorships, media appearances, endorsements, stuff like that."

"What would I say?"

"Just that we'll get to responding to everyone at the end of the season but not before. Nothing at this time, as I'm dedicating myself full-time to playing baseball."

"Okay. You come up with the statement you want me to say, and I will read it on your behalf. But wouldn't the team press person be better at this than you or me? I don't know anything about the media."

"No, you're the best person I know to do this. I trust you."

"Okay, if that's what you want. Now tell me more about the cancer. Are you in pain? Are you being treated? Aren't you tired? How can you still play?"

Melvin and Winnie talked for another two hours. Winnie asked a ton of questions, all of which Melvin fully and honestly answered to the best of his ability. Both men were emotionally if not physically drained.

Winnie's cell phone rang. It was an angry Alva. "Where the heck are you, Winnie? It's nearly ten o'clock."

"Alva, honey, I'm on my way. It's been a crazy night. I'll tell you more later."

"Okay, just get home."

"On my way." He ended the call and turned to Melvin. "Melvin, can I tell Alva? I think I need to if you want me to be able to do the things you've asked of me. She needs to know what I'm doing and why."

"Okay. As long as it's only Alva."

"Alva is like the CIA. She doesn't tell anybody anything. So no worries on that front. Okay, so we have our signals straight? Let's talk as often as possible when you're on the road. We need to stay on the same page."

Melvin hugged Winnie and said, "I can't thank you enough, Winnie."

"Yeah, yeah, yeah. Get some sleep, Melvin."

Sitting at the dinette table looking at Martha, Melvin repeatedly reviewed the advice given to him by Winnie—step by step in the exact order laid out by Winnie. Melvin knew it would be difficult and uncomfortable having these conversations, especially with Grace and Billy, but he accepted the reality that at this point he no longer had a choice—starting tomorrow.

CHAPTER 27

Tuesday, August 16
Springfield

Melvin had not slept well, anticipating the various conversations he would be having in the next twenty-four or so hours. Going over them in his mind all night, he knew it was going to be tough on him and those he cared about, especially Billy. But he was going to stick to the plan set out by Winnie. At this point, he really had no choice. The last thing in the world that Melvin wanted to do was upset or to disappoint Billy.

At 7:45 a.m., Melvin placed a call to General Manager Gus Christianson. Melvin knew that Gus came in early. Because his secretary did not come in until about 8:30 a.m., Gus answered the phone.

"Gus Christianson."

"Good morning, Gus. It's Melvin Klapper."

"Hey, Melvin, how're you doing?"

"Gus, would it be possible to come see you this morning?"

"Aren't you supposed to be on the road with the team?"

"Yes, but I need a day here in New York."

"Anything wrong?"

"Probably best to discuss it in person. And if Mr. Carter is in town, I'd like it if he could join us."

"Now you've got me worried. I hope you're not changing your mind about being examined."

"No, not at all. But I think we need to discuss it."

"Okay, let me reach out to Lang, but let's say my office at eleven."

"Thanks, Gus. I'll see you then."

After getting off the phone, Melvin immediately called Grace, who was already at school. So Melvin left a message asking if he could come over around 4:00 p.m.

About 9:00 a.m., Melvin received a call from Dr. Mendelsohn. It was unusual for Dr. Mendelsohn himself to call directly rather than have his office get the patient on the phone first.

"Melvin, it's Stan Mendelsohn. How are you doing?"

And to be using his first name, no less, something Melvin had never heard before.

"Okay, Doc. I think the day off yesterday helped. I needed the rest."

"Did you start the Tramadol?"

"No, not yet. I was hoping not to need it. I'm a little scared of it."

"I understand, but it works better if you take it before the pain sets in. So don't wait until you're really hurting."

"Thanks, Doc."

"Melvin, one more thing. Now that you're going to be examined by the league doctors, I expect a call from them asking questions about you. Do I have your permission to speak with them?"

"Sure, Doc, that's fine. I'm not going to hide anything. It's all going to come out sooner or later, one way or another, so we might as well do it right."

"Thanks, Melvin. I knew you would say that, but I had to check with you before talking to them. I'll keep you posted. Call me if you need anything."

"Thanks, Doc, I will."

Grace must have been on a break because she returned Melvin's call at 9:55 a.m.

"What's up, Dad?"

"Hi, Grace. I was hoping to speak with you later today. Does 4:00 p.m. work for you?"

"Sure. We'll all be home by then."

"I was hoping for a few private minutes with you first. Is that doable at the house?"

"Is everything all right, Dad?"

"Yep," Melvin fibbed, knowing that this was neither the time nor the place to have such a serious conversation, but Grace knew that her father's voice was not quite right.

"We just need a few minutes," said Melvin.

"Okay, we can sit out back while Chris helps Billy with his homework."

"Great, sweetheart, see you later." The call did not go as smoothly as Melvin had hoped. Grace was suspicious.

Melvin made his way to Gus's office by 10:45 a.m. and was surprised yet relieved to see Lang there. It would be easier to have Lang included in the conversation because at the end of the day, it would be Lang, not Gus, who would make any significant decision regarding Melvin.

"Good morning, Melvin," said Lang Carter, standing and not smiling. Lang did not know what prompted this urgent meeting and was obviously uncomfortable with the situation, although he maintained his customary air of courtesy.

"Good morning, Mr. Carter. Good morning, Gus."

"Have a seat, Melvin. Tell us what's on your mind," said Lang, who from experience knew how to be prepared for difficult conversations, including whatever Melvin was going to tell them.

"Thank you," said Melvin. "First, I apologize for bothering you gentlemen. I know how busy you both are. Second, I want to thank you both for how you've treated me these past six or so weeks. It's a dream come true, and I couldn't ask for better people to work for than the two of you."

"Sounds ominous," said Lang. "I hope you're not quitting on us."

"Oh no. You may fire me, but I'm not quitting," said Melvin. He had certainly gotten their attention. The ball was squarely in his court.

"Okay, so where to begin? As Gus and I discussed earlier this morning, I'm still on board with being examined by the league doctors. But I felt you should know what I expect will come out as a result of these examinations and blood tests."

Lang and Gus offered no response, not knowing what Melvin was about to tell them.

Melvin continued. "I have pancreatic cancer, stage four, and I've been told by my doctor that I could be looking at a couple of months."

Gus, reacting uncharacteristically, blurted out, "You're dying?"

"Now hold on, Gus," said Lang, raising a hand. "Melvin, how long have you known this?"

"I found out a day before I came to the game with Billy, but I was feeling fine, and frankly, I don't know if I actually believed what I was being told. It has gotten worse, so I don't know how fast it will go or how it will affect my play."

"How have you managed to play so well these past six weeks?" asked a confused Gus.

"I don't know. I can't explain it to you or myself or my doctor."

"Can you still play?" asked Lang.

"Yes, I think so. I certainly want to."

"What do you want us to do?" asked Gus, clearly flustered and unsure where the conversation was headed.

"Nothing, I guess. I just wanted you to hear it from me first. I intend to disclose it up front to the league docs if they ask. If they don't ask, I expect they will discover it on their own."

"Is there anything else you think we should know?" asked Lang.

"No. That's it."

"Who else knows about this?" continued Lang, thoughtful and composed.

"My regular doctor, Roland Benedict, my oncologist, Stanley Mendelsohn, and my friend Winnie, whom you've met. That's it. I plan on telling my daughter and her family later today. With your permission, I'd like to join the team in Baltimore tomorrow to tell Russ and then the team—if it's okay with him."

"This obviously comes as quite a shock," said Lang as he slowly took a seat. Melvin could tell that Lang was distressed by the sudden and unexpected news, probably for a myriad of reasons. Melvin and Gus knew that Lang was a careful listener, someone who would think quickly and intelligently about what had been disclosed and then succinctly issue the team's position.

No one spoke until Lang looked at Melvin and said, "The most important thing here, Melvin, is your health. Would you like to see pancreatic cancer specialists at Memorial? I can get you in there tomorrow."

Melvin's confidence and trust in Lang Carter had been reaffirmed. "Thank you, Lang. Can we discuss it again after the team returns to New York from the road trip? I really don't want to miss any more games."

"Melvin," said Lang, "you're an amazing guy, and I don't say this because of how you somehow manage to hit a baseball. The entire Yankee organization has great affection and admiration for you. In just a few short weeks, you have become a part of our family. So on behalf of all of us here, thank you for coming in this morning. I'm sure it wasn't easy. We'd like to help you if we can and if you want, but that's of course your call. Would you mind if we reached out to Dr. Mendelsohn just to hear what he has to say?"

"Sure, I understand. That would be okay with me. As long as it's you or Gus making the call."

Standing up to shake hands with Melvin, Lang said, "Melvin, you have our full support." Gus nodded, acknowledging his role in following up on Lang's directive.

"By the way," added Gus, who following Lang's cue had recovered his composure, "your appointment with the league docs is at 2:00 p.m. on the twenty-seventh with doctors Martin Lewis and Jack Hoffstein. Both highly regarded. We've been told that the commissioner will have their report within a week and that the commissioner will share his decision with us and then the public a few days after that. So this process will be concluded rather quickly. Would you like me to go with you on Saturday?"

Melvin was sincerely touched. "No, but thanks, Gus. I've taken enough of your time."

Gus continued, "Your flight to Baltimore is at 10:00 a.m. tomorrow. Let us know at every step of the way how things are going."

"Thank you both. I will."

Melvin left as quietly and respectfully as he had entered.

*****

Melvin was starting to tire more often and more quickly. It was only noon, but Melvin felt like a nap was in order. He still had four hours before seeing Grace. After eating half of a two-day-old egg salad sandwich he had brought from home, Melvin found a quiet spot in the empty Yankee locker room to stretch out and grab a snooze.

Waking up a few minutes past 2:30 p.m., Melvin called an Uber to go to Grace's house. When he got there, no one was home yet, so Melvin sat in one of the chaise lounges in the backyard. Amos, fenced in the backyard, wagged his tail and came running over.

"Hi, boy," said Melvin as he scratched Amos around his neck and ears. "This is not going to be easy."

He loved looking at the house where Grace lived, remembering how much she had accomplished in her life, how successful a mother and wife she was, and what a great daughter she had been. Melvin was glad she had taken after Martha. Melvin felt blessed to have had these two extraordinary women in his life.

"Hi, Grandpa," shouted Billy, running toward Melvin after exiting the sliding glass door in the kitchen. Engrossed in his thoughts about the upcoming conversations, Melvin had not heard them arrive home.

"Hey, my favorite grandson."

"Your only grandson," said Billy, knowing Melvin's joke.

Melvin and Billy hugged like they always did, but Melvin wondered if he was starting to hold on too long. How many more hugs with Billy would he have?

"Hey, Melvin," Chris said from the deck off the kitchen.

Not much affection there, thought Melvin. *He won't miss me*.

"Hey, Chris, how ya doing?" said Melvin, trying to be upbeat.

"Aren't you supposed to be on the road? Isn't there a game tonight in Baltimore?"

"Yes to both questions," replied Melvin, "but I needed a personal day in New York. I'll be in Baltimore tomorrow morning."

"Okay, good luck on this road trip. We need a few wins. C'mon, Billy. Homework time."

"How long will you be here, Grandpa?"

"About an hour or so."

"Can you stay for dinner?"

"I'll ask your mother. I see her pulling up now."

"Stay, Grandpa. We're hanging meatballs and spaghetti. And we have pistachio ice cream in the freezer."

"Thanks, Billy. Now go do your homework."

"Hi, Dad," said Grace as she walked down the deck stairs toward where Melvin was sitting.

They kissed and hugged. "Must be pretty important for you to miss a game. What's up?"

Melvin did not want to beat around the bush. He needed to say it straight out.

"Grace, it's not easy for me to tell you this, but I've been diagnosed with cancer."

"Cancer? Oh no, not like Mom all over again." Grace began crying. All the painful memories of her mother's suffering flooded her heart and her brain. The nightmare had returned.

Melvin had not anticipated that response.

He quickly realized how traumatized Grace must have been watching her mother endure her last few months before finally succumbing. It had remained very present in her mind.

"I'm sorry, Grace," said Melvin as he put his hand on her shoulder.

"How long have you known?"

"Just recently," Melvin responded, not wanting to get into details as to why he hadn't told her sooner.

"How serious?"

"Unfortunately, it's serious."

"Are you going to tell me more or do I have to keep asking questions?" Grace was clearly distraught.

"Pancreatic, stage four."

Grace burst out crying. "Goddamn it, Dad. I'm going to lose you now too?"

Melvin was silent.

Through her tears, she said, "Billy is going to be scared and upset like you can't believe."

"I know, but what can I do? It's the hand I've been dealt. I'll do the best I can do."

"Is there anything that can be done?"

"Apparently not. It sounds like radiation is out because it looks like it's spread, and I don't want to do chemo."

"Oh, Dad, this is horrible, absolutely horrible. Is there anything we can do for you?"

"Just be here for me."

Grace gave Melvin a long embrace, crying the entire time and making Melvin feel the worst he'd felt since Martha passed.

"I need to tell Billy myself," said Melvin.

"He's going to be devastated," responded Grace.

"Can I stay for dinner and then talk about it afterward?"

"If that's the way you want to do it. Let me tell Chris before dinner."

"Okay. Maybe Billy can take a break from homework to have a catch with me while you tell Chris."

"Right." Grace went to the porch steps, trying to stop her tears.

Five minutes later, Billy came running out with his glove and a ball. "Grandpa, you ready?"

"You bet, Billy. Let's see your best throw."

After a few tosses, Melvin looked up at the house. Through the kitchen window, he could see Grace talking and sobbing while Chris listened.

After about ten minutes, Chris came out onto the deck, trotted down the steps, and strolled toward Melvin, who just stood there until Chris said got closer.

"I'm so sorry, Melvin." For the first time since Billy was born, Melvin and Chris had a hug that felt authentic and sincere.

"Can I hug too?" yelled Billy, running toward Melvin and Chris.

"Come on in here. We'll all hug," said Melvin.

Billy squeezed both his dad and his grandpa.

Melvin thought he saw a tear in Chris's eye. If Chris was looking, he might have seen a tear in Melvin's. He knew that the most difficult and emotional conversation was yet to happen.

CHAPTER 28

Tuesday, August 16
Springfield

"Hey, Billy, how 'bout you and me take Amos for a walk around the block?"

"Sure, Grandpa. I'll put his leash on."

"Dinner in thirty minutes, boys," said Grace out the sliding glass door, trying to sound like her usual cheerful self.

"We'll be back soon. Just going around the block with Amos," Melvin said to Grace, who was struggling to maintain her composure.

As they were walking away from the house, Melvin said to Billy, "I have something to tell you. It's not good news, but I think you're old enough and smart enough to understand. I figure the best way to tell you is to tell you the truth, straight up, man to man. And then if you have questions, I'll answer them all as best as I can. Okay?"

"You're not on the Yankees anymore?"

"No, I'm still on the Yankees," said Melvin, laughing. "I leave for Baltimore tomorrow, and you can watch the game on

TV." After a slight pause, Melvin continued, "That's not it. Billy, have you ever heard the word *cancer*?"

Billy thought for a while and then said, "Don't people die from cancer?"

"They can, yes. But a lot of people don't. It depends on how sick you get."

"How sick are you, Grandpa?" asked the very perceptive ten-year-old. Melvin was once again reminded how sharp and astute this kid was.

"Pretty sick, Billy."

"Why?"

"I don't have an answer for that. It's no one's fault. It just happened. Remember I'm almost seventy-five, which is a ripe old age."

"Are you going to die?"

"Not today, not tomorrow, but probably someday in the future. I just wanted you to hear it from me first before you heard about it on TV or at school. There's nothing to worry about. I'm actually feeling pretty good."

"So I'll never see you again if you die?"

"Not physically like today, but you will see me in your heart and in your mind. You'll have all these memories of me. And you'll be able to tell me stuff just like I do with Grandma Martha. In the meantime, let's just enjoy every day and have as much fun as possible."

"Will you see me?"

"I hope so. I'm certainly going to try. Remember, you'll have your mom and dad to take good care of you."

Billy took his time to understand the answers to his questions. After a while, he asked, "Do Mom and Dad know?"

"I just told Mom, and she told your dad."

"Is that why you were hugging?"

Before Melvin could answer, Billy stopped walking and started to cry in a way that Melvin couldn't recall seeing Billy do before. Melvin took Amos's leash and put his arms around Billy. Then a wailing Billy fell into Melvin. It broke Melvin's heart to see his grandson cry, especially when he was the cause of it. Amos stood close by, sensing the sadness of the moment.

"It's okay to be upset, Billy. I know how much you love me, and you know how much I love you. It's natural that we would both be sad."

Melvin and Billy started to walk again. No words were spoken, but Billy grabbed onto Melvin's hand. Melvin could hear the wheels turning in Billy's very orderly mind.

Then Melvin said, "I'm trying very hard not to think about it because I need to focus on playing baseball and winning games. Right now for me, it's all about the New York Yankees and my contribution to the team."

"Grandpa, are you going to be able to play?"

"I think so. I'm certainly going to try. Are you going to watch me?"

"Yep. Every game."

"That's my boy. You're the best grandson in the whole world, Billy."

They were now back at the house. Walking back in, Billy ran to hug his mother, who was quietly sobbing.

"Let's sit down and have some dinner, boys," said Grace after a moment.

Billy loved his mom's meatballs but didn't eat any that night.

"Is it something we can talk about?" asked Chris.

"Absolutely," said Melvin, "absolutely. Nothing to shy away from. We're family. We can discuss anything."

Chris was ready. "What will happen with the league doctors? What's the latest on that?"

Melvin liked that Chris was asking questions, hoping that was a sign of sincere interest and concern—if not for himself then at least for Grace and Billy. Maybe this would help Grace and Billy cope with a difficult situation. They needed Chris to step up. Melvin hoped that was what he was doing.

"I'm due to be examined on Saturday, the twenty-seventh, at New York-Presbyterian Hospital. I plan on telling those docs the truth, which I assume they would find out anyway."

Chris replied, "Sorry to be blunt, Melvin, but won't the Yankees fire you?"

"You never know, but I don't think so. And if they do, they do. It's been a great six weeks, and no one can ever take this away from us."

"Good for you. You always have a positive outlook no matter what's going on," said Chris, shaking his head as if wishing he too could be that way.

Grace, who had not said much since learning her dad was dying, said, "Dad, we love you and will do anything we can to help."

"I know that, sweetheart. I couldn't ask for a better family. I love all of you. Okay, it's time for me to get my beauty sleep. I have an early morning flight to Baltimore. I expect to be in the lineup tomorrow."

"Would you like me to go to the hospital with you that Saturday?" offered Grace.

"No. Winnie will be with me. He's such a terrific guy."

"He really is," Grace agreed.

"I love Winnie," added Billy.

"That's great because I know he loves you too. Okay, guys. Wish me luck on the road trip. See you when I get back. Billy, make sure to root for me every game, okay?"

"I will, Grandpa. I promise."

"Okay, Billy, here's one for you. Do you have your thinking cap on?"

"You bet, Grandpa."

"Two baseball teams played a game. One team won, but no man reached base. How could that be?"

Grace smiled, knowing the answer while giving Billy time to work on it.

"What's the answer, Grandpa?"

"They were both women's teams. Gotcha."

"Aw. I should have figured that one out."

"Okay, big hugs all around now." As soon as Melvin had hugged Billy, the boy ran upstairs to his room and closed his door.

Melvin then held his loving daughter with an embrace that lasted longer than usual, with Grace quietly weeping.

"C'mon, Melvin. I'll drive you home," said Chris.

"Thanks, Chris, that would be great."

In the car, Melvin kept the conversation going with light banter, mostly describing what it was like to be in the locker room without giving away any secrets.

"Melvin, how have you been able to do all this with stage four pancreatic cancer?"

"I don't really know, but I'll do it for as long as I can. It's as if someone is watching over me. It's all going to work out just fine. I can feel it in my bones."

They had reached Melvin's house. Officer Finnerty was on tonight. As Melvin left the car, he said, "Good night, Chris, thanks for the ride. Listen, promise me you'll take good care of Grace and Billy so that I have nothing to worry about. Okay?"

"Melvin, I love Grace and Billy. I may not always show it, but they are my life."

Melvin smiled, closed the car door, waved to Officer Finnerty, and walked into a house that was still unlocked.

*****

It had been quite the day for Melvin. His early morning call with Gus, his meeting with Yankee owner Lang Carter, telling Grace, and then the most difficult part of the entire day—having to tell Billy. That conversation actually made Melvin's heart ache. Melvin was understandably exhausted but not too tired for a few spoonfuls of pistachio ice cream.

CHAPTER 29

Wednesday, August 17
Baltimore, Maryland

Up and raring to go by 7am, Melvin called for an Uber ride to LaGuardia Airport. He boarded a first-class seat for the Baltimore flight, which had been arranged for him by Gus's office. The flight gave Melvin some quiet time to reflect upon recent events and plan how he was going to approach his teammates. Before long, the plane landed at Baltimore/Washington International Airport. A car service, provided by the Yankees, took Melvin to the Convention Center Hilton, which was located across the street from Oriole Park at Camden Yards, where the Yankees were to play the Orioles at 7:05 p.m.

Fans were already beginning to congregate on Eutaw Street, where brass baseballs were embedded into the sidewalk, marking the spot where long home runs cleared the right field wall and landed on the street. A bronze statue of Babe Ruth stood guard outside the ballpark. Melvin found this curious since the Babe's best years were with the Yankees. Loving the Babe, Melvin paid his respects by patting the statue several times, hoping for good luck. He waited for just a second to see if the Babe would wink back, but he didn't. Melvin needed some time to unpack, get to the ballpark, talk with Russ who would be in his office all day, and then if given clearance, talk to the players when they came in around four or five.

Using his Yankee identification card, Melvin checked in at the hotel and decided to leave his bags with the front desk as he was anxious to meet with Russ. Melvin wondered if his manager already knew. It wouldn't be surprising or wrong if Gus had informed him of what was going on with Melvin, but he hoped they would have left it up to him to inform his manager. Melvin knew that Higgins and the team had been told that Melvin needed a personal day as do all the players from time to time. And since the Yanks had beaten the Orioles 7–2, the night before, his absence would not be an issue.

As usual, Higgins's door was open. Russ believed in an open-door policy, wanting to make players feel that they had access to him. Melvin looked in, saw Russ at his desk, knocked twice, and took one step in.

"Hi, Russ, got a minute?"

"Sure, Melvin. We missed you last night."

"Well, scoring seven runs you didn't," Melvin said. Higgins smiled.

"Can I close the door, Russ?"

"Sure, Melvin. C'mon in, sit and relax."

"Russ, I know your time is valuable, so rather than drag it out, I'm just going to come out with it. I've been told by my doctor that I have cancer and that it's pretty far advanced. The only reason I'm telling you this is because it's definitely gonna come out when the league docs examine me and run their tests. And I didn't want you caught short."

"Jeez, Melvin, I don't know what to say. I'm speechless. Whenever I saw you tired, I thought it was just an age thing. Are you still able to play?"

"Absolutely, Russ. I can't wait to play tonight if you have me in the lineup."

"Oh, you're in all right. Batting third in right field."

"I was hoping you'd say that. Thanks, Russ."

"Just so you know, I met with Gus and Lang yesterday. That's why I stayed back in New York, to tell them and my family. It was an awful day."

"What did Gus and Lang say?"

"Oh, they were great. Lang offered to help me get doctors that specialize in cancer. Both said I had their full support."

"I'm not surprised," said Russ. "Lang is a stand-up guy when the chips are down. And knowing Gus, he probably cried when you left the room. How did your grandson handle it? I know you two are close."

"He was quiet, asked his usual insightful questions, and then cried. We'll have to talk about it again when I get back off the road trip."

"You know Melvin, I had a cousin who was diagnosed with cancer, and he was told it was hopeless. That was thirty years ago, and he's still selling cars in Cleveland."

"Thanks. As we used to say in Vietnam, let's hope for the best and prepare for the worst."

"Do you want me to tell the coaches and the players?"

"I would appreciate it if you would tell the coaching staff, but let me tell my teammates."

"Sure. That makes sense. I have our coaches' meeting at four. You can tell the players either before or after the game."

"I'm thinking before because they like to get out once the game is over. It'll only take five minutes. Okay with you?"

"Sure, that's fine. I'd like to be in that meeting, okay?"

"Sure, Russ."

Even though it was only 3:00 p.m., Melvin changed into the uniform he so loved to wear and went onto the field. What was once rail yards was now a beautiful ballpark that would seat nearly 45,000 cheering fans tonight. He just walked around the bases, breathing in the air he truly believed was found only on a ball field. From second base, he could see an Oriole pitcher limbering up with a catcher on the Baltimore side of the field. Melvin recognized the tall, lanky pitcher as the ace of the Baltimore team,

Trevor Stallings, a perennial all-star. Stallings, scheduled to pitch tonight, was throwing easily, just warming up.

Walking past third base, Melvin nodded, and Stallings nodded back.

"You pitching tonight?" asked Melvin.

"I got nothing else to do. You playing tonight?"

"Course. Go easy on me, will ya?"

Stallings laughed and kept tossing.

Melvin completed his walk around the bases and sat in the dugout. He needed batting practice, having not swung a bat in a few days.

At around 4:00 p.m., players started strolling in, all greeting Melvin with smiles and sarcastic remarks about his absence. "We thought you retired, or did you miss the plane?"

Melvin just smiled, taking the good-natured ribbing in stride. It was a sign of affection, and Melvin knew it. He was glad to see Pete and Terry and Glenn and the teammates he had come to know and like. In such a short time, against all odds, he had somehow managed to become a part of the Yankees.

After batting and fielding practice, it was now approaching 6:00 p.m., and all the players were going through their pregame routines and waiting for game time. Russ Higgins was by the door and nodded to Melvin, who nodded back.

Melvin asked Pete if he could have a few words with the team. Pete said, "Is everything okay?"

"Yeah, I just need a few minutes. Can you call us all together?"

"Okay, boys," called out Pete, "let's huddle up."

After everyone got closer in a circle, Pete said, "The floor is yours, Melvin."

"Boys, first of all, I want to apologize for not making last night's game. I missed not being with you. But we won, and that's all that counts.

"I needed the day in New York to speak with Gus and Mr. Carter about the upcoming exam by the league doctors.

"I want to tell you what I told Gus and Lang yesterday and Russ a few hours ago. I've been diagnosed with cancer, stage four, so my future is somewhat unpredictable and most likely somewhat limited. Since I'm assuming this will be discovered by the league doctors and disclosed to the public by the commissioner or eventually leaked to the press, I felt it was better to tell you all now. I don't want you to feel sorry for me or cut me any slack. I remain one hundred percent committed to you, to the Yankees, and to winning. I'll be glad to answer any questions you may have, now or later."

There was total silence, which Melvin broke by saying, "Okay, thank you. We've got a game to win. Let's go get 'em!"

Almost silently, the players returned to their lockers, but gradually, one by one and then in small groups, Melvin's teammates came over to him. They patted him on the back, gave him fist bumps, extended well-wishes, did high fives, even a few hugs. Melvin could only say thank you.

And then it was game time.

ESPN knew how to take advantage of the moment. Millions of new and enthusiastic baseball fans were wanting to see Melvin Klapper in action. Yankee games were now the most-watched television event by far. Other channels were rearranging their schedules so as not to clash with Yankee games. Advertisers were outbidding each other just to get a piece of the action. Corporations that had never before even considered advertising during a baseball game were now clamoring for ad content that had anything at all to do with baseball or baseball fans.

Companies that sold services or products to those over sixty-five were willing to pay just about anything to be seen by the millions of new and active eyes focused on anything to do with Melvin. Vitamin supplements, insurance, healthy food and drinks, sneakers made especially for the elderly, communities selling real estate for the fifty-five and older crowd, even CBD (with or without THC), were now the dominant force in commercials for ESPN and other media outlets that covered baseball.

Fortunately for ESPN, they had the best in the business in their booth and were ready to cover an event that was attracting a remarkable number of viewers, young, old, and in between from all over the country. You didn't have to be a Yankee or Oriole fan to watch Melvin Klapper. You didn't even have to be a baseball fan. The story of Melvin Klapper was bigger than all that.

Scott and Dan never gave into yelling or histrionics. They knew the game, knew the players, and knew what their audience wanted to hear. They were well aware that their audience was growing exponentially and that the importance of each game as late August approached was surpassed only by the excitement of the story evolving around Melvin Klapper.

Scott did all he could to land an interview with Melvin but no dice. No one had gotten that yet as Melvin was not comfortable with doing an interview and knew that once he opened those floodgates, he would get drowned with requests. So when Scott couldn't land Melvin, he did the next best thing and got a promised five-minute interview with Yankee manager Russ Higgins, which would take place in the dugout prior to tonight's game.

At 6:35 p.m., the pregame show went on the air. The atmosphere was like that of a World Series game. An eager and energized crowd was filling in. The field was getting its final dressing and watering. The umpires were gathering. The new voice of Camden Yards was Adrienne Roberson, the first female public address announcer in Orioles history and only one of five in all of major league baseball. The scene was set.

"Good evening, folks. I'm Don Earling along with Scott Whaler. Welcome to Camden Yards, where the streaking New York Yankees will be up against the Baltimore Orioles and their best starter, Trevor Stallings. The Yanks won here last night despite the absence of their seventy-four-year-old right fielder Melvin Klapper. Klapper was not in the ballpark last night, and we'll try to find out why when Scott will talk with Yankee manager Russ Higgins just before game time. You won't want to miss that interview.

"So let me set the scene for you," continued Scott. "The American League pennant race is tightening in the East Division, where the Yankees have closed the gap with the Red Sox from fourteen games to eight games. Tampa Bay is also making a run but lags behind the Yanks by five games. Baltimore has played well of late but got off to a rocky start, which hampered their chances this year. The White Sox have a commanding lead in the Central division as do the Astros in the West division.

"So the excitement right now in baseball is focused on the Yankees. Can they catch up to the Red Sox? What role will the elderly Melvin Klapper continue to play?

"Dan, Klapper has played in only eleven games, has had just thirty-seven at bats, not including six walks. And don't forget the now famous incident of his getting hit by a pitch. He's had thirteen hits for an average of .361, which would lead the league if he had the required minimum of at bats, which of course he doesn't. He has had two home runs and three game-tying or winning hits. He has made no errors in the field and has thrown out two runners. Scott, what do you make of Klapper so far?"

"It's pretty incredible for any player at any age in any major league sport to come right in and have such an impact. To be honest, he's turned the Yankee season around. He's caught the attention and imagination of the entire country. Whether it will continue remains to be seen."

"Scott," Dan chimed in seamlessly, "you and I had the extraordinary experience of seeing Klapper catch that ball back on July 9 and then saw the throw he made. As unbelievable as all that was, who would have dreamed that this is where we would be six weeks later? What a story!

"With forty-four games to go until the end of the season, the full story of Melvin Klapper has yet to be told. It's going to get tougher for the Yankees and Klapper as teams will bear down on them and pitchers get to know Klapper and his weaknesses at the plate.

"Scott has left the booth to join Yankee manager Russ Higgins. So let's switch down to the Yankee dugout. Scott?"

"Thanks, Dan. Russ, my first question is obvious. Where was Klapper yesterday?"

"Scott, like all players, including I'm sure you when you were playing, Melvin needed a personal day, and because it was personal, I don't think it would be appropriate for me to say more."

"Fair enough, but will Melvin be a regular in the Yankee lineup down the stretch?"

"We'll take it one game at a time. He's batting third tonight, and as far as I'm concerned, I'll play him as often as possible. You know, Scott, Melvin is not used to the rigors of our schedule with the travel and all, so he's been doing a great job adjusting."

"How do the Yankee players view Melvin?"

"Oh, they love him. To a man, he's probably the most popular guy on the team."

"Will he be undergoing the league-ordered exam when he returns after the road trip?"

"Absolutely. Remember that both the Yankee organization and Melvin voluntarily agreed to this exam when they probably didn't have to. Hopefully, this will put to rest the spurious and vicious rumors started by a journalist looking for publicity."

"Are you referring to Victor Coleman?"

"It's almost game time, Scott. I need to be with my team."

"Thank you, Russ."

Russ Higgins had already walked away.

"Well, Dan. You heard it. I'd say Russ was pretty emphatic. Back to you in the booth."

"That he was. Great interview, Scott. I loved the way Russ avoided your question about Vic Coleman."

"Yeah, I knew he would, but I had to ask."

Melvin had not heard the interview of his manager, but he knew Russ Higgins well enough to imagine how it all went. He would soon need Winnie to make a short but definitive statement regarding the press and its demands upon Melvin, but the timing would be as important as the words. Melvin, feeling better for not having played the day before, tried to clear his mind of Winnie, Alva, Grace, and Billy. It was time to focus on winning baseball games.

After a slow start with only two hits (none for Melvin) in the first six innings, the Yankees scored four runs in the seventh to chase Stallings and two more in the ninth to go on to a 6–3 victory. Since the Red Sox won their game that night, there was no blood. The Yankees remained eight games behind Boston.

The road trip consisted of three games in Baltimore, four games against the always-pesky Tampa Bay Rays, and finally three in Pittsburgh. Melvin had never been to Tampa (as Melvin learned, the Rays actually played in St. Petersburg), but the Yankee players all liked playing in gorgeous Tropicana Field. It was the only major league park to feature an artificial surface with all-dirt base paths. And the air-conditioning was perfect on a hot day or humid evening.

It was a successful and encouraging road trip with the Yankees winning eight out of ten games and Melvin getting timely hits. By picking up another two games on Boston, they cut the deficit down to six games.

The Tramadol, which he had been reluctant to use before, was now needed to subdue enough pain to allow Melvin to play. Melvin was anxious to get home to his chair, to his routine at home. He needed rest that only home could provide. Having Friday off after a long road trip was just what he needed. It would provide him with a day to gather his strength for the physical exam set for the next day. He would connect with Winnie as to where and when to meet. He was filled with trepidation, but knowing Winnie was going to be with him calmed him down. It would be what it would be.

Every day Melvin was on the road, he called Grace to assure her all was well. He needed to hear Billy's voice to know how he was handling the news. He wanted Billy to hear a strong and healthy Melvin. Both Grace and Billy were hesitant at first, but both warmed up gradually the longer the call went. Melvin took his time, making sure not to rush Grace or Billy. He wanted the conversation to be as usual as those in the past. While Grace kept asking her father how he felt, Billy just talked about baseball, which was exactly what Melvin wanted.

CHAPTER 30

Saturday, August 27
New York-Presbyterian Hospital

Returning to New York-Presbyterian late Thursday night, having won eight of ten games on the road, the Yankees were feeling good. They were now out by only six games. Their spirits were high and their juices flowing. Melvin had amassed thirteen hits including three home runs. His batting average was a solid .351. His limp was noticeable, but since it apparently did not affect him at bat or in the field, it seemed not to matter to Melvin or anyone else. What was not apparent was that Melvin's back, side, and occasional belly pain was starting to bother him more often. While in Tampa, Melvin began taking the Tramadol prescribed by Dr. Mendelsohn. It brought some relief, which Melvin welcomed. He decided to take one a day, a few hours before each game. It seemed to have little effect on him other than quelling the pain.

The schedule was demanding. They had three games at home against Milwaukee and then would host Detroit for a quick two-game series then a much-needed day off. But today was going to be a huge day. Melvin was to go to for the tests and examination. Although he was still fatigued from having played in ten straight games, he was anxious to get this day over with. He had nothing to hide since he had disclosed the truth to everyone who mattered to him. The team made no mention of it other than a call from Gus, who inquired how he was doing. Gus reiterated Lang's gracious offer to get Melvin to oncologists at Memorial. Melvin appreciated the call and assured Gus he was well. Somehow, in a most inexplicable way, Melvin had been able to continue his high level of performance.

By 6:00 a.m., the morning papers were on the newsstands. The headline in one paper was "Today's the Day." Another one read, "Melvin Goes to the Doctors."

No one had forgotten the league's decision that Melvin be tested and examined. He wasn't going to read the papers, but a lot of the other players would want to know what was being said. Knowing this, Melvin reluctantly read one of the papers. He was actually surprised and glad to find the story to be factually accurate. The paper carried short bios of the two doctors, both of whom were highly regarded and clearly impartial. Melvin knew that Dr. Mendelsohn had received a call from one of them and assumed that they already knew of the cancer situation. Because there was a game scheduled for 7:05 at the stadium that night, Melvin was hoping that they would be done with him in time. With the exam starting at 2:00 p.m., there should be more than enough time to get back to the stadium in time for the game.

Melvin and Winnie had arranged for Winnie to pick Melvin up at home at noon. Melvin was waiting at the door from 10:30 a.m. on and was relieved to see Winnie pull up in front of the house at 11:30 a.m. Winnie honked once, and Melvin walked as quickly as he could to the car.

"Boy, are you a sight for sore eyes," said Melvin, leaning over to give Winnie a hug.

"How you feeling?" asked Winnie, concerned.

"Not too bad for an old man."

As soon as they got going, Winnie said, "Nice road trip. I saw all the games, including two I watched with Billy, Grace, and Chris. They invited me and Alva over. Alva wasn't comfortable with the whole idea but was okay with just me going. Man, you've got a nice family. Even Chris is starting to warm up to me. But that kid, I tell ya, is a pistol."

"Thanks, Winnie. That's good to hear. Maybe Alva will come around. I think she and Grace would like each other."

"I think so too. So are we ready for New York-Presbyterian?"

"Yep. The sooner the better. I wrote up a statement like we discussed. I can read it to you later and make whatever changes you want."

Winnie and Melvin chatted nonstop on a ride that took a little over an hour. It was typical NYC traffic for a summer Saturday. On the way from the parking lot a block away from the hospital to the front entrance of the hospital, Winnie and Melvin could see there were reporters, photographers, and police everywhere. For some reason, neither of them had anticipated this.

"Oh, crap," said Winnie, "I should have realized this would be a circus."

As they approached, a police officer spotted them and offered an escort. With the help of four of New York's finest, Melvin and Winnie walked into and through the hospital as if no one else was there. But even inside the halls of the entry area, well-wishers yelled out, "Good luck, Melvin. We love you, Melvin!" Melvin smiled and waved softly.

After passing the huge reception desk, a very doctorish-looking middle-aged man with a striped bow tie walked toward Melvin and said, "Are you Mr. Klapper?"

"Yes, I am."

"I'm Dr. Clark Alexander, chief medical officer here at New York-Presbyterian Hospital. I'm here to welcome you and show you where your examination will be."

Looking directly at Winnie, Dr. Alexander said, "And you are who, sir?"

"I'm Aaron Winfield, Mr. Klapper's friend."

"Well, you can't come into the examination suite, but I can arrange for you to have a room nearby. Is that acceptable with you, gentlemen?"

Winnie looked at Melvin, who said, "Sure, that'll be fine. Doctor Alexander, do you have any idea how long this will take?"

"No, I'm sorry, I don't. I will not be involved once I escort you to the examination. Your questions would best be directed to Dr. Lewis and Dr. Hoffstein. If you're ready, let's go."

After a five-minute walk and short elevator ride to the third floor, where Winnie was deposited in a room with a television and several magazines, Melvin went to the end of the hall with Dr. Alexander. The dark-wood door Dr. Alexander opened said 330 in white numerals. Upon walking in, Melvin saw two gentlemen and what appeared, judging by her white uniform, to be a nurse. Dr. Alexander introduced Melvin to Dr. Lewis and Dr. Hoffstein and Chief Nursing Officer Elizabeth Hastings. Everyone seemed formal but friendly, thought Melvin.

"I leave you in good hands." said Dr. Alexander, addressing Melvin as he departed the suite.

"Good day, Mr. Klapper. I'm Dr. Martin Lewis, and this is my colleague Dr. Jack Hoffstein. Nurse Hastings will assist us as needed. Please have a seat. Let us explain what we're doing here and what you can expect. As you know, the commissioner has asked us to examine you to see if you are taking any performance-enhancing drugs or anything else that would explain your ability as a seventy-four-year-old man to play major league baseball. You understand this, correct?"

"Yes."

"Good, so Dr. Hoffstein is a neurologist, and I'm an internal medicine physician with expertise in geriatrics. We will each examine you separately, and Nurse Hastings will assist with the blood draw and anything else that's needed. Nothing we do will be painful or invasive in any way. So far so good?"

"Yes. About how long will I be here? I have a game tonight at seven."

"Oh, you'll be fine. We should be done in about three hours."

"Thank you."

"Mr. Klapper," said Dr. Hoffstein, "as to confidentiality, today, for all intents and purposes, you are our patient. We are bound by the rules of doctor-patient privilege, which means that without your approval, we are not allowed to disclose what went on here today or any of the results or our opinions. Is that clear?"

"Yes."

"That confidentiality applies to any time in the future as well. The privilege of confidentiality continues. Now that having been said," Dr. Hoffstein continued, "it is our understanding that you have given permission for us to share our findings with the commissioner's office. Is this your understanding?"

"Yes."

"Which we will do as expeditiously as possible, no later than seventy-two hours. However, we need to tell you that we cannot be responsible for the confidentiality of our report once it leaves us and goes to the office of the commissioner. Do you understand this?"

"I think so. You're saying that you're not responsible if your report goes public once it leaves your hands."

"Unfortunately, that is the case. You can be sure that we won't disclose anything about you or today, but others may. That having been said, do you still want to proceed?"

"I do."

"All right then," said Dr. Lewis. "Nurse Hastings will ask you to sign a few forms and take your history. Then you will provide a urine specimen. After that, I will examine you, and then Dr. Hoffstein will examine you. Some blood work will be necessary, which Nurse Hastings will attend to. That is the procedure. Are you on board with everything we've said so far?"

"Yes, I understand and want to thank you all for taking the time on a beautiful summer Saturday to take care of me."

"May we call you Melvin?" asked Dr. Lewis.

"Sure."

"Thank you. Melvin. We're both big baseball fans. I'm a Met fan, and Dr. Hoffstein is a Yankee fan. But of course this has nothing to do with our professional responsibilities. We just wanted you to know that you're in a room with friends and admirers. You're older than we are, but we couldn't hit a ball if our lives depended on it." The doctors laughed. Nurse Hastings and Melvin smiled. Melvin wasn't sure if the doctors were trying to relax him, themselves, or everyone, but these were good people, and Melvin felt comfortable being with them even under these unusual circumstances.

"Before Nurse Hastings takes your history," Dr. Hoffstein went on, "we want you to know that Dr. Lewis spoke at length with Dr. Mendelsohn. Dr. Mendelsohn is an excellent physician, and with your prior consent, he discussed your medical situation in detail, so we are intimately familiar with your current condition. Do you understand?"

"I do."

"Very well. Nurse Hastings will talk with you about your current status, any complaints you may have, any medications you are taking. Shouldn't take very long. Then our examinations will begin."

Nurse Hastings, in as respectful a way as possible, handed Melvin a plastic cup and cap and pointed him to the lavatory. Afterward, she walked Melvin into a small office where she sat across but near Melvin and asked him questions he had expected. Melvin was able to answer all her questions truthfully and fully. She then walked Melvin back to another room where Dr. Lewis performed a forty-five minute examination of Melvin from head to toe. When that was done, Dr. Lewis exited the room, and shortly thereafter, Dr. Hoffstein entered. Much of Dr. Hoffstein's exam was in the form of questions apparently to assess Melvin's mental and cognitive state. Both doctors were polite, courteous, and professional at all times. Melvin never felt pressured or intimidated. He knew they were just doing their job and were doing it as nicely and as calmly as possible.

After Dr. Hoffstein was finished, Nurse Hastings came in and drew enough blood from Melvin's left arm (not his throwing arm) to fill five vials. She apologized but said it was necessary to get the lab results the doctors wanted to see.

She then walked Melvin into a room he had not been in yet. It was a small conference room with two windows, four chairs, and a round forty-eight-inch diameter wooden table with glass protection on it. "The doctors will be in momentarily," said Nurse Hastings, smiling for the first time. "Thank you, Melvin. It was a pleasure meeting you. I wish you well."

"Thank you, Mrs. Hastings."

A few minutes later, both doctors entered the room.

"Now that wasn't too bad, was it?" offered Dr. Lewis.

"Not at all. How'd I do?"

"We've agreed to share our findings with your physician, Dr. Mendelsohn, so it would probably be best to discuss it with him."

"Can you at least give me a hint?"

Dr. Hoffstein said, "Subject to the results of the blood and urine, which is a significant part of today's exam, you seem to be a rather average man of seventy-four. You're actually in pretty good health for your age. Other than your cancer, which is obviously very serious, we couldn't find anything on examination that would affect your physical ability one way or the other, other than your slight limp, which does not seem to impede or limit your functions. So to be quite frank with you, so far we can't find an explanation for the extraordinary level of your athletic performance. But we will not say that in writing until all your lab work is in."

"When will that be?"

"It's being expedited, so we expect it tonight or within twenty-four hours at the latest. We will then write up our report and hope to have it to the commissioner's office by Tuesday. And a copy to Dr. Mendelsohn at the same time. Does that sound reasonable to you?"

"Yes, you doctors and Nurse Hastings have been very kind, thank you."

"Melvin," said Dr. Lewis, "it's not our role here today to mix into your personal situation or discuss your medical condition, but it is quite unusual for a stage-four pancreatic cancer patient to be hitting baseballs and running around bases. So we were and remain perplexed about that. We have no medical explanation. But as I said, until we see your lab results, we take no formal position."

"I'm just as perplexed as you, Doc. I'm just taking it one day at a time."

"You need to stay in touch with Dr. Mendelsohn and let him guide you as best as possible."

Melvin stood to leave. Wanting to shake his hand, both docs came toward Melvin and said, "We wish you well, Melvin. We'll be rooting for you."

*****

It was now about 4:30 p.m. Winnie was waiting out in the hall and was glad to see Melvin with a smile on his face.

"How was it?"

"Fine, nice guys."

"Any idea what they're going to say?"

"So far so good, but they emphasized the importance of the lab results, which they won't have for another day. But I think we're okay."

"To the stadium?"

"I'm sorry to impose on you, Winnie, but…"

"I'd be glad to pick up, Billy. Can you call Grace once we're in the car?"

"You're a good pal, Winnie."

The crowds outside the hospital had dispersed. An officer greeted Melvin and said, "About an hour ago, we told the reporters you had already left through the back. Old trick, but it still works. Makes our job a lot easier. You playing tonight?"

"I hope so."

"Just keep hitting. I want to see a World Series in the Bronx."

As soon as the car pulled out of the garage, Melvin called Grace.

"Hi, Dad," said Grace, answering after the first ring. "How'd it go?"

"No problem at all. Listen, can Billy come to the game tonight? There's no school tomorrow, and Winnie can pick him up and bring him home."

"Billy is dying to see you as I am. I'll run it by Chris, but I don't see why not. When will I see you?"

"How about tomorrow morning? Our game doesn't begin until 8:00 p.m. tomorrow, so how about ten at your house for breakfast?"

"Wonderful. I can't wait."

"Love you, Grace."

"Love you, Dad."

At the game that night, buoyed by how well he felt the exam had gone, Melvin had three solid hits, including an opposite field home run as the Yankees coasted to a 9–3 win. The team did not pick up a game in the standings since the Red Sox won their game as well. Melvin was so happy to see Winnie and Billy in the stands cheering for him.

Higgins asked Melvin how it went as did several players. Melvin kept his answer short and sweet. "Thanks for asking. I think it went well. We'll know in a few days."

Melvin was looking forward to a good night's sleep. He felt the worst was behind him. He was feeling well thanks to the Tramadol he took a few hours before each game. Thankfully, he had not felt any side effects or adverse reactions.

Melvin was already thinking ahead to seeing Grace the next morning, and with it being Sunday, he would get to spend time with Billy. While in Tampa on the recent road trip, Melvin was strolling along some shops on Bay Street and came across an 8" × 15" sign made of wood that had the following black letters on a white background:

> Fear less, hope more; whine less, breathe more; talk less, listen more;
> Hate less, love more; and all good things will be yours.
> Never regret.
> If it's good, it's wonderful. If it's bad, it's experience.

Sing your song; dance your dance; dream your dream. Hope your hope.
The future depends on what we do in the present.
Never ever give up. Fall down seven times; get up eight.
No matter what you do, there will always be critics.
So be who you are and say what you want because
those who mind don't matter, and those who matter don't mind.
Go with confidence in the direction of your dreams.
Live the life you've imagined.
Believe deep down that you are destined to do great things.
If you are loving, hopeful, and optimistic, you can change the world.

Melvin had stared at this sign in the window for several minutes, reading it over and over. It said what he wanted to say to Billy but knew he was not capable of expressing it as well. He hoped Billy would feel the same about these words as Melvin, who would have paid just about anything for this sign, the last one the store had. It was not expensive. They wrapped it in plain brown paper and tied it with rough twine. Melvin carried it home like it was a precious diamond. He would give it to Billy on Sunday morning.

CHAPTER 31

Sunday, August 28
Springfield

At 5:45 a.m., Melvin was woken by the cell phone resting by his nightstand. Melvin wondered who could be calling him on Sunday morning before 6:00 a.m. His first thought was about Grace or Billy. Was someone sick? Pressing the green button, Melvin said, "Yes?"

"Melvin, it's Gus. I just had to call you. Sorry if I woke you."

"That's okay, Gus," said Melvin thinking Gus just wanted an update as to Saturday's examination. But Gus had something else on his mind.

"Coleman has done it again. Another nasty article by the Vulture. The guy is such a jerk. All I can say to you is don't let Coleman distract you. That's all he's trying to do. So let it go, have a peaceful Sunday, and we'll see you at the ballpark later on. Big game tonight."

"Okay, Gus, thanks for the heads-up."

By now, Melvin had learned how to use his cell phone to pull up articles, and there it was. From the *Boston Globe* but syndicated in over one hundred newspapers across the country, including New York, the headline read:

MLB Coverup
Vic Coleman

In response to this reporter's demanding an investigation into the Yankees and their 74-year-old star Melvin Klapper, MLB reluctantly but finally did the right thing and ordered Klapper to be examined by two NY doctors. At least that's what they tell us.

Now I don't know how qualified these doctors are or how they were chosen or whether they may be connected to the New York Yankees in some way, but the public has a right to know the results of any tests conducted on Klapper. This is a public matter, not a private matter. The integrity of baseball is on the line. And the public has a right to know if what they're seeing is real or a stunt.

Billionaire Yankee owner Lang Carter is a mighty big financial force in New York and specifically at New York hospitals, having given many millions of dollars over the past decade. So was Lang Carter involved here? If so, how?

The bottom line here is very simple. The public in general, especially baseball fans, have a right to know exactly what's going on. Will the results of the exams and tests be shared with us? Will the findings of the commissioner be fully and publicly disclosed? How can this matter be put to rest if it's kept quiet by MLB?

Once again this reporter demands full disclosure and nothing less. No secrets, Mr.

> Commissioner. We need you to go public, immediately and tell the complete and unvarnished truth about Klapper.

The article went on, but Melvin had read enough. *What's with this guy?* thought Melvin. Why was he so hell-bent on stirring up trouble by throwing around baseless allegations? As Gus said, it was an attempt to upset and distract the team.

Melvin showered, got dressed, had two cups of coffee, and sat on the porch reading his Jackie Robinson biography book. That always centered and inspired him. If Jackie could go through what he went through, Melvin had nothing to complain about. *Just go about your business, Melvin,* he thought. Just like Jackie did.

Since it was early on Sunday morning, everything was quiet. Two officers, neither of whom Melvin recognized, waved to Melvin when he walked onto the porch, who responded with a cheerful "Good morning, gentlemen. Looks like a beautiful day." At about 9:30 a.m., Melvin decided it was time to get going. Planning to go directly to the stadium from Grace's house for the night game, Melvin took with him all he would need for the rest of the day and evening. But most importantly, he carried the special package meant only for Billy.

Billy and Amos were standing on the front lawn outside their home when Melvin arrived via Uber. Melvin had become so accustomed to getting around by Uber that he was starting to know the drivers in his neighborhood. They often offered to comp him, but Melvin would politely say no and then give an extraordinarily generous tip. It was the least he could do.

Seeing Billy made Melvin's heart skip a beat. Although he had spoken to Billy several times while on the road trip, including on a Zoom call, it wasn't the same as hugging his grandson.

"Grandpa, want to have a catch?"

"Let me say hello to your mom and dad, and then after breakfast, we'll throw the ball around, okay?"

"What's that?" Billy asked, noting that Melvin was carrying a package in addition to his overnight bag.

"Oh this? Well, it's for you. Let's go inside and you can open it."

Billy ran inside, and Melvin followed him. Happy to see her father, Grace gave him an unusually long embrace. Chris patted Melvin on the back. "Nice game last night."

"Mom, Grandpa got me a present. Can I open it?"

"Would you rather wait until after breakfast?" asked Melvin almost sarcastically, knowing that Billy would reject any suggestion of waiting.

"No, let's open it now."

Billy tore it open as any ten-year-old boy would. Seeing a plaque with a bunch of words, Billy was silent, trying to figure out what it was. Melvin could see that his grandson was disappointed. "Grandpa, what is it?"

"It's meant to be hung on a wall in your room so you can look at it whenever you want to read it to yourself or out loud. Those are meant to be good thoughts for you. When I saw it in Tampa, I thought it would be nice to share it with you. If not today, I hope there will come a time in the future that you like it. I'm sorry if you're disappointed."

"Did you thank Grandpa Billy?" said Grace. "He carried it all the way back from Tampa for you."

Billy went through the motions of hugging Melvin and said, "Thank you, Grandpa." It was obvious to all that the gift had not gone over as well as Melvin had hoped. Melvin consoled himself by hoping that maybe someday Billy would appreciate it.

Changing the subject, Grace asked everyone to sit at the table. It didn't take Chris long to say, "I read Coleman's article today. He's really after you. That guy is just relentless."

"Doesn't really bother me. The team is laser focused," said Melvin as he ate a bowl of fruit Grace had prepared for him.

"Dad, how are you feeling?"

"I actually feel pretty good."

Grace followed up, "Are you taking any medication?"

"Dr. Mendelsohn prescribed Tramadol, a painkiller, for me, which I take on game day. Makes me feel a lot better."

"Is your situation going to get worse?" pressed Chris. Grace grimaced at the bluntness of the question.

"Yes, that's what I'm told, but so far, so good."

"Grandpa," Billy jumped in, "are you playing tonight?"

"I think so. We have two more games against Milwaukee. Will you be watching?"

"For as long as I'm allowed to stay up," Billy said, looking at his parents.

"We like your friend Winnie," added Chris. "He's quite a guy. And he thinks you're the nicest person he's ever met. For a big guy who was a cop, he sure is a softie. What's his family like?"

"I don't know. Never met his wife, and if he has kids, he's never mentioned it to me, and I haven't asked. He'll tell me if he wants to. Otherwise, none of my business."

"How did the exam go?" Grace asked.

"I think it went well but won't know until we get the report. The doctors, two very nice fellas, were very careful about what they said. They couldn't commit."

Chris kept asking questions. "Any truth to what Coleman was implying, a connection between the doctors and the Yankees?"

"Not that I know of," replied Melvin, "and why would Lang Carter risk his reputation over me? The Yankees have a long and honorable history. They're not going to jeopardize that for Melvin Klapper."

"Okay, Grandpa, time for a catch?"

"You bet. Grab your glove."

After a few minutes out back and wanting to leave Billy on a high note, Melvin said, "Okay, my brilliant grandson, I have a riddle for you. What was the spider doing on the baseball team?"

Billy thought about it for a moment and then shouted, "Catching flies." Melvin and Billy laughed.

The present that Melvin had lovingly carried back from Tampa that he couldn't wait to give Billy was left lying sideways on the floor under the table. It wasn't what a ten-year-old wanted. After Melvin left, Grace picked it up, carried it to Billy's room, and leaned it on a wall where Chris would hang it later that day.

Grace read it and knew that Billy would cherish it someday in the future.

*****

When Melvin got to the stadium around three, Higgins was in his office with about five newspapers spread out on his desk.

"Melvin, you're here early. What's up? How you feeling?"

"You know, Russ, I feel my best being right here. Walking through these doors, seeing you and the boys, it can't get much better."

"I don't think I've ever heard anyone say that before. Not even my wife. So you're not bothered by Coleman?"

"Not really. He's doing his job trying to sell newspapers, and I'm doing mine trying to hit baseballs."

"Good for you, Mclvin. Arc you anxious about how thc commissioner is going to handle the situation? I know Gus is up at night worrying."

"It will all work out. My mind is right here, right now. I'm having the time of my life, and I'm not going to let anything or anyone spoil it for me. I mean, who wouldn't trade places with me?"

"By the way, if you care, Coleman is getting crushed out there by the fans and the rest of the baseball press corps. I learned a long time ago that the difference between intelligence and stupidity is that intelligence has its limits. You have a lot of defenders out there, Melvin. Never forget that. Lang asked me how you were handling the pressure. He really likes you."

"Makes me feel good to hear that. I realize this hasn't been easy on the organization or the team. I'm just trying to keep my head down and play baseball."

"Melvin, you're doing fine. Just keep on being who you are."

"Thanks, Russ. I'll go suit up."

That night, on a game carried nationally to more than seventy-five million viewers by ESPN and announced by Scott Whaler and Dan Earling, the Yankees won 5–3. Melvin had two hits and two ribbies. The Red Sox had lost their game against the Phillies, so the Yankees trailed by only five games.

Monday was a makeup game from a rain/snow day back in April. The Red Sox had the day off, which gave their pitching staff a much-needed rest going into the stretch run. The Yankees continued their winning ways with a 6–4 win, led by home runs from Pete Warner and Terry Miller. Melvin had two singles out by four and a half games.

CHAPTER 32

Tuesday, August 30
Springfield

After enjoying a relatively quiet and restful day at home just reading and watching old movies, Melvin was looking forward to tonight's game against the Tigers. Although the night before had been rough due to back and side pain, Melvin only cared about his ability to keep playing well. As long as the pain did not interfere with his performance on the field, Melvin could deal with his pain off the field. At about 9:30 a.m., while sitting in his favorite chair reading about Churchill as a brilliant chess player and master mason, Melvin got a call. On the other end was Gus Christianson and Lang Carter.

They seemed not just happy but ecstatic. After their joint hello, Melvin just listened.

"Melvin, we just heard from the commissioner," said Lang. "You got a clean bill of health. Nothing in your system that would improve your play. Nothing illegal, period. Congrats, Melvin. It's over."

"So what now?"

"That SOB Coleman better apologize as publicly as he made his ridiculous allegations," added an angry-sounding Gus. Melvin had never seen or heard Gus agitated like this before.

Lang continued, "The commissioner will issue a report probably in the next day or two, but he hasn't yet decided how to do it. At this point, we want him to go public, and we told him that flat out. Since the allegations were public, so should the repudiation of those allegations. He seemed to agree but wouldn't commit. Said he had to confer with legal."

"Well, that's good news," said Melvin.

Lang laughingly replied, "You can be the master of understatement sometimes, Melvin."

What was important to Lang and Gus was not all that important to Melvin. He knew there would never be a showing of performance-enhancing drugs, which was where Yankee management was focused and rightfully so. But this was not Melvin's focus. He was concerned if his cancer was about to become public fodder and once again distract him and his teammates. Melvin just wanted to play baseball. He didn't want his personal life to be bandied about or trivialized.

"Is he going to mention the cancer?" asked Melvin.

"That we don't know," replied Gus. "He didn't say anything about that, and we didn't think it was our place to ask."

"No, you're right. I understand." Melvin did understand. Why bring it up if the commissioner didn't? Maybe the performance-enhancing drug issue was all that the commissioner's office was looking at. No need for him to go further, hoped Melvin.

"I hope he doesn't. I'm not looking for any sympathy."

"We know that. We have no control over what he says or how he says it, but this is a big day for the Yankees and for you. So let's enjoy it," said Lang, who was clearly relieved that this irritating and worrisome issue was now behind them.

"Thanks, guys, for calling."

As soon as that call ended, Melvin's cell phone rang again.

"Good morning, Melvin. It's Stan Mendelsohn. How are you?"

"Pretty good, Doc. I just heard from the Yankees that the exams went well."

"Yes, Melvin, that's why I'm calling. I just received a copy of the report written by Dr. Lewis and Dr. Hoffstein that went to the commissioner. All in all, a very good report. Unfortunately, it confirms your cancer. And they of course do mention the gunshot and shrapnel wounds, the medications you're on, and your general overall health."

Melvin asked, "Doc, do you know if that report will become public? I was hoping it would remain private."

"I have no idea, but I wouldn't worry about it. The people love you, Melvin, and knowing that you're playing while struggling with cancer will only make them love you more. Is the Tramadol working?"

"Yes, but not quite as well as when I started it. I use it only on game days."

"If it's not giving you sufficient relief, let me know. We can increase the dosage or step up to other meds, which we can do cautiously and only if necessary."

"Thanks, Doc. Say hello to Helen and Louise for me."

Melvin was enjoying the good news of the day. The Yankees were happy, and that made Melvin happy. The two docs had done their job, and now it was just a question of what the commissioner would say and how he would handle it. And it would be interesting, thought Melvin, whether Coleman would accept the report or continue his smear campaign.

By the time Melvin got to the ballpark, word was starting to leak out, as it always seemed to, that the docs had found nothing irregular or suspicious about Melvin's medical condition. The press already knew that the doctor's report was in the hands of the commissioner. Where it would go from there was a matter of speculation.

Unfortunately, the Yankees lost 8–6 as their bullpen struggled to hold onto a 6–5 lead. Melvin had two more hits and made a great throw from right field to third base to catch a runner trying to tag from second. But no matter how well Melvin did personally, if the team lost, Melvin was disheartened. Fortunately for New York, the Red Sox, still mired in a semi-slump, lost as well, so no blood. Billy couldn't be at the game because it was a school night, but Winnie was there. Melvin kept hoping that Winnie would bring Alva on those nights, but the seat next to Winnie remained empty.

After the game, Winnie and Melvin huddled up outside the players' parking lot. The players were starting to know Winnie and liked seeing him around. They viewed him as Melvin's close friend and confidant, which he was. The players who interacted with Winnie both liked and respected him.

"You played well, Melvin. How are you feeling?"

"Not great but I got good news today about the exam."

"Yeah, I know. It's all over the news. Supposedly the commissioner is holding a press conference tomorrow at 10:00 a.m."

"I hadn't heard that. Can you come over and we'll watch it together? I'd rather not be alone listening to this."

"No problem, I'm off tomorrow. I'll be over around nine. C'mon, I'll take you home."

"Thanks, Winnie," said Melvin, halfway home.

"For what? I'm the one who owes you thanks."

"How do you figure that?"

"Melvin, you've changed my life and for the better."

"To be honest, Winnie, this has been a roller coaster. Every day is something new but not always good. I just want to play baseball, but between the hip and back pain, the cancer, the doctors, the meds, this guy Coleman, and of course the sadness I bring to my family, let's just say it's a lot to deal with."

"Hang in there. It's almost September. Only thirty-one games to go. Forget the other stuff. It's just life. And believe me, you're bringing a lot of joy to millions of people, including your family, so stop whining."

Melvin thought about that. Once again, Winnie was spot on. Melvin smiled. Thank goodness for Winnie.

"Okay, Winnie. See ya in the morning."

CHAPTER 33

Wednesday, August 31
Springfield

A little before nine, Winnie showed up with a bag of donuts that he could probably devour without any help from Melvin. Winnie seemed more nervous about the press conference than Melvin.

Neither the Yankees nor Melvin had any idea what the commissioner was going to say, but of course, the sports media in New York and frankly across the country couldn't help but to predict, guess, and hypothesize. After all, they had a column or airtime to fill. Although each had their own take on what the day would hold, they at least agreed that Melvin had been brutally savaged by Coleman and that if Melvin had been playing for the Red Sox instead of the Yankees, Coleman would have hailed him as Babe Ruth or Ted Williams reincarnated.

At exactly ten o'clock, the networks and cable cameras focused on the conference table and center chair that the commissioner would soon be sitting at. The tension built as all cameras were on that chair. At 10:03 a.m., Commissioner Wendell Steinhouser strode with purpose to his chair. Known as "Wendy" to his family and close friends, Steinhouser had been general counsel representing major league baseball for many years before becoming commissioner. Looking every bit the wise judge, Steinhouser was both liked and respected. Although some accused him of doing the owners' bidding, the truth was that he often sided with the players. His punishments were rarely harsh. Most importantly, he always gave the players an honest hearing and the benefit of the doubt.

Sitting to the right of Steinhouser was Assistant Commissioner Lawrence Jaeger, and on his left side was Benjamin Lowerson, current legal counsel for MLB. They were a potent trio. All had attended Harvard Law School and had been colleagues for many years. Bright and tough, they were not a bunch to be messed with.

Steinhouser wasted no time.

"Good morning. I'd like to read the following statement that is being issued on behalf of Major League Baseball regarding the matter of Mr. Melvin Klapper and the New York Yankees.

"Recently, serious allegations were made against Mr. Klapper and the NY Yankee organization. My office felt that in response to those allegations, it became necessary and appropriate to look into the allegations to determine their validity, if any.

"On August 22, the league retained the services of two highly esteemed and impartial physicians, Dr. Martin Lewis and Dr. Jack Hoffstein, to conduct a thorough mental and physical examination of Mr. Klapper, including any and all laboratory tests that they felt were germane to their examination. No limitations, restraints, or conditions were requested or imposed by Major League Baseball, the New York Yankees, or Mr. Klapper. These physicians were chosen by the league without any prior discussion with Mr. Klapper or the Yankees. Subsequently, both Mr. Klapper and the Yankees consented to these examinations by these doctors at New York-Presbyterian Hospital.

"Five days later, on Saturday, August 27, the examinations proceeded. Mr. Klapper appeared on time. No representative of the Yankee organization attended the examinations, which lasted about three hours.

"An extensive joint report was subsequently rendered by Drs. Lewis and Hoffstein, which was received by my office at 5:00 p.m.

on Monday, August 29. After a complete and thoughtful review of the medical findings with Assistant Commissioner Jaeger and our legal team led by Mr. Lowenson, I prepared the statement I am reading to you now.

"Both doctors agreed that the examinations and tests conducted on Mr. Klapper showed no evidence of performance-enhancing drugs or any substance that could affect or improve his performance on the field. In short, there is no evidence to support the allegations that have been made against Mr. Klapper and the Yankees. As far as MLB is concerned, the matter is closed. Now I'll answer a few questions. Steve?"

"Thank you, Mr. Commissioner." Steve Greenspan was one of New York's most respected sports journalists. "Did the doctors explain or discuss how a seventy-four-year-old man with no prior baseball experience to speak of could be hitting .385 with six home runs against major league pitching?"

"Steve, that was not the objective here. The goal was to discover if Mr. Klapper's performance was legitimate or a sham somehow supported by illegal substances. The doctors could find nothing about Mr. Klapper that indicated any type of irregularity. Wayne?"

"Wendell, will you release the doctor's findings?"

"Frankly, I don't know if we have the authority to do that. After all, it's the medical record of a player. Would this mean that every player's personal medical record would or should be disclosed to the public? Does anything like that exist in any sport or in any part of our society? Are you prepared for your personal medical history to become part of the public discourse?"

"No, sir, but this is a very different situation," continued Wayne Connolly of the *Sporting News*. "Obviously, we're all looking for an explanation as to how this very unusual situation could be happening. You have to admit that we are talking about a most remarkable and maybe inexplicable moment in American sports history."

"That may be, but as far as the league is concerned, the matter has been addressed and resolved. If Mr. Klapper wants to release his medical information, that's up to him. Didi?"

Didi Bellardi was a former college all-American, now covering major league baseball for *Sports Illustrated*. "Thanks, Wendell. Was there anything else in the report pertaining to Mr. Klapper's medical condition?"

"Like what, Didi?"

"Well, like heart disease or diabetes or arthritis or any other condition that would not be uncommon in a man of Mr. Klapper's age?"

"I don't feel it's appropriate for me, not a doctor, to sit here with other non-doctors discussing the personal medical condition of one of our players. It feels improper, quite frankly, and guided by legal counsel, it may even be illegal for me to do so."

A reporter for the *New York Post* jumped in. "Mr. Commissioner, what medications, if any, is Mr. Klapper taking?"

"I'm not going to go beyond the medical findings I've already reported to you today. These findings clearly and fully address the allegations and put them to rest. There is simply no evidence of any kind to question the integrity of the performance of Mr. Klapper. Thank you all. Have a good day."

And that was that. More questions were shouted at Wendell Steinhouser, which he and his colleagues ignored while exiting the room. Noticeably, Victor Coleman had not attended.

It had been a good twenty minutes for Melvin. Winnie stood and applauded. Then he patted a sitting Melvin on the head and said, "That is over, baby. Done and done. Back to baseball."

"You really think so?"

"Most definitely. If Coleman continues with this crap, he'll become a punch line. His credibility is shot."

"Maybe this is a good time for us to make a short statement," said Melvin. "What do you think?"

"Whatever you think best. Let's write one up and hear how it sounds when read out loud."

Within minutes, ESPN was reporting that fans as well as legendary sports writers were calling for Coleman's head. Since few people in the business liked Coleman to begin with, they saw this as a golden opportunity to get rid of him. But Coleman remained silent as did the *Globe*. Some papers announced that they would be dropping his column.

By 5:00 p.m. that day, while Melvin was in the Yankee locker room, he was told by one of the coaches that Coleman had been suspended for thirty days without pay, pending an investigation into the basis for his columns accusing the Yankees and Klapper of a stunt—if not downright fraud.

Melvin felt awful. He did not enjoy seeing anyone, including Victor Coleman, harmed or hurt. He certainly wanted the matter over, but by suspending Coleman, it was being kept alive. Nor did he want to see anyone lose their income for a month. The statement that he and Winnie had drawn up earlier in the day was no longer timely or on point. A new statement was needed. Maybe Melvin was distracted or in pain. Those paying attention noticed a wince or two. Melvin went hitless, and the Yankees lost 4–0. The Red Sox had won against Baltimore, and so their lead went back to 5½ games.

Melvin sat on the chair by his locker talking with Pete, Glenn, and Terry. Though disappointed by the loss and lack of hitting, they all seemed confident that they could catch the Red Sox. Each teammate, in his own way, made the other guys feel better, including Melvin, who was now looking forward to the weekend series against the Tampa Bay Rays in Florida.

As Melvin was getting ready to leave the locker room and head home, Russ came over to him.

"Sorry, Melvin, but it's out."

"What's out?"

"The cancer stuff."

"What do you mean?"

"Someone leaked it. By the morning, it will be everywhere. You're probably going to have to say something or have your doctor say something. Otherwise, it will just continue. Think it over.

I'm always here if you want to run it by me. Or call Gus or even Lang. They'll back you up."

Sure enough, within fifteen minutes, Gus called. "Did you hear?"

"Yeah, Russ, just told me."

"Sorry, Melvin. Do you want me to say something?"

"Any idea how it got out?"

"Probably someone in the commissioner's office who got a few bucks. We live in a generation of leakers. That's just the way it is. Actually if you think about it, it's not that big a deal. Think of all the hope and inspiration you are going to bring to other cancer patients."

"You know, I never thought of that. Maybe you're right. Maybe some good can come from this."

"Attaboy, Melvin. You always turn lemons into lemonade. Go home and get some sleep."

CHAPTER 34

Thursday, September 1
Springfield

It was now September. With only thirty games remaining in the regular season, the Yankees trailed the Red Sox by 5½ games. That was a lot of territory to make up but not insurmountable. The Yankees had six games left against the Red Sox, three in Boston and three at home the last weekend of the season. Whoever made up the schedule years in advance had a sense of foreseeability and adventure. Tickets for those games were being scalped at twenty times face value, and no one was complaining. The month of September was traditionally crunch time in baseball, although this season, it was more exciting than usual because of the Yankees' late-season surge and the sensational story of Melvin Klapper. Could Melvin maintain his pace despite his deteriorating physical condition?

Just as Russ and Gus had predicted, the news coverage had switched to nonstop talk about Melvin's cancer. Did he have cancer? Where? For how long? Was he being treated? By whom? How come the cancer was not affecting his play? Did the Yankees know about this before the exam by the league? Did Melvin know about it? Did his teammates know about it?

And on and on it went. Endless media attention. The cancer story was just the latest fodder.

Melvin needed the day off as the team prepared for a potentially pivotal three game weekend series against Tampa, returning for a seven-game homestand beginning Monday. More than ever, Melvin and Winnie felt that a statement on behalf of Melvin was due. At about 2:00 p.m., Winnie called ESPN and other media outlets to say that he would be releasing a statement on behalf of Melvin. The statement read as follows:

> Hello, everyone. Melvin Klapper here. Thank you for your concern and well-wishes. I appreciate you all. I'd like to share my thoughts with you so you know what's going on.
>
> First of all, I do have cancer. Pancreatic, in fact, which I'm told only gets worse and rather quickly. But don't feel bad for me. I'm doing okay. I have wonderful doctors. It will be what it will be.
>
> In the meantime, I love playing for the Yankees. It's a dream come true. I'll continue to do my best. I need to stay focused, so I probably won't make any more statements until the season is over. Thank you for your support. Baseball is wonderful. Let's all enjoy it.
>
> Melvin

The public response was immediate and unanimous. Just like that, Melvin had done it again. He had become more popular than ever. Even opponents were singing his praises. Melvin had managed to transcend baseball. He had raised the conversation to a higher level. Seeing a good human being succeed lifted all boats. Melvin was named baseball's player of the month for August and was on the cover of more than forty magazines, including *Ladies*

Home Journal, *Vacation Homes of the South*, and even *Popular Mechanics*. Melvin had become a national feel-good phenomenon. The country was smitten by seventy-four-year-old cancer patient Melvin Klapper.

CHAPTER 35

Friday, September 2
St. Petersburg, Florida

"Welcome to beautiful Tropicana Field on a warm and humid evening in St. Petersburg, Florida," said Scott Whaler to open the broadcast. The former Dodger great would be doing the color for ESPN with his colleague and play-by-play veteran Dan Earling.

Melvin loved visiting these cities and these fields. On the flight down, he had read all about the oddities of Tropicana. It had the smallest seating capacity, 25,000 in the major leagues, and the only non-retractable dome in the majors. Rarely found anywhere else was its 10,000-gallon tank of stingrays that fans could touch. But the fact that really tickled Melvin was that it was not even in Tampa but actually in nearby St. Petersburg.

"This is the opening game of a three-game weekend series between the soaring New York Yankees and the Tampa Bay Rays, who are still not mathematically eliminated from the American League Eastern Conference pennant race. We have another night game tomorrow and then a day game at 1:00 p.m. on Sunday. While it's a muggy eighty-six degrees outside, it's a very comfortable seventy-two here inside the Trop. Looks like we'll have a capacity crowd tonight with many millions more watching from home."

"Should be a terrific game, Scott," added Dan. "The Yankees starter will be Lyle Little, who was acquired from the Cubs last month as the Yankees make their pennant charge. Little has been around the league and has pitched in some big games. He was 6–9 with the Cubs with an ERA of 3.98 before the trade. Since joining the Yanks, Little has won two, lost one, no decision in two with an ERA of 3.42. So he seems to be doing what the Yankees were hoping for in acquiring him."

Dan continued, "The Rays will be countering with their rookie sensation Hector Cruz. Cruz has won twelve games and lost only four. With a wicked fastball clocked at 100 mph, he has struck out 126 batters in 126 innings. Cruz is in the running for rookie of the year, and tonight will be a good test for him. In his only other outing with the Yankees, he was on the losing end of a 2–0 shutout, but the Yankees say they were impressed with his poise and ability to spot the ball.

"And of course the big talk in baseball today," picked up Scott, "as it has been since early July, is Mr. Melvin Klapper. What a story. It just seems to keep unfolding and in dramatic, almost storybook-like ways. What are your thoughts about Klapper, Dan?"

"Every time you think you've heard something about Melvin Klapper that can't be topped, there's more. Now we find out that this seventy-four-year-old man is suffering from pancreatic cancer. Pretty serious stuff. Yet at the same time, he's knocking out hits and to some extent carrying the Yankees on his back."

"I take his statement yesterday at face value," added Scott. "He just loves playing baseball, and I honestly believe that in just a few months he's probably done as much for the game of baseball as just about anyone else. He's increased the fan audience by millions, he's increased the revenue at every Yankee road game, he's energized our elderly community, and now cancer patients and survivors have a new hero. Baseball is now everywhere, and it's mostly because of one man, Melvin Klapper."

"Right, Scott, and on top of all that he goes out of his way to publicly defend Vic Coleman, the *Globe* columnist who started the call for the investigation of Melvin and the Yankees. I don't know that I could be that classy. So you've got to give the guy a world of credit. He's got the whole country pulling for him. And I understand that the Yankee brass and players love the guy."

The game went slowly, as there wasn't much hitting. Little was sharp, but Cruz was sharper. Cruz was dominating with a fastball and tight slider. Yankee bats were struggling. The Rays scored two off Little in the fourth and knocked him out in the sixth, scoring two more. The Yankees ended up losing the game 5–3. Melvin had two walks and a soft single to center.

CHAPTER 36

Saturday, September 3
St. Petersburg, Florida

Melvin liked his room at the recently renovated Renaissance International Plaza Hotel, having the day to just take it easy, do some slow walking and window shopping to stay loose and maybe catch a movie in an air-conditioned theater.

When he came down from his room for breakfast, he grabbed the *Tampa Tribune*, which on the bottom of the front page carried a story about Melvin, Victor Coleman, and the Boston Red Sox.

Would this ever end? thought Melvin to himself. The article rehashed all that had occurred since Coleman's first article back on July 11 and was clearly focused on the statement issued by the *Boston Globe* the night before. It read,

> The *Boston Globe* issues a sincere public apology to Mr. Melvin Klapper and the New York Yankees. Several recent columns printed in our paper went beyond the boundaries of the journalistic standards we here at the *Globe* have met for more than 150 years. The colum-

> nist who authored those columns has been suspended for thirty days without pay to give us time to consider what additional steps, if any, are necessary and appropriate at this time.
>
> While one may root for the Red Sox to do well, that determination should be made on the field, free from interference by outside forces. We consider this matter regarding Mr. Klapper to be resolved in his favor, and we wish him well in his ongoing battle with cancer. Similarly, we recognize that the New York Yankees are an outstanding organization deserving of our respect and admiration.

Melvin felt good that he had not sullied the reputation of the Yankees. After all they had done for him, causing them embarrassment or humiliation was the worst thing Melvin could do. He knew that Lang and Gus would be pleased to see the apology. Yet Melvin felt badly for Coleman. Yes, he had gone far out on a limb. Yes, he was trying to be provocative. But at the same time he had the courage to say what was on his mind and maybe the minds of others. And what if he had been right? Melvin thought the *Globe* was maybe overreacting, but he realized that the fans were calling for Coleman's head, so Melvin guessed that the *Globe* had to do something to quiet the crowd.

Melvin called Gus. After they rejoiced about the *Globe* apology, Melvin said, "Gus, can you do me a favor?"

"What do you need?"

"Gus, I don't want to be responsible for anyone getting fired or losing their salary, so would it be possible for you to call someone at the *Globe* and let them know that both the Yankees and Melvin Klapper would like to see Coleman returned to work? Could you do that for me?"

"Melvin, you're really something. Frankly, I think the guy needs to cool his heels, but if that's what you want I'll make the call. And, Melvin..."

"Yes, Gus?"

"We need a win tonight."

"Got it, Gus, thanks."

Melvin knew that he had to remain strong for the stretch run. The pressure was on, and his health was only going to get worse, not better. Russ had been offering Melvin an occasional day off, but so far, Melvin had resisted. He was relying on the four off days coming up over the next few weeks to provide the respite his body so badly required.

The *Globe* apology was blown up to a 3' × 4' poster size and tacked on the bulletin board in the Yankee locker room. Every player saw it and enjoyed it, each in his own way. Almost all the players went out of their way to greet Melvin, see how he was doing. Saturday night was a good night for Melvin and the Yankees. They had their hitting shoes on. The Yankees scored eight runs in the first three innings and coasted to an 11–3 win. Melvin had three hits, including a three-run home run. Melvin took his time trotting, almost walking, around the bases, but no one, including the Rays, uttered a word of criticism regarding Melvin's extraordinarily slow pace. They all just stood and watched him with admiration and wonderment.

CHAPTER 37

Sunday, September 4
St. Petersburg, Florida

The Sunday day game was pretty much a repeat of Saturday night. The Rays pitching staff got beaten up by Yankee bats, as the New York team knocked out fifteen hits, including three home runs, one by Melvin. The Yankees went on to a win 9–5 and picked up a game and a half on the Red Sox, who had lost a doubleheader in Texas to the Rangers. Boston's lead was down to four. The Yankees had picked up ten games since Melvin started playing.

Melvin was anxious to get home. To sleep in his own bed, to see Grace and Billy and to catch up with Winnie. Although Melvin used his phone and texted to stay in touch with Winnie, his family, Dr. Mendelsohn, and Gus, it was no substitute for actually seeing and being with the few people who truly cared about him. On this road trip, he bought a book of baseball facts and figures for Billy. Hopefully, this would make up for his faux pas of last time when Melvin had brought Billy a plaque of words meant to be inspirational that in reality didn't mean much to a ten-year-old boy.

Unfortunately, there was no day off between this last game of the road trip and the start of the homestand on Monday. It was going to be seven games in seven days, six of which were at night against the Minnesota Twins and the White Sox, two teams that played hard against the Yankees. Melvin much preferred day games. They gave his body more time to recover and allowed him more time to sleep. He also thought that he saw the ball better in the daylight, and it gave him more time to recover between games. It was going to be a tough week. Melvin was tired and getting more tired. He was surprised he was playing so well.

He had called Grace to make arrangements to come over for dinner on Monday night after the day game, but she, Chris, and Billy were going to a school function. Then he texted Winnie to see if he was around for lunch on Tuesday, which was to be a night game, but Winnie was working days all that week and the coming weekend. Security at the bank was 24/7, whether the bank was open or not. Being the head of security, Winnie worked more hours than his crew. Melvin asked Winnie if he could use the seats for Saturday or Sunday, suggesting that maybe Alva would like to see a game and then they could all have dinner together afterward. Winnie told Melvin that he would talk to Alva about Saturday and let him know.

The Yankees did well that week, winning five of their seven games. Melvin played in six games and had eleven hits, including a home run and a double that missed being a home run by inches. He also threw a runner out at the plate with a spectacular throw, his third such achievement since he started playing right field. But Melvin knew that time was running out. His batting average was still above .350, but he felt that he was losing power. He wondered if anyone else had noticed.

He had heard gossip in the locker room before Sunday's game that the suspension of Coleman by the *Globe* had been lifted. Melvin was glad. No one but Gus (and probably Lang) knew that Melvin was the reason the *Globe* did what it did. That was fine with Melvin. He wasn't looking for any credit. But it did make him feel better to know that maybe he had helped the guy get his job back.

As Melvin was leaving the locker room after the win on Sunday, his cell phone rang. Expecting Billy or Winnie, Melvin was taken aback when the caller said, "Is this Melvin?"

"Yes," said Melvin. "Who's calling?"

"It's Vic Coleman."

"Hello, Victor, how are you doing?" Melvin was probably the only person, other than Victor's parents, who ever called Vic by his full first name.

"Listen, I called first to apologize for making you have to go through that exam and then the release of your personal stuff. I'm really sorry about that. I just thought the whole thing with a seventy-four-year-old was fishy, impossible actually, but I let my emotions run away with my professionalism. So it was a big mistake, and I want you to know that I'm truly sorry."

"Okay, Victor, no problem. I appreciate your calling."

"Wait, there's more," said Vic.

"More?"

"Yes, I also want to thank you."

"For what?"

"For helping me get my job back. My editor said the only reason they were reinstating me at this time was because you and the Yankees requested it. That's pretty stand-up in my book."

"Victor, I wish you well."

"No, Melvin, I wish you well." And then he hung up.

Melvin felt good about the day and was looking forward to Saturday's day game when he could hopefully meet Alva.

CHAPTER 38

Monday, September 12
Springfield

The homestand was over on Sunday. Melvin was exhausted. Thankfully, the team had Monday off, so Melvin would use the day to regroup and get ready for a trip up to Boston to play a brief but important two-game midweek series against the Red Sox. Melvin enjoyed playing in Fenway because of how unique the ballpark was and because the fans were so appreciative of their players. He loved talking to the fans out in right field. Even his wearing a Yankee uniform didn't upset die-hard Boston fans, who just wanted to talk to Melvin. Fans all over the country did not see Melvin so much as a Yankee but as Melvin Klapper, a seventy-four-year-old man playing major league baseball. What he was doing fascinated baseball fans and that he was a decent man made it all the more attractive and nonpartisan.

It felt good, Melvin thought, just to lie around the house, read and prepare mentally for the games ahead. Around 11:00 a.m., there was a series of loud knocks at the door. With the police car still parked on the street across from Melvin's house and at least two officers present, it was unusual for someone to be able to get to Melvin's door without him knowing in advance. So Melvin thought it was probably someone he knew or maybe one of the officers wanting to ask or tell him something.

As soon as Melvin opened the door, the man standing there said, "Recognize me, Klapper?"

"I'm sorry, but I don't."

"It's your old Marine Corps buddy, Odom Briggs."

Melvin hesitated and then said, "Odom, it's been a while. Sorry, I didn't recognize you."

"Aren't you going to invite me in?"

"Sure," said Melvin, opening the door wider. "That was rude of me. I was just surprised to see you after all these years." Melvin realized that Briggs had somehow managed to sneak around from the back of the house, avoiding the eye of the police stationed out front.

Briggs strolled in and sat down in Melvin's chair. It had been nearly fifty-five years since Melvin had seen Odom Briggs. Melvin's initial impression was that Odom looked like a hardened, bitter, angry old man in desperate need of a shave and shower. His corded arms with prominent veins partially hidden by tatted sleeves jogged Melvin's memory as to whether he had had tattoos in Vietnam. His clothes were dirty and disheveled. His hair was long, stringy, oily, and unkempt. Odom had seen better days or maybe not. He stunk from tobacco and alcohol. Melvin had a flashback of Briggs chewing and spitting tobacco. And now he was sitting in Melvin's chair, acting like it was his house.

"Would you like a cold drink?" offered Melvin.

"How about some bourbon?"

"Sorry, but there's no alcohol in the house. I don't drink."

"Yeah, but how about for special guests like me?"

Melvin remained silent.

"So what's it like being a big, famous dude?"

"Odom, why are you here?"

"Life's been tough on me, Melvin. Unlike you, I have no house, no family who will speak to me, and no job. I live off government scraps and a pickup job here and there, but it ain't much.

So I figured my old Marine buddy Melvin Klapper, who has now hit it big, could help me out."

"Okay, how?"

"Well, I'm down and out. Pretty much no money. I could use a helping hand from a fellow Marine." Even though Melvin and Briggs had definitely not been buddies during the war, he was still a fellow Marine, and if Melvin could help him he would.

"I'd be glad to help you, Odom." Grabbing his wallet, Melvin said, "I've got about $400 here, and I'm glad to give you $300 of it. Would that help?"

"Melvin, Melvin, Melvin," Briggs snorted. "You were always a bit innocent."

"What does that mean?"

"I know you signed a multimillion-dollar contract with the Yankees. So I think you can afford a bit more, actually a lot more, than three hundred bucks."

"I haven't taken any of that money. It's being put into a trust account for my grandson's education."

"That's awfully sweet of you, Melvin, but that's not my problem. You have access to that money."

"Odom, what is it you want?"

"I was thinking, oh, one million dollars has a nice ring to it. And I want it in forty-eight hours," Briggs said with a sneer, displaying his contempt for Melvin.

Melvin was now starting to recall the Odom Briggs he knew in Vietnam. Briggs was a bad Marine. Not in times of combat, where he was ferocious and courageous, but the rest of the time, he was a man to be avoided.

"What? Odom, even if I had the money, why would I just give it to you?"

With a face contorted with evil and a snarling voice to match, Briggs said, "Melvin, it goes something like this. If you don't give me that money within forty-eight hours, I'll go to the press and tell them about the massacre of poor, innocent civilians you were part of in Vietnam."

"I was never part of any massacre."

"Yeah, you know that and I know that, but the press and the public don't know it. Overnight, you will become the most hated man in America and booed everywhere you go. You will be disgraced and humiliated. Your friends and family will turn on you." And then, changing his voice from harsh and gravelly to soft and almost whisper-like, he said, "And all I'm asking to spare you all that embarrassment is a measly one million dollars. So how about it, old pal, old Marine Corps buddy?"

"You would lie about me for money?"

"Hell yeah, I would," said a smiling Briggs. "I need that money, and you don't. So let's make life easy for both of us, dude."

"Odom, I wouldn't expect this from a fellow Marine. I have to think about it. I don't even know how to access that account. It's all being handled by the Yankees."

"You know, Klapper, I never liked you. You were always a goody-two-shoes type of Marine. Following orders, doing the right thing, making guys like me look bad. I wouldn't piss on you if you were on fire."

Melvin had no response because he couldn't believe this was happening.

Starting to rise from Melvin's chair, Briggs said, "You have forty-eight hours, Klapper. And then I go public." Walking to the door, Briggs continued, "Semper Fi man and all that crap." He slithered out the door like the snake he was. After being frozen in place for a moment, Melvin went to the door to look outside, but Briggs had vanished as stealthily as he had appeared.

The calm and peaceful day that Melvin had just begun to enjoy had come to an abrupt and crushing halt.

He could not believe that after all these years Vietnam was coming back to haunt him. Although he had nothing to hide and was never part of any civilian massacre, he also knew that Odom was right about the media. They would grab hold of this story and run with it for days, if not weeks. It would be his legacy, how Melvin would be remembered, as a disgrace to himself and all those around him. It would hurt Melvin, but more importantly, it would hurt the Yankees, his teammates, and Winnie. Thinking of how Grace and Billy would be affected by such a story was more than Melvin could imagine.

Melvin needed help. With the time deadline imposed by Briggs, he needed help quickly. He thought of going to Lang, but he had already burdened Lang and the Yankees so much that he felt it would be unfair to lay yet another problem on Lang or make this a Yankees problem.

"Winnie?" Melvin texted. "You there?"

"Yeah, buddy, at work. What's up?"

"I'm sorry to do this to you, Winnie, but I think I may have a really big problem and need your advice."

"Okay, how about Saturday?"

"No, it can't wait. How about tonight?"

"Tonight, huh? I have to run it by Alva. Where to meet?"

"It may take some time, and it's personal, so would you mind coming over here?"

"I'll talk to Alva. I'll bring some Chinese in. Okay?"

"Great. Thanks, Winnie."

For the six hours it took until Winnie showed up at the door, Melvin continuously paced the floor thinking of all the reasons he should pay Odom Briggs and all the reasons he shouldn't. Neither option seemed viable. It was blackmail, pure and simple. For the first time in years, since Martha was dying, Melvin felt so helpless. There was going to be no easy way out of this mess. Maybe Winnie would know what to do.

By 6:30 p.m., Winnie and Melvin were opening containers of spicy orange chicken, shrimp with lobster sauce, and everything fried rice.

"Melvin, what the heck is going on?"

"I'm being blackmailed."

"What? By whom?" said Winnie, stopping a fork midway to his mouth.

"Over something that's untrue."

"Whoa, start from the beginning."

So Melvin brought Winnie up to speed, retelling the entire conversation that had transpired between Melvin and Odom Briggs. "What should I do?"

"Tell me about this guy, Briggs."

"He was one of those Marines who liked the power and opportunity to shoot people. He didn't care about rules. He had no respect for authority and was always quick to pick a fight. He was a tough guy, and in times of combat, everyone else looked the other way. You don't want an enemy in your ranks. That's how you get killed from behind. He had a whole bunch of Article 15s, and I heard he was a Section 8."

"What's an Article 15?"

"Article 15 allows a commanding officer to discipline a Marine for misconduct without having to go through a court-martial. For convenience in combat zones. Briggs had several of these. He got busted twice that I know of."

"What's a...what did you call it? A section what?"

"A Section 8 is a discharge for being mentally unfit. It happens, but in the Marine Corps, you have to be really crazy, I mean batshit crazy, to get thrown out because of Section 8. That's Odom Briggs."

Winnie lowered his eyebrows.

"Melvin, I have to ask you a very tough question, and you must, must give me a totally truthful answer, leaving no part out. Without my knowing the absolute and unvarnished truth, I can't give you sound advice. Understood?"

"Understood, Winnie. Ask me anything."

"Listen, I understand things happen in war, in the heat of battle, okay, but did you, in any way, shape or form, participate in a massacre of civilians while you were in Vietnam? I repeat, in any way? At any time? Whether you got caught or not? Please think long and hard before answering. I know it was more than fifty years ago, but that's not something you'd forget."

Melvin didn't need a long time to think about it. He'd already spent six hours going over it all.

"Winnie, I was never involved in a civilian massacre. I heard about them but never actually saw one. There was one incident where there was a court-martial and a trial. I was on the ground at the time and called as a witness, but that's it. I was not even alleged to have done anything wrong. I along with about six or seven other guys were at least a click away guarding the perimeter with my helicopter crew and another crew. We were there for about two hours. We did hear gunfire, but that wasn't unusual. Villages had to be cleared. It doesn't necessarily mean that anyone, let alone civilians, were shot. We saw nothing and never moved from where we were. Later on, I think a few days later, we heard that there had been an incident in the village. I think Briggs was somehow involved, but I don't know for sure. That's the whole truth as best as I remember it. I swear it."

"So you have nothing to fear should the public hear about this, right? There's nothing that can be used against you? Did anything else happen while you were in the Marine Corps that could be discovered and used against you?"

"No, but the damage would be the same whether true or not, wouldn't it? Probably half the people will believe it. It will embarrass the Yankees, and can you imagine what it will do to Grace and Billy?"

"Let me think out loud," said Winnie. "If you pay this guy, and the public finds out, you'll look guilty. They'll say you wouldn't have paid him if you were truly innocent. Plus, if you pay him once, he can keep on blackmailing you. If he knows he can get money from you, he won't stop. If you are truly innocent, I'd tell him to take a hike. The question is whether you are ready, willing, and able to do that. Think it over, Melvin. This is a big decision, and it ain't going to be easy. You're in for a rough time, my friend, no matter what you decide here."

Winnie gave Melvin time to think over what Winnie had advised.

After about thirty seconds, Winnie continued, "Consider going to the police. Consider telling Lang and Gus. Leave everyone else out for the time being."

"I'm not ready to go to the police because I can't prove anything. I have no evidence. It would be his word against mine. If I tell Gus and Lang, it will just be another lousy situation that I've brought to them. They are going to get tired of me pretty soon. So I'd rather not do that."

"Do you want me to pay him a 'friendly' visit?" volunteered Winnie.

"No, I don't want to get you involved with this guy. I know you can take care of yourself, but Odom Briggs is pure danger. He likes violence and is willing to kill if necessary. He took joy in that over there. For him, it was fun unlike most other Marines, who were just doing their job. And I'd bet he's armed and just looking for an excuse to hurt someone. I don't want you to be that someone."

"Okay, think it over and let me know how you want to play this, but my advice, if you've got nothing to hide, is to play it straight and let the chips fall where they may. People who know you will believe you. That's all that counts. Fans are fickle. Don't base your decision on them. Look, I gotta get home. Alva is waiting up for me. She knew this was an emergency, but I gotta go."

"Thank you, Winnie, for being here for me. I've got a lot to think about."

CHAPTER 39

Tuesday, September 13
Boston, Massachusetts

The Yankees won a hard-fought, tension-filled opening game at Boston 3–2. Melvin had two singles and drove in a run. He was playing better than he felt. New York was now out by three games. The Red Sox lead was shrinking, and the Yankees were bubbling with confidence. Melvin was playing in pain but was so appreciative and grateful for this moment of opportunity that the pain seemed to be a small price to pay for the experience of a lifetime.

Wednesday, September 14

It had now been two days since Odom Briggs tried to blackmail Melvin. There had been no further contact from Briggs, which Melvin took as a good sign. Maybe Briggs had thought it over and decided not to take the risk. Melvin was encouraged.

The Red Sox rallied for two in the bottom of the eighth for a 5–4 lead. They made it stand up behind their closer, Ellis Demarie. Melvin made the last out of the game, getting called on a third strike that everyone thought was outside except the home plate umpire.

The ump yelled, "Yer out."

Melvin said, "Oh, c'mon, that was outside."

"Sorry, Melvin," said the ump, who turned and walked away. The Sox had renewed their four-game lead.

The Yankees had been hoping for a two-game sweep in Boston. Losing the second game cost them two games and canceled out the victory of the first game. Though somewhat down, the Yankees knew they were playing well and that they could catch the Sox, with whom they still had six games left to play. With the next day being a day off, Melvin was hoping to see Grace and Billy and relax a bit to get prepared for three games against the Brewers and then three hosting the Pirates. The schedule was only going to get tougher from here to the finish line, and Melvin's condition was steadily deteriorating.

The Yankee charter plane was waiting for the players at Logan to make the quick flight to LaGuardia. Melvin and the team were in good spirits. Melvin's pain had now become more of a constant dull throb with unpredictable, occasional jabs of sharper pain, mostly in his abdomen and side. The increased dose of Tramadol he was taking seemed to keep it in check.

As the players disembarked in New York and headed to their cars or cabs, Melvin spotted Odom Briggs leaning up against a vending machine and chewing on a jaw of tobacco. He looked just as mean and ornery as he had on Monday.

For a moment, Melvin thought of ignoring him but knew that wouldn't work. Briggs would not be ignored, and Melvin decided it was better to deal with this irrational and surly guy in public rather than in private. Melvin couldn't remember the last time he'd been in a fistfight, but he readied himself for that possibility.

"Klapper, what's it gonna be? I'm waiting for Mr. Green."

"Who's Mr. Green?" asked Melvin.

Rubbing his right thumb and forefinger together, Briggs snarled and said, "The money."

"I can't do it, Odom. I'll gladly help you out, but I can't let you make up a lie to extort money from me. That money is for my grandson. Sorry." Melvin started to walk away.

"Pal," fumed Briggs, raising his voice, "you just made a big mistake. I think I'll give a call to Victor Coleman. This time, he'll nail you good."

Melvin stopped and turned back to Briggs. "Don't do it, Odom. Please."

"You had your chance, Klapper. You'll regret this. I promise."

And just like that, Briggs was gone. Melvin knew that Briggs would do as he threatened. He would gladly, probably convincingly, tell his story to Coleman, who would see this as a chance to finally get rid of Klapper and tarnish the Yankees. Melvin stood there wondering if he had just made the worst mistake of his life.

CHAPTER 40

Thursday, September 15
Boston

"Hello, Mr. Coleman?"

"Yeah, this is Coleman. Who's this?" Coleman grunted through an unlit Cohiba dangling from his mouth.

"My name is Odor Briggs. I was a US Marine in Vietnam in 1968. I was serving with Melvin Klapper, who did something very bad and got away with it. Want to hear more?"

"Yeah, you bet I want to hear more," responded Coleman, "but why now after all these years? Where you been all this time?"

"I'm getting older and want to clear my conscience before I die."

"That's it?"

"That and I think it's only fair that I be compensated."

"What are you looking for?"

"One hundred thousand dollars," replied Briggs.

"The *Globe* will never go for that."

"How about $10,000?"

"I'd have to hear the story first before talking to my boss, and he'd probably have to go to his boss. The *Globe* doesn't like paying for stories. But if your story is worth it, I'll pitch for you to get paid. When can you come in?"

"How about tomorrow at 10:00 a.m.?"

"I'll be here. Fifth floor."

Coleman didn't like the tone of this caller nor his supposed reason for suddenly wanting to tell his story. His experience had been that people needing to tell the truth rarely asked to be paid. They just wanted their story to be heard. But rather than hang up on him, Coleman thought it would be better to hear him out. Could be a Pulitzer just waiting to happen.

At exactly ten o'clock the next morning, a clean-shaven, reasonably well-dressed, and coiffed man of about seventy-five appeared at the office of Vic Coleman on the fifth floor of the Boston Globe building in downtown Boston. They shook hands, and Odom Biggs told Coleman a story filled with lies that took about twenty uninterrupted minutes. Basically, Briggs was saying that Melvin was psychologically unfit and that he had used his position as a Marine to hurt and kill civilians. Briggs even exaggerated the story he originally concocted because he saw Coleman as a rapt listener.

Briggs went on to say that he thought Klapper had been court-martialed but couldn't say for sure. He said that Melvin was one of those Marines whom other Marines didn't like and couldn't trust. Briggs must have been thinking about himself.

"Do you have any proof of this, Mr. Briggs?"

"No, it was half a century ago."

"When was the last time you saw or spoke with Mr. Klapper?"

"I saw him on TV, which jogged my memory. Haven't spoken to him since Vietnam."

"What do you do for a living, Mr. Briggs?"

"Retired now. I was in law enforcement for a while. Then I taught school."

"I'd have to give Mr. Klapper a chance to respond. You understand that, right?"

"Oh, sure, but he'll lie. What about my ten grand? You have to admit it's front-page stuff."

"Let me do my homework, and I'll get back to you. Do you have a cell number where I can reach you at?"

"I'd rather I called you. Today is Thursday. How about I call you Saturday?"

"Sure, that works," said Vic.

The whole thing smelled, thought Coleman, as he leaned back in his wooden swivel chair with a number-two pencil perched atop his right ear, figuring out what to do next. As much as he disliked the Yankees or any New York team for that matter, he didn't dislike Melvin Klapper and found it hard to believe that Melvin was the kind of guy Briggs described.

Thursday, September 15
Springfield

Even though it was a day off, Melvin had a bad feeling about what the day would bring his way. He expected trouble, knowing that Odom Briggs was not going to just go away. That wasn't Odom's style.

He called Winnie at work to update him about Briggs and then told Winnie he was going to call Gus. Winnie agreed that Melvin had no choice at this point.

"Gus? It's Melvin."

"Melvin, can't you enjoy a day off?"

"I wish I could, but unfortunately something has come up, and I feel it's only fair to let you and Lang know about it."

"Well, Lang is out on Nantucket, and I have meetings all day, starting in a few minutes. Can it wait?"

"I'm afraid not. Would you mind talking now, Gus?"

"I guess we'll have to."

At that point, Melvin told Gus the entire story, how Briggs had come to his house, tried to extort money with a made-up story, and then was waiting for him at the airport last night.

"Holy cow, Melvin, what is going on?"

"I think this guy saw me on TV or read about me and thought he could cash in."

"What do you want me to do?" asked a perplexed Gus.

"Nothing. The story is untrue, but if it comes out, as I'm expecting it will, the Yankees will come under attack, as will I. You and Lang can do what you have to."

"I've got to call Lang right now. I'll call you back."

Melvin's phone rang. Expecting it to be Gus, he was surprised to hear the caller identify himself as Vic Coleman.

"Klapper?"

"Yes."

Without introducing himself, Coleman said, "I just had a friend of yours, Odom Briggs, in my office telling me you're a war criminal. Any truth to it?"

"No, absolutely not. He came to my home on Monday and tried to blackmail me for a million dollars. He said if I didn't pay him, he would tell this made-up story to the press. I guess he then reached out to you, knowing we've had our differences in the past."

"I figure I owe you one, Klapper, so I'm passing on the story. This may cost me a Pulitzer, but deep inside, I don't see you as a murderer of women and children. I hope I'm betting on the right horse here."

"You are. It's untrue. Thank you for calling me."

"Just so you know, he won't stop with me. He'll find someone to run with the story, so be prepared. But as far as I'm concerned, the story is dead."

"Thanks, Victor," said Melvin. Victor had already hung up.

While Melvin was catching his breath, the phone rang again. This time, it was Gus. Melvin knew that this call was important because Gus would be relaying whatever decision had been made by Lang. Melvin knew it could be the end of his time with the NY Yankees.

"Hey, Gus," said Melvin, very tired and frustrated.

"I spoke with Lang. We're going to stick by you at least for the time being. Please understand that if any facts come out or witnesses come forward that substantiate this guy's story, the Yankees will have to do what's in the best interest of the organization. You understand what I'm saying, Melvin?"

"Absolutely, Gus. I appreciate everything you and Lang have done for me. I'm sorry to keep bringing all these problems to you. I never imagined there would be people trying to take advantage of the situation."

"Lang said to tell you that people who make things worse are just trying to get back at people who make things better."

"Thank you, Gus, and please thank Lang. You may want to know that I got a call from Victor Coleman. Briggs reached out to him, but Coleman rejected the story because he didn't believe it was true."

"That's a side of Coleman I never saw before. Keep me posted. Goodbye, Melvin."

"Goodbye, Gus."

It had become a rough day for Melvin. What had started out as a day meant for rest and relaxation had become a mess. And he feared the worst was yet to come. Briggs was a loose cannon, and Melvin knew it was only a matter of time before the Yankees had enough.

He looked at Martha's picture while sitting at the kitchen table, explaining to her what had transpired and the predicament he was in.

As if that were not enough, his pain had escalated to a new level. He had called Dr. Mendelsohn but had not heard back from him yet. He was becoming afraid to eat because of the pain it caused. Similarly, he had to sleep sitting in his chair rather than lie down in bed, which also increased the pain. The worst thing that was bothering him was that he could still smell Odom Briggs in his house, especially in his chair.

Not feeling well enough to make the trip over to Grace's and not wanting to tell her all this over the phone, Melvin fell asleep in his chair, only to be startled at around 10:00 p.m. by the ringing of his cell phone. Calls that late always scared Melvin. There were no good calls late at night, thought Melvin.

It was Gus.

"Melvin, it broke. Everything you told me and more is in the paper and online. It's going to be bad. Really bad."

"What paper did this?"

"The *Insider.*"

"Never heard of it. Is that a real newspaper?"

"Yes and no," said Gus. "It's a rag, but it gets the story out. You know the old adage, 'If it bleeds, it leads.' This story is a doozy. It's not about journalism. It's about sales and ads, and the *Insider* has plenty of both. The point is the story will be carried nationally by tomorrow morning. You better fasten your seat belt, Melvin."

CHAPTER 41

Friday, September 16
Milwaukee

As Gus had correctly predicted, the story about "War Criminal Melvin Klapper" was everywhere—all over the television, the front pages of all the newspapers, even on Melvin's phone. Reporters and the public were demanding answers. And as you would expect, the talking heads were at it already, attacking Melvin and anyone who would employ him, demanding that he be tried as a war criminal and arguing that that statute of limitations for war crimes never expires.

Briggs, being hailed as an innocent man with a conscience, was in demand for interviews. Stations like CNN and the networks, even *60 Minutes*, were vying for Odom Briggs. *How could this possibly happen?* wondered Melvin. *Has the world gone mad? How could anyone believe this derelict?* Melvin was amazed how, without a scintilla of proof, based on the unsubstantiated allegations of one man, people not only had strong and definite opinions but wanted the harshest possible punishment to be imposed immediately on Melvin Klapper, the supposed war criminal.

The team was boarding their charter to get to Milwaukee for a three-game series starting at 7:00 p.m.

The Yankees trailed the Red Sox by four games, but they felt that it was well within their ability to catch the Boston team.

Yet the latest Melvin Klapper blockbuster could upset the winning rhythm the Yankees had finally achieved. While most players supported Melvin, even they realized that they didn't know the truth, and maybe Melvin had been a different guy fifty years ago. Obviously, no teammate wanted a war criminal playing alongside him no matter how good a player he was. Although the Marines were in fact extremely well disciplined, they had a public image that too often fed into a story of violence and brutality.

During most of these team trips, players talked, played cards and video games, or hung out with a teammate who played the guitar or harmonica. But this trip, the players were glued to their seats, quiet and content to let their earbuds give them some peace.

Halfway into the trip, Russ Higgins strode to the middle of the plane and started clapping. It got everyone's attention as it was intended to do.

In his usual foghorn voice, Higgins said, "Listen, men, we've been up against it this entire season, but we've persevered because we've hung together. Call me old-fashioned, but a man in my book is innocent until proven guilty. Especially a teammate. Melvin totally denies the allegation and says Briggs is a liar and con artist who came to Melvin's house on Monday trying to extort a million bucks. Melvin refused, knowing he had nothing to hide and that the people who know him would believe him, not this other guy. I say we back Melvin. My money is on him, and I'm a pretty good judge of character. Now let's open the floor to comments. Speak your piece, gentlemen."

After a moment or two, one of the senior and more respected team members, Carlton Bailey, said, "I'd like to hear it from Melvin."

Melvin stood up slowly. All eyes bored in on him. He was embarrassed that it had come to this. "I would never lie to you guys. I was a good and proud Marine. I did not participate in any civilian massacre or war crime. The story is totally untrue. I don't know how I can prove it to you, but I ask that you trust me. Give me the benefit of the doubt as I would you."

Bailey spoke up again. "That's good enough for me."

Pete then jumped in. "I'd rather support Melvin and be wrong than not support him and be wrong." That one line coming from Captain Pete Warner settled the matter.

Higgins knew it and said, "So are we okay on this?" Players started applauding. Higgins sat back down, next to Melvin.

"Thanks, Russ."

Knowing full well that hope was not a strategy, Russ nevertheless looked directly into Melvin's eyes and in a most serious whisper said, "I only hope to God that you're telling the truth, Melvin, or we're both in big trouble."

Melvin did not know what to say in response, so he just sat there quietly.

During the game, Melvin was booed almost continuously by the usually courteous Milwaukee crowd—when he touched the ball, every time at bat, when he left the dugout for the batter's box, and every time his name was announced. It was without mercy. The name-calling and throwing of objects onto the field was beyond the pale. It intimidated Melvin and traumatized the team. A judgment had been made based on almost nothing. But the public had spoken loudly and clearly. Melvin was guilty. End of story. It was devastating. Melvin went hitless, and the Yankees were shut out 5–0.

Covering every Yankee game were ESPN announcers Dan Earling and Scott Whaler. They had been a part of the Melvin Klapper story since the "catch and throw" (how it was referred to now) back on July 9. They had come a long way with the story and were still the best, most reliable source for understanding what had and was transpiring.

"Scott," began Dan, "the Yanks lose 5–0 and fall another game behind the Red Sox, who beat the Phillies tonight 5–1. In the meantime, it's been a tough day for the Yankees and Mr. Melvin Klapper—a day marked by an extraordinary event, not only for baseball but for the country. Some very serious allegations have been made against Klapper, which, if true, go far beyond baseball. And of course it brings back the whole debate of our involvement in Vietnam, which many people would like to forget."

"Dan, this story, however it unfolds, will have a significant impact on players, fans, and frankly all of us. Now we have to say right from the start that we sitting here in the booth have no idea whether these claims are true or not. We're not attacking Mr. Klapper or defending him. We're just here to report the story and assume that the truth will come out sooner or later, probably sooner."

"The question for me, Scott, is how can the Yankees and Klapper possibly handle this amount of pressure? How does the organization respond? How do the players handle it? Can Klapper play? Should he play? There is talk of benching him, possibly even suspending him. And how will the fans react? They used to love him, but will they love him tomorrow?"

CHAPTER 42

Saturday, September 17
Springfield

Back home, Grace and Chris were going at it. Chris felt he had finally found a flaw in good old Grandpa. Chris, though a fundamentally good person, just couldn't resist the opportunity to divide Billy and Melvin. He was envious of their relationship. He knew it was wrong but, being only human, couldn't get himself to support Melvin in his moment of need. Even worse, he wasn't there to support Grace and Billy.

"Dad," asked Billy, "is it true what they say on TV, that Grandpa killed innocent people?"

"We don't know, son, so I can't really say one way or the other."

"Would it be really bad if it's true?"

"Oh yeah. It would be very, very bad."

"What would happen? Would Grandpa be arrested and go to jail?"

"I don't really know what would happen, but it wouldn't be good for him or for us."

"I don't want to go to any more games or watch on TV."

"Not a bad idea, son," said Chris.

Billy turned and ran all the way up to his room. He threw his glove against the wall, same with his hat that had been resting on a bedpost. He then took the plaque that Melvin had given him off the wall and threw that too. Then he jumped on the bed and started crying.

Grace, hearing the commotion, went to Billy's room. Seeing him crying, Grace said, "Billy, is this about Grandpa?"

"I don't want to be his grandson. He's a bad man."

"No, he's not. He's the person you've known and loved all these years. Don't let other people who don't know him change how you feel about him."

"Mom, is it true? Did Grandpa kill innocent people?"

"Why don't we ask Grandpa and see what he says?"

"But maybe he'll lie."

"He's never lied to me. Has he ever lied to you?"

"No."

"Let's not jump to conclusions. Let's stick together. We're a family. That's what good families do in tough times. They stick together." Grace hugged Billy then went looking for Chris.

"Chris, what did you say to Billy that upset him so much?"

"He asked me questions, and I tried to answer them honestly."

"You made Melvin look guilty. Why would you do that?"

"I was preparing Billy for the worst."

"Why? Do you believe that my father is a war criminal?"

"Grace, I don't know, and you don't know. What if it's true?"

"This is my father you're talking about, and even if it is true, I've got his back all the way, same as I would for you. It's about loyalty and family. You've always resented Dad's relationship with Billy, and now you're using this unfounded and unproven accusation to hurt not only my father but me and Billy. I'm disappointed in you, Chris, deeply disappointed. I thought we could count on each other. Do the right thing, Chris, and fight for Melvin, not against him."

Grace walked away angrily while Chris just looked at her, realizing that he had screwed up big-time. He knew that Grace was right and that he had to do the right thing…and without Grace having to say anything further on the matter.

Saturday night's game was delayed by rain for about one hour. The Yankee locker room was much more subdued than usual. Despite the discussion on the plane ride out to Milwaukee, doubts about Melvin lingered and brought an unnecessary and untimely burden upon the Yankees with just two weeks to go in the season. The game was a snooze fest. The Yankees with only two hits (none by Melvin) had no energy. Their spirit had been sapped. They were lifeless. The Yankees lost 2–0 and were shut out for the second game in a row. The team had clearly been affected by the accusations against Melvin.

CHAPTER 43

Sunday, September 18
Milwaukee

Following two lackluster and lethargic performances, one would have expected the Yankees to bounce back for a Sunday day game, but that was not to be. Once again, the Yankees seemed in disarray as if they were just going through the motions. Melvin was booed incessantly as was the whole Yankee team. The fans had turned on him. The country, led by an aggressive and judgmental press, had turned on him. His teammates were taking it on the chin. They didn't know what to make of the situation other than that Melvin was hurting the team. The Yankees lost 6–1. Melvin went hitless and barely made contact. The Red Sox, although not playing well, had managed to increase their lead over the Yankees to six games.

After the game, Russ asked Melvin to stop by his office.

"Melvin, we need to talk." said Russ, sounding awkward and uncomfortable. "In the interest of the team and you, I think it's best that you ride the bench for now. It will give you a much-needed rest and maybe take some of the heat off all of us. You okay with this?"

"Sure, Russ. I understand and agree. Whatever you want me to do, I'll do. The team comes before me. I just feel so ashamed, although I've done nothing wrong. I'm not sure why, but I'm so embarrassed and humiliated."

"Is there anything you want to tell me, Melvin?"

"No, I'm just being honest. An innocent person shouldn't feel guilty, but I do. I'm not angry, which I ought to be, but I'm very upset and sad. Look at all the trouble I've caused."

"Melvin, if you haven't done anything wrong, hold your head up high, your shoulders back, and don't let this get to you. We'll get through it somehow. I for one believe in you. Don't worry. Everything will turn out okay in the end."

"Do you really think so, Russ?"

"I hope so, for you, for me, for all of us."

The team flight home seemed to take forever. The team had dropped all three games to a mediocre Brewers team and trailed the Red Sox by six games. Half the players looked like they were going to a funeral. The other half like they were coming back from one. Melvin felt responsible for the depression that had afflicted the team, but there was nothing more he could do.

When he got off the plane in New York on Sunday night, Winnie was at the airport to greet him. *Ah, finally a friendly face*, Melvin thought, but Winnie wasn't smiling his usual big smile, and he didn't seem particularly friendly.

"Winnie, what are you doing here?"

"Melvin, Chris wouldn't let me see Billy this weekend. Neither Chris nor Billy would even talk to me. Grace had to be the one to tell me. She was crying. She apologized for them. I told her it was okay, but it wasn't. Then Alva was all up in my face, telling me I got this all wrong and that I've been a fool. Melvin, this is getting rough—even for me."

"I'm sorry, Winnie. I don't know what to say. Just walk away. I'll be fine."

"I just want to ask you one more time, do I have your solemn word on Martha's grave that I'm backing the right horse here?"

"Winnie, I almost don't know anymore. I'm confused. It's been very frustrating. I'm ruining the team's chances. Everyone is booing me. I'm not feeling well. I have to go lie down," said Melvin as he started to walk away.

Winnie followed Melvin. "I spoke with Gus," he said to Melvin. "He wants you to issue a statement about what's going on. I'll do it if you're up to it."

"Not tonight, Winnie. I'm done for today. Maybe I'm just done, period. Tomorrow is a day off, and I need it real bad. I need to think things through and whether this baseball stuff is worth all the trouble I'm causing. If you want to continue this conversation, let's try tomorrow, but if you don't want to, I'll understand. You don't owe me anything, Winnie."

CHAPTER 44

Monday, September 19
Springfield

Despite plenty of reasons to stay away, Winnie showed up at Melvin's door at 9:00 a.m. He had gotten another security guard to cover his shift for the morning. He found Melvin as he had left him the night before. Tired and morose, Melvin was sitting in despair at the kitchen table and staring at Martha's picture as if for advice and counsel. Winnie figured he had been talking to her about the situation.

Melvin was surprised but pleased to see that Winnie was standing by him, at least up until now.

"Okay, Melvin, time to get our act together. Enough self-pity. Time to buck up, Marine. So what should we say? How about the truth? I'm told that sets us free. I jotted down some notes last night when I couldn't sleep. I didn't know if you wanted to mention anything about Briggs or the blackmail attempt."

"No, I don't want to give that guy any publicity, and I don't want to look like a victim."

Winnie read out loud what he had written. "I just want you all to know that the allegations about me are totally untrue. At no time would I or did I participate in any such misconduct. I'm proud of my service in Vietnam and proud to be a US Marine Corps veteran. I hope you will believe in me and support me during this very difficult time. Thank you."

"Yes, that's real good. Short and to the point."

"Okay," said Winnie, "I'm going to let this fly. Now you have to rest, and I have to get back to the bank."

"I have to go see Grace and Billy," said Melvin. "This is going to be horrible."

Winnie could see that Melvin was despondent. "It's going to be tough, but you can do it. You have to do it."

"But I'm just an ordinary person in extraordinary circumstances. I don't know how to respond, how to act, or what to say. To be perfectly honest, the truth is that I've never really been good at taking on challenges. Frankly, I get scared."

"Scared? Scared of what? What are you talking about? How about fighting in a war?"

"That was different. I was trained for that. I just did my job. Real life is actually much tougher than combat. Now I'm on my own, out there all alone. People are attacking me, and I can't shoot back. I'm defenseless. Totally defenseless."

"First of all, Melvin, you're not alone. I'm standing right here, right next to you. Second, what I learned early on the street was that it's not brave or courageous to do something unless you're scared of doing it. We're all scared, but you gotta fight through it."

"Winnie, my whole life, I've pretty much ducked every opportunity that has come along. I stayed a grocery store clerk for fifty years. Why do you think? I even turned down Mr. Wilson's offer to make me store manager. I've never really felt good enough or smart enough to step up to anything. I've always been Melvin Klapper, the nice guy who just wants to be liked. I've always wanted other people's acceptance of me, while I've never really been able to accept myself. I've been using kindness to avoid taking any risk whatsoever. It was just an excuse to allow me to back down, back off, and back away."

Winnie closed his eyes and took a deep breath. His sigh was audible.

"Melvin, the point is you can do both. It's not an either-or choice. You can be as nice as you want but still try to succeed. No one begrudges you for that."

"I realize now more than ever that I haven't really achieved much in my seventy-four years. I've never felt a sense of accomplishment. I don't even know what success feels like. I've never really felt it. Isn't that terrible for a grown person to say? This is the first time I've actually said this to anyone, including Martha, although I've been saying it to myself for a very long time. It's disappointing to feel this way at any age, but after a lifetime of almost seventy-five years, it really hurts. How many chances do I have left?"

"Melvin, we all get a chance to do something great. We just don't see it at the time. I'm here to tell you that this is your moment, your chance to do something great. This is your opportunity to put all that other stuff in the past. For once in your life, wouldn't you like to know how it feels to be a winner?"

Winnie sat down across from Melvin, who was sagging into his chair. "Melvin, think of Martha, your wonderful Grace, and your terrific grandson, Billy. That's a lot to be proud of. That's a lot to achieve in a man's lifetime. A good family is worth a lot. It takes a ton of work, but you did it. Something I always wanted but never had. My parents were not the greatest. My dad left us early with no support. Then Alva and I tried for years to have children of our own, but that wasn't meant to be. So appreciate what you do have. How can we discover what we're capable of if we hide from ourselves every time an opportunity presents itself? You have to take risks to find out who you really are and what you're made of. What is Melvin Klapper made of?"

After a long pause and a deep exhalation of breath, Melvin looked at Winnie with a look Winnie had never before seen and said, "Winnie, I know you're right. This is my moment of truth. It's taken a long time to get here, but now is the time for me to prove to myself that I have what it takes to be the best I can be and let the chips fall where they may. So maybe I should be thankful to Odom Briggs for forcing this moment upon me. He has placed this obstacle in my path, and it's up to me to face up to it and get past it."

"Melvin, I believe in you. You're much more than you think you are. This is your time, man. Just remember, Melvin, it's never too late."

"Thanks, Winnie. I'm scared, but I may never have another chance. It's time for me to find my backbone, meet life's challenges, and not be afraid of the outcome. I love you, Winnie."

"I love you, Melvin."

Winnie left to get back to the bank. Melvin showered and dressed, wearing his favorite shirt that Martha had given him. Melvin was ready to go see Grace and Billy. He knew it would be a difficult and emotional conversation, but it was a good starting point for Melvin to meet this challenge head on. He waited until he knew they would be at home.

When he got to Grace's, Billy was outside sitting on the stoop. When Billy saw Melvin, he started crying and ran inside the house. Billy had no baseball glove and wasn't wearing his Yankees cap. Amos ran with him. Melvin knew he had his work cut out for him. Grace came to the door, holding it open for her father.

"Hi, Dad, you off today?"

"Yes, sweetheart, I am. I wanted to talk with you today as we have nine games coming up before I have another day off. Would it be okay to sit with you, Billy, and Chris all at one time?"

"Chris is out back. I'll get him. It may be tougher getting Billy down here, but let's try. You should know that Billy was in a fight at school today. He has a shiner."

"A fight?"

"Yep, about you. The other boys were calling you names, and Billy was defending you. Billy got in trouble, and Chris had to go speak with Mrs. Locklear, the principal. It all got worked out, but I wanted you to know. Boys will be boys."

"I'm sorry to hear that, but at least Billy fought for me, which is more than I've been doing for myself."

Grace left Melvin sitting on the couch in the living room, while she went to collect Chris and then hopefully Billy.

When Chris came in, he was aloof and standoffish. There was no warmth, affection, or support for Melvin, almost a grudging acknowledgment of Melvin's presence.

"Hey, Chris, how are you?"

"Things could be better, couldn't they, Melvin?"

"Yes, they could, but that's life. I'm here to try and make things better."

Chris did not respond, nor would he look directly at Melvin.

Grace was walking Billy down the stairs.

"Hey, Billy," said Melvin, "you still talking to me?"

Billy did not respond. Grace sat in a chair opposite where Melvin was sitting. Billy stood close to the chair Grace was sitting in. Chris remained standing with his arms folded across his chest. Not a sign of receptiveness, but Melvin was way past worrying about what Chris thought.

"Okay," said Melvin, "let's clear the air. You know that some terrible things have been said about me. They are not true. I was never involved in anything where innocent people were hurt. It never happened. You three should know me well enough by now to believe me rather than someone you don't even know. So that's it. There should be nothing more I need to say."

"That's it?" asked Chris. "Do you realize how this has impacted our lives?"

"Yes, and I'm sorry for that."

"Dad, what's going to happen now?" asked Grace.

"Grace, I honestly don't know. So far, the Yankees are sticking with me. Winnie has been a great friend. My back and side are killing me. My grandson is ashamed of me. I'm playing terribly, I'm letting my teammates down, and I'm being booed everywhere. Other than that, everything is fine."

"I'm proud of you, Dad. Always have been. Being the daughter of Melvin Klapper is an honor, so I don't care about the controversy. Is there anything we can do for you?"

"Thank you, Grace. I knew I could count on you. Billy, do you believe me? Do you still love Grandpa Melvin?"

Billy started to cry as he ran over to Melvin and hugged him tightly. Tears came to Melvin's eyes.

"I love you, Billy. Don't worry, this will all work out. I want you to be proud of me. That's very important to me. Maybe the most of anything in the world. I want you to know that."

Melvin stood up to go. He had barely survived the ordeal of having to tell his daughter and grandson that he wasn't a war criminal who killed innocent women and children.

Chris, prompted by Grace, went over to Melvin to shake hands.

"Melvin, I have no idea what's going on, but I pray for you and for us that this somehow works out."

"Chris, you have to have confidence in yourself and in others. That's something I'm learning too. When thc chips are down, you need to believe in yourself and that it will all work out, and I believe it will. So you just take care of my daughter and grandson. Fair enough?"

"Fair enough," said Chris, looking perplexed.

Grace hugged her father with extra special love while weeping on his shoulder. Billy was holding on to Melvin's pant leg, so Melvin knelt down and hugged Billy. Chris stood a few feet away and listened to Melvin talk with Billy.

"Don't you worry, Billy. I'll come through for you. You'll be proud of me, I promise. Think about this one and text me the answer. A baseball bat and a ball cost $1.10 together. And the bat cost $1 more than the ball. How much does the ball cost?"

When Melvin arrived home, the television was blasting the statement that Winnie had disseminated to the media. At least it was getting coverage. Maybe it would somehow help to blunt the accusation, Melvin hoped. Melvin sat in his chair to get some much needed sleep. At least the house was beginning to smell less of Odom Briggs.

CHAPTER 45

Tuesday, September 20
Yankee Stadium

The Yankees were at home for a quick but important three-game homestand against the visiting Pittsburgh Pirates. Then they would be on the road for three games at Fenway, three in Toronto, and finally three in Baltimore, a grueling nine games away from home.

These twelve games would be crucial for the Yankees if they were going to make a run at the Red Sox. The Red Sox were not playing well, but the Yankees were playing even worse. Since the story broke of Melvin being involved in a civilian massacre in Vietnam, the Yankees had looked and played their worst of the season and were now six games out.

For the first time since joining the Yankees on July 12, Melvin was not looking forward to going to Yankee Stadium. He was actually scared. He felt small and old and weak. His limp was now more pronounced. His back, side, and abdominal pain had worsened. Equally as important, maybe more so, he had lost that confidence and positive attitude that he had so enjoyed since playing for the Yankees. He learned in the locker room that the players called it "drip," which meant a cool sense of style. But today, he was only filled with fear—fearful of the crowd, fearful of the fans booing him and yelling out nasty and hurtful remarks and for Billy to have to listen to this on television.

At 11:00 a.m. New York time, a group of earnest elderly men were gathered outside the front entrance to Yankee Stadium. There were five men in all. Three were white, one was Hispanic, and one was black. They all looked very serious. They were all impeccably dressed in suits and ties. They all had purple heart lapel pins. They had set up a lectern with a microphone. Two hours earlier, they had contacted the news media, several networks, Major League Baseball, and all those outlets they felt should hear what they have to say. By 11:00 a.m., there were hundreds of reporters, photographers, and microphones surrounding them. It turned out to be a flash mob but an orderly one as it didn't take New York's finest very long to get there and take charge of the scene.

A distinguished-looking, handsome lack man in his seventies went to the podium. He looked at the people gathered in front of him, took his time, nodded a good morning, and began to speak without the aid of notes.

"My name is Ezra Johnson. I retired from the US Marine Corps in 1986, having served twenty-four years and attaining the rank of major. In 1968 and 1969, I was a helicopter pilot stationed in Danang, Vietnam. During that time I met and served with Mr. Melvin Klapper, who was a door gunner in my crew. I'm here today to say to the world that Melvin Klapper did not—I repeat, did not—participate in any civilian misconduct. If he did, I would have made sure he was held accountable. The Melvin Klapper I know is an honorable man who served our country with distinction and pride. And anyone who says otherwise either doesn't know Melvin Klapper or is lying."

Johnson stepped away from the lectern and was replaced by a tall, fit, gray-haired man.

"James Woodling. I served with Melvin in Vietnam. I was a gunner on the other side of the chopper. At no time did Melvin or any member of the flight crew that I served with take part in any civilian misconduct. It just never happened. Period, end of sentence. I am proud to have served with Mr. Klapper."

One by one, Major Ezra Johnson, Captain James Woodling, Gunnery Sergeant John Jay Brown, and staff sergeants Felipe Fernandez and Ollie Coolidge stood ramrod straight as proud Marines did. They each spoke clearly with assurance and conviction. Anyone who heard them speak knew they were telling the truth. These were men whose words carried weight. They all liked and respected Melvin Klapper. They were there to tell the country that there was no truth to the story made up by Odom Briggs.

Melvin was watching this press gathering in Russ's office, which was now filled with about twenty players and coaches. Melvin was crying. So were others in the room. These five Marine veterans had chosen to go public to defend a fellow Marine from a lie, a lie that was just about the worst lie that could be leveled against a veteran Marine who served with honor.

"We'll take a few questions," said Major Johnson. "Yes, sir." He pointed to a reporter in the crowd.

"Have any of you spoken with the New York Yankees or Mr. Klapper since your time in the Marine Corps?"

"No. You, sir." He pointed at another member of the press.

"Do any of you know Odom Briggs?"

"We do but will not comment on him other than to say that his accusation about Melvin Klapper is untrue."

"Are you receiving remuneration for this?"

"No. Next question."

"Can you prove what you've said here today?"

"We are the proof. Secondly, the USMC knows what we're saying here today is the truth. So we're calling upon the Corps to do the right thing and come to the aid of a Marine in need. We leave no man behind, and that includes Melvin Klapper. Thank you."

And just like that, they were gone. The crowd was silent and unmoving, mesmerized by what they had just witnessed.

At just about the same time, Vic Coleman's latest column hit the wires. Coleman said what Melvin had yet to say. Coleman told the whole story about Briggs, that he had tried to blackmail

Melvin, that Briggs's story was not believable, that he had no evidence and no witnesses, that he had demanded $100,000 from the *Globe* for his story, and finally, that he, Vic Coleman, believed that Melvin was totally innocent.

Of all people to be giving a lesson to the press about doing the homework and digging for the facts before recklessly ruining a person's reputation, Coleman was front page again—but this time in a good way.

The press went looking for Briggs to get his reaction to these developments, but Briggs was nowhere to be found. He had vanished. The tide had turned. The media had heard enough. They quickly came to the realization that they had been duped and had prematurely and wrongfully "convicted" a seventy-four-year-old veteran of being a war criminal, a man who had served honorably and proudly.

Melvin felt relieved mentally, but his body was still in agony. A huge burden had been lifted off of Melvin and in turn the entire Yankee organization. Although Russ decided to give Melvin another night off, the Yankee bats came alive and pummeled the Pirates 11–2. There was no booing, and the crowd revived the "Melvin, Melvin, Melvin" cheer that had become popular in every park the Yankees played in. Melvin, sitting in the dugout, didn't mind if fans were fickle. That was their right, and if they were now cheering for him, so be it. Melvin admitted to himself that he was once again enjoying the moment.

With the Red Sox losing in extra innings, the Yankees picked up a game and were out by five games. Melvin went home tired but pleased. Winnie's advice had been right. That Melvin's fellow Marines from fifty years ago had come forward was incredible. Melvin wanted to thank them but had no idea where they lived or how to contact them. He would ask Gus if he could help.

Even though his pain was steadily increasing and requiring more medication, Melvin had a peaceful and restful night's sleep, probably because the day had been exhausting but had ended well. Unusual for Melvin, he slept until 8:00 a.m., when he was abruptly awoken by the ring of his cell phone.

CHAPTER 46

Wednesday, September 21
Springfield

"Good day yesterday, Melvin." It was Winnie. "I was going to call you last night, but I figured you were exhausted. I taped those Marines and replayed it last night about five times. Even got Alva to watch it. She didn't say anything. She didn't have to, but she got the message. Man, that was really something."

Melvin was glad to hear from Winnie. All his advice had turned out to be wise. "Yeah, those guys were great. Do I look as good as they did?"

"Well, sorta." Winnie laughed. "I think we may have some more good news. I just read online that the Marine Corps is issuing a statement today about your situation."

"Really? They hardly ever go public with anything."

"Yeah, well, they are this time. Maybe Vietnam is still a sore point. Listen, I'm off to the bank. I'll see you in Boston for the Saturday afternoon game. Maybe Chris and Grace will let me take Billy. I spoke with Grace. I think your family is back on track. So whatever you said to them seems to have worked. Okay, got to run, good luck tonight."

"Thanks for everything, Winnie. I can't tell you how much you mean to me. See ya Saturday. Dinner on me."

"That's a promise I'm gonna hold you to after all the crap you've put me through. How about a big juicy steak at Capital Grill?"

"You're on."

As Melvin ate his bowl of cereal and watched the news, the Channel 4 anchor announced that they had just received a statement from the USMC, which read in typically terse Marine Corps style.

> Due to the recent public allegations against Marine veteran Melvin Klapper, the USMC has reviewed his record for the entire period of time that Mr. Klapper was in service and states as follows. At all times, Mr. Klapper served his country with honor and distinction, having been awarded numerous medals and commendations, including two Purple Hearts and a Bronze Star. At no time was Mr. Klapper involved in, or alleged to have been involved in, any misconduct or civilian incident. The Marine Corps will make no further statements regarding this matter.

Now Melvin felt fully exonerated. There was nothing more Briggs could do or say that would be believed. The Marine Corps had come through for him as had his fellow jarheads.

Melvin went over to Martha's picture and kissed her. He thought he saw her wink.

Melvin's phone rang. He was shocked to hear the voice on the other end.

"Hey, Melvin, you came up smelling like roses," said Lang Carter. "I'm sitting here with Gus. What an amazing couple of days. You must be feeling as relieved as we are."

"It was extremely upsetting, and I saw no way out, but my fellow Marines came through for me. And thanks for standing by me, Lang. That took guts."

"You're a national hero again. They're going to love you more now than ever."

"I just want to get back on the field and win some games."

"Russ just told us you'd be playing tonight."

"Great. I can hardly wait." Melvin could hear Gus in the background saying something, presumably to Lang.

"Hold on. Gus just told me that the FBI arrested Briggs for attempted blackmail. There was also a federal warrant out on him for other crimes he committed, including bail-jumping. They found him drunk in a motel in West Virginia. He's going away for a long, long time."

"Thanks for calling, guys. You don't know how much it means to me to have friends like you."

"We're with you, Melvin," said Lang as he hung up.

Melvin called Grace. She was probably in class and couldn't pick up, but he left a message.

"Hi, sweetheart. I hope by now that you and Billy have heard the good news. Talk later."

Yankee Stadium

When Melvin got to the Stadium, Russ waved him into the office.

"Did you hear from Lang?"

"I did. He and Gus called me."

"Melvin, we all believed in you. You have a lot of friends here. Don't you ever forget it. You're in the lineup tonight. We need a win."

"Thanks, Russ. I'll do my best."

As soon as Melvin walked into the Yankee locker room, the fifteen or so players and coaches already there gave Melvin a standing ovation. One by one, they hugged Melvin, patted him on the back, and offered fist bumps, which Melvin was only too glad to do.

The life and spirit of the team was back. Better than ever. The ordeal about Melvin was not only over but ended in a way that was motivational for Melvin and his Yankee teammates.

The world now knew that Melvin was a war hero, not a war criminal. He had never bragged about his time in the Marine Corps or in Vietnam, which made it all the more precious and valuable. He was the only person on the entire team—in fact, in all of baseball—who had been in the USMC, served in Vietnam, and received two Purple Hearts and a Bronze Star. The affection and admiration for Melvin was now even greater than it had been before. Melvin was legit, and everyone in that locker room was proud of him and thankful for his presence on the team. Melvin's military achievements, about which he never spoke, seemed to almost overshadow the famous "catch and throw."

The ESPN pregame show started promptly at 6:35. It seemed like Scott and Dan couldn't wait for their airtime to begin. They had so much material to work with as the last twenty-four hours had been nonstop news about Melvin, frankly, the biggest story in the country. At each game, the viewership increased, giving Dan and Scott publicity that no marketing could buy. After a brief greeting, Scott went right to the statement issued by the Marine Corps.

After reading it aloud, he turned to Dan and said, "That pretty much wraps up that fiasco. Imagine Klapper having to go through this agonizing ordeal at his age with the media prosecuting and convicting him and the fans booing him and who knows who else questioning his conduct and his ethics. And he never raised his voice in retaliation. He never told us about Briggs and the attempted extortion. And he never told anyone about his valor and bravery during wartime. He's a person of rare character. Melvin Klapper simply astonishes us at every turn. The story of this man goes well beyond baseball, and hopefully, we will all learn from him a little something about how to conduct ourselves."

"Yeah, Dan, this baseball season has been like no other. There's just never been a story like Klapper, and I think that we're witnessing baseball history that will be talked about forever."

Dan said, "That's absolutely true, and we still don't know how a seventy-four-year-old man dying of cancer and limping from gunshot wounds is able to play major league baseball. Can anyone explain this? I certainly can't."

"The Yankees are taking the field," said Dan. "There's Melvin jogging his usual slow jog out to right field. Almost like a fast walk. Folks, the entire stadium is standing up and applauding Melvin Klapper. As are the Yankees on the field, in the dugout, even in the bullpen. I see some of the Pittsburgh players also applauding. Good for them. That's the kind of sportsmanship we need more of in this country."

Melvin finally took his cap off and waved to the stands, causing an even louder eruption of applause. Melvin had not forgotten the booing of just a few days earlier, but he understood how people could be sorry for having made a mistake. Melvin believed that most people were good and just doing their best to get by, one day at a time. Melvin reminded himself that there was a game to play.

The standing ovation started all over again when Melvin came out onto the on-deck circle in the bottom of the first. When he went to the plate, Pittsburgh catcher Larry Young and home plate umpire Vernon Dietz gave Melvin some extra time to enjoy the moment. "Way to go, Melvin," said the Pirate catcher, looking down so the fans wouldn't know what was being said.

The home plate umpire was the same one Melvin had tried to shake hands with on his first major league at bat. Now it was Dietz who sarcastically said, "I'd shake your hand, Melvin, but I can't do it in front of all these people. It would make me look like I'm favoring you."

"You do favor him," jumped in Young, chuckling.

"No, I don't. Now shut up, Larry."

"That's okay, guys. I'm just glad to be here. Frankly at my age, I'm glad to be anywhere." Hiding behind their face masks, Dietz and Young laughed.

On the second pitch, Melvin hit his first single of the two he would get that night, and the Yankees romped 8–1. After the second single, Young turned to Dietz and said just one word: "Unbelievable."

Dietz responded by saying, "We'll be telling our grandchildren about this someday."

When Melvin got to first base after his first hit, the Pirate first baseman tapped Melvin on the thigh with his glove, turned partially toward him, and subtly holding out a magic marker said, "Could you please sign your name right here?" He pointed to where on his glove he wanted the signature.

"Sure," said Melvin.

When the game was over, Melvin checked his cell phone and saw that Grace had left a message.

"Hi, Dad, it's been a great two days. We're so happy for you. You're going to have to talk to Billy. He feels ashamed that he didn't believe in you right from the start. I think he's learned an important lesson about loyalty, family, and friendship. Even Chris realizes he made a terrible mistake. He actually cried about it last night. He can't believe how poorly he's behaved. My two boys have learned some big lessons this week. Chris wants to apologize to you but doesn't know quite how to do it. So please make it easy for him, okay? He's trying.

"He spoke with Winnie and told Winnie it was okay for him to take Billy to Fenway on Saturday for the day game. That was big for Chris, so he's making progress. We'll see you on your next day off, which the calendar on the fridge says is the twenty-ninth, a Thursday. In the meantime, I hope you're feeling okay. Take your meds. Call or text whenever you can. We love you, Dad. You've always been my hero and always will be."

Tears of joy poured from Melvin's eyes. That was all he ever wanted, to be a hero to his family. Sure, it was nice to hear others speak well of him, but now, he was starting to feel good about himself. What else was there? What else mattered?

CHAPTER 47

Thursday, September 22
Yankee Stadium

The stadium was standing room only. The rhythmic chanting of "Melvin, Melvin, Melvin" began fifteen minutes before the game started.

The Yankees were hot and felt confident that they could close the gap the Red Sox held over them. It was a good night for Melvin, who hit a three-run homer in the seventh inning, helping the Yankees to a 4–2 victory. The sweep of the three games with Pittsburgh brought the Yankees to within four games with twelve to go.

CHAPTER 48

Friday, September 23
Fenway Park

"Folks," opened Scott Whaler, "it doesn't get much better than this. Here we are on a cool, crisp late-September evening in Boston, and we've got a packed house to watch the surging New York Yankees against the hometown Red Sox. As if we didn't have enough excitement with a tight pennant race, there is of course the biggest story in all of sports and maybe in the whole country. That of Melvin Klapper, number 75 for the Yankees."

"Now we all know," continued Dan Earling, "that a lot has transpired in the past few days concerning Melvin Klapper, so we'll spare you the lengthy version and simply say that Mr. Klapper was wrongly accused of misconduct while serving in Vietnam, and as far as we are concerned, and we believe we speak for the vast majority of people, that issue has now been to put to rest. So nothing further needs to be said about it."

"Getting our heads back in the game," said Scott, "let's set the stage. Including tonight there are twelve games left in the regular season for both the Yankees and the Red Sox. And interestingly, Dan, six of those games pit the Yankees and the Red Sox against each other. Those games will in all likelihood determine who wins this race."

"Yessiree, Scott, and we'll be there for all of them. I can't believe I get paid to do this." After a slight pause, Dan added, "I hope our producer, Ryan, didn't hear that."

Scott laughed. "Too late, my friend. The Yankees trail the Sox by four, but that lead was fourteen on August 3 when Klapper got his first start as a New York Yankee. Too bad he sat on the bench for so many games. But the Yankees are closing the gap, and the pressure seems to be on the Sox to hold off the Yankee momentum.

"Now as to Klapper, he's played in forty-one games, had 156 at bats, and delivered fifty-seven hits, including ten home runs, and has driven in twenty-nine runs. He's hitting a solid .365, which would lead the league except he hasn't met the minimum number of at bats to qualify. But I don't think Melvin Klapper will feel good about his contribution unless and until the Yankees win the World Series."

"The Sox take the field," said an exuberant Dan. "Lew Barnett takes the mound for the home team. Barnett, a wily sidearmer, has a 9–4 record so far this season, and has been very effective against righty batters, very important here at Fenway with that short left-field wall. And it will be Luis Caramone for the Yankees. Here we go."

The game went seven innings without either team scoring. A good old-fashioned pitchers' duel, both had thrown close to ninety pitches and were starting to tire.

Relief pitchers were brought in. Usually reliable Sox reliever Ellis Demarie was greeted by a towering fly ball off the bat of Pete Warner, which bounced just short of the right center field wall. Wagner could possibly have made it to third but knew the baseball maxim that a player should never make the first or last out of an inning at third base. Pete Warner stopped at second base, happy to have led the inning off with a hit and already in scoring position.

The next batter moved Wagner over with an excellent bunt, a seemingly lost art in today's baseball slugfest. With a man on third, Willie Niles lofted a deep enough fly ball to left field for Wagner to tag up and score the game's first run. But would it hold up?

In the bottom of the eighth, the Red Sox loaded the bases. Yankee relievers were unable to stop the Sox from scoring three runs.

In the top of the ninth, the Yankees had a bit of a threat going, getting two runners on, but the game ended on a called third strike, allowing the Red Sox to draw first blood and increase their lead over the Yankees to five games. Yet both teams could feel the Yankee momentum.

CHAPTER 49

Saturday, September 24
Fenway Park

It was 6:05 a.m. when Melvin woke up at the Copley Plaza Marriott, where the Yankees stayed when they were in Boston. Despite the loss the night before, Melvin felt refreshed. The pain medication prescribed by Dr. Mendelsohn seemed to keep the pain tolerable, although he was no longer pain free. He enjoyed the experience of staying at the different hotels when the team was on the road. In the past ten weeks, Melvin had stayed in more hotels than in his prior seventy-three years combined.

He was excited because he knew that Winnie and Billy would be in the stands today. Gus had helped them get two really good seats, and Melvin hoped that being at this game would help get Billy back to his usual self. He and Winnie loved being together, which made Melvin thankful. Knowing that he wouldn't be around for Billy that much longer, it was gratifying to know that Winnie and Billy would continue to enjoy each other's company and hopefully maintain a relationship they both apparently needed and wanted.

Before the game, Melvin scoured the area behind the visiting dugout where Gus said they'd be. But Melvin saw no Winnie and no Billy. Melvin started to get concerned as Winnie was supposedly picking Billy up at home and then driving several hours from Springfield to Boston. Maybe they ran into traffic and would show up later. Melvin knew he had to get his focus back on baseball.

In top of the first, Melvin hit a line drive off the "monster" in left field, driving in two runs. The Yankees carried that 2–0 lead into the fifth, when Red Sox slugger and Yankee nemesis Brock Dennison hit his forty-fourth home run of the season, knotting the game at two.

In the sixth, Melvin hit another bullet onto the wall that missed being a home run by inches. Most runners would have made it to second, but Melvin stopped at first. Russ wanted to put in a pinch runner for Melvin but didn't want to take his bat out of the lineup as Melvin would get at least one and possibly two more shots at that short left field wall.

Going into the top of the ninth, Melvin would be the third batter up. Yankee leadoff hitter Caesar De Conto had a good eye at the plate and took a close pitch for ball four and jogged to first. The next batter, Jesse Wolcott, flubbed two attempts at a sacrifice bunt and then struck out swinging. Now it was Melvin's turn to hit. Melvin was having a good game. Two hard hit balls, two RBIs, and a walk.

Red Sox pitching coach Sparky Sykes lumbered out to the mound. Surrounded by his catcher and the infielders, Sparky said, "You want to walk Klapper?"

"Not really," replied reliever Dean Smith, who still remembered their last game.

"Look, he's hit the ball hard every time up," said Sparky.

"I think I've got this," said Smith. "I just won't give him anything too good to hit." With Warner hitting behind Melvin, maybe walking Melvin was not such a good idea.

"Okay, boys," Sparky said as he turned and hustled back to the dugout.

The first pitch to Melvin was low and outside. As was the second pitch. Melvin knew he wasn't going to get anything good. The third pitch was low, 3–0. Melvin stepped out of the box and glared at third base coach Lou Hudson. To his surprise, he got the "hit away" sign. *Try not to look like you're going to swing*, thought Melvin. *Don't look anxious*.

Melvin appreciated the confidence that Russ had shown in him letting him swing away on a 3–0 pitch, but Melvin knew not to swing unless it was a really good pitch. And a good pitch it was, right down the middle, belt high. Melvin's eyes widened as he got ready to make contact. Then there was that wonderful, almost magical sound of when a bat made that perfectly sweet contact with a fastball. Melvin swung, and everyone in the park knew it was gone. Clearing the left field seats, the ball landed on Lansdowne Street. Some lucky kid got a souvenir, Melvin hoped as he slowly loped around the bases.

The Yankees held on to win 4–3. Melvin had gone three for three, knocking in all four Yankee runs and with a game-winning home run. Russ patted himself on the back for not pinch running for number 75. The Yankees were back within four games. Melvin should have been as elated as his teammates were, but without Winnie and Billy at the game, the joy was less than it could have been.

Melvin just couldn't understand why they hadn't shown up. When he got back to the Yankee locker room, he noticed that he had received three text messages and three calls. This was unusual. Now he was really concerned. What was going on? He went to the text messages first. Melvin was taken aback when he saw the text was from Alva. In fact, all three texts were from Alva. Melvin had never before received a call or a text from Alva. Still to this day, they had never even spoken.

Alva had written, "Mr. Klapper, this is Alva Winfield, Winnie's wife. Last night, Winnie was stabbed in the stomach and chest by some crazy guy trying to rob the bank. Winnie was operated on at Springfield Hospital at midnight. When he awoke this morning, he asked for you. I think you are in Boston, so maybe you can give Winnie a call to cheer him up. Thank you, Mr. Klapper."

The phone calls, two from Alva, said pretty much the same thing. The other call was from Grace, explaining that Winnie never showed up, so Billy watched on TV with Chris.

"That's not like Winnie," said Grace. "We called his phone, but he didn't answer, so we left a message. They tell me you won the game for the Yankees. See you soon, Dad. I hope Winnie is okay."

Melvin was traumatized by the news. Not sure what to do, he went to see Russ and told him what had occurred. "I need to go back to Springfield right away. I'll be back in time for tomorrow's game. Can Gus help me with travel plans?"

"I'll call him right now."

"Thanks, Russ."

While his teammates were congratulating him for how he performed, Melvin was consumed with worry for Winnie.

He texted Alva, "Got your message. I'm on my way. Melvin."

Alva couldn't believe it. She read the text to Winnie, who, half asleep from medication, smiled, and gave the thumbs-up sign.

Thankfully and true to form, Gus had come through again. A small charter plane was waiting for Melvin at Logan. The plane took off within ten minutes of Melvin boarding. Melvin would have enjoyed the experience were it not for the worry. What if Winnie died? Melvin couldn't even entertain that thought. No way. Winnie was too big and strong to let a few stab wounds bother him. Before Melvin knew it, the plane was about to land in New York. A car arranged by Gus was waiting to take Melvin directly to Springfield Hospital.

When Melvin arrived at the hospital, it was about 9:30 on an unseasonably chilly and breezy night.

"Fourth floor, east wing," said the receptionist. Melvin made his way up to Room 406. Hospital halls were eerie, especially at night, thought Melvin, feeling uncomfortable hearing the snores and the groans on his way from the elevator to Winnie's room.

Melvin knocked softly on the door of room 406 that was closed halfway and then entered slowly only to see Winnie asleep with tubes hanging from his arm and nose. Machines and equipment surrounded him. Melvin never thought he would see his formidable friend lying in a hospital bed like this.

"Mr. Klapper?"

"Yes."

"I'm Alva Winfield." She stood from a bedside chair to shake Melvin's hand.

"How do you do, Alva? I'm Melvin. How's Winnie doing?"

"They say the next twenty-four hours are critical."

Winnie went over and touched Winnie on the chest. He then held his huge hand.

Alva saw this but said nothing. She sat down. Clearly, she was emotionally and physically drained.

"Is there anything I can do for you, Alva? Do you need food?"

"I haven't eaten since yesterday."

"I'll go downstairs and get you a sandwich. Coffee?"

"I'll eat anything."

"Be right back," said Melvin.

Melvin was able to find a tuna on whole wheat and a cup of coffee for Alva.

"Okay, here we go," said Melvin, returning to the room, "a little something. Just try and relax. I'll watch Winnie for a while."

"Thank you," said Alva as she sipped the coffee, holding the cup with both hands.

After a few minutes, Melvin said, "What happened?"

"The police said some guy around twenty-five came into the bank around three o'clock and started screaming at everyone, waving a machete. Winnie tried to calm him down, and it seemed to be working, but this guy suddenly lashed out, cutting Winnie in his chest and stomach. Then he ran. The cops are still looking for him."

"The world has gone crazy. I'm sorry, Alva."

"When Winnie woke up from surgery, you were the first person he asked for."

Melvin was silent. He wasn't sure how to take that comment.

"So I called and texted you. I never really expected you to call me back."

"Why not? I love Winnie."

"And he apparently feels the same about you."

"We just hit it off, and he has been such a good friend to me the past few months. I would have been lost without him. He's changed my life…for the better."

"I can't say I understand it, but do you know what matters to me?"

Melvin waited for Alva to continue.

"That you're here. That says it all. You left Boston and somehow made it here. Actions do speak louder than words, so you being here confirms what Winnie told me about you."

"Thank you, Alva. I'm going to sleep here tonight, hopefully see Winnie in the morning, and then I have to head back to Boston for a 7:00 p.m. game."

Melvin could see Alva relax just a bit knowing that he was there. She finally got some shut-eye.

Melvin quietly pulled in another chair and quickly fell asleep.

CHAPTER 50

Sunday, September 25
Springfield Hospital

"Melvin. Hey Melvin," Winnie repeated, this time loud enough to wake Melvin.

"Hey," said Melvin, getting up stiffly from his chair on the side of Winnie's bed, "how are you?"

It took Winnie a moment to collect his thoughts and find his voice. He looked around at the tubes and monitors connected to him. "I feel like a truck ran over me. Am I going to live?"

"Are you kidding? You'll be better than new," said Melvin, smiling.

Alva, hearing voices, groggy from a deep sleep, said, "Winnie, you're awake. Thank God."

"Alva, I'm fine. Melvin said better than new. Right?"

"Right, Winnie."

"Hey, Melvin, what the heck are you doing here?"

"Alva reached out to me, told me what happened, so here I am."

"What time is it?" asked Winnie.

"Seven thirty in the morning," said Alva.

"What day is it?" asked Winnie.

"Sunday," replied Alva.

"Hey," said Winnie, looking at Melvin, "aren't you supposed to be in Boston?"

"Yes. I was and will be again."

"Melvin left after yesterday's game," added Alva, "and came right to the hospital to see you, Winnie. Not many people would do that."

"He's my man," said Winnie. "Melvin, you're all right."

"Breakfast time," said a nurse carrying a tray and interrupting the conversation.

"Good, I'm starving," said Winnie.

"That's a good sign. I worry about this man when he's not hungry," said Alva to the nurse.

"Any extra breakfasts around?" asked Melvin.

"I think I can find two more," said the nurse.

Alva fed Winnie, while Melvin updated Winnie about Saturday's game.

Then two cops who knew Winnie from his days in the department came in to tell Winnie that they had nabbed the stabber. "The guy was high as a kite, has no recollection of being anywhere near the bank. But we found the machete on him with blood on it, probably yours. It's over at the lab now. How you doing, Winnie?"

Before Winnie could answer, one of the cops looked over at Melvin and said, "Hey, aren't you that guy Melvin Klapper? Can we have your autograph?"

"Not right now. I'm here for my friend."

"Right," said one of the cops, who wished Winnie good luck and nudged his partner out of the room.

As they exited, Melvin and Alva laughed, while Winnie tried to crack a small smile.

After eating everything on his tray, Winnie fell back to sleep. He needed to rest.

"I could use some air," said Alva.

"Me too," said Melvin.

As they walked outside onto the hospital sidewalk, Alva said to Melvin, "I may have misjudged you, Mr. Klapper."

"Please call me Melvin."

"I was worried that my Winnie was getting caught up in something. I don't know what, but he's all I got, and so I'm overly protective." She turned to Melvin. "You understand what I'm saying?"

"Yes, yes I do. Winnie is one in a million. He's become part of my small family. It's just my daughter, Grace, her son, Billy, her husband, Chris, and Winnie. And now you. We're a small but tight-knit bunch. We make plenty of mistakes, but we learn from them."

"Melvin, I think I like you."

"I like you too, Alva."

They turned back toward the hospital and went back to Room 406 without saying another word. Nothing more needed to be said.

Winnie was still asleep.

"Alva, I have to get back to Boston now. Okay?"

"Of course. You go play baseball. I'll keep you posted."

"May I hug you?" asked Melvin.

Alva just smiled and opened up her arms. They embraced warmly. They had reached an understanding of each other and the situation. Alva knew that Melvin was battling cancer and that he didn't have long to live, which made his coming to see Winnie all the more meaningful.

Melvin patted Winnie on the chest and said, "See you later, pal."

Melvin called Russ. When Russ didn't answer, Melvin left a message.

"Russ, I'm leaving Springfield Hospital now. I'm on my way. I'll get there as soon as possible. Thanks for understanding."

Melvin still hadn't arrived by game time, so Russ went into the locker room and informed the team why Melvin wasn't there.

"Gather around, men. Melvin's not here because his friend Aaron Winfield—some of you know him by now, formerly NYPD, now bank security—was stabbed the other day while doing his job and is recovering from surgery at Springfield Hospital. Melvin left after the game yesterday to see him and cheer him up. That's a friend. When things like that happen to people we care about, we should drop whatever we're doing and get ourselves to where we're needed. Everything else can wait. Melvin teaches us things even when he's not here. Melvin left a message that he's on his way back. So I just wanted you all to know where he was and why. We should all have friends like Melvin Klapper." Russ turned around and left the locker room. The players returned to whatever they had been doing. There wasn't much else said. There was no need.

It was now game time. Still no Melvin. Russ waited as long as he could and finally decided that Tony Tucker would start in Melvin's place. Tony could field, run, and throw but wasn't much of a threat at the plate. So be it. That was what they said about a guy named Lou Gehrig when Wally Pipp missed a game because he had a headache.

The game was tied 3–3 in the seventh.

"Melvin's here," said Coach Homer Burgess.

"Sorry, Russ," said Melvin. "There was a delay landing at Logan."

Russ could see that Melvin was limping.

"How's your friend doing?"

"I think he's going to be okay."

"You up to playing a little baseball?"

"You bet, Russ."

It was now the top of the ninth, and the Yankees needed a base runner. With two outs and no one on base, Russ decided to use Melvin to pinch-hit. Melvin was mentally ready but tired from the travel and lack of a good night's sleep. His hip and side were really troubling him. He tried not to limp.

"Get up there, Melvin," said Russ.

Trying to avoid giving Melvin anything too fat to hit, they chose to walk him on four pitches. Melvin literally walked to first base before he was taken out for a pinch runner.

The Yankees did not score in the ninth. The game went eleven innings with the Yankees scoring three in the top of the inning. The Sox came roaring back in their half of the inning but fell short by a run. The Yanks had won an important game 6–5 and were now just three games behind the Red Sox.

CHAPTER 51

Monday, September 26–Wednesday, September 28
Toronto

The Yankees were on to Toronto for three games against the pesky Blue Jays. Melvin was happy just to lie down as soon as he hit the bed in his hotel room. He ordered room service, a bacon and cheese omelet with french fries, toast, and a big bowl of pistachio ice cream. Melvin didn't mind the calories. No matter how much he ate, he seemed to be losing weight, although his belly seemed more bloated than ever. His arms and legs seemed to be losing whatever muscle mass he had left. He felt himself becoming more frail and fragile. The increased dosage in medication was helping, but Melvin was pretty much in pain most of the time. He was adjusting the best he could.

After he ate some of his bacon, a few french fries, and all of his ice cream, he called Alva.

"How's the patient?" asked Melvin without saying who was calling.

Immediately recognizing his voice, Alva said, "Complaining as usual."

"That's a good sign, right?"

"Oh yeah. How'd you do today? Did you get back in time?"

"Everything went well. We won."

"He fell asleep halfway through the game. He'll be glad to know you called. Take care, Melvin."

"Okay, Alva, call me if you need anything."

Melvin then called Grace.

"Hey, Dad, I heard you won again today. Chris doesn't miss a pitch. He and Billy are glued to the games. You got two big fans there. Plus me of course."

"Of course. Billy's not mad at me anymore?"

"Oh no, that's long over. He says the kids at school apologized to him."

"Really? Glad to hear that. I feel terrible when Billy has to defend me."

Changing the subject, Grace asked, "How are you feeling?"

"I'm okay. Tired. I need to sleep now. Just needed to hear your voice."

"Thanks, Dad. You're in Toronto, right?"

"Yep."

"Okay, call or text when you get a moment. I'll tell Billy and Chris that you called. Love you, Dad."

"Love you, Grace."

Thinking of how many more times he would see Grace and feel her warmth and kindness, Melvin fell asleep fully dressed.

Despite Melvin not feeling well, the Toronto trip went well. Melvin got to the plate thirteen times. He had four hits, including one home run and three RBIs. The Yankees won all three games and gained another game on Boston.

The team made it to Baltimore late Wednesday night. Thankfully for Melvin, Thursday was a day off. The three-game series against the Orioles would begin Friday night. In the meantime, even though he was on the road, Melvin could stay in his room all day, read and watch TV, and most importantly catch up with Winnie, Alva, Grace, and Billy. Ah, finally a day off. Melvin needed it desperately. He was tired, and the body aches were worsening. It took more medicine than before to calm things down.

It had been a week since Winnie was stabbed. He was now recuperating at home under Alva's watchful eye. Melvin had spoken to Winnie almost every day, and he was sounding stronger each time they spoke. Melvin planned to see Winnie as soon as the team got back to New York.

Speaking with Alva had become almost as smooth and easy as talking with Winnie.

Grace was sounding her usual wonderful self, and Billy was back to loving his granddad. Even Chris was now getting on the phone, all excited about the pennant race. All was well, felt Melvin. If only his prognosis were better.

CHAPTER 52

Friday, September 30–Sunday, October 2
Baltimore

Friday morning, Melvin was awoken at about 4:15 a.m. by a sharp, dagger-like pain that extended from the left side of his belly to the left side of his back. He had trouble getting out of bed. He had never before taken the Percocet prescribed by Dr. Mendelsohn, hoping he would never need it. Rather, he had just increased the dosage of the Tramadol. But now he needed more. The Tramadol wasn't working anymore even though he was taking the maximum amount prescribed. Hunched over, Melvin made it to the bathroom, found the Percocet in his Dopp bag, and swallowed one. He was afraid to take two.

The instructions on the bottle said one or two 5 mg tablets every six hours. He then made his way back to the bed. He knew he had to be at the Oriole ballpark by around four, so he had the day to just relax and try to regroup. The Percocet, acting quickly, helped him fall back asleep until noon. He was feeling better, with the sharp pain now more of a dull throb.

At around 11:00 a.m., he ordered up a turkey sandwich and though he wasn't hungry knew he had to eat. He made it halfway through before feeling nauseous.

By 2:00 p.m., Melvin was starting to feel the pain return, but he decided to wait before taking another Percocet so he could make it through the game. If it brought him six hours of relief and he had to be good until around 10:00 p.m., he decided he would take another dose at around 4:00 or 4:30 p.m.

Making his way to the park in discomfort, he went right away to see Russ.

"Hey, Melvin, how you doing today?"

"Russ, to tell you the truth, not so good. I'm really tired. I don't think I can play all six games remaining on the schedule. I don't think I can play in the field."

"Okay, how about designated hitter?"

"Yes, I can do that. I think I can still swing the bat. I'd prefer not discussing this publicly, okay?"

"Sure, no problem, but I have to tell Gus, who will tell Lang."

"I understand. I just don't want it to look to the fans that I'm looking for their sympathy."

"Understood," said Russ.

Leaving Russ's office, Melvin took another Percocet. He took a somewhat abbreviated batting practice and managed to hit the ball well, although everyone could see Melvin was struggling. Despite his smile, usual positive attitude, and a good word for everyone, Melvin was getting weaker quickly.

The Yankees were ready for the Orioles but knew not to look past them to the Boston series coming up in New York starting Monday. With too much firepower against a weak Oriole pitching staff, the Yankees swept all three games and left Baltimore on Sunday night tied with the Red Sox, who lost two of three over the weekend in Toronto.

Remarkably, New York had made up the fourteen games that they trailed by when Melvin joined the team back in early July. Everyone knew that it was Melvin who had ignited the Yankees and inspired the players. It wasn't just his bat. It was the way he conducted himself on and off the field. It was the way he treated others. He made everyone around him that much better.

Batting third in the order as the designated hitter, Melvin hobbled up to the plate eleven times in the three games and had three hits and two RBIs. Just having him in the lineup made the Yankees a better team. Still hitting .358, Melvin timed the taking of his Percocet to allow him to be as pain-free as possible at game time no matter how much pain he was in at other times. The Percocet brought relief, but without it, the pain was intense.

Flying back to New York on Sunday, the players were glad to be coming back home. They had been on the road since September 23. No matter how nice a hotel room, it was no substitute for being at home. Going 8–1 on the road trip, however, did make being away a bit more palatable. They all knew the pennant was now on the line, coming down to three games against the Red Sox in the stadium.

"Okay, boys," said Russ to his players as they got ready to disembark, "I want everyone to go home, no drinking, no partying, just sleep and eat well. And especially you, Melvin, no late-night carousing." Everyone laughed as did Melvin.

CHAPTER 53

Sunday, October 2
Springfield

By the time Melvin got home Sunday night, it was too late to call Winnie or Grace and Billy. But he had stayed in touch with everyone during his time in Toronto and Baltimore. Winnie was now at home feeling good again and getting mentally prepared to get back to work. Melvin and Alva continued to have warm and affectionate conversations, some lasting a half hour. Winnie listened, knowing that Alva and Melvin were starting to like and trust each other, which made Winnie a very happy man.

Despite his now almost-constant left-side, hip, and abdominal pain, Melvin sat back in his tartan-colored chair and thought about how everyone he cared about was doing. Grace, Billy, and Chris were doing well.

Chris was like a new man. His entire demeanor had changed toward Melvin for sure but even more importantly with Billy. Through all the unpredictable and bizarre events of the past few months, they had grown closer, giving Melvin a good feeling about their father-son relationship going forward. Now Chris went out of his way to speak with Melvin whenever he was on the phone. Chris was much more upbeat, complimentary of Melvin, and asked Melvin really good baseball questions. Billy was back to his usual precocious self as always a loving grandson who made Melvin's days a joy. Grace was the only one who would actually ask Melvin how he was doing medically. Not wanting to saddle Grace with his issues and ailments, Melvin tried to play down his pain and deteriorating condition. Grace knew otherwise. She had seen it before.

Melvin left a text message on Grace's phone.

"Hi, hon, it's Dad. All is well. Three big games starting tomorrow night. Let's catch up. Big hugs to Billy and Chris."

He would reach out to Winnie and Alva in the morning. Because it was too painful to eat, he didn't. He'd rather be hungry. Because it was too painful to lie down in his bed, he knew he would sleep in his chair. Melvin was running out of time. After one tablespoon of ice cream, he looked at Martha, kissed her, and said, "See you soon, my love."

CHAPTER 54

Monday, October 3
Springfield

After a rough night falling in and out of sleep, Melvin knew he had to try to be ready for what would undoubtedly be the last time he would be playing at Yankee Stadium for the NY Yankees.

Melvin sat in his tartan chair and relived the incredible chain of events that had occurred since the day he took Billy to his first baseball game, the same day he met Winnie. How his life had changed in such a short period. Call it a miracle, a gift, an opportunity. How or why all this occurred, Melvin did not know for sure. But no explanation was needed. Melvin understood and embraced the moment for what it was. He was not going to let this moment pass him by. He now knew that if you try hard enough, you can achieve anything. It just takes guts. The point is you're never too old to take on challenges, set new goals, and be the absolute best you can be. It's never too late.

It may have taken a long time, but Melvin Klapper finally got to enjoy the feeling of being a winner—in the game of baseball but more importantly in the game of life. He would savor this feeling for as long as he had breath.

Melvin was now taking a Percocet every six to eight hours along with two Aleve. At least they were dulling the pain and allowing him to swing a bat. About two hours before game time, Melvin would take two Percocet along with three Aleve. So far, these pills were doing a reasonably decent job. Melvin was not getting nauseous or foggy, although he was almost always tired.

It was about 8:00 a.m., and Melvin, still in his chair, tried to grab as much sleep time as possible. His cell phone rang and woke him. It was Dr. Mendelsohn, who had been calling himself "Stan" for the past month or so.

"Good morning, Melvin. It's Stan. I'm just checking in with you to see how you're doing."

"Thanks for calling, Doc. It's a bit of a struggle, but I'm okay. The Percocet is helping, but it's starting to lose its impact. What's next for me?"

"Melvin, I'd like to see you tomorrow. We'll be watching your games. Good luck. Call Helen later today."

"Thanks, Doc, will do." Melvin could never get himself to call Dr. Mendelsohn by his first name.

He also knew there was no point setting up an appointment, so there was no need to call Helen.

Melvin knew Winnie was returning to work today, so he texted him.

"Good luck today, big guy. I'll be rooting for you."

Melvin included Alva in his text to Winnie as had become his and their custom since Melvin and Alva took their walk.

Almost immediately, Alva responded, "Big day for both my men today. Winnie, don't be a hero. Melvin, be a hero." Melvin chuckled. He now knew why Melvin and Alva were together. They were smart, strong, and loyal. Melvin couldn't believe how lucky he was to have met Winnie. *My, how things work out*, thought Melvin. Meeting Winnie was what Melvin remembered the most about that day sitting in Yankee Stadium on Billy's birthday. Winnie had become more than a friend to Melvin, like an uncle to Billy, and was now part of Grace and Chris's life.

"Hey, Melvin," wrote Winnie, "how about tickets for tonight's game?"

"They're yours," replied Melvin, "but only if Alva is with you."

Winnie then texted a big thumbs-up and about five other emojis that Melvin would have to ask someone to know what they meant.

"The tickets will be at Will Call. See you guys later."

Melvin then texted Grace.

"Would you and Chris like to come to the game tomorrow night? And if okay with you guys, can Winnie take Billy to Wednesday night's game? I know it's a school night, but it's the last game of the season, and Billy might not get to see me play again."

Melvin didn't like playing the sympathy card but knew Grace would understand. They both knew he was running out of time. That clock never stopped ticking.

CHAPTER 55

Monday, October 3
Yankee Stadium

Melvin got to the stadium at around three. He wanted to just look around and remind himself of what he had become part of over the past three months. The crowd was already starting to swell. The excitement of a final three-game series in New York to determine the American League champion was always a major event but even more so when it was against the Red Sox.

"Hey, Melvin," said Russ, "come on in. Take a load off. Did you hear you were named Baseball's Player of the Month for September? That's two months in a row. Only a few players in baseball history have done that. Congrats."

"Thanks, Russ," said Melvin, never sitting down. "Three big games. It's exciting."

"You ready to play tonight?"

"Oh yeah, I'm good to go."

Melvin walked away slowly, very slowly. He was more hunched over than ever before. It did not go unnoticed by Russ.

When Melvin got to his locker, there was a bag of mail like there was just about every day. Melvin had been receiving approximately five thousand pieces of mail a day—everything from marriage proposals to potential business deals, movie scripts, as well as pleas for money and the usual autograph requests. Melvin had even received offers to play in Japan and for minor league teams in the States. Didn't they know he was almost seventy-five and dying of cancer?

One team in Nashville asked if he was interested in a front-office position. It was estimated that the Yankees had received over two million pieces of mail from all over the world since Melvin had joined the team. It was Melvin's plan to respond to each and every person who took the time to write to him but not until the season was over. The Yankees had offered to send a form response thanking each letter writer, but Melvin felt it was his responsibility to show his appreciation of those who took the time to write to him, which he would hopefully do with the help of Grace and Chris. He thought that maybe Billy could respond to the kids that wrote to Melvin.

The locker room buzz had begun. Players were filing in. There was an air of confidence in the room. Just about everyone walked around greeting each other. Melvin loved it when his teammates came over to him, hugged him, and fist-bumped him. He felt like one of the guys even if that could never actually be. He watched these great athletes prepare for battle, each in his own way. Some remained quiet and pensive, others laughing and outgoing. A lot of tape was used on ankles, wrists, and fingers. A lot of Voltaren and other balms were used to soothe aches and pains. Trainer Eddie Montero was in constant demand, running from one player to the next. Eddie was a great guy, always there for the players. He knew how to take care of these guys, and they relied on him in order to be ready to play.

Pete had become like a son to Melvin as had many of the players. They enjoyed his company and his style. Having put his locker next to Pete was a smart thing to do. Whether that was Gus's or Russ's idea, it brought Melvin into the fold right away. Melvin couldn't ask for a better locker room neighbor than Pete Warner, who was now having one of his best years with twenty-five home runs and 102 RBIs. Pete credited Melvin for his productive season, which always made Melvin laugh, followed by Pete laughing.

"So, old man," said Pete, "feel like playing today?"

"You bet," said Melvin. "How about you?"

"I feel great," Pete said. "Can't wait to hit against Brown. I hit well against this guy. He throws hard, but it's pretty much over the plate, not a lot of movement. Just swing easy. The ball will fly outta here."

Batting practice came and went. Melvin took only a few swings, wanting to preserve his strength. To his amazement, he was still hitting the ball with authority. He couldn't run much anymore but was still somehow potent at the plate.

"Listen, Melvin, I need a few minutes of your time."

"Sure, Pete, what's up?"

"Come take a walk with me." As Melvin followed Pete out of the locker room, he noticed that Terry and Glenn and a few others were following, and then the whole team was following, including Russ and the coaches.

"What's going on, Pete?"

"You'll see." And then Melvin saw. They were at the Wall of Fame. All the players and coaches were huddled around Pete and Melvin, who started to tear up.

"Before you get too emotional, Melvin, here's the special indelible ink pen you need to sign the wall."

Melvin held the pen, found a spot, and signed his name. He kissed the wall. His teammates broke out into applause, chanting, "Melvin, Melvin, Melvin." Then they headed back to the locker room.

"Thanks, Pete. That was a thrill of a lifetime."

"You earned it, Melvin. Let's go play baseball."

The pregame show began at 6:35 p.m. for a 7:05 first pitch.

"Welcome to the Bronx," crowed Scott Whaler. "If you're a baseball fan, or even if you're not, this is as exciting and electrifying as it gets. This is the first of a crucial three-game series between arch rivals Boston Red Sox and the New York Yankees.

The teams are tied for first place in the AL East division. All of the other teams for the playoffs have been determined."

"So tonight," added Dan, "we'll see Red Sox hurler Kamau Brown with an 11–6 record against Yankee veteran Carlos Rojas, who comes in 13–5. Should be a whale of a game, Scott.

"We also have the leading home run hitter in the AL, Brock Dennison, whom I guess will remain forever famous in baseball trivia for being the batter who hit the home run ball caught by Melvin Klapper back on July 9, which I think is fair to say turned this season around in a way that baseball has never seen.

"And of course we have Melvin Klapper. As we used to say, that's Klapper with a *K*. No need to say that anymore. Everyone knows how to spell Klapper. No doubt the story of the year, the impact he has had on the Yankees, all of baseball, and in some ways the entire country. But Melvin just keeps on being Melvin."

Scott picked right up on what Dan was talking about. "Earlier today, Klapper was named Player of the Month in the AL for the second consecutive month, a rare feat in baseball. But his whole story has been an incredible feat. As of today, Klapper has played in only forty-nine games, has had 187 at bats with sixty-seven hits, twelve of which were home runs and has knocked in thirty-eight runs. He's batting .358. Simply unbelievable stats for any player, let alone a man about to be seventy-five.

"Clearly an MVP year if Klapper played a full season and was able to maintain that pace. Of course no one knows if Klapper could keep these stats for a whole season, but if he could, it would be as good an all-around season as any player has ever had in the history of baseball. There's really no way to explain it, Dan, so I've given up trying."

"His role seems to have changed lately, Scott. He doesn't play the field anymore, and he seems to have become the Yankee's designated hitter. How that will work out for the Yankees is yet to be seen. He's batting third tonight, so you could say that Russ Higgins still has high expectations of Klapper's ability to swing the lumber."

"Okay, here we go. The Yankees are taking the field. A packed crowd in the stadium tonight. It's going to be loud. Rojas has taken the mound. Red Sox leadoff hitter Corey Kendrick is in the box. Rojas takes the signal from battery mate Glenn Worthington, nods in agreement, and the first pitch is outside, ball one. The tension is palpable, Scott. I'm nervous just watching."

"Having played in many games like this," Scott said, "I can tell you firsthand that most players will be nervous until they get their first at bat or field one ball."

It was a well-played ballgame. Melvin received a standing ovation every time he was visible. It was as if the crowd knew that their days of enjoying Melvin Klapper were coming to an end. The Yankees scored first when Melvin singled to center and came home on a two-run blast by outfielder Terry Miller. The Sox came back, scoring one run in each of the next three innings. But in the seventh, Melvin hit a two-run homer, giving the Yankees the lead on their way to a 6–3 win.

Melvin waved to Winnie and Alva as he entered the Yankee dugout. Alva had become a big fan of Melvin's. His teammates made him go through the gauntlet. Melvin loved every high five, fist pump, and back slap.

"So the Yankees are in first place for the first time since May third, when they began their slide, allowing the Red Sox to build a fourteen-game lead by July. But as of tonight, the New York Yankees are at the top in their division. It's been an amazing season, Scott."

"Truly an incredible pennant run, one of the best ever," added Scott. "Tomorrow's game should be a dandy. We'll see you all at 6:35. Good night, folks."

Melvin was thrilled that he had contributed to the team's win. The locker room was alive with loud reggae music, laughter, pranks, and a heartfelt belief that they were destined to win the pennant. The players filed out quickly as did Melvin. Pete offered to drive Melvin home. Knowing that Winnie would be exhausted, still recovering from his stab wounds and surgery, Melvin accepted

Pete's offer. They talked about family and what Pete would do after his baseball career was over.

"Good night, Melvin."

"Good night, Pete. Thanks for the ride."

"It was my pleasure, Melvin. Now get your beauty sleep."

After eating a big bowl of ice cream, he kissed Martha and fell into his chair, exhausted but elated.

CHAPTER 56

Tuesday, October 4
Springfield

After a good night's sleep, assisted by three Aleve PMs, Melvin felt rested. He had started using pillows as buffers for his hip and back, which seemed to help—maybe just psychologically. The pain in his side was tolerable. Maybe it was the late-night ice cream, thought Melvin, smiling. Whatever it was, the relief of even a few hours was welcome. The longer Melvin could go relying upon less opioids, the better it was. He hadn't had a Percocet since 4:00 p.m. the day before. So it had been about sixteen hours. Hesitant to do anything that might possibly revive the pain, Melvin sat still in his chair and watched ESPN. They were reporting on the game the night before that the Yankees had won 6–3, They kept showing Melvin's seventh-inning home run. Melvin couldn't believe how slowly he rounded the bases. They showed the cheering crowd and the look of wonder on the face of the Red Sox pitcher as he watched a little old man riddled with cancer crossing home plate.

When Melvin watched these programs, he often wondered whom he was watching. How could this have happened? Was it real or just a dream? Melvin really didn't know anymore. And he didn't really care. Whether real or not, it was simply magical. The thought ended when Melvin received a text. It was from Winnie and Alva, congratulating him on the win and saying how great it was to be at the game. Melvin was thrilled to see Winnie and Alva on the same page about him. Winnie had been able to get Alva to look at people in a whole new way. Melvin thought that Alva was enjoying her new relationship with Melvin as much as he was enjoying her and Winnie. What a wonderful thing to happen, thought Melvin.

Tonight's tickets were going to Grace and Chris. This would be the first time and probably the last time they would see Melvin play. Melvin was thrilled that Chris was coming around after all these years. He had long wanted a close relationship with Chris, but Chris never felt much for Melvin. Chris saw Melvin as a grocery store clerk who stocked shelves. So whatever Chris saw now, Melvin didn't care as long as it brought Grace, Billy, and their small family closer together.

*****

"Another exciting evening here in the Bronx folks," said Dan. The pressure is on the Red Sox tonight. They'll have to come up big."

And they did. The game was lost early on. The Red Sox scored four times in the top of the first, and the Yankees never recovered, losing 8–2. Melvin walked twice and had a bloop single to right field. It was just one of those nights. Russ gave Melvin a rest after three at bats. The teams were once again tied for first place. Tomorrow night's game, the last game of the regular season, would decide the pennant. After 161 games and about 1,500 innings for each team, it could all come down to nine innings or twenty-seven outs. The Yankee locker room was subdued. They knew they had just blown an opportunity to clinch the pennant had they won tonight's game. But the players seemed determined to make Wednesday night a celebration.

Melvin returned home tired. He wasn't sure whether it was the emotional drain of the game, the Percocet, the cancer, or just his age catching up with him. Maybe it was a combination of everything. Enjoying pistachio ice cream from right out of the container, something Martha lovingly told Melvin not to do, he knew he needed as much rest as possible to perform well the next night. Realizing it could very well be his last game, Melvin wanted to finish in style. If there was ever a game to play well for his teammates, this would be it. If there was ever a game that Billy and Winnie would remember, Melvin wanted it to be this game. Thinking about these things and with his side and back pain getting more severe, Melvin took a Percocet and two Aleve and fell asleep in his chair.

CHAPTER 57

Wednesday, October 5
Yankee Stadium

It was estimated that the television audience for this last game of the season would surpass one hundred million, possibly greater than that of any Super Bowl. It was just about the only story covered by the media. No matter what was happening with world events or the economy or the weather, it seemed as if it would be the second biggest story. The *Springfield Press* devoted thirty-six front, middle, and back pages to the game, the players, the history between the teams, and of course the incredible journey of Melvin Klapper.

Even the nose in the air *New York Times* had four different articles devoted to some aspect of tonight's game, including one on the front page about how America had become entranced by baseball. The author acknowledged that the baseball season was really all about Melvin Klapper, who had turned the country into one big fan club rooting for a seventy-four-year-old man. Interestingly, the story went on to observe that while many baseball followers were looking forward to this deciding game, many others wanted this historical season to continue forever.

On his way into the stadium, Melvin must have been greeted by hundreds of well-wishers. He had a smile or a thank-you for everyone despite not feeling well. As Dr. Mendelsohn had warned, the increase in the dosage of the painkillers was starting to make Melvin nauseous and queasy. But this was no time for allowing that to happen. So Melvin saved his Percocet to take it at 4:00 p.m., which would hopefully carry him through the game. His phone rang. To his surprise, he saw Lang Carter's name come up.

"Hey, Melvin. Gus is sitting here with me. We just wanted to wish you luck tonight."

"Thanks, Lang. That's very nice of you. I appreciate it."

"There's one more thing," said Lang.

"What's that?"

"We want to thank you."

"Thank me? For what?"

"For being a great Yankee. You've done a lot for the team and the organization. The good will you've created throughout the country will last forever. You're now part of baseball legend."

"Well, it's me who owes the thanks to you, to Gus, to so many good people who have been there for me."

Lang continued, almost ignoring Melvin's comment, "And whether you know it or not, you've done a lot for me personally. You've renewed my spirit and inspired me, Melvin. You're not too shabby a ballplayer either. We're just so proud to know you."

"Wow, Lang, don't make me cry. I have a ball game to play."

"Listen, no matter what happens tonight, I want you to know how I—how we—feel about you. Win or lose, you've become very important to me and many others. More than you'll ever realize. Much more than just baseball."

And then Lang hung up. Melvin held the phone to his chest and began to well up. Who would have thought this was possible?

And with Winnie and Billy coming to the game, Melvin felt that tonight was going to be his night.

The locker room was alive. The atmosphere was electric. Everyone was sky-high for this game. Melvin was thrilled to be part of the excitement. He knew he would never have this feeling again.

Russ called everyone together.

"Boys, I just want you to know how proud I am of this team, maybe more than any team I've managed. This was a tough season, but we came back. More importantly, we cared about each other. We stuck together. We never pointed fingers. We didn't get down on ourselves. We acted like men, like family. We'll remember this season for the rest of our lives, no matter how it goes tonight or from this point forward, because a season like this will never happen again. As far as I'm concerned, we've already won, so yes, do your best out there tonight, but most importantly, have fun out there." The clapping and cheering that ensued gave Melvin chills.

*****

"Welcome, folks, to ESPN," said Scott Whaler. "This is the night baseball fans and maybe all Americans have been waiting for. No regular season game could be bigger than this. After 161 games, we're down to one game, winner take all. The Red Sox and the Yankees in Yankee Stadium on a beautiful crisp, clear October night. Temperature of about sixty-two at game time. No wind to speak of.

"Both teams have all their pitchers ready to go. The Yankees will start Luke St. Germain, and the Sox will send their star hurler, Olivio Otero, to the mound. St. Germain has been injured much of the season but has pitched well in September. And he likes pitching in big games."

"Scott, I can hardly wait. The last ten weeks of this season have been like no other season I've ever experienced. And of course the story of Melvin Klapper has made it all the more memorable."

"Yes, Dan, this is truly a season to remember. I think it will become part of baseball history no matter how it turns out. The increased interest in baseball from all segments of the country has been extraordinary. To be perfectly honest, it's affected my life. I never thought I could be this enthralled and enthusiastic once my playing days were over. I thought I had done it all and seen it all. But I was wrong. I could barely sleep last night in anticipation of this game. I slept better the night before my own World Series games."

"I know what you're saying, Scott. I couldn't wait to get to the stadium today. I got here two hours earlier than I usually do. I see the Yankees getting ready to take the field, and there they go. So buckle up, fans, we're in for a ride."

The frisson of excitement in the ballpark was palpable. It was not just a game but an event. The game got off to an anxious beginning. The players were tight. No one wanted to make a mistake. Neither team had a hit for the first three innings. The batters were feeling the pressure.

In the top of the fourth, the Sox managed to get a run on a walk, a stolen base, a wild pitch, and then a sacrifice fly to left. Still no hits, but they had a 1–0 lead. The Yankees responded in their half of the inning when Pete hit a towering home run to left field with a man on, giving the Yankees a 2–1 lead. While the hometown crowd was still jumping, screaming and clapping, Pete and Melvin were hugging in the dugout.

All was quiet in the fifth except for a ground ball single between short and third, giving the Sox their first hit. But in the sixth, the Boston batters got their hitting shoes on. The Red Sox scored three runs on five hits chasing two Yankee pitchers.

With the Yankees trailing 4–2 in the bottom of the seventh, Melvin hit a solo home run, bringing the Yankees to within a run. It took Melvin a while to circle the bases, but it just allowed the applause to go longer. The Red Sox bench looked on with silent awe while the Yankee bench emptied out onto the field, almost to home plate, to greet Melvin and help him back to the dugout.

Seeing Winnie and Billy standing and clapping was all the thrill Melvin needed.

In the bottom of the eighth, Yankee first baseman Jesse Wolcott hit a line drive down the right-field side that just made it past the foul pole for a game-tying home run: 4–4 in the eighth inning. The crowd and the television audience had already gotten their money's worth.

"What a game, folks," said Dan knowing he and Scott had run out of superlatives. "We're going to the home ninth with the game tied at four."

"The Red Sox, Dan, have brought in crafty veteran Ed Turley, who has a wicked slider and a sneaky fastball."

Leading off the Yankees was Caesar De Conto, whom Melvin had gotten to know and like. Not knowing English, Caesar kept mostly to himself or other Spanish-speaking players. But for some reason, he and Melvin got along. Melvin learned a few words of Spanish just to be able to communicate with Caesar, and that was all it took for him to smile every time he saw Melvin.

On the second pitch, De Conto hit a slow ground ball up the middle over second base, fielded cleanly by the Red Sox shortstop, but Caesar's speed and hustle beat the throw by a whisker. The Red Sox did not challenge the umpire's call at first, although they thought about it. With each manager allowed only one unsuccessful challenge per game, a manager had to reserve that decision to when they were almost certain that the call had been wrong. Even though it was the ninth inning with maybe the game on the line, the call looked too good on replay to risk the challenge.

"Will the Yankees try to bunt him over?" posed Scott to Dan.

"Scott, that's old baseball. Nowadays, I'm not so sure."

De Conto was taking a big lead at first, possibly too big. His run was the potential winning run. Turley took a long look over at De Conto and threw to first just to let De Conto know he was being watched. It was close, but Caesar dove headfirst and got back just in time. Russ could breathe again.

Turley wound up again. Anticipating that De Conto might try to steal a base and get into scoring position, the Sox called for a pitchout, but it sailed over the catcher's head, allowing De Conto to go over to second without drawing a throw or having to slide.

With first base now open, the Sox chose to intentionally walk Terry Miller to set up a possible double play or at least a force out. The next batter, Willie Niles, struck out swinging on a ninety-eight-mile-an-hour fastball as did the next Yankee batter Jay Jones. Turley was not kidding around. Two on, two out. Batting third tonight, Pete Warner was coming to the plate, and the crowd was standing and roaring. Melvin was in the on-deck circle. Yankee hopes were high.

Turley pitched carefully to Warner, trying to get him to go after a bad pitch. After fouling off three pitches, Warner worked a walk. Bases loaded, and up stepped Melvin Klapper.

In his short time playing baseball, Melvin had become accustomed to hitting with the game on the line, only now the entire season was on the line. Everything that Melvin had achieved since early July was on the line. It had all come down to this one at bat.

"Strike one," called umpire Lou Lamirello. Then two pitches low and away. The next pitch, Melvin ripped down the third base line. It was foul by inches, 2–2 count. The hopes of millions of fans, holding their breath, had been dashed.

Turley fired, Melvin checked his swing, but Lamirello yelled, "Yer out."

Melvin had been called out with the bases loaded in the bottom of the ninth of the most important game he would ever play. As was his custom, Melvin did not argue. He simply walked back to the dugout holding his bat at his side. His head was down. He couldn't look at Winnie and Billy. The crowd was in mourning. Melvin felt numb. He wondered if it had been the Percocet that affected his judgment at the plate or dulled his senses just enough to make a difference. But without the opioid, Melvin couldn't play at all.

With the crowd of fifty thousand, including Winnie and Billy, staring at him, Melvin knew he just had the opportunity of a lifetime and came up empty.

Returning to the dugout with his head down, Russ said, "It's okay, Melvin. It's only one at bat. You'll get another chance."

Several of the players gave Melvin a pat on the back or backside. Melvin sat down on the bench as the game would now go into extra innings.

The tenth inning went quickly and quietly. In the eleventh, the Red Sox scored a run to lead 5–4 after having the bases loaded with no outs. So keeping the Sox to one run in those circumstances was somewhat of a victory.

The Yankees knew they had to score at least one run to keep the game going.

The first batter popped up to the catcher. The second batter struck out. The next batter jumped on a fastball and lined it to center field for a solid single. Pete Warner strode to the plate as Melvin took his spot in the on deck circle. Pete had hit a home run earlier in the game and was not afraid to come to the plate in big pressure situations. Russ, knowing that Pete was a hot hitter and that Melvin was struggling, had decided to switch them in the batting order for tonight's game. Russ was a smart manager. Pete was a savvy hitter in these situations, had a good eye at the plate, and was not prone to swinging at bad pitches. Plus, he knew Melvin was on deck, so he didn't feel that he had to be the hero. Getting on base was his objective.

On a 2–1 count, Warner smashed a ball between the right fielder and the center fielder. In for a hit, but was it enough to score the runner from third to tie the game? Third-base Coach Bert Lansing thought not and held the runner up. It would have been close, but Coach Lansing knew that Klapper was next and didn't want to take the bat out of his hands. It was a gutsy call. Because of the right fielder's throw to home, Warner loped into second.

With runners on second and third and two outs in the bottom of the eleventh inning, Melvin Klapper walked slowly to the plate. It was his moment again. His memory of striking out in the ninth was long gone. Was he up to the challenge? Could he come through? He remembered what Winnie had said. This was Melvin's chance, his moment. It may never happen again. Did he have one more hit left in that magical bat?

Melvin was feeling nauseous and dizzy from the Percocet but knew he had to clear his mind for just one more at bat.

The Red Sox had gathered at the mound to discuss whether they should walk him since first base was open. Should they bring in a fresh pitcher?

Melvin stood outside the batter's box, praying they would pitch to him. Home plate ump Lamirello scurried out to the mound to break up the meeting. What had they decided?

They chose to pitch to Melvin, sensing he was not quite the Melvin of earlier in the game. Baseball people and savvy fans knew that Melvin tired as the game went on. He had struck out his last time up, and Turley was confident that he could strike him out again. But with first base open, Turley knew that walking Melvin didn't really matter. The only runs that mattered were the tying run at third and the winning run at second.

The first pitch was way outside. The second pitch was low, almost in the dirt. The third pitch caught the outside corner. The next pitch was a perfect strike right down the middle. Melvin had been caught off guard. He hadn't been expecting such a good pitch. He was momentarily disappointed in himself. Was that the one good pitch to hit most major league batters get each time up?

The count was now 2–2. Melvin didn't know what to expect, but he was ready. The windup and another tough slider followed, which Melvin managed to foul back.

It had been a decent cut but not with his usual authority.

The next pitch just missed the inside corner. It was too close to have been taken, but luckily for Melvin and the Yankees, it was called a ball. Maybe Lamirello was making up for his called third strike on Melvin in the ninth.

"Good eye, Melvin," Russ yelled out, trying to reinforce the umpire that he had made the right call.

Melvin stepped out and took a deep breath.

In that one passing moment, Melvin heard fifty thousand fans all clapping in unison. He saw the entire Yankee dugout on its feet. Pete, Terry, Glenn, and Russ crowded together as close to the field as possible. And there were Winnie and Billy. Winnie had his big arm around Billy's shoulder while Billy stood silently, his glove covering his face up to his eyes, Melvin could feel the love.

In just a few short months, professional athletes he admired had become his teammates, his friends, his supporters. Now they were cheering for him. He couldn't let them down. They looked worried but confident that Melvin would come through. They wanted the bat in Melvin's hand. The pressure was enormous.

He looked up and saw Lang and Gus standing in the owner's box looking at Melvin.

It was a frightening but glorious moment in Melvin's life to know all these people were counting on him to come though. That was their role. His role was to meet the moment, to face the challenge. He knew it, welcomed it, savored it. This was what it had all been about. It had all come down to this moment in time in the life of Melvin Klapper. And he knew it wasn't too late to make up for all the missed opportunities.

If Melvin was dreaming, he wanted the dream to continue for just one more hit.

Although he felt like throwing up or lying down, Melvin stepped back into the box, knocked dirt from his cleats, swung his bat a few times, and waited for the 3–2 pitch from Red Sox hurler Turley.

It was a slider, Melvin could tell from its spin. He could see that it was heading for the outside edge of the plate. It was going to be a strike. It was a nearly perfect pitch from the pitcher's point of view, but on this day in October in Yankee Stadium in front of fifty thousand screaming fans and more than a hundred million witnesses watching on television, it was a perfect pitch for Melvin to get his bat on.

As if in slow motion, Melvin saw the rotation of the ball and the direction in which it was moving. Timing his swing as only Melvin Klapper could do, Melvin swung and drove the ball into right field. The runner from third scored easily, and then came Warner who had never run so fast in his life. The right fielder picked up the ball and fired a peg home. It was going to be a close call at the plate. But Warner slid home, beating the throw.

The Yankees had won 6–5, and with it took the pennant of the AL East division. The crowd was beyond delirious with joy. Not only had the Yankees won, but once again, it was seventy-four-year-old Melvin Klapper who had magically driven in the tying and winning runs—a perfect ending for a miraculous season.

The Yankee players ran out onto the field to mob their hero. But something had happened. Something really bad. Melvin had fallen after touching first base. A hush fell over the stadium. Even Red Sox players were out of their dugout trying to see what had happened. Russ and trainer Eddie Montero ran to Melvin, who was now unconscious, ashen, and sweating profusely. Lying next to the first base line about ten feet past the base, his cap was off. He wasn't moving. Yankees were all around him. In seconds, the stadium had gone from a deafening roar of joy to the silence of a funeral. Billy wanted to run onto the field, but Winnie held him back, not wanting him to see Melvin in distress.

There were calls for a stretcher and an ambulance, which seemed to take forever to get to the scene of where Melvin was on the ground. Water had been splashed on his face and head by the trainer with towels of ice placed under the back of his neck. The top buttons of his jersey had been loosened to make room for a cold towel. After a frightening minute or so, Melvin started to come around. Holding his head up, trainer Eddie Montero gave him some water. Several doctors who had been sitting near the field had come running out of the stands to see if they could help.

Many Red Sox players and coaches as well as their manager and trainer joined the Yankee players huddling around Melvin. Their concern for Melvin seemed at this moment in time greater than their disappointment in losing. Even though the game was officially over, the umpires remained on the field.

When the EMTs and ambulance arrived, Pete, Terry, and other players assisted them in lifting Melvin onto the stretcher. Melvin was now conscious but not yet in full control of his facilities. He was embarrassed. He never wanted Billy to see him like this. A standing and tearful ovation continued uninterrupted for the ten minutes it took to place and secure Melvin on to the stretcher until the time he was no longer visible to the crowd.

Melvin was taken by ambulance to St. Michael's Hospital, the closest major medical facility to the stadium. Pete and Russ got into the ambulance alongside Melvin. No one had left the stadium except Lang and Gus, who went directly to the hospital to meet the ambulance. Winnie and Billy were not far behind. Grace and Chris, who had watched the game, jumped in their car and raced to St Michael's. Over the next hour or so, almost all of Melvin's teammates went to the hospital, as did Victor Coleman.

Melvin was taken to the emergency department, where he was given electrolytes by IV. The Percocet was still working enough that Melvin wasn't in severe pain, but the side effects of the drug were still making him sick to his stomach. Melvin was given Compazine for his queasiness, which seemed to be working. But none of this spoiled the moment for Melvin. He realized that his playing days were over, but he was comforted by the thought of knowing what he had done, and he was proud, the proudest he had ever been. Proud of himself. Proud of what he had accomplished. Proud of repaying the Yankees for the opportunity. Proud to be a winner. Finally, after all those years of not knowing how it felt to meet a challenge, to overcome it, and to taste victory, he liked the feeling. It was better late than never.

Melvin ended the season with 196 at bats in 52 games, 72 hits, 14 home runs, 43 RBIs, and a batting average of .367. He had taken the Yankees from fourteen games back in July to winning the pennant in October. While in his hospital bed, watching the television replay of how the game ended and then seeing himself lying unconscious on the field, he could not help but replay the events of the past three months. Some of the worst and best days of his life had occurred in a span of about ninety days. Not only had he survived, but he had thrived. He knew he had triumphed over himself, his fears, and his lack of self-confidence. He never felt as good as he did at that very moment while in a hospital bed with tubes sticking out of him. Melvin fell asleep with a smile on his face and a smile in his heart.

CHAPTER 58

Thursday, October 6
St. Michael's Hospital

At 3:00 a.m. on Thursday, Melvin woke up with agonizing pain in his ribcage. The Percocet that he had last taken at 4:00 p.m. the day before had finally worn off. And the doctors at St. Michaels had been focused not on Melvin's cancer but on stabilizing him. With Melvin crying out in pain, the attentive and well-trained staff at St. Michaels realized that Melvin had far more serious issues than nausea, so they quickly called Dr. Mendelsohn, who arranged for an immediate transfer by ambulance to Memorial, where their cancer institute was known for its quality care. Given a shot of morphine, Melvin felt somewhat better within minutes and was told that he would be moved over to Memorial within the hour. Melvin could barely make out what they were saying, but he knew what this meant.

By 10:00 a.m., Grace accompanied Dr. Mendelsohn to Memorial, where they met with Dr. Gary Feldman and Dr. Nancy Beckworth, two of the finest medical oncologists in the Northeast. Melvin was still asleep. It was clear that Melvin's pancreatic cancer had metastasized and that he would not recover from the inevitable path he was on. Every effort would now be made to ease his pain and provide as much comfort as possible. Grace held back her tears as best as she could. She had been through this with her mother and understood that doctors and hospitals could only do so much.

When the consultation concluded, Grace and Dr. Mendelsohn went to talk with Melvin now that he was awake. Grace and Melvin hugged and shared their tears.

"Please don't cry, Grace. You'll only make me feel worse. How's Billy?"

"He's very scared. He wants to come see you. Winnie and Alva have called several times. They're anxious to see you too. You may not remember, but Lang and Gus were with you at St. Michael's and will probably visit you later. Everyone is just waiting to hear from me that you're up to visits."

"Oh, absolutely. The more the merrier. Whatever they gave me is working. I have no pain at all for the first time in months."

Dr. Mendelsohn, who customarily played it close to the vest when talking with patients, said, "Melvin, I envy you. You've got so much to be proud of. You've accomplished so much in your life. I hope you realize this. I'm honored to know you. I'll be by every day to see how you're doing. Drs. Feldman and Beckworth are very fine doctors, so you'll get the best of care. You need to rest now." They shook hands, leaving only Grace in the room with her father.

"Well, that went as well as expected," offered Melvin sarcastically. "What did you think?"

"I like the docs and have always liked Dr. Mendelsohn. He was great with Mom and now you."

"I'm more concerned about Billy than about me," said Melvin.

"Other than worrying about you, he's on cloud nine because the Yanks are in the playoffs. Even Chris is into it. Boy, has he changed over the past few months."

"Yep," said Melvin, "Father of the Year award is in his future."

"I'm glad you two finally had a meeting of the minds."

"More like a meeting of the hearts. We both love you and Billy. That's our connection."

"So what was it like?" asked Grace.

"What was what like?"

"The past three months. I didn't want to ask you before, but I'm really curious."

"It was great, Grace. Better than great. It gave me an opportunity to take on challenges, to be afraid but keep on going, to achieve something for myself and others. Wow, what a feeling."

"You were always great, Dad. You just didn't know it."

"Thank you, but I never felt great. Just the opposite. I let too many opportunities pass me by. This was a last chance to make it all right. And I did it. At this moment in this hospital bed, this is the best I've ever felt about myself."

"But how was this possible? How did this happen?"

Melvin didn't answer right away, not sure what Grace was asking. "What do you mean?"

"I mean, how did my seventy-four-year-old father suffering from cancer end up starring for the New York Yankees?"

"You'll have to ask Billy, although he might not tell you."

"Billy? What did Billy have to do with this?"

"I'm not sure, but I think he may know."

"I don't understand, Dad."

"Neither do I, sweetheart, neither do I. I need to sleep now. I'm very tired. Will I see you tomorrow? Can you bring Billy and Chris?"

"Of course. Get some rest, Dad," Grace said as she kissed Melvin on his head.

Melvin was asleep by the time Grace made it to the door.

To Melvin's pleasant surprise, he woke up the next morning to see Bart Slaughter sitting in the chair by his bedside.

"Bart, what are you doing here?"

"Just wanted to come see you, Mr. Klapper. To thank you for everything."

"Nothing to thank me for, Bart. You still at Wilson's?"

"I'm full-time now, supporting my mom, going to school at night. They say I could be an assistant manager someday."

"I'm proud of you, Bart. I knew you could do it."

"I have to go to work now, but I just wanted to say goodbye, I mean hello, and to thank you."

"Thanks, Bart. I always knew you were a good kid. Keep up the good work."

Later that morning when Grace came to the hospital, she brought a framed picture of her mother, as Melvin had requested, to sit by Melvin's side.

She also brought another picture—this one suggested by Billy—of Melvin and Billy on the Jumbotron after the now-famous catch and throw. Melvin loved looking at these pictures.

It brought back all the wonderful thoughts and feelings of joy that Melvin had been fortunate enough to have since July. These few months had added a dimension to a life that had always been good but never great. Melvin knew what had happened and how it had happened, but that didn't diminish his joy, sense of satisfaction, or gratitude one bit.

Over the next few days, there was an endless stream of visitors. Winnie and Alva came with homemade cookies. Winnie had always been a big fan of Melvin's, but now Alva had joined the club. Melvin was glad to know that he and Alva had formed a friendship of their own and that she understood how he and Winnie had made each other's lives better.

"Melvin," Alva said, holding Melvin's hand, "I'm glad that Winnie here finally found a father and son. I just never thought they'd be white." They all laughed.

"We're family, Alva. Winnie is the best friend I've ever had. I'd be proud to have a son like Winnie and a daughter like you." Alva cried, hugged Melvin, and walked out of the room, leaving Winnie and Melvin alone.

"Melvin," began a soft-spoken Winnie, "whether you know it or not, you've changed our lives. We see the world differently now. God blessed you. You can't do better than that." Starting to cry, Winnie patted Melvin on the chest, turned, and left the room.

Melvin thought to himself, *Why do I make everyone cry? I better die soon or they'll all be disappointed.* Although half asleep, Melvin had heard Dr. Feldman tell Grace and Dr. Mendelsohn that he had a few weeks at most before his other organs would start to fail. But Melvin was feeling very little pain, mostly just numb, which he didn't mind. They didn't like him getting out of bed on his own, but he snuck into the bathroom as needed. He just couldn't get himself to bother nurses doing far more important stuff than walking Melvin so he could pee.

So Melvin kept busy. He was signing autographs for anyone who asked, and there were plenty of people asking for his signature on gloves, caps, bats, and clothing. Melvin couldn't get over the fact that people actually wanted his autograph. He thought it was funny.

He watched the playoff games but usually fell asleep halfway through, so the nurses recorded the games for him to watch later. That way, Melvin could watch the game the next day, which he enjoyed immensely. He watched knowing what it was like to be a player, to be on the field, to get a hit, to be cheered on by fans. That feeling was like no other. He rooted on every pitch, calling the players by their first names. Every once in a while, an announcer would mention Melvin's name, how much the team missed him, how much he meant to everyone in and out of the game. Melvin just smiled. It made him feel so good.

Winnie and Alva visited regularly, and they always brought something Melvin liked. Oftentimes, it was homemade cookies or meatballs from Randazzo's or a pint of pistachio ice cream in one of those freezer bags. Every time Alva and Winnie came to see Melvin, they showered him with affection. In turn, Melvin thanked Winnie for teaching him so much, for giving him advice, for sharing his wisdom. Melvin knew he never could have gotten through the Odom Briggs accusation without Winnie's guidance. And on each and every visit, Winnie thanked Melvin for the incredible experience of the past three months, which both Winnie and Alva told Melvin had changed their lives.

Melvin was watching a lot of television these days because it was easy, requiring no effort. His name was getting mentioned less and less as time passed. *As it should*, he thought. Life went on.

He was awoken early one morning by a bald, neatly dressed, serious-looking gentleman of about fifty looming over him. Melvin assumed he was another doctor.

"How are you feeling, Mr. Klapper?"

"I was okay until you woke me. Do we know each other?"

"I'm Roger Cunningham, the CEO of the hospital. I just wanted to come by and say hello."

"That's very nice. Thank you," said Melvin as he wondered whether the CEO of a 450-bed hospital said hello to every patient. But he seemed friendly enough, although a bit formal.

"Is everyone treating you well?" Cunningham was a habitual throat clearer, which made him hard to listen to.

"Oh, it's been just terrific. You run a fine hospital. Feels like I'm in a five-star hotel."

"Good. If you need anything, just tell a nurse you want to see me."

"Thank you, Mr. Cunningham. Thank you very much. Very kind of you to stop by."

Melvin thought it odd that the CEO would visit him, but two hours later, he realized why.

As Lang and Gus strolled into his room with Cunningham trailing behind like a puppy, Melvin remembered what a big donor to the hospital's Cancer Institute the Carter family had been over the years. The Carter Foundation donated millions of dollars a year to the study and research of cancer at the institute, the finest of its kind in New York and maybe the country, and was the hospital's biggest benefactor, a Board of Trustees member for many years and a former Chair of the Board. Without the Carter stamp of approval, Cunningham would be calling a headhunter.

Lang walked in with all kinds of goodies in a big basket for Melvin. He and Gus had big smiles on their faces that didn't come close to covering up their worry and concern.

"We miss you, Melvin," said Lang.

"The team is doing pretty well without me."

"We couldn't have gotten to this point without you. You made this a Yankee year to remember."

"The boys miss you," added Gus. "They're always telling Melvin Klapper stories."

"I miss them, the locker room, being in the dugout. What an experience."

"They'll come visit you soon," offered Gus.

"Do you need anything?" asked Lang.

"No, I'm doing okay."

After a few minutes, seeing how tired Melvin was, Lang and Gus left.

Outside in the hall, they stopped. "Roger," said Lang, "anything that man wants, he gets. Understood?"

"Of course, Lang. I'll stay on top of it."

And so it went. Just about every day, Melvin had an endless stream of visitors—television producers, talk show hosts, magazine photographers, publishing companies, baseball card manufacturers, all looking for interviews or endorsements for everything from caps to cereal to cruises. Melvin had never even been on a cruise, although he and Martha had discussed it several times, but they couldn't afford it. Melvin even had a visit from an exec at AARP asking Melvin to recommend membership to everyone over fifty-five.

Melvin respectfully declined all offers. For those who were really insistent, he referred them to Chris or Winnie just to get rid of them. Melvin thought that was funny. Even Vic "the Vulture" stopped by more than once. He shared a few funny anecdotes with Melvin with the goal of getting Melvin to laugh. Vic was shaken by how different Melvin looked from the last time they were together. It was as if Melvin had aged by years, although it had only been a few weeks. Vic knew it was probably the last time he'd see Melvin.

"Melvin, you're really something. I still don't know how you did it, but there's no doubt about it. You changed baseball, the whole freakin' country, and even nasty old Vic. Thank you is all I can say. Knowing you has been quite the learning experience."

Grace, Chris, Billy, Winnie, and Alva would, in various combinations, spend time with Melvin each and every day. It made Melvin's time, however much he had left, that more livable. Of course Dr. Mendelsohn stopped by every day. He brought regards from Helen.

He even had a visit from Drs. Lewis and Hoffstein, who had examined him for the league. They came to see Melvin with the commissioner. It was a short visit but one that everyone enjoyed despite heavy hearts. Melvin thanked everyone for taking the time to stop by. He had always thought he would die a lonely and defeated man, but life had changed for him these past three months, and he was no longer lonely or defeated.

The Yankees went on to win the playoffs and would soon be facing off with the Dodgers in the World Series. Melvin was sleeping more these days and was not able to ambulate without assistance.

Now that the playoffs were behind them, the Yankee players had three days off while waiting for the World Series to begin in New York. Leading the way into Melvin's room were Russ and Pete. Behind them, there were about thirty players, coaches, and staff. Having advance notice from Gus, Roger Cunningham waived the regulation that limited the number of visitors at a time.

All the players and coaches were wearing Melvin's number 75 jersey. Seeing them in his jersey made Melvin cry.

And then Russ, Pete, and some of the players cried—grown men crying just for knowing each other and sharing an adventure that only lasted a few months but would be remembered and appreciated for a lifetime.

The gathering went on much longer than it should have considering Melvin's condition, but no one wanted it to end. Russ and Pete told stories about Melvin that made everyone, especially Melvin, laugh. They remembered how it all started and how no one could believe this guy was a ballplayer. Russ told a funny story about an old man who showed up at the stadium one Sunday wanting to play for the Yankees. He had no glove, no cleats, and no experience. Who the heck was this guy? And everyone laughed, including Melvin. But they all acknowledged that he was a great Yankee and a person of great character, integrity, and humility whom they would remember and cherish forever. Players took photos and then gave Melvin a big blown up picture of him hitting a home run in the stadium to win a game. They all signed it taped it to the wall under the TV so Melvin and everyone else would be reminded of what it meant to all those involved. Melvin had touched the lives of so many people. He had given them joy and inspiration and, maybe more importantly, hope—hope of what could be achieved at any point in one's life He was just beginning to realize this.

"Melvin," said Russ, "we're devoting this season and the World Series to you. We're going to win this as our thank-you for making us a better team and better people. We love you, Melvin."

There wasn't a dry eye in the room. The players applauded and filed out with Russ and Pete remaining behind.

"Melvin," said Russ, "I meant all that. You made us all better in so many ways. We can't thank you enough. You're a great Yankee and even better person. I'll come visit after we win the World Series."

As Russ left, Pete said, "Melvin, it was fun having you next to me in the locker room. It brought a little too much traffic to our neighborhood, but everyone just wanted a piece of you.

"Having you bat after me, the pitchers had to pitch to me, so thanks for that too. My kids talk more about you than me, which my wife and I laugh about. It was my great good fortune to meet you and learn from you. Remember that when I'm at the plate during the World Series, I'll know you're watching and cheering me on. That alone should get me a few hits. I'll come back with Russ after we win it for you."

Hugging Melvin goodbye, Pete said, "Number seventy-five, we'll always be with you."

Melvin wondered whether he would ever see Russ and Pete again. He knew he was fading a little more each day, some days more than others.

The hospital was all a-flutter having Yankee ballplayers walking around the corridors. Nurses and doctors, a rare bunch to get starstruck, just kept looking and smiling at the players. They knew it was all because of Melvin, whom they had gotten to know and adore.

Because so many people in the hospital as well as those visiting Melvin wanted to watch the World Series, CEO Cunningham—probably "encouraged" by a call from Lang Carter—cleared out an underutilized storage area on Melvin's floor, creating a large television viewing venue that could seat at least sixty comfortably, not counting ample standing room in the back. A giant-sized screen was brought in and affixed to the wall, and a long buffet table was set up and frequently refreshed for people to enjoy at their leisure. Melvin would be wheeled in on his bed with his headrest elevated so he could easily see the big screen. Melvin's embarrassment at having to be wheeled in was somewhat alleviated by the standing ovation he received from others in the room every time he entered. The doctors were just praying that Melvin would make it through the end of the series.

Chris, Grace, and Billy watched every game of the World Series at the hospital sitting next to Melvin. Winnie came when his bank schedule permitted, and Alva always accompanied him. Melvin slept in the afternoons so he could stay awake during the night games, which he managed to do as best as he could. Doctors, nurses, and staff walked in and out of the room to grab a sandwich or a bowl of fresh fruit, almost always staying for an inning or so before getting back to work. Other patients asked if they could watch and were of course welcomed by Melvin.

Some patients walked in and took a seat. Others came in by wheelchair or a wheeled bed. Almost everyone made their way to Melvin just to say hello. Melvin greeted everyone with a smile or a wave. He was still aware enough to know what was going on. His pain now was more of a dull throb blunted by medications. His loss of weight continued, leaving him gaunt and fragile. He could see the veins sticking out of his arms and legs. Nurses tried to get Melvin to consume high-calorie food, but Melvin's diet was pretty much down to ice cream and an occasional cookie. The doctors said he could eat as much as he wanted of whatever he wanted.

Dr. Mendelsohn, true to his word, visited nearly every day, and Melvin was always glad to see his old friend who had been through so much with him and Martha. Oddly, Melvin noted how much older and smaller Dr. Mendelsohn now looked compared to when he met him a few years earlier when Martha was ill. Melvin realized that doctors age and get sick just like everyone else.

Dr. Mendelsohn informed Grace that Melvin was down to a few days, his systems were shutting down, and there wasn't much more that could be done. The morphine drip, now in place, eased the passage of time. Melvin knew what was happening. His time had come, but he was a satisfied man. No, he was much more than satisfied. He was joyous and grateful and appreciative. He had been afforded one last opportunity to accomplish something with his life, and despite the roadblocks and the obstacles placed along the way, he overcame them, demonstrating to himself his desire and ability to succeed. It may have taken him nearly seventy-five years, but better late than never, he had finally achieved a sense of self-worth. Melvin was a happy and content man.

His thoughts now were constantly about Grace and Billy. That Chris had come around gave Melvin comfort. Chris had grown as a husband and father. Melvin knew that Billy was going to be a great success. He had all the traits and qualities necessary for success and happiness. Billy didn't yet know what he wanted to be when he was older, but Melvin was confident that Grace and Chris would be proud of him, whatever he chose to do.

Winnie and Alva had special meaning to Melvin. That he could be close friends with a young black couple who previously had no white friends in their life gave Melvin an internal warmth and glow. His admiration and affection for Winnie and then Alva had grown quickly and by leaps and bounds. They were kind and loving people whose wise advice helped Melvin navigate his way through the difficult moments of the past few months. They had made him a better, more fulfilled person, and he hoped that in turn, he had done something that made their lives richer.

The Yankees took a 3–0 lead in games over the Dodgers. They were just unstoppable. The team was playing with supreme confidence in themselves and in their destiny. Whatever magic Melvin had brought to the New York Yankees that season was continuing. No one enjoyed it more than Melvin.

Although his visitor list had been curtailed by the doctors, Melvin was happy to see Lang, Gus, Russ and Pete stop by just to say one last goodbye to Melvin as did Winnie and Alva. Chris asked Grace if he could see Melvin alone.

"Of course," said Grace.

Melvin was now in and out of wakefulness.

"Melvin, it's me, Chris." Half-awake but still aware, Melvin listened.

"I just wanted to tell you what I should have said many times before. You're a terrific guy, and I should have seen that before this baseball thing happened. Maybe I felt I was in competition with you for Grace and Billy. But now I know better. There's plenty of love to go around. I'm sorry I wasted all those years. I could have learned a lot. Most importantly, I want you to know that I will take care of Grace and Billy because I'll always be thinking of how you would do things. Thanks for everything, Melvin." Melvin smiled and grabbed Chris's hand as Chris bent over and kissed Melvin on the forehead, the first time Chris had ever done that.

Chris came out bawling. Grace hugged him. Billy understood the moment.

After Chris calmed down, Billy asked if he could say goodbye to Grandpa.

"Yes, Billy, but not too long, okay?"

Unlike other ten-year-olds, Billy wasn't afraid to walk into a hospital room where his grandfather was dying. He knew full well that this was probably the last time they would get to talk. And he wanted to tell Melvin what was on his mind and in his heart.

"Hi, Grandpa." Melvin loved hearing his voice.

"Billy, Billy, Billy. My lifesaver. Thanks, Billy, that was really something."

"Grandpa, I love you. You're the greatest grandpa ever."

"Billy, I owe this all to you. I got to play for the Yankees."

"Huh?"

"I know what you did, Billy. The wish. You did this."

"Sorry, Grandpa, you know we aren't allowed to talk about our wishes. There are rules, you know."

"By the way," said Melvin, "I wouldn't mind playing quarterback in the NFL for a season."

Billy and Melvin laughed.

"Billy, you made me a very happy man. You gave me something I couldn't do for myself. I know you're going to be a good son, a good husband, and someday a good father. I'll be looking down and helping you along the way. Think of us as friends forever."

"I'll always think about you, Grandpa. I love you."

"Billy, you taught me that it's never too late to just keep trying, to never quit. The impossible can become possible. Thank you, Billy. Thank you for everything."

Now crying, Billy and Melvin hugged for a long time without either making a sound.

Grace came into the room. Without saying a word, she hugged Billy and Melvin. Then Chris came in and hugged all of them. Melvin fell asleep. For the last time.

The Yankees won that night, sweeping the Dodgers in four straight. The Dodgers never even had a chance. The Yankees had become unstoppable. Melvin never got to see the game or see the Yankee celebration. On October 25, the day of Melvin's seventy-fifth birthday, he passed away as quietly, politely, and respectfully as he had lived.

But the champagne celebration was on the huge screen in the hospital as it was just about everywhere else in America. Every player who came on television toasted Melvin. Manager Russ Higgins thanked Melvin for making it all possible. Lang said this had been the most gratifying and personally rewarding year in his tenure as Yankee owner. He said it was because of Melvin Klapper, a great baseball player but an even greater human being. Gus was in tears talking about Melvin as were many of the players.

Even though Melvin was physically absent from the Yankees' locker room, his presence there was incredibly powerful. His locker was purposely kept open with his number seventy-five uniform draped on the door. The players gleefully sprayed champagne all over Melvin's locker.

There was no funeral. Melvin wouldn't have wanted it. There was no memorial service or celebration of life. Melvin was discreetly buried next to Martha in a quiet, private ceremony with Grace, Chris, Billy, Winnie, and Alva in attendance.

Several weeks later, the family was informed by the Memorial Hospital Cancer Institute that the Carter Foundation had donated $100 million in honor of Melvin and that there would be a dedication ceremony naming that part of the hospital the Klapper Cancer Institute.

CHAPTER 59

About six months later
New York City

A lawyer by the name of Spencer Smith wrote a letter to Grace and to the Winfields that there was a will left by Melvin that was going to be read and that their attendance was requested at his office at 2:00 p.m.

Smith, coincidentally, was one of Lang Carter's attorneys. Apparently, Melvin and Lang had talked about how Melvin wanted his compensation from the Yankees to be distributed in case of his death. It turned out that Melvin had told Lang what he wanted done with the money, and Lang suggested his estate attorney, Spencer Smith, draw up the necessary paperwork, which was precisely how Melvin proceeded. No one other than Melvin, Lang, and Smith were aware there was a will.

The British-accented receptionist of the white-shoe law firm of Smith, Jamison, and Featherwell escorted Grace, Chris, Winnie, and Alva into an oversized wood-paneled conference room. The green leather chairs and plush rust-colored carpet were meant to remind you of the success and power of this firm founded in 1875.

After about a ten-minute wait, Mr. Smith, a descendant of the firm's founder, Elias Smith, strode in, going right to the head of the table. A secretary with a stenographic machine sat next to him. Apparently, she was going to record what was said. Since the table sat sixteen, the first remark made by Smith was when he asked the four guests if they could please move closer so he wouldn't have to shout.

They all rose and shuffled toward Mr. Smith, who was an unsmiling, formal, all-business chap, nattily attired in a three-piece pinstripe suit and a pocket watch on a fob for carrying in his vest.

Grace, Chris, and Winnie had taken the day off, and Alva certainly wasn't going to miss this for the world.

"I'm Spencer Smith. I represented Mr. Melvin Klapper in drawing up the document that I'm holding in my hand. The purpose of this document is to express the intentions of Mr. Klapper as regards the assets in his estate.

"You were all invited here today because you are all named in the disposition as well as William, whom I understand is in school today but is represented by his parents, Christopher and Grace. Is this correct?"

"Yes," Grace said.

"Thank you," Smith continued. "I'm going to skip the usual formalities and get right to it. And I might add that a copy of this document will be in the mail to each of you by the end of today's business. Should you have any questions, feel free to contact me.

"Now the bequests:

"'I, Melvin Klapper, being of sound mind, hereby bequeath my estate as follows. To my dearest friends Aaron and Alva Winfield, $1 million.'"

Alva's gasp was so audible that everything else in the room stopped. Winnie just smiled. Alva grabbed his hand for support.

"May I continue?" asked Smith rhetorically.

"'I bequeath $3 million to Chris and Grace Walker.'"

Chris and Grace sat there stunned. Alva was still sobbing. Winnie was still smiling at the thought of Melvin's generosity and goodness.

"'I bequeath the remainder of my estate to my beloved grandson, William Walker, to be held in trust until William is twenty-five or sooner if needed for health or educational reasons. The trustee shall be Mr. Lang Carter or his designated representative.'"

The room was silent.

"Are there any questions?" asked Smith.

The room remained silent.

"Very well then. You will need to call my office within the next seventy-two hours to instruct us how you want to proceed regarding your bequest. If there are no further questions, ladies and gentlemen, that concludes our meeting. I bid you adieu."

Smith and his secretary walked out of the room as briskly and as officiously as they had walked in. The four remaining people just sat there and stared at each other. Alva was still sobbing, while Winnie had his arm around her. Winnie was still smiling. He always got a kick out of Melvin. Even in death, Melvin was Melvin.

Finally Grace broke the ice. Standing, she said, "I don't say this very often, but I need a drink. Anyone going to join me?" The three others wasted no time in following Grace, who had already begun marching to the door.

A few months later, it was announced that Melvin Klapper had been named by the Baseball Writers of America as the American League Rookie of the Year. It was fitting that Melvin's hero, Jackie Robinson, had received the first ever Rookie of the Year award back in 1947.

Melvin was also the first recipient of the Player of the Year award, recognizing a player's overall contribution to the game of baseball. Shortly thereafter, Lang and Gus invited Grace and Chris to lunch, at which time Lang presented them with the World Series ring awarded to the winning team. The Yankees had voted unanimously, in Melvin's absence, to give the ring to Melvin's family. Lang told them it was for Billy on his twenty-first birthday.

Clutching the ring to her chest, Grace cried, comforted by Chris's arm around her.

Grace and Chris continued teaching and remained in their current home. They asked Lang for the name of a financial advisor, who provided monthly reports. They rarely spoke about the money again. They told Billy of Melvin's generosity without mentioning numbers. Billy asked if it would pay for college. When Chris said yes, Billy asked, "Enough to pay for medical school?" Once again, Chris said yes.

"Good, because I want to be a doctor and cure cancer."

"That would be wonderful, son," said Chris, "but you'll have to keep your grades up."

"I will," said Billy, bounding up the stairs. "I'm going to make Grandpa proud of me."

Back up on his wall was the plaque that Melvin had bought for Billy a few months before. Billy may not have been ready for those meaningful words back then, but he had grown up a lot since then. He felt badly that he hadn't appreciated what Melvin had brought to him that day, but Melvin had known that eventually the words would be as powerful to Billy as they were to him.

Grace and Alva made sure to maintain their relationship. They got together on birthdays, holidays, and as often as possible. As Billy got older, his relationship with Winnie got closer. Chris was totally supportive as he had gotten to know how great Winnie was with Billy. Winnie had in effect become Billy's uncle.

Although Lang often invited them to sit with him in the owner's box, the Winfields and the Walkers were happy to sit in the bleachers, close to where Grandpa Melvin sat with Billy and Winnie back on July 9, the day his life and the lives of those around him changed forever.

About a year after Melvin passed, Winnie had another incident at the bank, and although he wasn't seriously injured this time, he followed Alva's advice and retired. Because they did not want to lose contact with Billy, Grace, and Chris, they decided to stay in Springfield, fix up the house, get the SUV they always wanted, and just take time to reflect upon the past and plan how best to enjoy the future.

Grace and Chris never spent any of the money Melvin left to them. It just sat accruing interest. They both retired from teaching at fifty-five and decided to travel, something they had never done. Whether they were in Lisbon, Lucerne, or Lake Como, they took great comfort in thinking about what Melvin had accomplished and what Billy was about to accomplish. They were proud children and proud parents.

Billy went on to graduate from Harvard Medical School with high honors and, as Dr. William Walker, was now doing cancer research as director of the Klapper Cancer Institute at Memorial Hospital. The money that Melvin had left had been invested wisely by Lang Carter's financial people and was being well spent to fund laboratories, doctors, staff, and studies to cure and hopefully prevent cancer. Billy thought about Melvin just about every day. The picture of Melvin and Billy from the Jumbotron sat on his desk. The impact that one man had on an entire country always inspired Billy. He knew it was possible because he had witnessed it. Hanging in his office was the plaque that Melvin had given Billy when he was ten.

The line that always stuck out for Billy was "Love is better than anger, hope is better than fear, optimism is better than despair, so be loving, hopeful, and optimistic, and we'll change the world."

EPILOGUE

By now you've probably figured out that I've been telling you the story of my grandfather Melvin. I've set down everything I personally witnessed as accurately as my memory permitted. The rest I filled in based on my recollection of him and how he treated people, including me, as well as conversations with Uncle Winnie and others who knew him.

It's been twenty-five years since I lost Grandpa Melvin, but he is with me every day. As I sit here today in Yankee Stadium with my uncle Winnie and my soon-to-be ten-year-old daughter, Martha, I'm still in awe and wonderment how life can sometimes work out better than expected. It helps if you believe deep down that you are more capable, more competent, and more courageous than you might think.

I look out beyond the fence in center field and see my grandfather's jersey number 75 emblazoned on the wall, a number retired by the Yankees back in 2023. I try to imagine what it must have been like to experience all that he did. Not just the baseball part but his entire life, making friends wherever he went and always striving to make things better. A long and happy marriage with my grandmother, raising a daughter who became my wonderful mother, working hard for fifty years stocking shelves in a grocery store. Never a complaint. Never hurtful or mean.

And then one day, something special happened for this special person because of the wish of an adoring ten-year-old.

"Welcome to Yankee Stadium," blared the public address system. "Today we are proud to have with us Dr. William Walker, the grandson of New York Yankee great Melvin Klapper, sitting in the center field bleachers with his daughter, Martha, and family friend Mr. Aaron Winfield. Would Dr. Walker, Martha Walker, and Mr. Winfield please stand?"

And as they did, so did fifty thousand smiling, clapping people, expressing their recognition and gratitude for all the joy and happiness that Melvin Klapper had brought them. For many of them, Melvin had lived out their dream even if it was for just a moment in time. Martha wasn't quite sure what to make of it all, but seeing her father and uncle with tears in their eyes made it a special moment.

In the second inning, Martha turned to her father and said, "Dad, with all the people you know, why couldn't you have gotten us better seats?"

"Tell her, Winnie," said Billy with a wink.

"Sweetheart," said Winnie, turning to Martha, "this is where the real people sit."

ABOUT THE AUTHOR

David J. Meiselman, after serving in Vietnam as a proud US Marine, graduated college and law school and then founded and led a forty-five-attorney firm that successfully litigated cases all over the country. He subsequently had the honor and privilege of being elected chair of the Board of Trustees at Southwestern Vermont Medical Center while writing a children's book and a guide to success in business. Although a scary experience, David has acted in local theater, recently portraying the Scotland Yard inspector in Agatha Christie's famous *Witness for the Prosecution*.

Enjoying family and working on his next novel, a thriller featuring former military hero and legendary sniper, now off the grid, Luke London, David lives in bucolic Vermont with his wife Myra.

Printed in the USA
CPSIA information can be obtained
at www.ICGtesting.com
CBHW030353300724
12355CB00001B/4

9 781637 844649